The reptile was long and large, with a serpentine neck thrust low. It glided on huge, batlike wings, its tail hanging stiff. Elyana saw that it had no arms and knew then that it was no true dragon, but a wyvern. She'd faced one once before, a creature half this size, and that had been no easy day. Its poisoned sting had put two men in the ground. Wyverns were powerful, relentless, and hungry.

This one swung toward her and lowered its wings for a dive.

"Wyvern!" she screamed in warning, then launched two arrows. Even as the first was still arcing into the air she was running forward. She threw herself into the tall grass and landed with a whuff that knocked the air out of her.

The first arrow slammed home just left of the wyvern's breastbone, provoking a growl that was cut off as the second caught it high along its wing. Its hooked claws grabbed at the dashing humanoid, but Elyana was too swift.

The wyvern landed with an earth-shaking thump. Its snaky neck swung left and right as it considered its targets, its roar a piercing shriek so loud that Elyana felt a sympathetic vibration deep in her chest. She heard Renar call out to her in worry, but stayed low as the wyvern searched the air with its long snout . . .

The Pathfinder Tales Library

Plague of Shadows

Howard Andrew Jones

Cover art by Darin Bader.
Cover design by Sarah Robinson.
Map by Crystal Frasier.

Paizo Publishing, LLC
7120 185th Ave NE, Ste 120
Redmond, WA 98052
paizo.com

ISBN 978-1-60125-291-3

Publisher's Cataloging-In-Publication Data
(Prepared by The Donohue Group, Inc.)

Jones, Howard A.
  Pathfinder tales. Plague of Shadows / Howard Andrew Jones.

  p. ; cm.

  Set in the world of the role-playing game, Pathfinder.
  ISBN: 978-1-60125-291-3

  1. Imaginary places--Fiction. 2. Elves--Fiction. 3. Curses--Fiction. 4. Fantasy fiction. 5. Adventure stories. I. Title. II. Title: Plague of Shadows

PS3610.O62535 P38 2010
813/.6

First printing February 2011.

Printed in the United States of America.

For Darian and Rhiana.

Chapter One
Old Friends

Elyana knelt among the splintered wooden debris for only a few moments before discovering a claw mark scored deeply into one of the boards. Frowning in concentration, she laid the ruined planks in the grass, piece by piece, trying to reconstruct how the fence must have looked at the moment of its destruction.

She'd already studied the tracks and stains left in the trampled steppe grass, and a disquieting suspicion had dawned. So she searched carefully, hoping to find some sign that whatever had crashed through her fence was mundane.

Her work area was small. Debris lay between two sturdy posts, six paces apart. The remains of three horizontal planks littered a cart-sized area inside the fence line, leaving only a few jagged edges still nailed to the posts themselves. The rest of the fence stretched intact across the plain to the darkening east, and to the west, where the sun sank in a golden haze.

She could feel Renar watching as she worked. The boy—young man, now, she corrected herself—might think he was being calm and quiet, but his suppressed shifting from foot to foot was a distraction. It flattered Elyana that he tried to mirror her own calm when he was in her presence, but it was an act, not yet an attribute.

Renar waited only ten paces away, inside the fence line. She glanced up at him, hoping her disapproving look would communicate the need for silence.

He took the acknowledgment as permission to speak. "Was it a bear?" His questions were as rapid-fire as they'd been at half his age, though his voice was a rich alto now. "Is it still inside the pasture? I can see the horse tracks. Did it attack any horses?" Renar's fingers shifted down the reins of his mount, which was browsing a patch of wild rye behind his right foot. Elyana's mare waited obediently on his left.

"It was not a bear." Elyana looked down again at the ragged edges of the boards, then rose and considered the setting sun. There was not much time before nightfall. The servants were likely already laying out plates in Stelan's dining hall.

Renar released the reins and stepped carefully over the planks. He bent down near a hoofprint, examining it with great care. She tried to remember when it was that he'd begun to resemble his father so strongly. Renar was slighter than Stelan, with fuller lips. In truth he was better looking, for he had inherited his mother's high cheekbones, though they still weren't as sharp as Elyana's own elven features. Then, too, Renar's nose had not been broken in innumerable combats . . . But the hawklike eyes and the forehead and the hairline, those looked so much like a young Stelan that when she contemplated him at rest she sometimes felt an ache in her chest.

"What do you see?" she asked him gently.

Renar's mouth worked as his eyes roved over the tracks. "The horse has spun and bucked."

"Good. What more can you tell me of the horse?"

"Was it Calda?"

Elyana smiled and Renar beamed at the sight of it. She tried not to smile too often at him now, for she had overheard him saying to a friend, with the sighing ardor of youth, that her smile was bewitching. There were too many issues already between Elyana and the boy's mother to have her worrying about *that*. "How did you know?" she asked.

"The notch in Calda's right front hoof where she hit that stone last week."

She was more pleased than she let on. The boy was picking out details and integrating pertinent outside information as well. They had trimmed Calda's damaged left front hoof only a few days ago, and it left a small but telltale mark in the prints wherever she walked. "Tell me of her attacker," she instructed.

"Well . . . the paws are bear-sized."

"Yes."

"But these tracks don't look quite like a bear's. They look more like they were made by a dog."

"Correct," Elyana agreed. "It was not a bear." She did not manage to keep a grim note from her voice.

"So what was it?"

"There's the trouble, Renar. It had claws, for it used them to smash in the fence. You can see them here, and there—that long gouge." She pointed precisely at the ruined boards.

Elyana glanced up to check their horses. Renar's gelding had wandered a few paces on; her own animal waited patiently.

She returned her attention to Renar, who was ready with more questions.

"It's so large for a dog, though. Could it be a cat? Mountain lions come down from the hills sometimes."

"These paws are twice the size of a mountain lion's."

"Oh." From his meek tone, it was clear Renar had picked up on her disappointment. "So what was it?"

An answer would require too much explanation, and she wasn't sure she wanted to hear herself say it aloud. "Tell me the order of events."

He stood, hands on his hips. He was not so tall as his father, though the broad-shouldered youth might still gain a few inches of height. After another moment spent regarding the prints, he shook his head. "I'm sorry, Elyana."

At least he had the grace to admit his lack of skill this time.

"The creature smashed through the fence with brute strength. It attacked Calda on her left flank. You can see the blood here." She pointed to a few blades of grass. "And do you see here, as she runs?" Elyana paced away from the broken boundary, pointing at the grass. "She was favoring her off hind leg."

"Calda survived and fled," Renar announced.

"Is there anything else you find peculiar?" Elyana stepped past him and took up the reins of Persaily, her long-limbed brown mare.

Renar stood with a puzzled expression, seemingly intent on reaching his conclusion by scrunching his mouth in different ways. On foot, Elyana guided Persaily carefully through the boards, then stood and petted her, sliding long fingers along the animal's neck.

After careful deliberation, Renar finally spoke. "Um. Hmm."

"Calda was here alone. By the fence. Far from any others. What's odd about that?" Elyana swung effortlessly up into the saddle, long-legged and impossibly graceful to Renar, who stared in undisguised awe.

"You aren't going out there to look for her alone, are you?"

She couldn't help smiling. "The day I can't track down a missing horse, Renar—"

"But there's some mad beast out there! I should go with you."

"I was handling things much worse than this before you were a glint in your father's eye." That, she realized, was an unfortunate way to phrase things, for she had once been well acquainted with the glints in his father's eyes, and Renar was sure to know it.

Renar was too concerned to notice. "But you don't even know what it is," he sputtered. "I should go get father and Drelm and—"

"I'll be fine," Elyana said. She patted the curve of her bow, strung and holstered behind her saddle. "Round up all the horses and get them out of the north pasture until we can repair this fence."

"But—"

"And then get to supper. Your mother will be furious if you're late again."

A protesting noise began deep in Renar's throat, but Elyana had already urged Persaily into motion. The bottom curve of the sun now touched the horizon, and their shadows were long upon the grass as the mare cantered away.

She doubted Renar had the expertise to guess why a horse would wander so far from the rest of its herd that it would stand beside the fence as a large predator charged.

It was remotely possible that she'd missed some tracks, but to Elyana it looked as though no other animals had been anywhere near the edge of the north pasture recently. It was possible, if completely uncharacteristic, that Calda had wandered from the rest of the herd of her own volition. But at the very same time something crept down from the foothills? The coincidence defied belief.

Only one explanation served all the facts: sorcery had called the horse forth, and a sorcerous beast had attacked her. Elyana hadn't seen predator prints like those for more than twenty years, but she hadn't forgotten them. And a summoned shadow hound meant someone to do the summoning. The possible whos and whys tumbled through Elyana's mind as she followed the wounded horse's trail. None of them especially brightened her mood.

Twilight was fading on toward night when she found what was left of Calda.

Persaily gave the slashed and twisted corpse a wide berth as a grim-faced Elyana soothed her mount with whispers and scanned the death site. The colors might be drained from the land, but to her eyes, details still stood out sharply. Calda's body was missing most of its neck, and the haunches were stripped of flesh. Terrible raking wounds stood out all over her body, as if she'd been repeatedly slashed before she was finally killed. Flies were settled into the wounds and were already at the eyes.

Elyana frowned. Calda hadn't been the brightest of horses, but she'd been good-natured and swift. She had not deserved this death. Elyana resisted the impulse to bend down and look for the shadow hound's tracks, for the wind was blowing her scent toward a dense thicket of hawthorn and maple standing only twenty feet off.

Persaily pricked up her ears. Elyana had her circle the little stand of trees, and eyed the place warily. She brought Persaily to a stop downwind.

There was no missing the smell of horseflesh, which kept Persaily alert. The predator's scent was absent, which might have meant that a normal animal had moved on.

But Elyana was positive she faced no normal animal.

She drew her sword. The elven craftsman who'd fashioned the long, slim blade untold years before had known better than to announce its wielder's presence with showy magical energy. Instead its power pulsed through the hilt against her palm like a slow, steady heartbeat. As always, it set off a resonant thrumming in the coarse old armband hidden by her shirtsleeve.

She waited.

Suddenly, a hound bayed from inside the copse. The sound was deep and sonorous and strangely resonant, as though it echoed in from some far-off place. Elyana winced at the assault on her senses, and Persaily snorted in fear, laying back her ears and readying to bolt. Only Elyana's deep bond with the horse left her some modicum of control when the snarling hound charged.

It seemed more a shadow than a being, a huge springing darkness against the lesser blackness of the twilight. Elyana had a mere heartbeat to note the flashing teeth in its overlarge maw before it closed the distance and leapt for Persaily's newly presented haunches.

Elyana urged Persaily forward with her knees, praying the mare would respond. Persaily had never been in combat before, but she was no green mount; she'd been trained to ignore dozens of different kinds of loud noises, sudden movements, and strange shapes. They'd both soon learn whether it had been enough.

Persaily whirled at her command and the hound twisted in air to follow, missing by only a dagger's length. Elyana leaned out. The edge of her blade slashed deep through an ebon shoulder. The moment her steel met the flesh of the hound the blade glittered with silver energy, dimming to nothing as her weapon cleared.

The creature landed with a grunt and pivoted on its hind legs. Elyana spun Persaily to face it.

Again the beast howled. The sound was a sorcerous attack, and Persaily nickered in fear, dancing and tossing her head. Yet she did not bolt, and Elyana's mouth tightened with satisfaction.

The hound sprang again, its arc more shallow this time and its massive clawed paws reaching for horse and rider.

At Elyana's command Persaily kicked in a burst of speed, and Elyana's strike caught the hound a hair before the apex of its jump. The blow raked through the darkness that was the creature's head. A dark spray of blood trailed after the blade's silvery passage. The hound itself missed her by inches, for Persaily had veered left precisely as directed.

The hound shook the ground as it fell, keening. It clawed at the dirt and from its mouth came a mournful call, falling in pitch as life seeped away.

Elyana swiftly brought Persaily around and scanned the plains, suddenly fearful the hound might be signaling others. It was then she heard the tolling of the village bell. The distant, lonely sound seemed to evoke an answering response from the dying beast, which howled forlornly a final time before its head fell between two black paws. A moment later it dissolved into dark clouds that were carried and thinned by the wind.

She glanced quickly at her blade to see that the blood smeared there was transforming to smoke as well. She sheathed the weapon, then leaned down to pat her animal's neck, trying to decide why someone would be ringing the bells. "Good girl. Very good girl."

Persaily snorted in satisfaction, or perhaps relief. Elyana listened. Fourteen clangs. This was no late hour ring, but an alarm. The last time she'd heard them rung like this was six years ago, when that sky-swallowing storm had roared out of the north to rip roofs off of half the farmsteads.

Elyana cursed and urged Persaily into a gallop.

She could not guess what kind of emergency had set someone ringing the bells, but she feared any number of things. More shadow hounds. Shadow wizards. Galtans.

Or worse, her old friend Arcil.

Persaily's gallop ate up the miles, her gait so smooth it was akin to flying. Soon Elyana saw the bell tower of the temple limned against the stars. She cut through a dark pasture and thundered into the road, clouds of dust billowing out behind them. Persaily was winded now, so Elyana let her slow. It was just as well, for the villagers were gathered around the fountain in the square, nervously fingering farm implements and old swords. They looked at Elyana expectantly, and Odric, the balding headman, stepped out from among them with his lantern.

"What's happened?" Elyana demanded.

"Captain Drelm's ordered us to search the streets and houses," Odric reported. Elyana hadn't seen the man this tense since his granddaughter's birth three years back.

"For what?"

"Someone's poisoned the baron," Odric said, almost choking. "We're going to catch the rat bastard and string him up!"

"Poison?" Elyana repeated, stunned. It felt as though her stomach had dropped away. Her heart hammered in her chest like the beat of a mad drummer urging her to war. "Is he dead? Who did it?"

"The priest of Abadar is with him now, milady, and we'll all be praying—"

Elyana's voice grew uncharacteristically strident. "Where is he? In the keep?"

"So far as I know, milady."

"Yah!" Elyana kicked Persaily into action again and the tired mare leapt forward. A half-dozen startled farmhands scattered from her path.

She'd been a fool. The shadow hound and the missing horse had been an obvious ploy to lead her from the keep—a mystery intriguing enough to lure her out, but not one so dangerous she wouldn't be able to handle it. Who else but Arcil would have been so careful? The question was why. He had no reason to hate Stelan any longer. He'd been gone for twenty years. What could he possibly be after?

Persaily gamely worked into a gallop, though her breath came in heavy gasps. They flew from the village and pounded up the hill to the old keep. Elyana hated to overtax the animal, but if Stelan had been poisoned, he might not have much time left. She might already be too late.

The mailed armsmen at the portcullis lifted lanterns and stepped aside. She swept past them, ducking her head under the points of the gate retracting into the stone arch above. She reached the courtyard and swung down from the saddle as a gasping and trembling Persaily came to a halt before the stables.

"She's been ridden hard," Elyana said as the stable hand ran up. "See that she's rubbed down and given half a bucket of warm water. If I'm not back in two hours, start feeding her some small handfuls of grain."

The boy bobbed his head quickly, eager to please even at so late an hour. "Certainly, m'lady."

Elyana patted Persaily's neck as she stepped away, then held scabbard to hip and raced for the old wooden door to the keep's tower. She scarcely acknowledged the chamberlain's bow. He must have been told she was riding up, as he had no other reason to linger in the entryway.

"Is he still alive?"

"I think so, Lady, but—"

"Where is he?"

The chamberlain bowed his head respectfully and his hand swept out toward the stone stairs. "He is in his—" before he said the word "bedchamber" Elyana was already pelting up the crescent steps.

She found Stelan in the room that made up most of the keep's top floor. He lay under a thin linen shroud in his canopied bed. Waiting in the bow-shaped room with him were an anguished-looking Renar; a sturdy little cleric of Abadar, robed in white silk and sitting at the baron's side; and the baroness, wan and pale, an aging beauty whose dark locks were now threaded with gray. Elyana paid scant heed to the subtle turn of Lenelle's lip at sight of her and stepped to the side of her old friend.

His arms lay atop the cover; everything below his chest lay beneath. And that scarred face with its broken nose and graying beard was still.

Elyana reached out for his left hand.

"Don't touch him!" Lenelle said swiftly, and Elyana snatched back her hand, astonished Lenelle would be territorial over him even now.

"He bruises with but the slightest touch," the cleric said quietly, and Elyana felt a pang of guilt for assuming the worst of Lenelle until she saw the woman's eyes. She knew then that Lenelle might have used the same words regardless of Stelan's condition.

Elyana looked away from her and down at Stelan. She saw the slow rise and fall of the cloth above his chest.

"He lives," Lenelle told her, her Chelish accent sliding over the vowels.

Elyana looked to the cleric, who had risen politely. She ignored the bow of his head. "What's wrong with him?"

"I have been in prayer," the man said, adjusting his gold chain of office with pompous dignity. "I believe he has been cursed."

"What makes you say that?"

Lenelle answered sharply. "'Twas the letter, not prayer, that showed him that."

"My prayer confirmed it," the cleric countered.

"What letter?" Elyana asked.

Lenelle gently withdrew a folded piece of parchment from the table by the bedside, passing it across Stelan's body.

"It was addressed to you," Lenelle continued, "and I am sorry to have opened it." She did not sound especially apologetic. "It was lying beside him, where he lay on the floor."

There was no mistaking the handwriting, cramped and precise even though its wielder had attempted an elegant flow with his letters. Arcil had only ever been able to pretend gentility, never to feel it, even in his writing.

Elyana let out a sigh. Sometimes she hated being right. She unfolded the parchment.

Dearest Elyana,
    I regret that we must become reacquainted under such unpleasant circumstances, but since our old friend proved so unwilling to deal with me in any sort of reasonable fashion, I am turning to

*you. Neither you nor Stelan's family should grow
too alarmed.*

*The trouble that has afflicted Stelan is com-
pletely curable, and when he recovers he will be no
worse for the effects. He might even be more rested.
All you have to do is turn over that old statuette we
recovered from Athalos. I know that you remember
the one; you rightly found it hideous.*

*Had Stelan accepted my initial correspondence,
he would have been well rewarded for parting
with the thing, which I now find useful for my
researches. Instead, I have been forced into the
uncomfortable position of causing consternation
to his charming family, and yourself.*

*Be waiting before the castle gate with the
statuette at midnight. My familiar will collect it,
and then Stelan will be as he was before and we
shall all be happy.*

*Do not try to be clever this time, Elyana. I
am ever so much more skilled than I was when
you knew me, and as you used to say, I become
obsessive about my interests.*

The missive was signed, "Respectfully, Arcil."

Renar practically pounced on Elyana the moment she
lowered the letter, his words galloping. "Mother says
that Arcil was a friend of yours and father's. It doesn't
make any sense! Why would a friend do this? And what
statue is he talking about?"

Elyana, lost in her thoughts, did not immediately
answer.

"He was very proper and civil when he came for the
wedding," Lenelle said. "I would not have expected this
of him."

"This death threat's civil as well," Elyana pointed out, then dropped it unceremoniously on the bed. The cleric eyed the paper cautiously.

Elyana turned to Renar. "He *was* our friend. He rode with your father and me for many years, and helped Stelan restore these lands, but he was . . . not an especially nice man." Elyana could have backed up her point by providing the boy with several telling examples, but it *might* be possible for Lenelle to disapprove of her even more.

"How do you think he got in?" Renar asked. "Can you find him and reason with him? Can you catch him?"

Before Elyana could frame an answer to any of those questions, Lenelle asked one herself: "Do you know where this statue is?"

Elyana shook her head. She hadn't seen the ugly thing since before Renar was born.

Renar hadn't given up. "Can you find him?" he repeated. "Talk to him?"

"Arcil, or something he sent, got in and out via magic. He might be close, but he won't be in the keep." She paused for a moment, lost in thought. "And no . . . I don't think I can reason with him. Not anymore."

"What is this statue, exactly?" Lenelle asked.

"It's part of a . . ." Should she tell her it was loot they found in the keep of a shadow wizard? ". . . one of our recovery operations. We divided the spoils, and that ugly statue was one of the last things to go. It's fashioned in the likeness of a furred beast."

"Like a wolf?" Renar asked. "Or a bear, or something?"

She could have told him it was in the shape of a vile monster from another plane. The less Renar knew about any of that, the better. "It's only about a foot high, ornamented with silver filigree, and has two bloodstones for eyes. I would have thought your father had gotten rid of it years ago." She glanced at the paper. "But Arcil's methodical. If he thinks Stelan has it, he probably does." She eyed Lenelle. "Arcil says there's been some kind of contact between the two of them. Are there other letters?"

Lenelle stepped around the side of the bed. "There are."

"Stelan did not mention them to me."

"Does he keep you apprised of everything?" Lenelle asked coolly.

Elyana did not trouble replying. It was peculiar that Stelan had kept Arcil's contact secret. Why hadn't he told her?

"He's been troubled whenever they arrived," Lenelle continued, "but he would not discuss the letters with me, or share them."

"He expressly forbid her from looking," Renar said, adding, "that's what mother said when we were talking about them earlier."

So Stelan had kept them from everyone. He hadn't wanted anyone to worry. "Where are they?" Elyana asked.

Lenelle and Renar glanced about the room at the same instant. There was precious little furniture—a wardrobe, a table, and three chests. The boy took a lantern from a hook beside the door and hurried to the first chest.

Elyana could see nothing over the boy's shoulder but neatly folded clothing. She turned to the cleric. "Do you have any idea what's afflicted the baron?"

Lenelle again interrupted, speaking imperiously to the little man. "I am sure you recall that we recently donated the funds to repair the tilework in the bell tower." She stepped up to Elyana, the closest the woman had been to her in Elyana's memory. Elyana realized after a startled moment that Lenelle was ham-handedly striving to intimidate the cleric with a show of rank: the two leading ladies of Adrast standing together.

"We are well aware of the strength of your piety." The cleric cleared his throat, apparently uncomfortable under the dual scrutiny. "That's not the issue. The issue is that your husband, the noble baron, is suffering from a curse that I am unable to identify."

"Arcil doesn't mention a curse," Elyana said. "Not once. Are you sure that it's not a poison?"

A frown briefly crossed the cleric's features, then he bowed his head and fingered the key hanging from his neck chain. "I have laid hands upon him and summoned forth holy energy. The curative powers of Abadar would have healed any normal affliction. This is something different. In my experience, it must be a curse. A powerful one. You can see it—already his flesh sinks, and it is time to heal him once more."

Elyana turned swiftly to Stelan and perceived dark circles deepening under his eyes, hollows forming between cheekbone and chin. The skin was tightening as it did on the very aged.

The cleric turned to the bed, offered empty palms to the heavens, and with closed eyes began a prayer to Abadar.

Elyana tuned out the words, watching side by side with Lenelle as the healing magic began its work. After only a few moments, Stelan was restored, though he remained asleep.

"How often must you heal him?" Elyana asked.

"Several times a day," the cleric answered. "More often if he is moved or jostled."

"The mere act of lifting him into the bed covered him in bruises from head to foot," Lenelle told her.

There was a clunk from behind them, and Elyana turned to find Renar had finished rifling through one chest and moved the lantern close to a second. Stelan's clothes lay in a rough pile beside him, and more swiftly joined them as the young man dug into the second chest.

"Elyana." Lenelle was considering her through her long eyelashes. "I know that you have some skill with healing magics. Perhaps you can examine my husband?"

This was another first, but Elyana only bowed her head with grace. "I shall. But if Stelan's condition is as the cleric says, aiding him will be beyond my powers."

She stepped around Stelan's wife. She could not help trailing long fingers along the dark wooden footboard and past the slim decorative column that held up one side of the canopy. The bed was a heavy piece of furniture, but its carver had shaped it with a care and simple precision, and feeling it under her skin had always pleased her.

Lenelle's mouth thinned disapprovingly as Elyana drew off Stelan's covers, exposing a wrinkled beige shirt. Whoever had carried him to the bed had not bothered to change him into a dressing gown. They had likely been afraid to bruise him further.

The ties that closed the shirt over Stelan's pectorals were undone; it was interesting to see that the hair here was turning gray as well. She opened the shirt more widely and gently touched the fingertips of her left hand to the exposed flesh.

Lenelle sucked in a hissing breath, for dark marks appeared beneath Elyana's touch. What exactly had Arcil done to him?

Elyana closed her eyes, gathering her energy. Arcil was well acquainted with her own meager magical talents, and would certainly have anticipated she would try a healing. She therefore doubted she would be any use at all, except that she would learn the nature of the affliction. Why, then, had Arcil been so deliberately vague about what he'd done? Not because he meant to keep the matter secret, she thought, but because Arcil prided himself on his politeness. He had acted with cold-blooded calculation, but would have found discussing the sordid details gauche.

Once, long ago, Arcil's peculiar understanding of honor had wryly amused her. The sound of his sharp, surprised laugh rang unbidden in her memory, and her mind flooded with other moments: that slight, shy smile he shared only with her, his low voice on a late night watch, the frantic cry of her name as he searched for her in the fog after the hounds had come. These and other recollections rained down upon her like the shards of a stained glass window, and the pain of vanished moments and missed chances stabbed deeply bittersweet.

Arcil should have grown into someone better.

Gritting her teeth, she felt her own life energy extend through her fingertips and merge with Stelan's.

Stelan's heartbeat was slow and steady, his breathing regular and deep. She explored his life force with her own, feeling her way through muscle and bone. Here was a notch from that spear thrust along his ribs, inflamed again—why had he not told her so that she could ease the pain? She found scars from other old injuries as well. Folk said elves were more resilient than humans, but it was not quite true—human bodies just didn't last as long, and their scars had less time to heal without outside assistance.

She was hardly an expert healer, and she was reaching the limit of her abilities. Still, she extended herself further, trying better to sense the more complex systems of Stelan's body. Long moments passed as she reached through the web of veins, rich with life. She could detect no poison; there was, in fact, nothing odd about him at all except for the visible wounding he'd taken at her slightest touch, and his continued unconsciousness.

She opened her eyes to find the humans staring at her.

"Can you help him?" Lenelle's voice was still controlled, but Elyana heard a plaintive note. Whatever her faults, the woman loved Stelan.

Elyana wished for her sake, for Stelan's sake, that she had better news. "No. The cleric is correct. He's been cursed."

Chapter Two
Unfinished Business

You're sure?" Lenelle asked, then spoke on before Elyana could answer. "How can it be removed? Can you remove it?"

"It is far beyond my knowledge. Perhaps the cleric's superiors?"

The little man offered his open palms. "I am afraid that I am the best we have here. I can send word to Yanmass, but that will require weeks. I don't know if I can keep him alive long enough to await a reply."

Elyana wasn't surprised. Stelan's rule had invigorated the little village, but Adrast was still a backwater, and a healer or wizard skilled enough to counter someone of Arcil's power would probably be found only in a major city.

"What if we take him to Yanmass?" Renar offered. He had come up behind Elyana, and continued speaking at great speed. "Then we wouldn't have to wait for word to reach Yanmass. We could get him the best help immediately."

"He nearly died being carried to the bed," Lenelle protested. "How do you think he'd fare in a cart on a rutted road?"

"The local clerics could ride with him and heal him—" Renar began.

The little cleric was shaking his head, then talked over Renar, speaking with force for the first time. "I am sorry, my child. Your mother is completely correct. We would swiftly exhaust our store of healing magics. For the lord's own sake, he should not be moved."

"Then we have no choice," Lenelle said. "We will have to do as Arcil says. We'll leave off this pointless search for the letters and look instead for the statuette."

Elyana shook her head. "Your husband didn't want to hand over the statue, or he would have done so."

"He is not in charge now," Lenelle retorted. "I am. We will find the statue and turn it over to Arcil."

Elyana understood the woman's sentiment. "I want to help him too, Lenelle. But Stelan knew what Arcil was capable of. He didn't think Arcil should have the statue, or he'd have given it to him."

Lenelle's expression in no way softened, but she fell silent.

"What are we to do?" Renar asked.

Elyana stepped over to where Renar waited beside the chests and eyed them herself. It would not be there, under any of those clothes.

Two of the chests were all but identical, and it took a moment for her to recall which was the one until she lowered the open lid. Then, across one of their rounded heights, she spotted the reddish knothole. She pressed her thumb inside it, then raised the lid again to reveal a slim plank on the lid's underside that had swung loose. A parcel of papers sat within the gap. She removed them and stood.

"Is that them?" Renar asked.

"What do you have?" Lenelle asked indignantly. "How did you know those were there?"

Elyana sighed inwardly. After all these years, Lenelle was still envious, no matter that Stelan had been hers now for almost half his lifetime. Elyana kept her voice level, as though the matter were unimportant. "I know that chest of old. I didn't know he still used it."

The three folded papers had broken black seals with Arcil's signature. Ignoring the disapproving gaze of the baroness, Elyana leafed through them.

They proved to be variations on a theme. The first one was brusquely cordial. Arcil began by reminding Stelan of their years of comradeship and asking if he knew the whereabouts of the old statuette, for which he would be willing to pay a handsome sum. The next missive refused offer of coins in the statuette's place, increased the monetary incentive, and made a veiled threat. The third letter was much more terse and impatient. She handed off the letters one by one to Lenelle as she finished.

Renar stood at his mother's shoulder, reading with her. Lenelle studied every letter with elaborate care.

Elyana turned to the cleric, who held tightly to the key that was his holy symbol, as if by squeezing it he might find strength.

"You say you cannot cure the curse," Elyana said. "Can you forestall it?"

The cleric mused over that possibility and then nodded slowly. "I may delay it with countercurses and healing. Any such delay would be expensive, however, because it would be so draining. And it would not restore him."

Expense. Clerics of Abadar mouthed pretty things, but with them it always came down to money. Though she herself had been raised by humans and appreciated money as a resource, the hoarding of it remained

31

innately mysterious to Elyana, and more than a little preposterous.

Lenelle frowned at Elyana. "I don't care what you say about this Arcil. We've really no choice, have we? We've got to start looking for this statue. Is it, too, hidden in some special place you know about?"

"No. Lenelle, we cannot trust Arcil. And there is another alternative."

"There is?" Renar seized hold of this new hope eagerly. "What is it?"

Elyana met Lenelle's eyes. "Arcil deliberately kept me occupied today," she said, "though I didn't know it at the time. He sent a creature to kill my horse and distract me so I would be nowhere close when he struck Stelan."

For the first time that night, Lenelle took fuller stock of Elyana, searching for wounds or other signs of injury. There was nothing to see, and Elyana could guess the woman's thoughts by her changing expression. Elyana knew that she might as well have stepped whole from Lenelle's memory of the day she'd come riding up at Stelan's side twenty-one years before.

As an orphaned elf, Elyana had grown up awkward and gangly amongst humans, self-conscious about her appearance. As she'd aged into her slim height, she had at first been pleased and astonished by the attentions humans granted her. She had long since grown tired of them, however, and resented having to guard something so simple as a smile lest it be taken as an invitation to courtship. Worse were the reactions of some women. Elyana had never fully understood why Stelan would set her aside for the formal and sometimes autocratic Lenelle, and it was easy to guess that Lenelle wondered herself. At forty, the human was still pretty, though there was gray in her hair and her waistline had broadened. Still, she spent an inordinate amount of time on the appearance of things, be they the arrangement of furniture in the keep, the tailoring of Renar's tunics, or the arrangement of her hair. Elyana knew from the gossip of Lenelle's often disgruntled handmaids that the baroness had spent large sums on rare Chelish cosmetics for her skin, that she frequently tasked servants to brush her hair for a half-hour or more, and that she sometimes dropped a poisonous belladonna extract into her eyes to enlarge her pupils. Elyana had been aghast when she'd learned that, until she remembered Stelan once praising Elyana's eyes as huge and luminous, their violet so vibrant that their color might be seen from across a room.

Lenelle's competitive drive mystified Elyana—Stelan had long ago made his choice. If his decision had come down to appearance alone, surely he would have picked Elyana, whose auburn hair hung straight with minimal effort, whose skin barely tanned and never wrinkled, and who never had to be cinched into her daily wear with the help of servants. Elyana would never have bothered with the fussy, restrictive dresses that were Lenelle's custom. Today, as usual, she wore loose brown pants and calf-high riding boots. The ties of her weathered leather buskin were loose, and the white shirt with its tight sleeves was rumpled beneath it. Her hair was tied back with a simple leather strap.

"You look well," Lenelle said, her tone cool. "I'm glad you returned unscathed. What happened to the beast?"

"I slew the thing. Arcil must have been close, to have attacked Stelan and summoned the shadow hound. And he must remain close, if he plans to send a creature here later tonight. I can track the monster back to him."

"I thought you said he could not be found," Lenelle pointed out.

"He won't be found by Drelm." The thought of the half-orc blundering around in the darkness after Arcil with a handful of armsmen and a mob of villagers was almost laughable.

"What are you going to do?" Renar asked, then answered his own question with another. "You mean to find him and force him to cure father?"

"I do."

"I forbid it!" Lenelle's voice rose in anger. "What if you're wrong? What if you make this wizard angry? What will he do then?"

"We are in combat," Elyana said, barely polite. She breathed deep, forcing calm. "Arcil thinks our back is to the wall. It's time to strike."

"That's what father would say," Renar agreed. He turned to the baroness. "Mother, he would not permit blackmail. We shouldn't either."

"I don't mean for the wizard to go unpunished. Not forever. But now . . ." Lenelle's voice faltered. "I don't wish . . . your father . . ." The woman took a deep breath and raised her head regally. Elyana realized that Lenelle was close to the breaking point and that now, at this moment, their similarities outweighed their differences.

"Lenelle," she said gently, "I can find Arcil."

The gaze of the baroness measured her guardedly.

"I have never managed a household," Elyana continued, "nor raised a child, nor hosted a gathering of nobles. But tracking, fighting—these things I know. Give me your leave."

Lenelle's eyes softened, though she still frowned uncertainly.

"Let us ride," Renar agreed. "Elyana can track anything."

"No," Lenelle said sharply.

For a brief moment Elyana thought the baroness was forbidding action, and opened her mouth to protest.

But Lenelle spoke on. "I'll not risk losing you both."

Elyana understood that the baroness meant both husband and son. Not her.

"Mother—" Renar said, only to be cut off.

"You will stay." Lenelle lifted her chin. "Elyana will go." She turned to the elf. "But you should not go alone. We have our own magic worker, remember? Take Kellius. And take Captain Drelm and some soldiers."

Elyana bowed her head. "If you wish." So far as she knew, the young wizard Kellius was not especially powerful, but he might prove useful.

He might also end up dead, for Arcil surely outclassed him.

She wasn't nearly as worried about Drelm's survival. The half-orc was tough enough to endure a pounding, and there was an outside chance he'd be useful distracting any backup forces Arcil might have with him.

"We will ride light," Elyana told the baroness. "I want no others. And both men must know that I am in charge." She spoke on as Lenelle opened her mouth to object. "I know Arcil. They do not."

Lenelle cleared her throat. "The captain is a trained warrior."

Elyana's eyes narrowed.

"And the head of the baron's guard," Lenelle continued. "I'm sure—"

"I lead," Elyana snapped.

Lenelle's eyebrows rose in outrage. Elyana took a single step forward, and Lenelle, suddenly uncomfortable, retreated as the elf spoke on, her voice low, passion barely leashed.

"I've walked Golarion for almost two hundred years, Lenelle. I've faced things that would kill Drelm in a single blow and shatter your mind if you even glimpsed them. I will lead."

Lenelle cleared her throat. "Very well," she said, managing dignity.

Renar was either oblivious to the tension or incredibly single-minded. "Mother," he said, "I really think I should go with—"

"Do as your mother says," Elyana commanded. After a moment, she added more gently, "Find the statue. If this doesn't go well, you're going to need it. And besides, you need the rest. You've been helping me in the pastures all day."

"I need rest? What of you?"

Elyana bowed her head slightly. Renar had a point. "Allow me a few moments to center myself, and I will be ready. Perhaps a small meal."

Elyana's meager wants were quickly tended to, the cook understanding from long experience that she preferred her meat rare, her vegetables fresh and crisp.

She sat down to eat in the empty mead hall, dark save for the hearth fire. When Kellius and Drelm arrived she set down the slice of young green pepper she'd been chewing and tried not to look longingly at the cushioned bench left of the hearth. Fifteen minutes would have seen her a long way toward recuperating her energy.

Kellius bowed his head, restraining a quirky, lopsided smile. A leather pouch was slung over one shoulder and dangled to his waist opposite. Tall and rawboned, with large hands, he looked more like a farmhand who'd forgotten to eat for a few weeks than a wizard. Most magic workers of Elyana's acquaintance had been at best self-absorbed, but Kellius was neither prickly nor unpleasant, and his homely face spread easily in a grin. "Milady." He bowed his head to her.

Drelm's stocky frame and stance were far more imposing than the wizard's, no matter that Kellius was just as tall. A mixed heritage marred his otherwise even features with a blocky forehead and fangs that jutted up from his lower lip. His skin, though coarse, was nearly human in the flickering hearthlight, showing only a hint of green. His silvery hair, reddened by reflected flame, was thick and immaculate, tied back in a tail. The baron's cloth tabard concealed a goodly portion of Drelm's scale mail, but Elyana knew that the whole of it was polished to a high sheen even if only a few inches showed above the tabard collar. He carried his dark helm in the crook of an arm.

"Lady Elyana," Drelm said. His voice was rough, low and level.

"Captain. Mage Kellius."

"The baroness says we are to track the wizard who cursed the baron." Drelm's voice betrayed his eagerness. He was always like that, she thought, like a fighting dog. One with ferocious power and murderous impulses.

Her disdain for him did not show in her voice. "That we are, Captain. But we must take him alive if we are to save Stelan."

Drelm nodded once.

"We must ride swiftly," Elyana told them both. "And detour through the Plane of Shadow, to track the beast."

"The Plane of Shadow?" Drelm repeated.

"Lady," Kellius drawled, "I have no shadow magic."

"I do," she said simply, and saw the mage's face brighten in curiosity. The half-orc's narrowed in suspicion. He looked more bestial that way.

"We face a wizard well versed in shadow magics. I know him of old, and he is ruthless. He is likely to employ a handful of warriors to guard his person. Kellius, I've seen you create fire, and I've heard you can cast lighting. How well can you handle those spells?"

"I know what I'm about," he said easily.

She found it refreshing that the wizard was neither falsely humble nor arrogant, and she bobbed her head in approval. Kellius was more a horticulturist and scholar than anything else; Stelan had hired him three years ago as a matter of general principle, and the baron had warmed quickly to the wizard. "Arcil is clever," she told them both, "but tends to be linear with his tactics. He's smart, but I think we can outfight him if we're fast and wily. Do you understand?"

"Yes," Drelm answered gruffly. Kellius bowed his head.

"Good. Let's ride." Elyana started to turn away.

"The men will be ready shortly," Drelm said. "I sent a runner down to the village to gather them."

"We're not taking any others with us."

"Why not?" Drelm asked. "We have fifteen men-at-arms and forty villagers who can—"

"We ride swiftly, and we keep the expedition small, the better to sneak up on Arcil."

Drelm growled. "We have more than enough men to overwhelm him. If he is so powerful a wizard—"

Elyana cut him off. "If we take those men, all we do is condemn them to death."

Drelm's scowl deepened.

Elyana's patience had been stretched to the limit this night. She was tired and sad, and it took little to fan her simmering irritation to rage. "I am in charge," she said, her tone like ice. "Are you with me or not?"

The half-orc's lower jaw moved back and forth, shifting his projecting teeth. Finally he assented. "I'll follow you."

"Glad to hear it," Elyana said. "Let's go."

Chapter Three
Shadow Ride

Drelm was a practiced horseman, but the wizard was no great talent, and insisted on riding with his narrow shoulders hunched forward no matter Elyana's instruction. She gave up after the third attempt. There were more important things to worry about. If Kellius survived all this, he would be sore in the morning. So be it.

She trusted neither man to pick out her trail from the pasture, and chafed at the necessity of leading the wizard slowly through the darkness, his human eyes far inferior to hers and the half-orc's. At this rate it would be almost an hour before they arrived at Calda's body. Then the tracking would begin, and there was no way of knowing how long it would take, provided she would really be able to follow the beast's trail through the Plane of Shadow.

She still wore the ring that opened the portal to that strange realm, but the last time she'd actually employed it, she, Arcil, Vallyn, and Stelan were riding for their lives from Galtan soldiers. She couldn't quite recall if both twins had been with them. Probably. And it was probably before Stelan had begun courting Lenelle.

In the years since, she'd often looked at the dull black stone, thinking that she should drop it into a keepsake box, for it was hardly useful in her day-to-day life. She supposed it was a reminder of other days, and friends, and tried not to dwell too much on the fact that it was Stelan who'd slid it toward her while they divided Lathroft's spoils. Sometimes she wondered if he even remembered he'd given her a ring before Lenelle, and then she mocked herself for her sentimentality and thought it better to put the thing aside.

Somehow she always slipped it onto her finger each morning.

After they left the keep they stopped only once, at Elyana's cottage beside the stables. There she donned her leather armor and took up her silver arrows, a little surprised to learn the feathers remained in pretty good shape after all these years.

When they finally reached the battle site, Elyana found a wolverine growling over Calda's carcass. Typical of its kind, the animal was ready to fight any or all of them over the meat. Drelm grumbled and drew his axe, but Elyana bade him let be and led them to the back of the thicket.

Drelm dismounted and followed Elyana as she trod lightly over the ground, his heavy footfalls crunching down rotting leaves and sticks. Elyana waved him back. She felt his eyes upon her as she searched over the ground, his impatience like a spear at her back.

"Time's wasting." Drelm said loudly. "I thought you meant to take us to some magical land."

"Patience," she said.

She decided to ignore his low-voiced growl. On a clear night like tonight she saw almost as well as she did during daylight. After only a short while she discovered a print. Then another. And another. The beast had come from the north. She stood and whistled.

Persaily trotted over immediately and Elyana vaulted into her saddle.

"Find something?" Drelm asked needlessly.

"I have the shadow hound's trail," she said. "Follow me."

Follow they did. Drelm either had the good sense or the natural inclination to let her ride several horse lengths ahead. Elyana did not look up at the familiar twinkling patterns to find horse and hunter, monsters and prey shining in the firmament. Her focus was only upon the earth, and she tuned out the croaking of frogs, the occasional far-off call of an owl. Long years of practice and her inborn skill enabled her to detect the prints of the beast in the soil and its passage through the steppe grass from horseback. The task was made simpler in that the thing had proceeded in a straight line. She had but to trace that line to its other end to come upon the summoning point, and she could already guess where it was likely to be.

Another quarter-hour passed. The trail led up toward a rocky knoll. Elyana slid out of her saddle and stilled Persaily with a word. The horse waited patiently, ears erect, turning her head to search the distance. Lifting a hand to her allies to signal a halt, Elyana left them with the mounts and started soundlessly up the little hill alone.

She climbed through the sand and gravel and little bushes, reaching the flat top a few minutes later. Lying prone, she picked out the remains of the old watchtower perched on Ostivai Hill, raising its broken outline against the stars a mile to the northwest. Would Arcil really be that obvious?

Yes, she thought. Arcil habitually underestimated the intelligence of others.

She kept low as she crawled out to examine a flurry of prints. She did not want to alert any distant watchers to her position.

The tracks told her almost everything she needed, and a savage smile rose on her lips. From here the beast's tracks began. There were the tracks of its summoner, who'd come up the knoll from the north and then stood to work magic. Two large men wearing boots had accompanied him, but had stood well clear, likely because they were uncomfortable with the magical energies. Guards.

Her musings were disrupted by the sound of heavy booted feet scuffing soil and crushing sticks. Her hand slipped instinctively for a weapon and then she cursed softly, realizing it must be Drelm. She flung herself around and crawled swiftly, reaching the edge just as the half-orc rose into view on the slope. Her sudden appearance startled him and he lifted his throwing axe.

"I motioned you to stay put," Elyana hissed.

"What's taking so long?"

"I said to wait," she snapped. She slid down beside him feet first, readying a short lecture, but the half-orc spoke first.

"Have you found him yet?" he demanded.

"I think they're in the ruined watchtower."

"I could have guessed that, the way we were going."

"And if you'd stood up on the hill here, they'd have seen you."

Drelm grunted. "What were you doing up there?"

"Assessing our enemy, Drelm. One wizard and two trusted guards came up to the knoll. Likely there were a handful more about the bottom holding their horses.

The half-orc nodded slowly. Was that approval, she wondered?

"Well. If they're in the ruins, let's have the wizard throw a spell on us. For quiet."

He was at least aware of some of his deficiencies, then, which is more than she'd given him credit for. "I can do better. It's time to enter the shadow realm."

"You can sneak up on them that way?" Drelm's small eyes narrowed in suspicion.

"We can. Captain, when next I give an order, you must follow me, or someone may die. Do you understand?"

"You ride and track well," the half-orc admitted. "The baron says you are a great fighter." He sounded as though he were half-willing to believe the information, probably because he so admired the baron. "But you are a woman. I can see that you are not strong." He waved at her slim body with his free hand.

"Neither is a serpent," she countered. "But it's still swift and deadly. You forget I am older than I seem."

He said nothing, and his expression was unreadable. At least he was no longer wrinkling his brow at her.

The half-orc grunted, somehow conveying finality. He looped his throwing axe back onto his belt, and Elyana started down. As she descended, she wondered what she'd said that had proved more convincing than the last time. Shorter sentences and smaller words, likely.

Soon they were back beside their mounts, and Elyana quickly hobbled the legs of her companions' horses with lengths of rope. Persaily she trusted not to wander. "Don't forget. The shadow wizard must be taken alive."

"What can this shadow mage do?" Drelm asked.

"He will do his best to confuse your senses," Elyana answered. "Arcil was never good at seeing beyond his own senses. He thinks like a human. No offense."

"None taken." Kellius raised his hand good-naturedly.

Drelm only frowned, but whether that was because he was insulted to be considered other than human or because he remained impatient Elyana did not know. Or care. "His illusions are more sight-based than anything else," she continued. "Trust your nose and your ears. Stay close, especially as we approach our departure point."

"Shouldn't we ride?" Kellius asked.

"Horses aren't fond of the shadow realm," she said, though she did not add that unpracticed riders on those horses worried her more.

"What is . . . on the other side?" Kellius asked. "I have heard about the shadow world, but not very much."

"The darkness of twilight, and a crushing sense of isolation. Your senses will strain to make sense of it. Try not to pay much attention to the things on the edges of your vision—anything beyond your immediate sight is insubstantial and might well shift."

Kellius nodded once. His silence might have been meant to hide nervousness. Drelm, naturally, was still frowning. Stelan had called him dependable, and so far his irritability and sullen nature was unflagging.

"We shall not be there for very long." Elyana hoped that would be true. In her experience distances were always shorter in the shadow realm, though she had heard that sometimes they were longer, or warped, or utterly confused. No need to tell the others. "I'll take us to the ruins through the shadow realm and then into the real world for the attack."

"You said Arcil's a shadow wizard," Kellius said. "Is he going to be able to sense us coming?"

"He might."

Elyana stared down at her ring and tried not to think that Arcil himself had helped her deduce its use. Might he expect her? He had once complained that he could never anticipate her reactions; could she still trust that she'd surprise him?

Her eyes made contact with the ring, and the full power of it swept into the air surrounding her, like a dark, windblown fog. Focusing her will upon that energy was something like grasping hold of the shoots of a deeply rooted plant and pulling hard enough to feel its connection to the soil without ripping it free.

She took hold, whispered a word in ancient Azlanti, and reality spun. Persaily nickered in surprise at the formation of the whirling circle of black vapor. She heard Kellius exclaim behind her, and the other horses whinnied.

Elyana put hand to hilt and stepped through.

Beyond the portal lay a plain of waving black grass. A few miles to her left the ground twisted sharply, as though some deity had grasped hold of the earth and bent the plain in the middle until it lurched to one side.

Elyana scanned the grasses and waited for her companions. Kellius stepped through a moment later, his gaze roving wildly.

Drelm's eyes were narrowed in suspicion as he too took in the place. "May Abadar guide me," he said.

Elyana lifted her leather-clad arm toward the distant hill. Stone pillars stretched clawlike for the heavens. The stars here were points of flickering blackness in the gray sky.

"The sooner we're out of here, the better," Kellius said. His voice was dulled in the Plane of Shadow and did not carry far. About them was only silence. There was no wind, nor the creak of insects or the call of night animals. Nothing.

"I know you're eager to be done with this," Elyana cautioned, "but do not rush. There are things here that our senses may not detect." With that, she started forward.

The strange ebon grasses reached to her elbows, and the ground was dry beneath her boots. The stars themselves drifted slowly, like clouds. She tried not to look at them. From somewhere far to their right came what she took to be a keening wind, but it did not rise and fall—it just continued in a high, whistling moan for a long moment before ebbing away.

They were two-thirds of the way across the plain when her sharp eyes caught something moving in the ruin; a man shape half again as large as a man, with long swaying arms. It ducked quickly behind a stone wall and did not reappear.

Was the beast real or phantom? A guardian that Arcil had summoned? Had he anticipated her?

They walked to the back side of the hill. A gently sloping path was carved into the hillside parallel to the ruin itself so that the old stone stood sentinel above.

"Something moved in the ruins," Elyana told her companions, and they followed her gaze. Drelm sniffed the air and unlimbered his axe.

Elyana loosed her sword in the scabbard but did not yet draw it, knowing that the blade would gleam furiously in the Plane of Shadow. She lifted her bow out of the holster at her shoulder.

She started up the ramp at a jog, the others following.

Stone rumbled above them. They looked up in time to see a dark chunk of masonry plummet down.

"Look out!" Elyana shouted, and sprinted ahead. She heard the impact behind her as the ground shook. There were no screams, only a growled curse from Drelm and the rumble of the rock sliding farther down, so she kept her attention on the final leg of the old ramp. Nothing was left of the gatehouse but a jumble of masonry, though the wall to its right was intact. A long-armed figure rose up from behind shattered second-story crenellations and heaved up a man-sized hunk of stone. It let out a deep-throated roar of challenge.

Elyana raised her bow, then heard Kellius behind her.

"I've got him," the mage declared. Lightning flashed up from the man's fingertips. The spell struck the shadow man about head and shoulders, revealing a corpselike face with fangs half the length of its head.

Its roar transformed into a cry of pain. The beast dropped the stone to shield its eyes with clawed hands.

Elyana selected one of her silver-tipped arrows by the feel of its feathers and nocked it to the bow. In a heartbeat it was airborne. Even as the lightning faded and the creature hunched and sniffed toward them, the arrow took it through one eye and it howled and dropped to the slope. It did not rise.

Elyana readied another arrow and leapt a fallen pillar to move deeper into the ruins.

She stepped into an uneven rectangle of stone. Loose rock and entire sections of wall lay in shattered lines across the courtyard, overgrown with black grasses. Most of the tower's second story had fallen away, but a few narrow walkways still thrust out jaggedly alongside the merlons.

Something moved at the corner of her vision. She spun to find a second beast-man rising from behind a pile of tumbled masonry, hefting a broken tree limb.

Drelm roared a challenge behind her, and she stepped aside so the half-orc could face the charging creature head on. She coolly surveyed the rest of the site.

The captain ran past her, axe lifted in one thick hand. The beast gibbered and readied to swing its branch.

She was glad she'd taken her time. Another shadow beast rose up from along the second floor. Elyana threw herself clear as a large hunk of stone blasted into the ground where she'd been standing. She ignored the rocky shrapnel raining against her left leg, rolled to a kneeling position, and sent another silver arrow winging.

She had aimed for the creature's throat, but it bent to scoop up another rock and the arrow slid over its scalp and disappeared into the darkness.

On her left Drelm let out a whoop of triumph as his greataxe sliced off the beast-man's shriveled head. Its body roiled away in black smoke.

Elyana's second arrow caught her attacker through the throat just as it hefted its stone overhead. It too dissolved into vapor. The massive stone it held fell through the space where it had stood and took a chunk of the second floor with it into the ground.

Elyana scanned the rest of the ruins, then stepped slowly into the center, peering behind rubble. Nothing.

"Praise Abadar!" Drelm came over to join her. "A good battle, that!"

Not as Elyana saw it. Arcil must have anticipated her actions and placed these guardians. That evidenced a greater mastery of shadow magics than he'd ever shown. She'd have to plan their next move carefully.

Her mood dark, she climbed up one broken wall, then jumped nimbly to grasp the broken ledge of the second floor.

"What are you doing?" Drelm called up.

"Retrieving my arrows." It wasn't just that she'd crafted them herself. She had only a handful that were effective against creatures of darkness, and no longer traveled with a wizard who could enchant more.

The first arrow was completely serviceable, though the fletching would need repair. From the height she looked down on Kellius and Drelm wandering guardedly about the ruins. The dark, endless expanse of the plains twisted beyond . . .

In short order she'd recovered her arrows and rejoined the half-orc and the mage in the center of the ruins. Drelm was grinning, flush with the joy of his battle. She wished she could share his elation.

"I think Arcil set these things here as sentinels," she said. "He must know we're here."

Drelm growled. "You said this was the best way."

She partly agreed with his approbation. She had misjudged. Either Arcil had been planning this for a very long time, or he'd grown far more powerful.

Her question to Drelm showed none of her internal worries. "Have we failed yet?"

The half-orc glowered, but did not answer.

"They may know we're coming," Elyana told them. "However—" she turned to Kellius—"suppose a spell were to come through first?"

"What do you have in mind?" Kellius asked.

Elyana smiled. "What do you have on hand?"

Chapter Four
Distractions in the Dark

Elyana and Kellius came through the spiral from the Plane of Shadow at the same moment, Kellius casting forth a blinding light, Elyana sending arrow after arrow into the Nidalese mercenaries who threw shielding arms across their eyes. Drelm charged through on their heels in time to launch a throwing axe at an archer on a ledge.

After that surprise there were only four of eight men left, one of them the wizard. Elyana spotted him in the corner and sprinted his way, swaying clear of the arrow aimed at her from the darkness. The shaft skittered away against the stones. She closed her eyes to the prismatic blast of colors raining all about her from the column ahead and paused briefly to send an arrow in response. Someone cried out, and then from behind came the scream of men in pain—an old sound, and too familiar, though she was still unused to Drelm's triumphant war whoop.

Elyana spotted Arcil leaning against the column, his hand clasped around the arrow shaft embedded in his sleeve and upper arm. His lips moved, then closed up as she drew her sword and leveled it at his throat from two paces off. "Let's have none of that, Arcil."

Before she had even finished her sentence, she knew something was wrong; there was hatred in those hooded eyes, but no recognition, only a wary fear. This was *not* Arcil, despite appearances. "Where is he?"

"Where's who, Elyana?" The man's words were in a fine imitation of Arcil's voice.

On closer inspection, she saw more evidence that she faced someone other than Arcil, for the man in front of her could be no older than forty. Arcil had been the oldest human of their band, and must now be approaching sixty, if he had not surpassed it.

Yet this man *looked* like Arcil from the old days. The clean-shaven face was handsome in an arrogant way, with a thin, arched nose. His teeth were white and straight, showing now in a sneer. The tips of his dark hair were flecked with gray, less like actual age and more like the stage makeup of someone playing a distinguished gentleman.

"Arcil was a comrade," Elyana told him. "You are nothing." She pressed the sword to the man's neck. "Where is he?"

"I thought you said to go easy on him," Drelm commented, stepping into her field of view. The half-orc held his bloodstained axe almost casually in one large hand.

"Eyes sharp," she said. "This man's an impostor."

Drelm yelled for Kellius to look alive for skulkers, but Elyana guessed there'd be nothing more to see.

She pricked the impostor's neck with her blade and drew a bead of blood. The impostor's chin rose and his eyes—Arcil's eyes—showed their whites in fear.

"Let me save your time," she said. "You're an apprentice. He placed an illusion of his semblance upon you, then told you to hold this position."

"Yes," the man said.

"Why?"

His eyes considered her blade, faintly catching starlight. She withdrew it a handspan. He risked a breath and paled as she swirled her sword point before him. An elven blade forged for elven physique, it was intended for both slicing and thrusting, and Elyana kept the point razor-sharp.

The apprentice gulped with Arcil's throat. "He said to relay a message, should you come to me."

"Yes?"

"Do you promise not to slay me, if I give it?"

"Which of us do you fear more?"

The fellow was not without spirit. He considered her. "In the main, I fear my master."

"I'm of a mind to let you live," Elyana said, "if there are no tricks."

"My only trick is that the master watches, and stands ready with magic."

"There is no one here but us," Elyana countered, and did not care for the satisfied smile that played at the corner of the man's mouth. He did not bluff—either Arcil waited nearby, invisible, or he was ready, somehow, to cast a spell from afar.

"The message," Elyana prompted.

His eyes flicked briefly up and to his left in recollection, and then he spoke. This time, the words were so typical of Arcil that, as he said them, it was much easier to believe she faced the real man.

"You always liked to be kept busy, Elyana, so I arranged several divertissements for you this evening. I hope they amused you. Questioning this one at any real length will only result in his death, which will sadden you and frustrate me, as I've put considerable time into his training. There's no good way to trace me. I advise you to employ your considerable talent in locating the statuette our idiot friend has hidden so that I don't have to kill him."

Elyana stared hard at the man before her, wondering for a moment if it wasn't truly Arcil playing some kind of game. Then she saw the wary look in his eye and the way he held himself. This fellow was arrogant, but lacked Arcil's assured superiority.

"It seems your master places some value in you," Elyana said.

"Some." The impostor's voice held a hint of pride. "But I would give much to be held in the same regard he holds you."

Even still? Had Arcil remained infatuated all these years? It was hard to imagine.

Kellius drew up on her left. "Did you learn anything?"

Elyana lowered her blade and glared at Arcil's apprentice. "This was all a trap. Well, not a trap, but a waste of time. Arcil guessed my plan. There's nothing to be learned from this one."

"I can make him talk," Drelm said.

"My master would not permit me to live," the fellow said.

"So asking you what he really wants with the statue is right out, then," Elyana asked.

"It is." The man sounded insufferably pleased to be under a death threat. "Or where he's really staying, or what his strength is."

The false Arcil smiled at her, smugly, so she wiped the tip of her blade clean on the cuff of his robe. That went a long way toward adjusting his expression to one more palatable."

"Well then." Elyana sheathed her sword. "You'll just have to find your way back to your master yourself, and let him remove the arrow. That should be fun."

Drelm stood frowning beside her. "Couldn't Kellius work something out of him?"

Kellius glanced quizzically at the half-orc. "What do you mean?"

Drelm took a moment, clearly trying to decide how to communicate his idea. "She's afraid the wizard will be killed by Arcil. With magic. Can you protect him so we can question him?"

"You want me to protect this fellow?" Kellius asked.

"Arcil's watching right now," Elyana said. "I can guarantee it. We're done."

She studied Arcil's apprentice for reaction, but he wisely showed none. Even the hint of a smile might have shattered her composure and prompted violence.

"Let's go."

Drelm let out a dissatisfied grunt and turned to leave. Elyana started after, then halted, suddenly curious about a final matter. "What does he really look like these days?"

The apprentice's mouth opened silently before he spoke. "He's . . ."

As he hesitated, a stream of darkness erupted out of the shadows and snared about the apprentice's torso, coiling like a giant serpent.

"No, Master!" The man's voice rose plaintively. "I would not have said—"

Elyana leapt close, blade ready. For all her speed, she was still too slow. The apprentice's voice broke in a scream mingled with the crunching of bones. He fell silent as blood oozed and fluids dripped and spurted from his twitching corpse. The shadow tentacle that had wrapped him dissipated in black smoke. What was left of the body slumped to the ground.

Kellius leaned over and began to retch.

Elyana found herself shaking in anger. She raised her head and addressed the empty air. "If you could wield so powerful a spell," she snarled, "you could have teleported him back and slapped him!"

There was no answer.

She bent down beside the man. As she'd thought, there was nothing to be done for him. Arcil was as thorough as ever. She dug into the man's bloody robes and found the amulet she'd expected, slipping it over his head. At once Arcil's familiar face became the pockmarked features of a thin man in his early twenties.

The others looked down at her, even Drelm's face showing surprise. She understood then that Arcil's lesson had not been meant for the poor apprentice, who would never apply its teachings.

Arcil's power had grown. Tremendously. He had said as much, and she had forgotten to take him at the word he valued so highly. Neither she nor Stelan's household had understood the strength of his power, or the seriousness of his will.

They could not fail to do so now.

Interlude
Conference of Equals

Don't be so thick, Stelan." Arcil set the faded scroll down on the table and let the paper roll in on itself. Their plates sat on the floor, empty now save for a few chicken bones, which Stelan's hunting dogs cleaned with tail-wagging enthusiasm.

Elyana swept her fingertips gently along the side of an old goblet in front of her. One small part of her attention was focused on the changing texture of the vessel's surface. The rest gauged Stelan's reaction.

The new baron had grown used to Arcil's condescension. The young man reached out with one powerful arm and soundly patted the flank of the dog beside Elyana.

Edak hunched on the bench beside Arcil and gnawed a hunk of bread. He glanced back and forth between wizard and warrior through his tousled hair. Edak was no mental giant, but it took little intellect to sense the tension in the air.

Still Stelan did not reply; Elyana looked away from Arcil's gaze, now fastened upon her, to watch the dust motes drifting in a sunbeam angled from a high

59

window. The same sunbeam shone upon a single banner, the only decoration Stelan had left in place after his assumption of the keep last week.

Aside from the four of them and the hounds, the cavernous mead hall was vacant. The place was all but barren, and the fall wind whistled steadily through cracks in the mortar. She did not much care for it.

"We've a duty," Arcil continued emphatically. "It's not just this one shadow wizard. This letter proves it. There's a whole cabal of them, all in league. They should be stopped."

"Stelan's a baron now," Edak said. He chewed for a moment, and swallowed before setting the bread aside. "Can't he call on the grand prince and get troops?"

Arcil was already shaking his head. Edak continued anyway. "The prince should be looking into this problem. We can show him the evidence."

"The grand prince!" Arcil said with distaste. "The prince didn't lift a finger to help Stelan when his father was killed. He probably never even heard about it, Edak. Every letter to the court goes through a hundred bureaucrats, each of whom needs a bribe. They're not going to be remotely interested in helping us—we're too far from the center of their universe, and lack the wealth to lure their attentions."

Edak brushed hair away from his brow.

Stelan pushed back his arms and stretched his back, then looked across the table at the wizard. "Arcil, you nearly died when those hounds came at us. It's enough that you risked your life for me once."

Elyana loved the sound of that voice. It was not so much the alto timbre, though that was pleasing—it was his clear, honest delivery. Stelan was incapable of dissembling about even the simplest things, and she loved him for it.

"Stelan . . ." Arcil drummed his fingers against the table's edge. Elyana could practically see him working on a new line of attack. "I don't think these wizards will just let this go. They'll probably come after you when they hear what we've done."

"They're wizards," Stelan countered. "They'll be more interested in hiding than in vengeance. They've books to read."

Arcil shook his head. "You don't really believe that, do you?" He looked to the elf for support. "Elyana? You're being awfully quiet."

All three men turned to her.

Elyana slid her hand away from the edge of the mug. This was Stelan's choice, not theirs, and she could tell he was reluctant. She would not gainsay him. "We've already accomplished all we set out to do," she pointed out. "The baron here has recovered his ancestral lands." She used the new title as a light joke, but no one laughed. "His people are safe."

Stelan nodded slowly. Arcil's frown deepened, but he waited, for it was clear from Elyana's tone that she had more to say.

She turned her eyes to Stelan. "But I can't help thinking you don't know what to do with yourself."

Stelan turned up his hands. Elyana knew he was overwhelmed with the mundane responsibilities that were suddenly in his lap. Allying with a dark wizard was the least of his uncle's crimes. Everything was depleted: gold, animals, mineral resources . . . even timber.

"The coffers are almost empty," Elyana continued. "If we do as Arcil suggests, they can be filled."

"I never thought you worried about money," Edak said.

Elyana faced him. "Stelan's a baron now. And he's going to need gold if he wants to take care of anything."

Stelan sighed. He knocked once on the wood. "If I'm killed, who will rule after me? There's no one. Things would be even worse. I'm not sure I can do that to Adrast. They need . . . someone."

"Appoint the headman, then," Arcil suggested. "He's no dullard. You heard him yesterday. He knows exactly what's needed."

"He does," Stelan agreed, nodding. "But he needs money."

"There you go, then," Arcil said. "A good baron would get him some."

Stelan reached down to scratch behind the ear of one of the dogs loitering nearby in the hope more food would fall.

Elyana recalled a moment the week before when Stelan had leaned against the hearth beside her, his breastplate dented, face smeared in gore and blood. He had been drained and exhausted and pale.

Today he looked worse.

Stelan looked up from the animal and spoke slowly. "I swore to my mother that I would restore my family's lands and save my people. With your help, I've done that. But it's not as simple as I thought. I'll give what you've said careful consideration."

"The longer you give it," Arcil said irritably, "the longer these wizards will have to prepare. The furthest ones out might not even have heard yet."

"Don't rush him," Edak urged, prompting a frown from Arcil. But the wizard fell silent.

"We'll talk again over supper," Stelan said, rising. He nodded once and pushed out from the bench, then rose and strode slowly off.

Arcil caught Elyana's eye and tipped his head toward Stelan, as if she did not already plan to follow him. He and Edak stood and walked for the exit, their boot heels echoing on the flagstones. Elyana trailed after her lover.

She was glad to see that Stelan did not return to the cold stone room in the tower above; he strode instead for the tightly wound stairs of the musicians' gallery. Judging from the dust, it had not been much used under his uncle's reign. Stelan glanced out over the banquet hall, then stepped away from the balcony and out through the archway, where he could look down on the courtyard from a narrow window.

Elyana joined him. She crossed her arms to help shield against the wind, then watched the smooth, strong curve of his shoulders rise and fall as he breathed. Below, two men were dragging a two-wheeled cart over to the stables. She wondered why they had not bothered with a horse. The people of Adrast were strange to her.

"It needs shingles," Stelan said, and it took a moment for Elyana to realize he referred to the gaps in the stable roof. It needed much more than shingles. What had Stelan's uncle been spending all the area's resources on?

"By holy Abadar, Elyana, this is no life for me." Stelan spoke softly, without looking at her. "I know fighting best—it's what I want to do. But if I leave—if I die, what will happen?"

She did not answer.

He turned to meet her eyes. "I want to go—is it wrong of me? Am I just abandoning the responsibilities I don't like?"

"You pledged to your mother that you would set things right," she reminded him.

Those bright eyes of his fell, as if she were chastising him.

She stepped forward and put a hand on his shoulder, and felt the warmth of his skin through the shirt fabric. "Your people need more than this shell of a home that is left them, Stelan."

Hope shone on his face then, and he looked momentarily like a child suddenly granted permission to consume candies. "You think I should go?"

"You should decide, not I."

His expression evened. He did not speak for a moment. "What about what Arcil said?" he asked finally. "Do you think the wizards will seek vengeance?"

"Arcil's a wizard. Perhaps he understands better."

"But you don't think they will."

She sighed. "I don't. But if there is darkness elsewhere as we found it here, and we have the strength to destroy it . . ." her voice trailed off.

Stelan nodded once, and then again, more vigorously. "You're right, Elyana. It's not just about us."

Chapter Five
Last Wishes

The pounding of hooves and the jingle of tack took Elyana back to days long past as the trio rode hard up the dirt road toward the keep. For six years, she and Stelan and the others had maintained their makeshift campaign. At first they strove just against the shadow wizards, but when they saw firsthand the plight of the Galtans across whose land they sometimes rode, they could not help but become involved with their affairs as well.

Those days had ended long ago, and in the years since Elyana had ridden back and forth to the keep so many times that it did not normally make her think of journeys at the side of her old traveling companions. Yet this night she did. Perhaps it was because she once more rode with a wizard and a warrior after a battle, or because she had spoken with Arcil.

The perfectly ordinary eleventh bell of the night rang as they halted their foaming horses in front of the stable doors. Elyana whispered an apology to Persaily and instructed the stableboy to take special care with her, knowing even as she did so that it was unnecessary. He bowed, and as he straightened she patted the boy on the shoulder. He meant well, and loved the horses almost as much as she did.

Still, she was tired, and frustrated, and her temper was short. She ordered Kellius to place magical wards in Stelan's chamber, and Drelm followed them both up into the tower. The cleric was still there, sitting beside the baron. The chests lay open, contents strewn about the floor. The table was overturned, and if the cleric had not risen to give her a polite bow, she would have assumed foul play.

"What's happened?" she asked.

"The baroness and the young lord have searched the keep for the statue," he said.

"Have they found it?"

"Not that I have heard. Was your own mission successful?"

Elyana said nothing. From behind came the sound of running footsteps on the keep stairs, racing toward them in the hall, and then Renar burst in, holding a sheet of paper. The young man's face fell at sight of them. His expressions were even easier to read than his father's.

Elyana shook her head, and he frowned dejectedly.

Lenelle arrived a few moments later. She had donned a shawl. She favored Elyana with an accusing stare, then stepped over to the hearth and the fire, which was flickering low and doing little to stave off the chill in the air.

"Pardon, baroness," Kellius said, brushing past her to the middle of the room and drawing forth a scroll from his robe.

"What are you doing?" she demanded.

"Elyana told me to place protective wards upon the room."

Lenelle glared. "That's a little late, isn't it?"

"I believe Arcil can listen to us from afar," Elyana told her.

"I see that you did not find him," the noblewoman observed icily.

It was Drelm who spoke in her defense. "We found much, Baroness," he told her. "A wizard and a band of rogues waited in a ruined tower."

Lenelle's eyebrows rose in weary hope.

"There was nothing to be learned from them." Elyana shook her head. "It was all misdirection, devised by Arcil. He sent an apprentice who looked like him to wait for us, then killed the man."

"We found these," Renar said, and for the first time Elyana took greater stock of the paper held in Renar's hand, creased into three sharp horizontal lines where it had been carefully folded before its opening. Another lay open on the fireplace lintel. Lenelle lifted a parchment that lay beside it: a letter with a red wax seal.

"My husband's will and letters addressed to each of us," Lenelle said softly, indicating Renar as well with her eyes.

Elyana received her letter with great care. She took in the tactical sensation of the paper beneath her fingers and studied the seal of Stelan's house, a rearing horse on a flat plain under a radiant sun, pressed there in wax with his own hand. The seal appeared to have been broken and then restamped. She said nothing, for it would be impolite to mention she noticed Lenelle's tampering. She looked up at Kellius. "Are those wards up?"

"Yes," Kellius said. "I've placed a protective barrier about the room. It will prevent scrying for only a short while, though."

"Then we will speak quickly," Elyana said. "Baroness, what does your letter say?"

"It is advice on how to manage the property, and to see to the raising of our son . . . it is not especially recent. I think yours is, Elyana. It looks as though he has broken and then resealed it."

Though Elyana felt a momentary stab of guilt for again assuming the worst about Lenelle, her face remained untroubled. She glanced over at Renar. "What was the subject of yours?"

"I . . . father . . ." Renar collected himself and stood almost at attention. "It was advice, from a father to a son, on how best to be a man." His voice broke but he soldiered on. "I shall cherish it."

Elyana looked away before she too choked up. She steadied herself, then broke the seal.

She found two letters within. The first began with: "My dear Elyana—if you are reading this, I must be dead . . ." She placed it under the second. He was not dead yet. Would not be. Not now.

The second paper was of a lighter stock. That same steady hand, with its artful flourishes that Arcil had tried so hard to emulate, had composed a less formal note, dated earlier that week.

> *My dear friend,*
>
> *If Arcil has slain me, then my family is in danger. He seeks that ugly statuette from the shadow wizard's lair. You'll recall that Vallyn full expected me to scrape the silver off the thing—enough to buy a small pony, or half a horse, he said.*
>
> *The statuette is hollow, and something lies within. The enchanted visor on my helm showed me what I believe to be a scroll inside, or a map.*

If it were a spell, I did not wish Arcil to have it, because I no longer trusted him, and if it were a map, I did not want him involved in the finding of anything treasured by a shadow wizard. In later years I was tempted sometimes to break the statuette myself, but there was land to care for and a son to raise. I had no need for another map. We had earned treasure enough. I let it stand against my better judgment, unshattered and unburned, thinking sometimes that when Renar was grown, perhaps you and Vallyn and I might ride out on one last venture.

I still cannot quite bear to destroy the statue while there's a chance of salvaging the situation, but if you hold this page, then my foolishness has doomed me. Arcil wants the thing, and whatever it is, he must not have it. In a holding spot within the hearth I have secreted the statuette. Just below the worn stone under the far right side of the lintel is another of average size and color. Pinch midway upon its edge. When the statuette stands revealed, I want you to smash it and burn the paper within. I must ask you a final time to stand with my blood, and protect my family from Arcil's rage.

Your dear friend,
Stelan

Elyana lowered the papers and folded them crisply. All of them, even the cleric, eyed her expectantly.

No, not all, she corrected, for Stelan lay . . . no, he did not lay still as death, he lay *quietly*. That's all it was. Quietly.

She did nothing to relieve the watching humans. Instead, she stepped to the fireplace, her eyes sweeping over the stones. She placed her hand on that unremarkable light gray stone, nearly encompassing it with spread fingers. And then she pinched its edge. The thing swung soundlessly out.

"By the holy key!" The cleric said, and Renar let out a wordless cry of amazement.

There was a dark cavity between the stones. Elyana picked out the hideous old statue in the gloom, and tipped it forward so that it would fit through the opening. Nothing more was hidden within the space.

"Sacred Abadar," Lenelle said, the words almost rasping from her lips. "You found it!" Tears of gratitude welled up from her eyes, and she raised her hands in heartfelt prayer.

Then Elyana lifted the statue and hurled it into the flagstones.

Lenelle was already screaming before the statue shattered into hundreds of pieces. She hurled herself at Elyana, hands balled into fists, only to find herself held at arm's length by a confused Drelm, who'd swiftly interposed himself.

"She's killed him, you fool!" Lenelle shrieked. "The statue was all that was keeping Stelan alive!"

Elyana had lifted something from amongst the debris upon the floor: a tightly rolled parchment. At the sight of it, Lenelle fell silent. Drelm, glancing back at Elyana, grunted doubtfully.

"What is it?" Renar asked.

"*This*," Elyana said, "is what Arcil wants." She passed him the letter she had just read, but retained the scroll. "Stelan asked me to destroy the statue and burn the scroll."

"No!" Lenelle cried.

"The letter is a last request," Elyana continued reasonably, "but I'm not sure a last request need be

followed while the person who made it remains alive."
That was the kind of reasoning that Arcil might have
used, and her frown deepened at the thought.

She unrolled the scroll.

The parchment was aged but stiff, crafted of fine
vellum. Contained as it had been within the statue,
sealed from the elements, it was well preserved.

Here was no scroll with spells, but a detailed,
topographically marked map of southwest Galt and
southern Kyonin, the kingdom of the elves, and the
long, fanged run of the Five Kings Mountains. Someone
with spidery handwriting had ornamented it with
occasional phrases in Azlanti, showing a route through
the peaks to a location marked as the Vale of Shadows.
Inset upon the map's lower third was a primitive sketch
of a tower, with the cramped annotation: "Star Tower—
Twilight Crown." Elyana felt someone at her shoulder
and knew by the scent of flowers and grass that Kellius
had joined her.

"What's it a map of?" the wizard asked.

"I'm still reading," Elyana answered slowly. But
she felt a dawning awareness, and for the first time in
hours she knew a sense of hope. The Crown of Twilight.
This was what Arcil had so feared in the last of their
adventuring years. He'd learned the shadow wizard
Athalos had sought the thing, and had been terrified he
would wield it against them. The crown, Arcil had told
her, held power over life and death, the ability to mend
and warp flesh and spirit as only the gods might do.

So Arcil had kept up his searching. Elyana shouldn't
have been surprised. She studied the map and the
words, committing them to memory. After a long time
she let the parchment roll back in upon itself and
looked up.

Stelan lay unmoving in his bed. Drelm had released the baroness, and she and the captain waited expectantly.

"Father ordered her to destroy the statue and whatever it holds," Renar announced to the room as he lowered the letter. "Lest Arcil find it."

"Arcil will cure your father if we give him that paper," Lenelle said.

"Even if Arcil did honor his word," Elyana said, "I would be shamed to hand this over to the wizard, for Stelan has entrusted it to me. He would be very angry with us both."

"I would rather have him angry than dead," Lenelle snapped.

"No, mother," Renar said quickly. "We must honor father's orders."

"You're condemning your father to death!" Lenelle spat. "Are you so eager for his title?"

Renar bristled visibly. "Mother! How could you say that?"

"Arcil cannot be allowed to have this," Elyana said, brandishing the scroll levelly. "But if Stelan can be kept alive, it holds hope for him."

The baroness adjusted her shawl. "What do you mean?" she asked suspiciously.

"It's a map. A map to where an artifact Arcil seeks is likely to reside. If he lays hands on it, his power will only grow. If I recover it, the thing should restore Stelan to life, curse or no."

"What kind of artifact?" Lenelle demanded. "How do you know?"

Elyana looked past her and Renar to the others. Drelm's brow was furrowed as if thinking with great effort. Kellius waited tensely. The cleric pretended indifference but was clearly fascinated by all that he saw and heard.

"I know," Elyana replied slowly, "because Arcil once confided the matter to me. It was he who guided us in the destruction of so many dark places. Stelan and I did not realize at first that it was Arcil's interest in their magics that drove him. It might not have been, at first . . ." Elyana, about to lose herself in sad reverie, pulled herself back into focus. She lightly tapped the map against her hand. "The structure at the bottom of the map is a star tower. Legend says that the god Zon-Kuthon himself helped make our world safe from the beast-god Rovagug with the creation of these towers."

"Zon-Kuthon? Rovagug?" The cleric stood as tall as his plump little body could manage and wrapped fingers about the sacred key dangling from his neck. "These are dark and evil gods, Baroness." His head wagged back and forth in consternation. "Lady Elyana, how do you know anything of them, or their doings?"

"From the mouth of the wizard who cursed Stelan," Elyana said. "Zon-Kuthon sided with the other gods against Rovagug, who planned to destroy the world. The Rough Beast and his minions were caged within the earth, and Zon-Kuthon stitched it shut."

The cleric shook his head. "I have never heard of these star towers."

Elyana didn't really care what the cleric knew aside from his countercurses. "Have you the skill to stave off Arcil's curse?"

The fellow nodded. "But as I said, it shall be expensive."

"What is your price?"

The cleric cleared his throat. "Well. I must continually throw spells to cancel the curse, which shall be wearying. I would estimate it to cost approximately two hundred gold a day."

"I will do better. If you swear to keep Stelan alive and whole, I shall turn over the Crown of Twilight to you, to deliver to your church, after we use it to revive Stelan."

The cleric licked his lips. Any artifact of the power Elyana had described would undoubtedly pay for his magical expenditure many times over.

"I forbid this," Lenelle said. She shouldered past the half-orc, who had crossed his arms.

"You cannot, Mother," Renar countered. She turned on him, lips twisting in fury. He went on regardless. "The map is in Elyana's charge, as father wished. Father expressly forbade turning it over to Arcil. I mean to see that his wish is carried out!"

"You ungrateful little. . ." Lenelle became apoplectic with rage, and turned on Elyana. "This is your doing, witch! You bedeviled both of them! The only certain way to save Stelan is to deal with Arcil!"

"Your pardon, Baroness," the cleric interjected, "but I can keep him alive. It will be labor-intensive, but the temple will be most grateful for such payment. Think of all the souls we can save."

For the right price, Elyana thought, but did not say.

Lenelle's hands shook as she raised them and clenched fingers into fists. For a long moment Elyana thought the woman meant to strike her. Finally Lenelle screamed in fury.

"To Hell with all of you!" she said, sweeping past them and out of the chamber. The heavy door slammed shut behind her.

"Very well, then," Elyana said reasonably, as though nothing out of the ordinary had transpired. "Do we have an agreement?"

"We do," the cleric replied. "But how long shall you be gone?"

She could not help wondering if he asked so as to calculate the amount of money his temple would earn. "Ten to twelve days. Faster if possible. Word should likewise be sent to Yanmass . . . in case we do not succeed."

The little man nodded. "As you will. The price will have to be paid in either case, you realize."

She nodded her understanding and turned to Drelm. "I must ride before Arcil's messenger comes. I will have to rest on the road."

"I will go," Drelm said. "I would risk any danger for the life of my baron."

"I thought you might volunteer. I can use a skilled warrior."

Drelm grunted acknowledgment.

"Lady Elyana, I too will come," Kellius said.

She nodded in thanks and prepared to tell them just how dangerous this was likely to be. Then Renar stepped up beside them.

"I'm going with you."

She should not have been surprised. "You should stay here with your father."

"Why? There's nothing I can do for him, save help you to succeed." The boy's glance slid over to Drelm, and then Renar drew himself up. "I'm fair with spear, bow, and sword. You and Captain Drelm and Father have seen to that. I've been readying for a ride like this all my life. And besides, I'm technically your baron now, until Father recovers."

"I was wondering when you'd notice that," Elyana said. "Well, Baron, allow me to suggest, for your mother's sanity, that you remain."

He shook his head. "She will be insufferable until you return. I couldn't live with her any more than I could live with myself if I were to remain behind while you risk your lives for Father."

"Very well."

"I know Arcil's more powerful than I am," Kellius said thoughtfully. "But I know I can be of service. The baron has been good to me. I mean to ride with you and Captain Drelm and . . . the young baron." He bowed his head to Renar.

"We will be pleased to have you," Renar said, managing a regal bow of his own.

"We must act quickly, then," Elyana said "We have much to do in the next quarter-hour."

All three lingered for a moment beside the bed of the baron while the cleric looked on with folded hands. The half-orc began a prayer to Abadar to keep his lord safe and the cleric took it up smoothly; Renar and Kellius bowed their heads in silence. Elyana looked down upon Stelan, studying his face for the thousandth time. She fully planned to see him again, but if she did not, she wished to remember his features.

Elyana unrolled the map again, confirmed a few final features, then stepped to the hearth and tossed it into the fire. Kellius let out a little gasp. Elyana watched it crinkle in the heat and then brown and burn.

"Why did you do that?" Drelm asked.

"If anything happens to us," Elyana said, "the map is destroyed as Stelan wished."

"I . . ." Renar wasn't able to say anything more. Elyana turned.

"Come. Time's wasting."

Interlude
Death in the Night

The mountains stood tall and jagged on the horizon, dark fangs against the vault of the night. From the peaks came a biting wind, so cold it felt to Arcil as if it swept down from the stars themselves.

Arcil suppressed a shiver. His companions were motionless shapes stretched in a circle about the red embers.

Stelan lay on Elyana's right, snoring softly, cocooned in his blankets with his head facing away from her. Around the fire were the others: Edak and Vallyn and the two Galtan youngsters decreed enemies of the state because their uncle had once been a noble's bookkeeper.

They were all asleep. All but Elyana, quiet beside the dying fire. Arcil sat up slowly, gathering his blankets, and walked over, hunched, to her side. He smiled at her questioning look. "Is this patch of grass taken?"

"Join me if you like."

His smile widened into one of genuine satisfaction. Their camp rested in the rocky arms of a narrow defile. Only a few lonely oaks stretched bare branches skyward behind them. The border with Taldor lay two days west, and he was deathly afraid that the Galtans would catch them. But he would never tell her that he had wakened imagining the Galtan cavalry was riding them down even now. There were many things he hoped to share with the exotic beauty, but his weakness was not one of them. He quickly stilled his arms, shaking with cold.

"You do not need to hide your cold," Elyana told him.

He knew she detested liars and those who dissembled in any way; she should be made to understand that he was not one. "I am a man of learning, Elyana. Many men and women say that makes me a weakling. Thus I cultivate a manner that reveals no weakness."

"Weaknesses do not make you less a man, among your friends."

"Friends," he said bitterly. "Where are my friends? Vallyn lives to mock me, and Stelan does not trust me. I see it in his eyes."

"Vallyn mocks everyone," she said. "And Stelan thinks highly of you."

"Stelan thinks highly of my skill."

A slight nod indicated her concession. "Stelan considers you a friend."

He doubted that. "And Edak—"

"Edak is your friend."

"Edak is a fool."

Elyana sighed, and Arcil wondered what he had said to cause it.

"Is he foolish for risking his life for you?" she asked. "For he has done that more times than I can count."

They had all helped each other enough times that even he had lost count. They worked together, and thus they watched out for one another. But she was right— for whatever reason, Edak liked him, and Arcil might be forced to admit he was fond of the warrior, though more as a man might care for a dumb animal.

He glanced over at her, considering what that steady gaze might hide. She was the only one who could ever get him to question his decisions—even the obvious conclusions. She was like a fire: when she was pleased with him, he felt not just warm, but truly comfortable.

"Are you my friend?" He was aghast that he had blurted his question out like that. For a brief second his heart hammered in fear. Why had he asked that?

Her answer came without pause. "You know that I am."

He smiled, and Elyana frowned in response.

"What's wrong?" he asked. What had he done now?

"Sometimes your reactions trouble me," she said.

So that was it. He struggled to reassure her that he understood the boundaries of their relationship. "Don't worry, I know you're Stelan's." For now, he added silently.

"I do not belong to Stelan any more than he belongs to me."

His breath stilled. Could she mean that her heart was not truly pledged? Her expression remained closed, almost catlike. There was no guessing any woman's mind, he thought, much less Elyana's.

Somehow he knew that she was not inviting a changed relationship with him. Not now, at least. It saddened him, although he realized it was folly to have expected more. He faced away from her and changed the subject. "What do you want, in the end, from all this?"

"I wish to see these refugees safely into Taldor. I look forward to a warm bath, and boar meat."

She could be so literal. He cleared his throat, then forced himself to question on.

"No, I mean after all this. After you've had your fill of adventuring. Do you mean to settle down with Stelan? What do you really want?"

"That's a very personal question, Arcil."

"I mean no insult. You live so long. I know that you're lonely among humans. Do you never want friends who can live as long as you?"

She gave him a piercing look, then stared off into the distance. Her profile was so lovely that it cut the breath from him.

It was a moment before she spoke. "I have wished that many times, Arcil. But there's nothing for me to do about that, and my own people are strange to me."

He had heard about her sojourn among the elves, and how peculiar they seemed to someone who had lived all her life among humans. There was no home for her there, but he could offer hope that the coming years need not be as lonely. "What if I found a way?" he asked her, softly, daring to draw a fraction closer.

"What?" She turned to regard him.

"A way to live longer. A way to remain. I have heard tell of methods."

"I would very much like to have you as a friend in a hundred years," she said, and that set his heart speeding so surely that he barely heard the rest of her words. "But you are always too eager to take risks, Arcil. Sometimes—"

She held up a hand and shot soundlessly to her feet. Somehow her bow was already to hand and strung.

"What is it?" he hissed. His heart thudded within his chest, fear having chased out desire in a single breath.

"Something comes. Wake Stelan." So whispering, she grabbed an arrow and trotted forward, as certain and

focused as a panther. He watched her disappear into
the darkness, marveling at her grace. At his feelings.
Weakness, he thought, but did not care.

He stepped around her lover, deciding to first wake
homely Edak.

The thing had advanced softly into the valley, walking
on two feet, and Elyana had almost missed its coming.
It had appeared alone, so if there were others, it must
be the scout.

Elyana stopped beside a bush and watched it move
from behind a large stone, silhouetting itself against the
night. It moved like a man, yet while she saw the outline
of its body and the swing of its arms, she perceived no
head.

The wind blew its scent away from her, but she
needed no other clues—the moving thing was dead
already. Whether it was sorcery of the Galtans, whose
Gray Gardeners were blacker than any supposed, or
some wraith wandered down from a mountain crypt,
she neither knew nor cared. She swiftly replaced the
arrow she'd drawn and, feeling by shape of feather
alone, produced one of the enchanted shafts fixed with
a silver head. She nocked it and fired.

The string thrummed and the cast was true. She heard
the arrow thunk home. But the thing kept coming.

Elyana's flesh recoiled at the thought of facing the
undead once more. She fitted another arrow to her
bow, wondering where Stelan was.

Twice more she fired with the blessed silver arrows,
and then there was movement on her left. Almost too
late she realized she'd been drawn out, and ducked a
lurching swipe from a man-shape with burning eyes.
She fired point-blank and the arrow sank into flesh.

The rotting visage before her smiled. Starlight revealed a body garbed in the clothes of a nobleman, perfectly tailored but spattered with blood and mud, especially about the collar, where the head had been crudely stitched to the neck with thick threads.

Elyana fought against her fear before it rose into true panic. She knew that if she fell to the thing, she would rise again as a wight herself.

She retreated, aware now of a third figure, this one, too, with burning eyes. How many had the Galtans sent after them?

Elyana's final arrow tore into the neck of the nobleman wight. She retreated, breath escaping her mouth in a thin stream of vapor. The corpse stalked after.

"Lights!" Arcil cried behind her, the long-arranged warning for one of his spells.

Elyana narrowed her eyes so she would not be blinded by the dazzling explosion that spread across the area before her. Suddenly the three things moved in the light of day. They were dead nobles: one fat and headless; another nimble and coated, with long straggling hair and two arrows protruding from his body; the third a beautiful woman in a brown dress with petticoats and ruffles, creeping on bare feet.

Elyana heard Arcil curse, realizing too late that his spell—prepared for use against shadow wizards and their minions—had been pointless on the undead.

Edak shouted a battle cry. There was no sign of Edak himself, but the wight facing Elyana flinched as some unseen force slashed through his coat, cutting a long, clean line so that the upper and lower halves of one side of the fabric flapped independently. The dead flesh leaked black fluid, darkening its garments. Lanky Edak, armorless, long hair wild about him, appeared suddenly and stepped quickly backward, vapor trailing from his open mouth.

Just as suddenly, he vanished again as Arcil threw another spell over the warrior, a recent trick the two had worked on. Elyana wasn't altogether certain of its utility against the undead or creatures of magic, which might well use senses other than vision to perceive them.

Elyana tossed down her bow. Her elven blade came clear in a flash of steel. She advanced against the wight, discovering a problem with Arcil's spell—if Edak could not be seen, how could she be sure he was out of range? She solved the problem by charging against the headless body.

A burst of music rolled then out of the night, and Elyana knew Vallyn was slinging a spell with his lute strings. Stelan too was there, shouting for the glory of Abadar as his long blade slashed deep into the dead woman's flesh. He threw up his shield almost too late to block the woman's grab for his throat.

Elyana came in low against her opponent. Her first strike sliced half through one of the thick stocking-clad calves.

The wight was fast. Its hand smashed the side of her head and sent her reeling, chattering from the deathly chill of its presence, a cold so intense it made the wind off the mountain seem balmy. She shook her head to clear her vision as the thing came at her with outstretched arms.

Arcil, lingering outside the range of the wights, saw Elyana stagger and felt an entirely different kind of fear. He pulled free the fire wand they'd found in the River Kingdom ruins. He'd hoarded its final charges, but with Elyana in danger he spared no thought to that. One word later a lancing spear of fire streamed from the red mahogany shaft. It struck the wight along one wide shoulder and set it ablaze.

The corpse slapped its other hand against the flame. Elyana dropped low and swung again, cutting the thing's leg off. She rolled free as it collapsed.

"Arcil!"

Edak's voice; the warrior sounded panicked. Arcil whirled and pointed the wand at the snarling wight that stood twenty paces off, hands outstretched. He only realized his error when the jet of flame blasted into something in front of the wight, outlining a human shape in flame.

Edak. The warrior screamed in pain and surprise, becoming suddenly visible as he flailed at the wight which continued to attack him, fire or no.

Arcil knew no spells to stifle the flames. He could only stand and watch, feeling a mounting sense of horror.

Elyana raced to Edak's aid. The sleeves of the wight were ablaze, the skin on its hands smoking as they wrapped about Edak's throat.

Two swift strikes separated the corpse's head from its body, but the hands kept on their choking even as flame engulfed Edak. Elyana shouted in frustration and cut through first one wight arm, then the other. One dropped away, the other still clinging to poor Edak, who sank limply.

Stelan charged into the dying wight, slashing the thing near in half before kicking the flaming body away.

Arcil, still stunned, walked up slowly, staying clear of Elyana's frantic effort to roll the warrior on the frost-covered grass. Vallyn had come running up with a blanket. Arcil tried not to watch too closely—was that black stuff Edak's skin?—as the others set to smothering the fire. The smell was horrible, like burned and dirty pig meat. Elyana shouted at Vallyn to begin a healing spell as she patted, and the young bard complied with a song that sounded like a merry jig. It was completely incongruous to the frantic, pained expressions on Elyana and Vallyn's faces. Stelan stood by, his breath rising in quick gasps, his expression bleak.

The two teenaged Galtans wandered up, blankets clasped tightly about them. They watched with wide eyes.

Elyana finally tore the blanket from the smoldering figure and laid her hands upon him.

The whistle of the wind that followed after Vallyn stopped playing seemed absurdly loud. The bard stepped back beside Arcil and the wizard tensed. As he'd expected, Vallyn could only hold back his comment for a short while. "Nicely done. I thought wizards were supposed to be smart."

"I've one charge left," Arcil snapped.

"Silence," Stelan cautioned. "Vallyn, go scout the perimeter. See if there's more out there."

"Shouldn't Elyana—" Vallyn started to object.

"Elyana's busy," Stelan countered. "Go."

The bard jogged off, the neck of his lute bumping against his shoulder blade.

Elyana was shaking her head. She leaned back. Arcil risked a step closer and saw the whites of Edak's eyes staring blankly up from his blackened face.

"Can't you do anything?" Arcil was displeased by the high, quavering note in his voice. "Or Vallyn?"

"There's nothing left to do," Elyana said. "He's dead."

"But the fire . . . I didn't think the wand was that powerful. Maybe it was the wight . . ."

"It may have been," Stelan said softly. "We know you did not mean to harm him."

Arcil fumed at the implied rebuke. "Isn't there any— can't you try again? Sometimes your spells work better than others."

But Elyana was rising, and her gaze was bleak. Arcil looked away, ashamed and angry.

"We must bury him," Elyana said. "At least he won't rise again as a wight."

Stelan clasped Arcil's shoulder and squeezed, gently. "I know this must be hard. You were closest to him."

Arcil jerked his shoulder away. He wanted to tell Stelan to shut up, but no sound would come from his mouth. His throat was dry.

The wind blew down chill from the mountains and Arcil shivered.

Chapter Six
Equal Shares

The night was cold. Sitting on watch with her traveling companions asleep under the shade of the old oak dredged up the inevitable memories of past exploits. Elyana didn't mean to imagine that Renar, sleeping on his side, head pillowed on his saddle, was Stelan, but the image came unbidden. And if he were Stelan on her right, then Arcil would lie on her left . . . but there was Drelm, who presented an altogether different picture from the wizard.

It was too easy to imagine Arcil there beside her on one of their nighttime chats, where his basic decency, so often shielded from the others, had occasionally shown strong and clean. Had it always been an act to gain her affection, or had there once been something more?

A person could drive herself crazy with thoughts like that.

They'd ridden for only two hours before stopping to rest just off the road. Elyana let the wizard and the boy sleep, trading off with Drelm after she herself had lain still for two hours. She had never needed to sleep as long as most folk, though she'd learned after time among the elves that this was a personal quirk rather than an innate difference between elves and humans.

She spent most of her watch thinking about her mission and wondering whether it was folly to have brought Renar. She did not believe she could have dissuaded him, and Drelm would not have approved of restraining the young man physically. She really had no choice other than to guard Renar well, for both his sake and his father's.

She shook her head. Humans burned through their lives so swiftly. How many years did Stelan have left? Did she have any business leading these few forward to save him? It would likely be their deaths.

If human days were few, though, didn't it mean that each was precious, and that there was that much more reason to fight to preserve them? And it was Stelan for whom they rode—gentle, far-seeing Stelan, who had loved her. Whom she loved still.

It was folly to care so much for creatures with such fleeting lives, but she knew no other way.

She roused them at dawn and they muttered through their meal of hard rolls and sausages cooked a little too thoroughly. Elyana had never learned to appreciate most human preferences in food preparation, and inevitably over- or underprepared meals for them. She had blackened the sausages in her effort to get that crispiness Vallyn and Stelan had always claimed to prefer.

Everyone was sluggish that morning, even the horses. Elyana rode one of the spare mounts so that Persaily could walk at ease with the pack animals.

The skies were overcast as they rode north on the old road. Wildlife was scarce, although in the afternoon they spotted a herd of elk, a buck standing sentinel while the rest of the animals grazed.

As the sun began its afternoon drop toward the horizon they encountered a single cart, driven by a merchant heading southward. With him were a handful of children of varying ages, all stamped with the fellow's pug nose. Elyana asked him for news of the village of Tregan, and how it fared.

He was perfectly at ease speaking with her. Many in this region of Taldor had heard of the elf lady who raised horses for Baron Stelan, and knew a half-orc was high in the baron's service. While he answered Elyana's questions, his eyes strayed over to Drelm, and she saw the merchant noting the well-maintained tabard worn over the captain's spotless armor.

The merchant did not, however, lower his reins. His children shifted on piled crates and stared keenly at her and the captain.

The fellow told them that Tregan still prospered, and that the Hornet's Nest tavern still offered the best food and music within two days of the border.

After they left the merchant, they rode on for two more hours. It wasn't until they stopped for supper that Renar, chewing on sausages he'd insisted on cooking himself, got around to asking what the rest of them were wondering.

"What's our plan, and how long will it take? Aren't we headed the wrong way?"

"I did expect us to be heading due west," Kellius agreed. "But I'm sure you've a reason."

Elyana nodded once in confirmation. "We make first for the village of Tregan, in the woods just east of the border. I've an old friend there. An old friend of your father's," she added for Renar's benefit.

"A friend like the wizard?" Kellius asked. There was a small patch along the left side of his chin that he'd missed shaving this morning. Elyana tried not to stare. Arcil had been incapable of that kind of oversight. He might accidentally kill a friend, but his appearance was always immaculate.

"His name's Vallyn," Elyana answered. "He's a good man to have in tight places. He rode with Stelan and Arcil and myself. It's only half a day out of our way, and we'll be better for it."

"He's a warrior, then?" Drelm asked.

"He's decent with a blade. But he's better with traps and puzzles. We're likely to face a fair share of those."

"Isn't he going to be, well . . ." Renar hesitated. ". . . old?"

"Everyone's older than you, Renar," Elyana countered. She meant to sound playful, but though Drelm laughed and Kellius smiled, the boy's cheeks flushed.

Elyana was surprised. And folk said that elves were thin-skinned. She continued as if she had not noticed. "He should be in his early forties now, which might mean older than the hills or well preserved, depending on his luck and how he's taken care of himself."

Renar nodded minutely but asked nothing else.

"What of Arcil?" Kellius asked. "Should we be worried about him?"

"Yes," Elyana replied. "He'll have guessed by now what I'm doing." Likely he was hating himself for not having foreseen this . . . unless having her seek the crown had been his intention all along.

Drelm interrupted her musings with another question. "Will he attack?"

"Arcil's very clever. If you wanted something that was very dangerous to get, and someone you respected very much was after it, would you attack them?"

Drelm's brow furrowed. "I would attack them with care," he said, "analyzing their strengths and weaknesses."

"Possibly." She tried not to let her disappointment show. "Or you might wait until that person had found the thing." She watched the half-orc, seeing if he could reason out the rest.

The captain's face cleared. "He'll let us do the hard part before springing an ambush."

"Provided we survive to get the thing," Kellius added.

The others all stared at the wizard, and he shrugged, offering a thin smile.

"Abadar shall weigh us," Drelm said, his voice taking on a pedantic quality, "and judge us well, even should we fail, so long as we keep to his path."

Renar bowed his head. "Praise Abadar."

Elyana said nothing. The worship of Abadar, as with many practices and customs observed by humans, evoked in her only amused disinterest. To her, it was enough to revere the natural world, which seemed miraculous enough all on its own.

After lunch she switched her saddle to Persaily, who was excited by the journey and—as Elyana learned, for she understood the language of her horses—somewhat concerned that when they came to the big rocks that were mountains, there would be no grass to eat. Elyana assured her that they would pack food for both men and horses.

That night they spent at a humble roadside inn outlying a small but welcoming farming community. Elyana pushed them hard the next day, insisting on only one meal break. Even so, they reached Tregan before nightfall only by riding through the twilight.

A mile south of the village, they passed a battered old wall stretching into the darkness on either side of the road. Some sections stood untouched, but others were marred with large gaps. Time had worn the stone.

"Has Tregan been attacked?" Renar whispered.

"They've looted the wall for building material," Elyana answered.

"That's criminal," Renar said indignantly. Then he heard the music on the air. "It's kind of late for music, isn't it?" he asked. It was the middle of the week, after all. "Is tonight a Tregan holiday or something?"

"There are a lot of Galtan refugees here," Elyana told him over her shoulder. Renar had little to compare any settlement to but his own village and Yanmass, the great caravan city, which he had visited twice. Elyana kept her amusement at the sight of his wide eyes to herself.

Tall wooden buildings flanked the wide central street. Folk on second-story balconies looked down upon them with hard eyes. Yet music and light flowed out from the open doors and windows of the street's dozen inns and taverns, accompanied by the laughter of both men and women.

The place had grown since Elyana's last visit. The buildings were taller. Many were new, and the street was half again as long. Here, at least, the miserable Galtan government's policies had led to a kind of prosperity, for it had driven these folk from Galtan lands to thrive in Tregan.

She scanned the signs swinging before the shops and taverns, most of which were decorated with symbols rather than words. Halfway along the block she saw the dim shape of a gold hornet's hive, sketched colorfully onto a hanging placard with an artistic flair that brought a smile to her lips. Vallyn himself had painted that sign, she was certain.

She made arrangements for the overnight care of the horses at stables beside the inn, then walked for the tavern entrance, unstrung bow poking up over her shoulder, sword swinging at her slim hip. Drelm was on her right hand. Renar and the mage followed. Her eyes had no trouble adjusting, but she remembered to stop and let her human companions grow used to the change in lighting.

"Why aren't all these people in bed?" Renar sounded confused and a little scandalized.

Some two dozen men and women were up and dancing in twin lines, facing each other. The Galtan rondel required both shaking of leg and lifting of arm. A trio of musicians against the back wall wound a merry tune on a pair of lutes and a reed flute.

Most of the tables were pushed to the left wall. Behind the counter on the right stood a smiling, balding man nodding in time to the music. A handful of oldsters leaned against the counter he manned, their backs to the bartender, likewise watching the dancers, mugs to hand. Some even older than those at the bar were dancing in the long lines.

The bartender spotted the newcomers and waited as they approached. Elyana wondered what he made of them: a half-orc in livery, a young nobleman, a rangy mage who looked more like a farmer in his rumpled and rustic clothes, and an elf in her brown traveler's garb. It did not take long before all the old men leaning against the bar were staring. So were a few of the dancers.

All too soon the song ended, but another began as the notes of the first one died. One of the lutenists left his instrument with the other musicians and worked his way through the dancers.

Elyana smiled at sight of him. Vallyn had grown out of his gawky youth during the years he'd adventured at her side. He'd never been especially tall, and he'd broadened further in the intervening years, but judging by the way the women watched him as he moved through the dancers, they found him as handsome as ever. The gray flecking his brown beard and temples suggested a roguish wisdom.

Vallyn laughed at sight of her and opened his arms. She threw herself into the embrace with a grin.

"Hah!" he said, then continued in a smooth, calm voice as he pulled away, smiling up at her. "You're just as lovely as ever! What brings you here?"

"We need rooms and victuals," Elyana answered. "My friends are already tired of my cooking."

"Fed them once, did you?" He laughed again. "Come on, then. Any friends of Elyana's are friends of mine! Welcome to the finest tavern in all Tregan!"

Drelm grunted, which Elyana thought might have meant anything, but Vallyn read it as skepticism.

"That's a more impressive credit than it may seem, friend," Vallyn said, waggling his finger toward the half-orc. "The village is settled by Galtans, who have discriminating palates, and ask much of their chefs. If only," he added sadly to Elyana, "we had better wine."

Vallyn put them up in a two-room suite complete with tasseled draperies with gold-filigreed edgings. The four-poster bed frames were made of brass, and the pillows stuffed with goose feathers.

"You'd be surprised at the comforts some people flee with," Vallyn said, dismissing their astonished murmurs with a careless wave.

Vallyn spoke lightly to them all until servants arrived with an expansive meal featuring roast pheasant and potatoes, then motioned for Elyana to follow. She bade her companions farewell and left with her friend.

On the table awaiting them in Vallyn's wood-paneled sitting room she found nuts, berries, and boar meat slices so pink they were almost raw. Vallyn knew her preferences. She set to with undisguised pleasure while Vallyn watched with an amiable smile, sipping wine from a high-lipped glass.

She ate quickly, all the time scanning the room. It was hard not to notice that this room too was expensively furnished, from the writing desk with elaborate scrollwork to the dragon-headed curtain rod finials that looked down with staring eyes. The paneled door that presumably led to Vallyn's own bedchamber had been skillfully carved with mirrored leaf patterns.

The music below carried on merrily, though it was dulled by the wood through which it passed. The music and the stamp of dancers set the floorboards vibrating. She found her own foot tapping in sympathetic time, and she smiled.

"It is good to see you," Vallyn said.

His voice was even richer than she had remembered. But then he had been practicing his craft for twenty years; undoubtedly he'd gotten better since their wandering days.

"And you have done well for yourself," she replied. "That, too, is good to see."

Vallyn shrugged. "Folk still pay well for being smuggled from Galt. There aren't so many nobles left now, as you'd guess, but the mob's always ready to turn against some new faction." He gestured to the room at large. "Some of this is paid for; some of it was gifted to me by folk grateful to be alive."

"Have the Gray Gardeners come with any gifts?"

Vallyn snorted. "If you mean assassins' blades, there have been a few. Praise Calistria, they're too busy running their miserable country to worry much about me." He placed both elbows on the table and rested his chin on his hands, drawing down his heavy eyebrows. He studied her in silence for a long moment. "You're going to go back in, aren't you." It was not a question.

She nodded once.

"Even I'm not crazy enough to cross over the border much anymore. Mostly I sponsor other folk these days."

"Are you getting too old?" She followed this up with a thin smile.

"Huh! I'm as fit as a man half my age. Well, two-thirds my age. But I'll tell you something, Elyana, I'm a lot more fond of my skin than I used to be, and I mind more when I bleed. The Gray Gardeners play for keeps."

"I need your help," Elyana said. "For Stelan's sake."

"I'd noticed he wasn't here. I could've guessed that lad was his son, though. Practically a spitting image. So where's his old man?"

"He's in bed in Adrast, and he won't be getting up unless we find something for him."

"What is it?" Vallyn leaned forward, his brow furrowing. "How bad is he?"

"There's something Arcil used to talk about. The Crown of Twilight. It has powers over life and death. Stelan needs its curative powers."

"I'd be worried about anything that caught Arcil's interest. The Crown of Twilight, huh?" Vallyn's glance traveled down to the silverware beside Elyana's empty plate. "That table knife has powers over life and death. Don't be so prosaic."

"I thought bards liked that sort of thing."

"What does it do, really?"

"It will clear Stelan of a curse."

"Is it valuable?"

"I should imagine."

Vallyn mulled that over for a short while. "Is it a little valuable, or a lot valuable?"

She repressed a smile. It was typical of Vallyn to ask. "It's pledged already to the church of Abadar."

"Who pledged it? You?" At her nod he sighed. "You've already sold off your profit to the clerics?"

"The thing's in a tower. I'm guessing that there's more to be had inside than just the crown."

"Let me guess. Shadow magic, right? And hard knocks, and things that are trying to kill you."

"Probably."

Vallyn's chair creaked as he sat back. "I hoped to be through with shadows. They remind me of Arcil."

It was as good a time as any to tell him the rest. "Arcil's the one who cursed Stelan. He wanted the map to the crown and Stelan wouldn't give it to him."

"Damn . . . Arcil tried to kill Stelan? I never thought he'd take it that far."

"Why does that surprise you? You know he didn't like Stelan."

"Any fool could see that. He didn't like anyone but you, Elyana."

"He liked Edak."

"Whom he killed," the bard pointed out. "He probably liked Eriah, too. Arcil knew killing Stelan would anger you, or he'd have done it years ago. You ever notice that he only watched his temper when he was afraid *you'd* be upset?"

She wasn't sure that was quite right. "You're simplifying."

"You and Stelan made too many excuses for him for too long. He went bad long before you ever admitted it. You're the only thing that kept him with us that last year."

She'd heard Vallyn say that before, and didn't want to revisit the counterarguments. "Whatever the case, he's cursed Stelan, and this is the one way to save him. The clerics can't remove the curse. I know western Galt well enough, but you know it in more recent years. And I would be grateful for your eyes and ears in the tower. You were the handiest man I ever met with barriers and locks."

"I knew it was coming to this."

The eyes that considered Elyana now were much like those of her old friend's, but they studied her with abstract intensity, as if the mind behind them were gauging sums and weighing bars of gold.

"This crown," he said slowly, "is there any chance we can give these clerics something else? Treasures that equal its price, say?"

"I already agreed to the crown."

Vallyn smiled sadly and shook his head. "I thought you knew to leave all the bargaining to me. You've no sense of worth."

"Are you in, Vallyn? For Stelan?"

"Tell me about the lot you have with you. Is Renar any good?"

"Strong and fast. But he's unseasoned. Drelm—"

"The orc," Vallyn said with disdain.

"Half-orc. He's strong and sturdy."

"You can tell by looking at him that he's stubborn and mulish. And probably foul-tempered to boot."

For all that Elyana was inclined to agree about Drelm's stubbornness, she said nothing to confirm the bard's opinion. "He's Stelan's chosen captain of the guard."

"Really?" Vallyn's eyebrows shot up. "I can't say I should be surprised. He kept Arcil around for years. Why not an orc?"

"Half-orc."

"Sure. So now he uses a half-orc. And you're all right with that?"

"He's good in a fight."

"So you don't trust him."

"I barely know him. He takes my orders and is good in a fight. That's what I need." She didn't add that she felt like Drelm was a poorly trained game hound, ever ready to strain against the leash and tear off to do what he wished rather than what his master desired. She was trying to build a fighting unit, and she'd be a fool to divide it before it was even assembled.

Vallyn studied her for a long moment. She wondered if he could tell that she was concealing her opinion.

But the bard changed subjects. "What about the wizard? He looks like a country bumpkin."

"He's better than he looks. He's smart."

Vallyn smiled. "You need me because your team's stacked with amateurs."

"I need you in any case, Vallyn. For Stelan."

"All right," he said soberly. "I'm in. For Stelan." Then, almost as an afterthought, he added: "And an equal share of whatever else is in the tower."

Chapter Seven
Detours

Elyana dearly wanted to remain at rest in the feather bed, but she forced herself into motion as she heard a rooster crow. Every day, every hour, was counting against Stelan. She wasn't entirely convinced that the cleric and his acolytes had the skill and stamina to keep Stelan going, and there was the added wrinkle that broth and water would have to be spooned carefully into his mouth to keep up his energy. He would be growing slowly weaker.

At dawn, the others found her already awake with Vallyn and helping to supervise the packing of supplies. The bard explained that he didn't want to subject them to any more of Elyana's cooking, so he was bringing plenty of food he himself could prepare.

A half-hour after breakfast they were on the road. Vallyn guided them northeast, where, he assured them, they'd be less likely to meet with a patrol than they were on a straight east jaunt, where lazier smugglers and refugees were apt to cross.

Kellius had a violet petunia in his cap, and reported that he had rarely seen one of such a bright color. Vallyn then set to asking the mage questions about flowers and gardens, and the young wizard expounded upon them for almost an hour, demonstrating more expertise than Elyana had expected. Drelm, of course, remained quiet. If anything, though, Renar looked more suspicious than the half-orc, and Elyana could get nothing out of him. Finally, Vallyn announced to them all that they'd crossed over from the plains of Taldor to Galt.

"How do you know?" the young man asked.

"See that mountain to the north?"

Renar followed the bard's pointing finger to a snow-topped peak thrusting toward the clouds.

"I mark it."

"That's Mount Rein. Our angle's passed far enough that we're over now, you can be sure. Not that a Galtan patrol wouldn't chase you past the border if they didn't like your look, mind you. Or send something worse after—eh, Elyana?"

"True."

"Why are the Galtans so . . . mad?" Renar asked.

Vallyn answered before Elyana. "They're not mad, boy. They're angry."

"Well, they seem mad. First they kill their rightful rulers. Then they rise up every few years and guillotine whoever they put in place the last time."

"They're impatient, is what they are," Vallyn said. "They won't give anyone a chance to set the place in order. The old ones, the nobles, a lot of them had it coming. In my opinion," Vallyn added.

This was news to Elyana, and the bard must have sensed her surprise, for he hurried to explain.

"The Galtans went way too far," Vallyn said. "I'm not excusing what they did. I'm just saying that their government wasn't exactly looking out for anyone's interests but its own."

"It's not a good place," Elyana said to Renar. "There are spies everywhere. We must tread lightly even in the wilderness."

Renar fell silent for only a moment. "What are we really going to do about Arcil?"

If this was what had truly been troubling him, he would find no comfort from Elyana now. This was neither the time nor the place for that particular discussion. "Nothing I'd discuss without wards against scrying in place," Elyana replied.

"He didn't used to know that kind of thing," Vallyn said.

"He didn't used to be able to crush a man with shadows, either. From a distance."

Vallyn whistled. He rode in silence for a long moment, then said: "I always told you he was going to go bad."

So he had. And still Elyana sometimes wondered if there was something she might have said or done differently to help Arcil find the right direction. She didn't mean to mislead Vallyn or Renar, but she had no intention of admitting to them—or to Arcil, should he be listening—that she had no idea how to stop her old friend. She was still hoping she'd find something within the tower to aid her.

That night they set up camp in the Galtan wilderness and lit no fire, subsisting only on cold rations. Elyana arranged to take the middle watch, and lay down to rest. Sleep came quickly to her.

"Elyana."

She opened her eyes to find Kellius looking down at her. While his expression was calm, the wizard's face was strained. The stars shone in a clear sky. It was deep into the night.

Kellius pretended calm. "There's something out there. Something large. I saw it flying—"

"Wake Drelm first. Hurry."

"It's circled twice," Kellius said as he moved off.

Large and winged. Elyana ran over the possibilities as she slipped feet into boots and buckled into her leather cuirass. She climbed up to search the sky.

Dragons, wyverns, and giant birds could all be found near the Five Kings mountain range. Galt's constant chaos meant patrols and huntsman were not as plentiful as they once had been, and all manner of wild beasts had multiplied in the wilderness.

And there was always the chance that Arcil had sent something against them, calling it down from the peaks or even the Plane of Shadow.

She saw that the land was dark but for a distant light from the Galtan city of Woodsedge, miles to the south. Their camp sat under a scrubby stand of trees, which might explain why whatever it was had not dropped straight in.

The black wall of the Five Kings loomed on the western horizon. Elyana glanced briefly toward it, then looked skyward once more. It was then that she saw the draconic shape blotting out a swath of stars.

The reptile was long and large, with a serpentine neck thrust low. It glided on huge, batlike wings, its tail hanging stiff. Elyana saw that it had no arms and knew then that it was no true dragon, but a wyvern. She'd faced one once before, a creature half this size, and that had been no easy day. Its poisoned sting had put two men in the ground. Wyverns were powerful, relentless, and hungry.

This one swung toward her and lowered its wings for a dive.

"Wyvern!" she screamed in warning, then launched two arrows. Even as the first was still arcing into the air she was running forward. She threw herself into the tall grass and landed with a *whuff* that knocked the air out of her.

The first arrow slammed home just left of the wyvern's breastbone, provoking a growl that was cut off as the second caught it high along its wing. Its hooked claws grabbed at the dashing humanoid, but Elyana was too swift.

The wyvern landed with an earth-shaking thump. Its snaky neck swung left and right as it considered its targets, its roar a piercing shriek so loud that Elyana felt a sympathetic vibration deep in her chest. She heard Renar call out to her in worry, but stayed low as the wyvern searched the air with its long snout, snuffling.

Drelm praised one gift from his cursed heritage, and that was the ability to see not only in dim light, but in the deepest black. The humans might see the wyvern as a dark, threatening shape with a long neck, but he saw the glint of its eyes, the muscles along its chest as it thundered toward him. He heaved his throwing axe and ran to meet the beast. But the wyvern had hunched as it built speed for a charge, and the weapon soared over its shoulder.

The winged lizard lowered its head, its mouth widening in a display of daggerlike fangs. Drelm knew a burning thrill of action in his veins, a searing strength that left little room for anything but rage and power. He met the wyvern's strike with a sideways slash of his greataxe. The blow ripped into the side of the monster's head, tearing through scales in a spray of blood. The wyvern's teeth clamped down, narrowly missing Drelm's chest.

Drelm dodged left, his hands barely retaining hold of the axe as he leapt away. There was a blanket of darkness as the wing fell over him, and then the beast's tail lashed down. He caught sight of the long, long spike and rolled, but the thing slammed into his arm, penetrating armor, flesh, and bone. He roared not at the pain, but in anger, and climbed to his feet.

The wyvern somehow managed a swift stop. It spun, horned head twisting toward him. Drelm readied his axe, wondering why his right hand shook so.

A lightning blast underlit the beast's scaly maw, casting its brow ridge in shadow. The thing convulsed, then threw back its head in a deep-throated roar.

So close was the wyvern's head to Drelm when the wizard's lightning struck that he saw the beast's pupils shrink. Drelm raised his axe, snarling, then realized he was strangely dizzy. Dimly, he perceived that Renar was running into the fray. He heard the pluck of a lute, of all things, and Vallyn shouting for Renar to get back. Drelm agreed, and tried to tell the boy to stay clear, but couldn't quite find the strength.

Then a screen of shifting motes of light fell between him and the wyvern. Drelm did not understand where it had come from, but it was very beautiful, and he wanted to do nothing more than study the slowly changing colors, except that he was already feeling rather sleepy. He sat down, conscious that his arm ached and that he wasn't thinking clearly. For whatever reason, it all seemed unimportant.

Renar was two-thirds of the way to the monstrous, roaring beast when Vallyn told him to get back. But Renar wasn't about to retreat and be accused of cowardice. It didn't matter that he could practically feel his heart in his mouth, or that his pulse beat in his temples like a drum. He pledged to himself that he would not hang back while his friends struggled. His father would not have done so.

When the lovely rainbow screen dropped all about the wyvern, the creature's head swiveled his direction and Renar halted, thinking the thing had seen him. Then he noticed its eyes tracking after an especially pretty shimmer of blue drifting to the right. Renar had seen sorcery before, but never anything like this. Kellius had talent.

Renar steeled himself and advanced to swing at the beast's swaying neck. It was a glancing blow, but he'd connected. Somehow that granted him greater courage, and his second strike bit through the blue-black scales. The impact of it raced up through his arms, and he knew a savage exultation as blood spurted forth in dark rain.

He heard Elyana cry a warning. "Renar! Jump back!"

He was accustomed to obeying Elyana instantly—there was no room for hesitation when training horses. He did as bade, and the swinging tail and its bloody spike missed him by a handspan.

As the wyvern's head rose, Renar saw two arrows blossom along its neck like gruesome spines.

"Run, boy!" he heard Vallyn shout, and he leapt back, watching that tail and the head that was suddenly no longer fascinated by the shining lights. A clawed wing swung down as he backpedaled, and then a blazing ball of fire struck that same wing, filling the air with the sound of sizzling and the smell of burned meat.

The wyvern roared again, and at close range, Renar's ears rang at the sound. Smoke rose up from the flapping wing as the creature beat it rapidly to put out the flame.

Elyana raced up on its blind side, the long slim blade glittering in both hands. Renar saw the creature's nostrils flare open. Its head turned.

The elf's blow sliced deeply into the beast's neck a foot back from its head. Renar shouted warning as the tail swung up and then down at her, but Elyana threw up her sword. The tail spike clanged against it, and Elyana staggered, then dropped to her knee.

"Back!" she called to Renar in a strained voice. He'd assumed her first neck blow would kill the thing, but the wyvern beat the grass with its wings. Dirt, dry leaves, and grit blew out, stinging the boy's eyes.

Elyana stumbled backward, panting, and Renar went with her. The wyvern beat its wings once, twice, gave a little hop as though it meant to take flight, and then crashed into the earth.

Its wings fluttered, feebly, and its legs clawed at the grasses. Even after it stopped moving it moaned for several long minutes, in such a pitiful way that Renar actually felt a little sorry for it.

"Is it dead?" Kellius asked, trotting up. A ball of light floated just back of his left shoulder, and black smoke trailed up from the ends of the fingers on his right hand.

"Mostly," Elyana told him. "Stay back." She moved off into the dark. Renar followed.

Elyana found Drelm lying still in the grass, his breathing swift and shallow. As if that weren't a clear enough indicator of what had happened, the plate armor about his right arm was bashed in around a slim hole that leaked blood across the plate, the chain sleeve beneath it, and the tabard that covered both.

Poison. She had no cure for poison.

"Get Vallyn," she told Renar without turning. The young man dashed away as she bent down, centering her focus. There was a slim chance that the bard had learned greater healing magic in the intervening years. Certainly Arcil had improved—perhaps Vallyn had as well.

Elyana centered her focus with a deep breath. She lowered both hands to the wound and extended her spirit.

The injury was deep and painful, plunging through nearly the whole of the musculature, right down to the bone. The half-orc's arm was more than twice as thick as hers. She wondered if the spike would have passed all the way through hers.

She sealed the upper layers of his flesh first, so that the blood ceased its egress from the body, and then set to work lacing the muscles together. She was not as practiced nor as polished with more challenging wounds, but she knew that the injury was most of the way knitted. The real problem was the weakness caused by the poison. It marched slow and steady through his bloodstream like a procession of mourners halfway up the cliff to where they would inter the body.

"Looks like we'd best start digging," she heard Vallyn say beside her, and she snapped out of her trance.

The bard's lute was slung once more on his back. His nightshirt was rumpled, his hair mussed, and Elyana was surprised by how much older he seemed.

"He's poisoned," Elyana said quickly to him. "Are your healing magics—"

"I don't know poisons, Elyana." The bard cursed and passed a hand through his hair. "I never thought I'd be burying an orc," he finished, sounding bemused.

"We're not burying him," Elyana said, rising. She did not remind him, again, that Drelm was a half-orc. She considered the horizon, and the distant point of light that was Woodsedge.

"He's not dead already, is he?" Renar asked, dismayed. "Isn't there something we can do? And what do you mean we aren't going to bury him? He deserves a proper burial—"

Vallyn talked over Renar, paying him no heed. "That's a Galtan city, Elyana. Even if they didn't want to shoot you and me on sight, there's no way any healer would help Drelm. He looks too much like an orc."

"We can get him to a temple of Abadar."

"He'll be dead before we can make it," Vallyn countered.

"Not if we take a shadow ride," Elyana answered.

Vallyn winced. "A plague on shadows. You'd be mad to try."

She stared at him, hard, and he looked down.

"When I last saw you," she said, still staring at him, "you were working on spells that altered your appearance. Do you know them still?"

Vallyn nodded, reluctantly at first, then added a pleased little shrug. "I've gotten pretty good at it, if truth be told."

"Can you alter someone else?"

Kellius and Renar looked back and forth between them, wondering at the length of time it took Vallyn to reply.

"I can," he said. "But I can't alter us all. Only one."

"One will have to do."

"But there's three of us needing disguise."

"Two." Elyana produced an amulet from her pouch. "I have a little help from Arcil." So saying, she lifted the necklace and clasped it around her neck. Instantly Kellius beheld the face of the thin-nosed, arrogantly handsome man who'd confronted them in the ruins.

"Arcil!" Vallyn cried.

"He left this on the body of his apprentice," she said, astonished that her own voice had now taken on the haughty, male precision of her former friend. "Listen to me!" she said. Despite everything, amusement rang in her voice. "He's very good."

"He's very *bad*," Vallyn countered.

"Is this wyvern his work?" Kellius asked.

"Probably," Vallyn said. "It'd be like him. If he were listening and thought we had him pegged to attack after we found the crown, he might've sent the thing just to show us up."

"Wyverns are common in the mountains," Elyana noted.

"I know we've little time," Kellius said quickly, "but I have one more question. It's clear the Galtans want you two dead. Arcil rode with you. Won't they recognize his face?"

"Arcil was always good with concealment magic," Vallyn said. "I don't think any Galtan that lived ever saw his real face."

Elyana faced the bard. "Set a spell on Drelm so we can be on our way."

Vallyn shook his head. "I'm still wanted there, remember?"

"When's the last time you were on a wanted poster, Vallyn? Do you look the same?"

Vallyn's hesitation seemed to indicate more surely than anything else that her point struck home. But he nodded. "They know me even better than you, Elyana."

"Very well." She undid the necklace and passed it over her head, changing in an instant back to her true form and voice. "You wear it. I shall wear a hood. Place your spell on Drelm."

Vallyn considered her, then let the amulet sink into his palm, the chain dangling between his fingers. "He's probably not going to live," Vallyn cautioned. "This is—"

"The sooner we get moving," Elyana said coolly, "the better his chances. Cast your spell."

Vallyn thrust the necklace into an upper pocket on his shirt. He unslung his lute and stepped over to the prone captain.

In moments the bard was plucking at strings, singing a simple little melody, his voice rich and thoughtful. Drelm's features wavered and blurred, and Elyana suddenly found herself regarding a pale fighting man with dark hair. He did not look so much a different man as he did an image of what Drelm would have been if the orc blood were somehow stripped away. Fangs vanished, the brow ridge faded, the ears shrank down. He was still thick and muscular, but even in rest was somehow more peaceful.

"There he is," Vallyn said, a touch of pride in his voice. "It'll hold for a few hours. After that—they'll have a half-orc on their hands."

"He might be dead before then," Elyana told him.

They worked quickly to saddle the horses and gather their gear. Even so, it was not swiftly enough, and Elyana twice checked Drelm's pulse, so concerned was she that they were wasting time.

She herself held Drelm, knowing that she could trust Persaily to carry the extra weight and travel the strange terrain. She hoped she could likewise trust the mare to carry them through the Plane of Shadow. To the others she gave the lead lines of one pack animal each, hoping they were skilled enough to manage their beasts and lead another, then set her mind upon the ring and called forth the shadows.

Chapter Eight
Temples and Temptation

The spiraling gateway of darkness spun open before them, and Elyana urged on her mount. Persaily advanced at a trot, ears cocked forward. The other horses followed her example, whinnying back and forth to each other.

Persaily snorted in surprise but settled to Elyana's soothing whisper. The landscape through the barrier was flat and grassless, the sky gray. Mountains loomed on their left, but they were twisted and impossibly high. A strange blocky shape with immense bat wings glided high in the air, beneath the drifting stars, and its body trailed long hair or tendrils. Elyana couldn't tell which they were and hoped it would never fly close enough for her to learn.

As was common with powerful energy foci from the real world, the city dominated the plain on the shadow realm. In Elyana's experience, cities and landforms large enough to register in the shadow realm either compressed distances, or somehow attracted objects toward them. After only a minute of riding Elyana had already drawn close enough to the shadow version of Woodsedge to perceive the sides of its buildings. Homes and shops seemed fashioned in misshapen parallelograms, sometimes narrower on the top than the bottom, sometimes longer on one side than the other. Distant and lumpy man-shapes lurched between those buildings, and as their horses cantered toward them, Elyana saw two of those humanoids turn and point at their coming. Above, the winged thing turned in the air and glided down.

They would have to chance riding on a little farther. There might be no city wall in this shadowy reflection, but there was certainly one circling Woodsedge.

"Take us back!" Vallyn urged.

But Elyana rode on, and with that strange rippling of distance that happened all too often in the Plane of Shadow, she was suddenly before the figures in the city. The "men" were just as warped and twisted as their buildings, longer on one side than the other. One in front raised a bent staff to swing at her, but she leaned away, balancing Drelm's slumped form with her off hand, and Persaily sped past. She made for a dark alley, willing the gate to reopen. Whatever the creature was that flew above let out a high, trilling call that sounded like a concert played on smashing glass, with a chorus of female choking victims.

The gate between planes spun open in a counter-clockwise pattern before her. Persaily dashed through, her hooves clattering on the cobblestones beyond. The animal snorted in relief as Elyana drew her to a stop.

They'd come out in a winding side street. Multistory apartments crowded so far overhead that they blotted out all but a slim ribbon of the sky. She saw no watchmen. Scent was restored to her, but not the crisp, clean smell of steppe grass—it was the stink of a city with massed, unwashed humanity and overflowing sewers. Her mouth twisted in disgust.

She turned Persaily. Over her shoulder she found Vallyn and Renar riding clear of the portal. Kellius, exiting last, stared fearfully back as the gate rolled shut and vanished in a puff of smoke. Both the horse he led and the horse he rode showed widened nostrils and rolling eyes, and she took a precious moment to ride back and soothe them.

A bell tolled from within the city, a mournful sound. It struck three times.

"Now comes the hard part," Vallyn said tiredly.

"That wasn't the hard part?" Kellius drawled. He adjusted his hat, and Elyana noticed that it still boasted the petunia. She wondered if he'd been wearing it all the way through the fight with the wyvern.

"That was just a race," Vallyn replied. "Now we've got some talking to do." He took stock of his surroundings and lifted Arcil's necklace to his head. His voice changed in mid-sentence as he continued: "We can follow the bell to the temple district." As startling as it was to hear the sound of Arcil's voice, it was even more peculiar to see Vallyn's transformation into the aristocratic wizard.

Elyana pulled up her hood. A simple disguise, but adequate enough in the darkness.

Woodsedge was a small, remote city, but it was Galtan, and as such the tall black shape of a guillotine stood like a grisly beacon in the central square. Lights burned in high towers beside the three stories of the columned magistrate's building across from it, and lantern lights flickered in high windows of many tenement buildings. As they rounded a corner, two men wearing black sashes and drooping, knit liberty caps spotted them and hurried to the middle of the street.

"Citizens!" The larger of the pair called out to them in a booming voice. "What are you doing here after curfew?"

"Greetings, citizen," Vallyn answered smoothly. He'd already slung his lute across his chest, holding the reins with one hand and the instrument with the other.

The large man raised a hand and halted in front of them. The other raised a whistle to his mouth with one hand, though he did not blow it. With the other he brandished a cudgel crudely carved with the outline of a guillotine.

Vallyn pulled his mount to a stop in front of the guards, who peered suspiciously. Renar quietly asked Elyana what they should do.

"Listen," she answered.

Vallyn spoke swiftly while plucking a soft, bright melody. His voice rose in a singsong way. Elyana wondered if the real Arcil would sound as pleasant were he to chant or sing.

"We few but ride to aid a friend. He fell tonight and needs our aid. We know that you will let us by, for you can see we do no harm."

The man with the whistle lowered both it and the cudgel. His companion's arm fell and his expression softened. Both looked a little blank.

Vallyn kept strumming as he guided his mount down the street with his knees. Elyana and the others rode after.

She did not remember the city in its entirety, for it had been more than a quarter-century since she'd briefly walked its streets at nighttime like this. Yet she wondered as to Vallyn's course, because it veered from the temple district down toward the south end of the city.

Up ahead she heard the sound of music, and recognized that they had come to a neighborhood where they'd once lain concealed. It was a maze of streets, and if not quite lawless, less well patrolled than much of Woodsedge. Here, apparently, there was no curfew, for folk still walked the streets, albeit only in groups, and with sharp eyes for those who passed them. Many taverns and inns remained open, pale light shining ghostlike from upper windows, and music rose over strained and drunken laughter. Elyana likewise heard shouts and a single, distant scream that rose sharply and ended with abrupt finality. None of those they passed paid it any heed.

There was just enough room to trot up to Vallyn's side.

"What are we doing here, Vallyn?" she asked.

"The temple district's closed by curfew," Vallyn answered. "But we can reach the temple of Calistria."

Elyana's mouth tightened. She knew what a temple of Calistria was like here in the north. Of course it would remain open into the late hours, unlike a staid temple of Abadar.

They left their horses with twin stable hands they found awake and dicing in front of the barn beside the temple, then Kellius and Renar carried their heavy burden. Even stripped of armor, Drelm was no lightweight.

Vallyn led the way in; Elyana saw that he'd removed the disguise from his features and guessed that he meant to be recognized here by friends or allies. It troubled her that he'd changed their course of action without consultation, but now was not the time to question him. She fell back behind Renar, her hood drawn high.

Renar had heard of Calistrian temples, but had never seen one, much less walked through one's doors. Used to the austere stonework of a temple of Abadar, he was impressed first by the easy way the walls of Calistria's house were softened by silk banners, its benches by bright pillows.

Then he was struck by other things—the drifting clouds of incense, the little pools of light and the tables about which folk gathered, and most of all the attractive folk who moved among them and held court. These, he knew, were the priests and priestesses of Calistria, selected not just for physical beauty but for their intelligence and force of personality. The priestesses, with their scant yellow silk skirts and flounced, low-cut blouses, were some of the loveliest women Renar had ever seen, moving with long-legged ease, their hair swaying with their hips. When they smiled in response to offered questions of those come to the temple, it was like sunlight striking an altar or the opening of a flower. Off to the right he saw one lovely creature leading a man by the hand through an archway that led up a flight of stairs. He gulped, a flush creeping over his features. At that moment he had scarce thought for the dying captain whose shoulders he carried.

Vallyn stopped a passing priest, a well-muscled fellow wearing a yellow loincloth, matching vest, and sandals.

"One of our companions has been injured with poison," Vallyn said. "He needs help."

The man bowed. "We will be pleased to help, brother. Is he a follower of Calistria?"

"No, but I am."

Renar saw Vallyn tap at his chest.

"We shall donate to the temple upon his behalf," Elyana said. Renar started. He'd forgotten she was there. Had she seen him ogling the priestesses?

The priest looked past Vallyn at Elyana, as if trying to peer into the darkness of her hood, then smiled benevolently. "Please, come with me. I will help the fellow personally."

Renar was disappointed that the first time he was invited into a backroom of a Calistrian temple he was in the company of a male priest, and hoped that his friends would never hear of it.

Drelm seemed to be growing heavier in his arms as they walked nearly the whole of the temple, stepping around square columns and other templegoers. Renar couldn't be sure how worshiping was done here, save that there seemed to be a lot of lanterns and candles lit, that drinks were being served, and that priests and priestesses were talking with small knots of people.

They passed through little pools of light, arriving finally near the domed end of the temple where a throned statue of Calistria herself sat, three times life size. The sculptor had crafted a breathtaking elven beauty with a sly smile, one palm resting on the arm of the white marble throne, the other atop the head of a giant wasp, her fingers spread in mid-stroke. Her dress was not quite as revealing as that of the priestesses, but the gown hugged a curving figure and was slit up one side far enough to show one shapely leg from ankle to upper thigh. Suddenly aware that he was gawking— and at marble, no less—Renar forced himself to look away. He watched the back of Kellius's head bob as the mage struggled with Drelm's feet, and thought of the poor, brave captain. It was much more respectful to be solemn at a time like this, and so he frowned slightly in disapproval at Vallyn. The bard was taking in the room with undisguised pleasure, as though there were nothing at all to be embarrassed about.

Finally the priest pushed open a stout oaken door on the far wall of the room and hung the lantern he bore inside the room beyond. It swayed for a moment, now lengthening, now shortening their shadows, so that the small rectangular chamber crawled with movement.

"Set the patient there on the divan," the priest said in smooth, low tones. "Is he bleeding?" He hesitated by a chest to the right of the door.

"The bleeding has been healed," Elyana said. "We could do nothing about the effects of the poison."

Renar was only too glad to lay the fellow down. Kellius breathed a sigh of relief and lowered Drelm's legs.

There was little to the small room—a deep green couch wide and long enough to hold Drelm, a single chair, a chest, and a painting of a reclined Calistria, wearing even less than her statue and smiling invitingly. Renar was so engrossed studying her that he almost missed the large wasp depicted behind the goddess.

Vallyn slapped him on the back. "First time in a temple of Calistria, youngster?"

"Uh. Yes."

Vallyn chuckled. "Come on, then. Since your father's not here, I'll show you around myself. You too, wizard."

"Eh—" Kellius's narrow head rose. "Shouldn't we stay here?"

"Elyana will be fine," Vallyn said. "And Drelm wouldn't begrudge us."

Renar looked questioningly at Elyana. He could not see her face, and her voice was calm and measured. "Go. All will be well."

A little embarrassed, he followed the bard and the wizard out into the central chamber.

Elyana watched them depart, then dropped a slim coin purse onto the lid of the chest and withdrew a flattened emerald. It had once been one of four eyes in the statue of a lizard demon, pried free by Vallyn himself.

The priest's eyes rounded, then he held the thing up to the lantern light.

"Praise Calistria. I do not mean to turn a gift away, but—"

"It is only too much if you fail to keep a secret," Elyana said, lowering her hood.

The priest smiled. "I already knew you were an elf. You can't hide those beautiful eyes."

"It is the identity of my half-orc friend I'm concerned about."

The priest stepped to Drelm and looked down at him. "He is the most attractive specimen I have ever seen."

"He wears an illusion, and it may fade at any time. Now, please. Set to work."

"I shall."

Elyana dropped into the chair. She drank deep from her wine sack and listened as the cleric praised Calistria and asked for her aid. He then placed hands upon Drelm's thick neck. Elyana was reassured somewhat to see that although the cleric's eyes were closed he found the wound's entry point upon Drelm's arm without hesitation. He was no amateur.

She could not help studying the lines of the cleric's physique, from calf to waist, and admired the rounded biceps and triceps abstractly. How much energy did it take to keep such tone every day when there was no manual labor to do? Likely he spent hours at exercise, all to be beautiful for the men and women who took steps toward his temple. And for what reward? Elyana knew many elves worshiped Calistria, but the appeal of this deity remained as elusive to her as Abadar's. Too many worshipers of Abadar cared only about money, and too many worshipers of Calistria thought only of the flesh. Money she found a useful evil, flesh she enjoyed, but she knew that it was all too easy to lose one's path and seek either to excess.

She could weakly sense the power rolling out from the cleric as a pleasant, sensual tingle. That was a vast improvement over the staid warmth evoked by Abadar's clerics.

She sat and watched the man work. Sweat beaded on his forehead. He finished in only a few moments, and stood, wiping his face with the back of his hand. Sweat glistened on his pectorals.

He smiled down at her. "By the grace of Calistria, he has been healed. His strength was mighty, but failing. You were wise to bring him to us."

Elyana rose and stepped over to Drelm. The half-orc stirred fitfully but did not open his eyes. "How long must he rest?"

"You must give him at least the night." The cleric's hand reached out for her fingers and closed softly on them. "He will be safe, here."

Elyana slid her fingers from the man's grasp and looked questioningly at him.

"Come, my beauty." His voice was low, beckoning. "You have more than paid for this service, and others beside. Let us worship Calistria together, in far more comfortable chambers. I will see to it that your friend remains undisturbed, whatever shape he takes."

"You are kind," Elyana said. "But I will stay here."

The cleric's mouth twitched into a smile. "Is he your lover, then? Surely he would not begrudge you a holy union."

Elyana stiffened at the insult and tried not to let her anger show in her voice. "He is not my lover, though that is no concern of yours. I thank you for your service and for preserving the life of my friend."

The cleric's smile fell away and he straightened. Elyana sensed that he was unused to being rebuffed. "I will rest here this night," she finished.

"As you wish," the cleric said with a bow. He swept up the emerald and departed. Elyana realized then that she should have handled him better, and frowned at herself. It would surely not have hurt to have been more gracious. Yet she could not now picture herself having reacted differently to the man's assumptions.

She spread her bedroll on the floor under the painting of Calistria, then turned to take Drelm's measure with her own magic. She discovered that the half-orc had reverted to his true appearance. His eyes were closed. His mouth hung slightly open, exposing the protruding canine teeth almost to the root. It was easy to imagine him still as that handsome warrior Vallyn's illusion had painted. A mistake, she reminded herself. If pushed to rage, or tempted too far, the orc blood within him would undoubtedly burn hot enough to sear away the overlay of morality and civilization.

She set hands upon his arm. After a moment of concentration she confirmed that the poison taint had vanished from his system. His body surged once more with vitality. He stirred in his sleep and she lifted her hands away. Bad enough to be a human, whose life was so fleeting. What was it like to not even be fully so, and to have to strive to meet even that standard?

With that uncomfortable thought, she stepped to her bedroll and lay down. It was easier to center herself than she would have guessed, despite the half-orc, who snored from time to time, and the faint laughter from outside the room. She lay back, crossed hands across her chest, and closed her eyes. She fixed her mind first on relaxing her limbs, then the muscles of her back, neck, and chest, and within a quarter-hour she was sleeping.

She returned suddenly to full consciousness, eyes opening wide. Her hand fell immediately to the hilt of her sword. The room was cast in darkness save for a feeble line of light creeping through the gap between door and floorboards.

Someone stood outside the door; she felt a hesitation like the gathering of a storm cloud. She climbed soundlessly to her feet. Drelm lay now on his side, not snoring, exactly, but breathing heavily as if readying to grumble at any moment. One muscular arm dangled off the side of the couch, hairy knuckles against the floor. She sidled over to him, her feet bringing forth no squeak or shuffle from the old planks beneath the rugs. She crouched by his ear.

"Drelm," she said softly.

The half-orc stirred.

She bent closer, left hand still wrapped about her sword. "Drelm," she said forcefully. "Rise up! The enemy comes!"

The big eyes blinked at her, taking a moment to truly see her, and then she saw consciousness wrest him from his dreams. His bottom lip curled. Would he wake in time to act, and was he in shape to do so? She could not use her ring now; it would be hours before its magic recharged. They had only their prowess to see them through.

Drelm sat up.

The door opened.

The man in the doorway brandished a cudgel in one hand, a lantern in the other. His scowl shifted into a look of horror the moment the elven woman lunged at him. Her sword shone in the light of his lantern as it passed deep into his chest. He had time for a swift scream before he dropped, his curling Galtan cap landing on the floor beside his writhing body. The lamp shattered on impact and flaming oil rolled out across the carpet.

Elyana charged out, yelling for Drelm to follow.

A dozen Galtan soldiers in long cloaks and curled caps waited beyond the door. A man's voice shouted, "Now!"

Two soldiers darted at her and tossed a weighted net, but she rolled away, coming up in time to strike off a hand that bore a cudgel. Its bearer screamed and dropped, holding his bloody stump.

The nearest guardsman dashed aside as she advanced, and one of them shouted warning as Drelm emerged from his chambers, roaring. Elyana wished that she'd ordered his weapons brought in. Too late.

Drelm swatted out with the cudgel he'd swept up from the fellow in the burning chamber. The half-orc did not know where he was, or how he had come to be there. None of it mattered. These were foes, and they meant him harm. He felled a guardsman with one crack to the head. Ahead of him, the elf moved like water, slashing and ducking, and the guardsman that dared approach her fell. Drelm guessed her aim was the side door on the right. He did not know that it was the very door through which he had been carried only a few hours earlier.

Urged on by the shouting male voice at their rear, two other soldiers raced up. Drelm lacked both Elyana's speed and reaction time, and when the thick-fibered net descended around him, he misjudged. The net slammed home. Drelm roared and butted his head into the mouth of a man who ventured too close. The fellow fell back shrieking through cracked teeth and bleeding gums. Drelm bared his own teeth and shouted for the others to come, but the net tightened suddenly around him. Magic.

Elyana fought on, and Drelm saw to his surprise that all but three of the men were down. "Run!" he yelled.

He was not sure that she'd heard him. She had paused, staring at a figure in a tricorne hat and leather mask who stepped out from behind a pillar. Elyana's feet shifted as she readied to spring.

The masked figure raised a finger and a ray of darkness shot forth and struck her squarely in her chest.

There was no hint of physical force when the dark beam struck Elyana. Instead, an intense fatigue swept through her body. Her arms sagged with the weight of her sword, and her breath came in ragged gasps. Her muscles ached in protest, demanding that she sit down and rest them.

Elyana dared not give in. She stood, wavering, her eyes blazing.

"She is weak now," said the masked figure, the man who had been directing them all along. "Take her, and swiftly!"

The three who still stood hesitated for a moment, then rushed. One Elyana slashed deep with a shaking hand, and then a human stinking of fear and garlic crashed into her, bearing her to the floor. Before she could smash in his head with the pommel of her sword, a booted foot crashed down onto her wrist. She heard the snap of bone even as pain raced firelike through her body. She gritted her teeth to keep from screaming, and for a moment could focus upon nothing at all. She refused to ride the wave of pain into unconsciousness. She glared up at the grunting figure who sat on top of her. As of yet, his eyes still showed with fear rather than desire, but she knew the way of men.

"Search her for weapons," the man's voice continued. "Then bind her in the net, and bring her." Elyana said nothing as the commander drew closer and peered down through the mask that marked him as a Gray Gardener, one of the Galtan dispensers of justice. "There is much I would hear from you before you meet my mistress, elf."

By that she knew that the Gardener meant the guillotine, and Elyana bared her teeth.

The Gardener laughed shortly, then barked once more to his underlings. "Hurry with her, dolts!"

They hauled her to her feet, the motion setting her wrist afire. They bade her lift her arms, then searched her, roughly, while one inexpertly held her own sword ready to thrust at her. She tried not to sag under the magical weariness, tried not to focus on the web of pain pulsing from her smashed wrist.

They stripped her of her knife, bow, and money pouch, and growing bold with her seeming helplessness, one of the Galtans let his hands stray over her breasts.

"None of that," the Gardener snarled, but even as he spoke Elyana grabbed the back of the fellow's head with her good hand and introduced him to her knee. He crumpled. It was then that a heavy weight crashed into the back of her head. There came a sharp pain and a flash of light and everything slipped away.

Interlude
Together in Darkness

In street plays and fireside stories, and even in some ballads, Elyana had heard of heroes and heroines captured by their foes only to escape unharmed. They always returned to their families whole, their wrongs avenged.

Elyana knew that real prisoners rarely fared as well, and that a helpless woman was too tempting for the men who held power over her. She held no illusions about captivity. Thus she was pleased when she awoke and realized the presence she sensed over her was Stelan; she knew him by scent.

"Praise Abadar," Stelan said. His speech was distorted, as though he were talking with his mouth full. "I thought you were done for."

She was so happy to find him there that she pulled him down with two arms, realizing only then that she ached abominably. Her head felt as though she'd downed an entire cask of that wretched ale they served in Pitax, and she suddenly remembered the long slide into darkness. The floor in the shadow temple had given way, and then had come the impact of her body onto stone.

"Where are we?" she asked.

"I was hoping you could tell me." He still sounded as though there was something in his mouth, and she listened more intently as he continued. "I can't see a blessed thing."

"Neither can I. Is there something the matter? Why do you sound like that?"

"I've cut open my lip. Or bruised it. I can't really tell, but it's sore and swollen. You really can't see anything at all?" Stelan sounded almost comically disappointed.

"Nothing. Stand close. Let me see to your wounds." She reached out for his shoulder and gingerly felt his face. "We're not in prison?"

"Well," Stelan mused, "we're in a room without an exit, so I suppose we are. Elyana, you should always see first to yourself. Remember?"

They had argued over that before. She was in no mood for the argument again today, so she acquiesced.

She reached up to feel her forehead. Blood was crusted there.

Stelan was right—it was always easier to craft a spell if untroubled by pain, and he seemed in no serious danger, so she saw first to the swollen bump on her forehead, then her bruises and scrapes. She then turned her attention to Stelan. His lips were bloodied and swollen, and his ankle was sprained. She chided him for not mentioning the sprain, then kissed the lips she had mended. Stelan's mouth was briefly stiff in surprise before he returned her passion.

They broke apart at the same moment.

"What was that for?" Stelan asked.

"For the joy that we live and are together," Elyana told him, then paced out the room that neither could see.

Twenty paces wide, twenty paces long, and nothing within the room but some shards of stone and the rotted bones of the chamber's last occupant. She told this to Stelan.

"I learned as much. I was hoping you would detect something I had not. I'm under the spot where we dropped from, but I can't reach the ceiling. Can you climb up and see if it's sealed?"

"Where are Vallyn and Arcil?" Elyana scaled up his broad back and set her legs on wide shoulders. No catch plate was obvious to her fingers. The entry point was of the same rough stone as the ceiling, wall, and floor. There seemed no way clear.

"I saw Vallyn dive to the side," Stelan answered, weary not from holding her, but from the battles that had been their fare as they advanced through the temple ruins. "I don't know what happened to Arcil."

She directed Stelan to move around a little as she kept hands overhead, feeling the stone. They walked nearly the whole of the room, and she sensed that, strong as he was, her weight really was wearying him. She slipped off his shoulders. "I can't find anything."

"What about those bones? Are they . . . likely to stay there?"

She laughed. "How should I know? But if they haven't animated by now, I'm betting they won't. My guess is that only one poor soul ever wandered into this trap before, and either he came in with an empty wine sack, or he drained it before he died."

"What are we to do, then?" Stelan asked.

"Let us search more carefully. You feel around the floor, I'll examine the walls."

This they did, for a very long while. Elyana had no way to track time in that dark place, but it seemed to her that at least an hour sped on. They had yet to find any stone out of place upon any of the walls.

"Perhaps we should search the ceiling again."

"I've a better idea," Elyana told him, and surprised him with another kiss. He responded slowly, then with great interest, for she did not relent. Finally he pulled back.

"Elyana, what are you about?"

"I'm snatching a moment while we have one. We've not been alone together for more than two weeks."

"That's true. But it occurs to me . . ."

His voice trailed off. She ran a finger down his crooked nose. Even in the darkness she pictured the shape of his strong, kindly face.

"You distract me, Elyana," he said, trying to sound composed. "It occurs to me that we have not shown thanks. Here in this dark hour, I don't suppose I might ask you to pray with me?"

"Now?" The man had no sense of timing.

"Yes."

"I don't expect him to aid us, here," she said.

"That's the problem with most folk," Stelan said, sounding disappointed. "They think a prayer is a contract. The gods must tire of that. 'I'm praying to you, so you should give me a new saddle.' You don't honestly think—"

Elyana laughed. "No, I'm in agreement with you. Why do you pray, then?"

"To become one with something greater. To ease my spirit. To show gratitude. We were lucky to have survived that fall."

"Go ahead, then."

"And you cannot be made to join me?"

"Stelan, you are charming beyond measure, but if you wish a woman to join you in Abadar, you shall have to look elsewhere."

"I'm certainly not going to find another one here," he muttered. She heard him shuffle around, and the rustle of his clothing, and she pictured him sinking to one knee. Faintly amused, she returned to pace the walls, trying to tune out the low sound of the knight's prayer.

It was on her second circuit that she heard a faint chink, as of a rhythmic tapping of metal hammering on stone. She could not quite determine the source above the sound of Stelan's long-winded prayer.

"Stelan—quiet!"

The knight grumbled but fell silent. She heard the sound again, from farther off. Might someone be trying to signal them?

Quickly she lifted the knife from her belt and clanged the hilt against the wall three times. It echoed in that small chamber.

The noise outside stopped.

"What is it?" Stelan asked. He drew near, and she felt one of his outstretched hands brush her shoulder.

"I think—" Elyana fell silent as the triple knock sounded again, close once more. Elyana grinned and clanged on the stone beside her.

There came an answering ring from nearer yet.

"I suppose we can assume that's one of ours," Stelan muttered.

"We can hope." Elyana tapped again upon the stone, and whoever was beating it on the other side returned the call. Then she heard her name, shouted by Arcil's voice.

"Praise Abadar," Stelan said. "He has smiled twice upon us."

Chapter Nine
Galtan Entertainments

Elyana came to in a daze, wondering where Stelan had gone. Arcil had been calling to her, in that trap in the shadow temple. How had she gotten here, and why did her head ache?

"Praise Abadar," the deeper voice said, and everything came back to Elyana. Another head blow, another dark place, another voice thanking Abadar rather than blind luck. Abadar, she was certain, had no interest in her.

"Were you calling my name?" Elyana asked Drelm. She put a hand to her forehead as she sat. Her skull throbbed. That would need tending, and soon.

"I was praying for you to wake up," Drelm said. "I wasn't sure you would."

"Don't worry." She held her head in her right hand, then noticed that while her wrist still ached, it moved at her command. "The Galtans are expert at keeping prisoners alive," she told Drelm as she flexed her fingers. "It's not nearly as much fun lopping the head off a corpse."

Elyana centered herself as the half-orc said something about her having been out for a while, though he could not gauge the hours. She discovered that someone had performed simple healing magic on her—there was no other accounting for a wound that was already sealed, albeit inexpertly. Clearly they had not especially cared if she fully recovered, only that she did not die before her scheduled date with guillotine and crowd. Galtans. She pooled her magic, finished the healing properly, then stood and considered Drelm and her surroundings.

The half-orc seemed little the worse for wear. His eyes reflected the moonlight streaming in through a high, barred window in their cell, barely large enough for a fist to pass through.

Drelm waited, silent, while she inspected their surroundings.

The cell was fashioned of old worn stone. She sat on a single slab built into the wall. A hole in the corner smelled of waste, and a sturdy wooden door with a tiny barred window closed them in. That was the extent of their world.

"Are you well?" Elyana asked. She glanced down at her finger to see that her ring had been removed. Of course—the Gray Gardener sorcerer would have checked her for magic even if the other humans hadn't simply pawned the ring. A band of flesh paler than the rest was the sole reminder of her ownership.

"I'm fine," Drelm answered curtly. "What happened to me? All I know is that I passed out. And the next thing I knew you were waking me up while the Galtans attacked."

Elyana brought him up to speed and checked her pockets to see if there was anything the Galtans had missed. They had left her only her clothes, and these were disheveled, for they had turned out her vest and pockets and even searched her boots, though these were handed to her by Drelm.

"They tossed them into the cell with you," he said.

She slipped her footgear on, thinking. The bastard Galtans had even taken her hair tie, leaving her locks to hang loose and wild.

"Have they said anything about the others?" Elyana asked.

"No."

"A taunt? A question? Anything?"

"Nothing."

Elyana smiled grimly. "It might be that they got away. We can hope for them."

"What will we do?"

She finished pulling on her boots and rested an arm on one knee. "Keep them interested without saying much. The longer we do that, the longer we live, and the more chances present themselves. The moment we lose their interest . . ." she let her sentence trail off.

"I am not afraid of death," Drelm said. "But I do not mean to fail the baron."

"Death shall reach us all," Elyana agreed, "but you do not want death under a Galtan guillotine, Drelm. They say that the souls of those they kill are trapped in the blade that beheads them. I've heard the Galtans brag often enough that it may be true."

"Men lie to sound fierce."

"I don't think they're lying about this."

Drelm's sigh was something more like the rumble of a lion. He leaned against the stone wall. Elyana sat still, considering her options, which were not plentiful. Much would depend upon the others. "Did they leave us any food?" She was terribly hungry. The blood loss and magic use had drained her.

"No," Drelm said simply.

The half-orc seemed in no hurry to thank her for risking, and possibly losing, her life to save his. He was in no hurry to say anything at all. Arcil or Vallyn would have thanked her instantly, in which case the debt would have been dismissed out of hand by her as something comrades did for one another. Drelm's lack of gratitude rubbed at her like a saddle sore. Her irritation grew until she was almost happy when there were footsteps in the corridor.

Through the window in the door she saw more capped guardsman, one of them bearing a lantern that shone in the hallway like a pale yellow eye. Another carried a crossbow. Gone was the Gray Gardener, but there was no mistaking the sash about the short fellow in the lead. Some kind of officer.

They wanted only her, and she permitted them to march her out, feigning that she was hurt still by walking a little stiffly and pressing her hand to her head from time to time. The blood crusted in her hair and along one side of her face was real enough.

One floor down she was led into a small stone room with peeling yellow paint and pushed into a chair before a high desk. The officer retreated behind it, and the two guards left to stand sentinel on either side of the door. She realized her thoughts were too apparent on her face when the officer addressed her for the first time.

"There is no escape, Elyana," he said in a heavy voice, then raised a hand to his mouth as he coughed. Elyana guessed him to be in his early fifties. His forehead was high and square, and he had combed receding hair toward it in an awkward attempt to conceal oncoming baldness. The lanterns hanging behind him threw his shadow across the desk. He lifted an old sheet of parchment paper and shook it at her, then tilted it into the light for her benefit. On it she recognized a fair depiction of her face, and ten lines of text that described her height, features, and crimes against the state.

"It seems you have me at a disadvantage, sir," she said politely. "You know my name, but I do not know yours."

His eyebrows rose in surprise. "You admit, then, that you are the wanted fugitive and traitoress, the elf Elyana?"

"To whom," Elyana asked slowly, "am I speaking?"

"I am Inspector Ledarr." The fellow set down the paper, leaned forward, and steepled his fingers on the desk.

"I have never heard of you," she told him in truth.

"I have brought exactly sixty-seven men and women to the guillotine, traitors all. You will be sixty-eight. Do you deny that you are Elyana, the elven witch?"

"I deny that I am a witch. I am Elyana."

The inspector's eyes lit in triumph. "You were a fool to admit that," he told her smugly.

Galtans. She held back a sigh. The chance that she'd be questioned by someone reasonable had been infinitesimally small, but this man was insufferable. "You would have killed me for slaying the men you sent to arrest me, no matter my name," she said. "Or perhaps you would have had me arrested if I looked at someone oddly, or walked on the wrong side of the street."

Ledarr's expression soured. He wasn't used to a prisoner questioning his goals, she realized. Good. She'd keep him unsettled. "It's hard to track Galtan laws. They change as often as the government."

"The state changes to purify itself," Ledarr said, as if repeating a maxim for the benefit of his listeners. Perhaps he was. Knowing Galt, either of the soldiers could be an informer. "We of Galt climb ever closer to perfection in our pursuit of liberty, and we do not stomach the flaws other nations are forced to endure! When our government is corrupt, the people change it, and start afresh! We are slaves to nothing but liberty!"

He raised his hand in a flourish as if he expected applause.

"And you've done wonders with the place," Elyana said quickly. "It's no wonder everyone's clamoring to visit."

Ledarr clicked his tongue against the roof of his mouth, then lowered his hand. "Do not mock me. I can make your last hours very unpleasant, elf witch." He smiled comfortably, thinking her cowed, then lifted the paper with her picture and began to read. "You are hereby charged with the treasonous aid of seventeen criminals of the state."

"It was really more like thirty," Elyana said evenly.

He glared, then read on, squinting slightly. "You are likewise charged with the murder of loyal members of the militia, obstruction of duty, insult to the state, theft, and perjury, and are suspected in the death of two honorable Gray Gardeners."

"Five, actually," Elyana said. Her voice took on a cool, hard edge. "And there will be more."

"Do you think this is a joke, madam? Do you find yourself funny? Because I assure you that none of us are laughing." His open palm stabbed toward the silent guards, who were markedly grim. "And if you think that you have a shadow of a chance of leaving our custody alive, you are sadly mistaken. We inspectors are dedicated to the pursuit of justice, and we mean to enforce it upon you."

"Galtan justice is a bit sharp for my tastes."

"Do you ever tire of your tongue, madam? It will be hard pressed to wag once your head is sliced from your body."

"You've a poor method of information gathering, Inspector. How can you get any if you do nothing but promise punishment?"

He blinked at her and produced another clicking noise.

Good—she had his attention, at least. "I assume you want to know for whom I was spying, and what my aims were?"

"If you think to bargain for your release, or think that I, a servant of the state, can be empowered to offer mercy, then you are sadly mistaken."

"See, that's exactly what I mean. How do you expect to find out anything with that sort of approach?"

He set down the paper again. "I see that in addition to thinking yourself humorous, you are mistaken in believing yourself clever. Do you plan to fool me, Elyana?"

She leaned forward and lowered her voice. Her speech slowed and lost its sarcastic edge. "I think that you are a man who seizes an opportunity, Inspector. Especially an opportunity to advance the state." She glanced back toward the guards, then met his eyes. She was now a model of restraint. "Both you and I know that there is no hope for me in regards to clemency, but there is no harm, is there, in changing the manner I am housed, so long as I remain a prisoner doomed to execution?"

He studied her a moment, then spoke slowly. "Go on."

"I suggest a more comfortable room for myself and my companion—who, I might add, is guilty of nothing other than being wounded by a Galtan wyvern."

"Anyone found in your company has guilt enough."

"I assumed you would see things that way. A room, then, with clean linens and beds. A final day to reflect in prayer, and water for baths, and well-cooked meals. Not prison slop; meals a man such as yourself might eat."

"That is asking a great deal, madam," Ledarr said. "What would the state receive in return for an outlay extended to a spy and traitoress such as yourself?"

"What do you want to know?"

"I desire to know . . . everything. And I will make no bargains." Ledarr raised something from below the desk and set it before her with a thunk. When he unwrapped his fingers he revealed a small statue of a woman holding a sword aloft. Elyana knew the moment she set her eyes upon the thing that it was a charm.

"Now," Ledarr said affably, "I will hand you documents and you will sign, confessing your guilt. And then you will tell me anything I wish to ask."

Ledarr twisted the papers stacked neatly on the left-hand side of his desk so that they faced Elyana, then pulled free a quill pen from its inkwell and brandished it, offering it feather end first.

Elyana felt the pull of the statue and knew its exhortation. Someone had placed a crude compulsion upon the thing. Blunt, powerful, it demanded obedience and invoked love of the state and its agents.

"Are you ready to sign?" Ledarr asked, practically purring. He then added: "Do you now regret bringing harm to the state? If you wish to profess your love to lady liberty and myself, her agent, you have my permission to kneel."

"The state," Elyana said, "is a pox-ridden, mummified harlot and you are a worm writhing within her."

Ledarr's face reddened in rage. He shot to his feet. "Look at the statuette!"

"I am looking."

She heard the guards rustle behind her and managed to sound reasonable even as they seized her shoulders. "Doesn't your poster tell you that I'm immune to charms?"

In point of fact, she wasn't, not so far as Elyana knew. She was certain that prolonged exposure to the figurine would see her confessing to whatever Ledarr desired. So she bluffed.

Her delivery was so calm and assured that Ledarr appeared to believe her. His eyes all but bugged from his head and his lips struggled to frame words. The guards held Elyana and watched him, awaiting orders.

"Take her back to her cell," the inspector decided finally. He scowled. "We'll see how funny you think this is when the Gray Gardener returns to question you!"

Elyana smiled at him as she was led away. Two more guards waited outside, for a total of four, including the one with the crossbow. Together they marched her back. She was tempted to move against them; tired as she was, she still might be able to take them, so long as she could trip one into the path of the crossbowman. But if Vallyn had escaped, she knew that he'd already have a plan in progress. She decided to give him a little time.

Drelm waited, scowling. His large eyes roved over her after the guards slammed and barred the door. There was no sign of dawn yet through the window, but Elyana knew that it could not be far off. She felt it in the air.

"Did they hurt you?" he growled.

"Not yet. Their questioning's gotten more sophisticated, but they're still tripping over their own arrogance."

"Do you think they were on the alert for us?"

"I don't know how," Elyana said. "I suppose we were recognized. It's been twenty years, and they still had an identification poster for me."

He grunted. "What did you do to make them so angry?"

"We escorted a lot of frightened people to safety over several years," Elyana answered. "But specifically. . ." She chuckled. "Specifically, I think we made our biggest impression on our last visit. We escaped with ten prisoners and burned down a few blocks on the way out of town. And some Gray Gardeners along with them."

Drelm snorted. He opened his mouth as if to say more, then turned suddenly toward the door.

Elyana heard it a moment later: the tramp of approaching boots in the dungeon corridor. Drelm moved to the window in the door and peered out.

"Two guards," he said. "One with a lantern. One of those gray cloaked men is walking with them."

A Gray Gardener, already? She hadn't expected that. If one of them questioned her . . . She forced confidence into her voice. "Two guards. Those are better odds."

"You said the gray men have magic."

"Pretend you're weaker than you are," Elyana told him. He grunted acknowledgment.

She feigned nonchalance as she listened to the troupe march forward. Finally the footsteps stopped in front of the door.

"Leave me," a voice said. A man's voice. Elyana felt a thrill of recognition. Had she heard correctly?

"If it please your citizenship," one of the guards said gutturally, "I'm not sure we—"

"I said to leave," the voice repeated sharply, and one of his two companions set the lantern on the floor. Footsteps retreated the way they'd come.

The Gardener's eyes shone from deep in his mask as he peered through the window in the door. "We've not much time," he said.

"Nice costume," Elyana told Vallyn. "Did it come with a key?"

"It came with all kinds of perks," Vallyn answered softly from behind the mask, "but we'd best move fast. The boy and the wizard await us in the stables. I've even managed to recover most of our belongings. Though not, I'm afraid, your ring."

Elyana winced. "My sword?"

"In the stables. Now get back. I'm opening the door."

The bard soon had them out, and passed Elyana's knife over, apologizing that he couldn't have sneaked her sword in.

"I'm just glad you got in at all." Elyana's eyes passed over the darkened doors. The dungeon hall was long, dark, and narrow. Cell doors stood on either hand. "Who's in the rest of these?"

"No one right now."

"You're sure?"

Vallyn's answer was grim. "They just cleared everyone out yesterday evening."

He did not mean, she realized, that anyone had been freed.

"Not as many folk to execute as there were in the old days," Vallyn continued, almost conversationally. "They save them up. More interesting for the crowd."

"That's thoughtful of them."

"Now ready yourselves. When we round the next corner there's another door, and there are guards on its other side. I'll go through, and then you two will have to account for at least one of them."

"It will please me," Drelm said in his low voice.

Elyana and the half-orc held back from the door as Vallyn rapped on it. The eye panel slid aside and a bearded face peered at them. The door opened swiftly to Vallyn's Gray Gardener costume. The guard on its other side started to close it the moment Vallyn was clear, but Drelm was already charging.

The half-orc slammed into the door with his shoulder so hard that it swung back and into the wall. He lifted a guard with one hand in a chokehold and smashed him into the wall while the fellow kicked. Vallyn knifed the other when the guard whirled to check on the commotion. By the time Elyana was across the threshold, both guardsmen were down.

Drelm released his soldier to crash unconscious or dead against the floor.

"Good enough." Vallyn's eyes swept over the guards. "I'm afraid I'm fresh out of disguise spells at the moment. You might pull on this fellow's coat and hat, my dear. Drelm—"

"I can wear the other man's hat," Drelm said.

Vallyn shrugged. "Good enough."

Elyana took the bard's suggestion, helping herself to the man's sword. Drelm snatched up one himself. The weapons were wide cutlasses, not especially sharp, but better than nothing.

Their exit from the building proved uneventful. That early in the morning there were no other people in any of the halls, which Elyana supposed was natural enough. Still, the escape seemed too easy, and when Vallyn opened the door to the courtyard she was surprised to learn that it too was empty. A line of lighter darkness glowed faintly on the eastern horizon. Dawn was come.

Behind them was the prison. To her right were the stables, and on her left a three-story building hung with a regimental banner. Barracks. A wall topped with a walkway and towers stretched between barracks and stables, and below it was a high wooden palisade, closed and barred. A lone figure strode the battlement above the gate, his head turning to take the group in as they walked for the stables, Vallyn still in the rear. The bard had doused the light to help conceal the two who preceded him.

Renar waited just inside the stables, a liberty cap pulled a little too low over his forehead. Elyana could not help but return his glad smile.

"Praise Abadar!" the young man said in a stage whisper, then hugged her. He shook the half-orc's hand enthusiastically.

Kellius smiled at them. "All the gear's packed," he said. "Are you both all right?"

"We are well," Drelm said.

Their horses were saddled, Elyana saw, and after nodding a greeting to Kellius she returned Persaily's friendly nicker with a pat on the nose and a few words of praise.

She had just swung into her saddle when the alarm bell rang. And she'd been concerned that things were going too easily.

Some loud-voiced scion of liberty was shouting at the same time he clanged a great iron bell from high in the jail, and fine as Elyana's hearing was, even she could not determine what the fellow warned against. His words were lost in the titanic ringing. It was easy to guess, though.

Vallyn, cursing a blue streak, climbed into his own saddle and led them into the courtyard. He rode with self-assurance, head high, back straight as a polearm. The barracks boiled with activity as soldiers threw on jackets and dashed across the brick courtyard toward both gate and jail. A bugler sounded high, squawking notes to rouse sleeping guardsmen.

Four soldiers stepped from the gatehouse and halted in front of the thick oaken doors that barred passage from the courtyard. These four wore mailed helms and carried halberds. Their grizzled leader bowed his head briefly to Vallyn as his gaze swept over the rest of them. Elyana's cap was pulled down far over her ear tips, and she squinted to in an attempt to hide her monochrome elven eyes. Drelm slouched in his saddle, trying to look small, and sucked on his lower lips so that his fangs did not show. It lent him a demented and stupid aspect, but in the predawn light he looked human enough. Elyana guessed he was not the only hulking idiot the Galtans had ever seen wearing a liberty cap.

"We must pass," Vallyn said.

"The prison bell's rung, citizen," the officer said in a steely voice. "No one comes in or out."

"Fool," Vallyn said, "the prisoners are out already! We ride to find them!"

"I have my orders, citizen. No one comes in or out."

Vallyn leaned forward in his stirrups, the leather in his boots creaking as he did so. His voice was thick with menace. "If you let the elf girl escape me, *citizen*, I will have your head. Open the doors and stop quoting laws to me. I *am* the law."

The man actually quivered a little, then looked down at the toes of his shoes. He stepped away and waved sharply at his attendants, who scurried to unbar the gates.

The officer stepped off to the side, watching them.

Elyana's head swiveled as she took in the scene. Armed with halberds, dozens of guardsmen were forming a square in the courtyard. The bell ringer had finally left off his tolling, which Elyana was momentarily glad for until another Galtan emerged from the stable to shout that someone had tied up the stable hands.

Renar winced, then gave voice to one of the first curses Elyana had ever heard cross his lips. The chief gate guard's head snapped up and he stared hard at the Gray Gardener before him. His head turned toward the gate guards, mouth opening, but Elyana's sword thrust took him in the throat and he fell, his command unvoiced.

"Calistria's blessing only works so far," Vallyn said, and with a hearty yell kicked his mount into a gallop.

The guards had only opened one of the two palisade gates, and that a mere six feet wide, but Vallyn and Elyana were through it before the stunned guards still pushing it grew conscious of anything amiss. Elyana slashed one before he could answer shouts to close them, and Drelm rode the other down. In a moment all five of the companions were riding free into the cobbled streets.

Vallyn galloped into the main thoroughfare, scattering a militia patrol marching past the guillotine.

Kellius shouted eldritch syllables and Elyana looked back to see what he wrought. A glowing ball of flickering, shifting flame formed in one of his hands. Still shouting, the wizard hurled the fire at the base of the scaffolding holding the deadly guillotine. It landed amidst the timber and licked hungrily up the wood.

The wizard's mount was caught up in the thrill of the run with his fellows, or Elyana could guess it would have been more concerned by the shouting. Even a few days ago Kellius wouldn't have had the skill to ride while casting, but his days in the saddle had paid off, and he managed to keep his seat and control his mount. He grinned triumphantly at Elyana, who chuckled merrily in response.

Vallyn took the corner sharply, then rounded the next. Bells rang throughout the city, warning guards to seal the gates. Long ago, Elyana and Stelan's Galtan contacts had known a hidden way through the walls. Elyana guessed that the resistance would have had to find a new way to freedom, if any significant number of rebels remained. The Galtans were simply too practiced at hunting down their foes.

Vallyn's course wound them back into the quarter where they'd been captured. The streets were quiet, and the overhanging buildings kept them in deep shadow even as dawn's waking light reached into the urban valleys.

The bard finally slowed when he rounded onto a street that dead-ended against the gray stone wall of the city, looming mountainously. Thirty feet of sheer climb looked down at them.

The bard slid from his saddle, smoothly taking the reins and heading through the wide, curtained opening of a one-story building set flat against the wall. Elyana dropped from Persaily and looked behind her. The other three trailed only a few horse lengths back, Drelm bringing up the rear. She strained to listen for signs of pursuit and heard nothing. Strange. The bells still rang from towers spread through the city. She heard the crow of roosters, the lowing of animals and the shouting of people raised early by the racket. But as of yet, no one on this back street stirred.

She parted the curtains and led Persaily into the building. She doubted the fabric was a standard shop feature and guessed it had been added this morning to conceal whatever Vallyn had set in motion.

A cold blacksmith's forge stood in the gloom to her left, beneath a row of tools hung from a rafter. The stones beneath her must surely be crowded with various tools during the day, but now a path was swept clear, leading straight to an uneven doorway where a six-foot gap had been opened in the bricks themselves. Vallyn, limned by the light, held the reins of his horse while he spoke softly with a woman in the shadows. The stranger faced Elyana as she neared them, and the elf thought that she looked familiar. An instant later she recognized that the mature woman's features were similar to those of a young, reluctant ally from years before.

"Nadara," Elyana said in greeting. What was the shadow wizard Lathroft's niece doing *here*?

The woman bowed her head. "Hurry," she said softly.

"You heard her," Vallyn said, tipping his head toward the opening.

Elyana led Persaily through the gap and leapt to saddle. In a moment more the others were out, and Elyana glanced back in time to see the wall seal behind them.

There would be time to have her questions answered later. Now there was nothing for it but to ride as far and as fast as their horses could carry them.

Chapter Ten
In Among the Kings

They pushed themselves and their mounts, and by noon they had crossed a bridge over the river Sellen, which was coursing its long way down from the River Kingdoms. They drew up on the windward side of a hill and looked back toward Woodsedge. Elyana kept them from the height, where they would be silhouetted against the sky.

The humans sank wearily down for a rest. The horses cropped at the grasses. Elyana scanned the distance.

"No pursuers," Drelm said.

Renar looked up from the pockmarked boulder against which he leaned. "Vallyn had us cut all the girths and bridles in the stable while we were waiting."

Drelm produced a strange noise. Elyana glanced at him, saw the half-orc's lips open in a fang-bearing smile, and realized that he was laughing.

"That can't have stopped all of them," Kellius said. His voice was weary and soft.

"It hasn't," Elyana answered. "There's a line of cavalry after us. Three or four hours back."

Drelm narrowed his own eyes. "I don't see anything but hills and woods."

"You're not Elyana," Vallyn pointed out.

"I'm glad someone finally noticed," Kellius offered, and Drelm laughed again, then smacked the wizard on the back and laughed more deeply.

Kellius grinned at him and adjusted his hat. He'd long since discarded his liberty cap.

"As comfortable as this is," Elyana said, "we dare not rest long."

After a long silence, during which they all dug rations from their saddlebags, Renar's voice rose, quiet not with fatigue, but with worry. "Are they going to catch us?"

"We will reach the foothills today." She knew that was not the reassurance Renar was wanting, but could not muster the sympathy to console him. She was exhausted, and even the dried meat was glorious to her as she dropped down beside Renar and tore into it. It was good to be free, with her sword and her bow. Even the old dwarven bracelet wrapped about her upper arm felt good. When she had time later she'd slip the ugly bearded face back under a sleeve.

Kellius saw her fingering it. "What is that?"

"A dwarven ornament," Elyana said, then took a long sip of wine. She was delighted to discover it was some fine sweet Galtan vintage.

"Old, old loot," Vallyn said amiably. "It was probably some stubby dwarf woman's bracelet. It just fits about Elyana's arm."

Despite his fatigue, the wizard's curiosity was clearly piqued. "What does it do?"

"It boosts my strength," Elyana said, tearing off another bite of dried meat.

"You don't seem strong," Drelm said, dubiously.

"I'm strong enough to lead," Elyana reminded him.

The half-orc grunted thoughtfully.

The captain was right, she thought as she sipped her wine. Even with the magic from the bracelet, her strength was nothing remarkable, and she was glad Vallyn had been able to recover the charm. The Galtan wine was smooth down her throat, and she capped the wine sack with reluctance, for she might easily have drained it. "We should preserve our drink. I don't know these mountains. Water could be scarce once we reach the heights."

"We're not going to the heights, are we?" Vallyn asked, then sighed tiredly at Elyana's answering stare.

"That was Nadara," Elyana said to him, her gaze unwavering. "What was she doing in Galt?"

"Who's Nadara?" Renar asked.

"The woman who helped us escape," Elyana told him without looking over. She was in no mood to catch Renar up on old doings. Not right now. She continued to press Vallyn. "So she's a wizard, like her uncle?"

"She's not a shadow wizard, Elyana," Vallyn told her. "She's part of the resistance. She has been for years. She just put her life on the line for us tonight. That escape route is ruined now, and so might be the lives of anyone associated with it. Or even those living nearby."

Elyana's look softened. She nodded.

"Who's Nadara?" Renar asked again.

"An old friend," Vallyn said. Elyana heard something in his tone that suggested the woman might be more to him than that, but for once the bard did not elaborate.

"Thank her for me," Elyana said formally, "when next you see her."

Vallyn bowed his head. "I shall."

"And thank you, Vallyn," she said kindly.

The bard smiled and bowed his head again.

The whole exchange struck Renar as peculiar. The look in Elyana's eyes when she'd first asked Vallyn about the woman reminded him of the way Elyana had looked at him when he was ten and she'd inquired politely if it was he who'd been trying to punch new holes in the saddle girths with a dagger. Clearly he was missing something, but he did not ask explanation from Elyana, whom he was sure would not answer, and had risen to check over the horses in any case. He chose not to raise the matter with Vallyn, either. Instead he sat down by Kellius.

"What was that all about?" he asked the wizard.

Kellius looked up from the blade of grass he'd been studying. "I can't be sure."

"You can guess, though, right?"

"Possibly." The wizard's eyes drifted back down to the grass, and Renar was readying to ask him if there was something especially fascinating about it until the magic user cast it aside.

"I think," Kellius said, "that Elyana had been about to pry, then let Vallyn know that she had decided not to inquire further."

"I still don't understand."

Kellius shook his head and grinned. He provided no more answers, though.

They'd been up half the night and ridden half the day, and Renar had decided that he now understood the full meaning of fatigue. By the time they crossed into the foothills he discovered that every muscle in his body ached. He felt weary down through to the bone.

He could tell Elyana was weary herself, but the elf
held herself straight as she gazed back the way they'd
come. Renar could see nothing in the foothills. His eyes
flicked up to the peaks looming ahead of them, their
jagged lines sheathed in snow and ice. It was cool even
in their long shadows. How cold would it be along their
slopes?

Elyana permitted no fire, and they were reduced
to eating some rations Vallyn had liberated from the
stables. The Galtan wine the bard had also filched was
delicious enough that Renar offered a toast in its praise.
He was answered by all but Drelm, who announced the
drink lacked fire.

They ate in silence for many minutes. The horses
stood with heads bowed, cropping the grasses lazily.
They would need seeing to before bed, and Renar
sighed at the thought.

"They're still following," Elyana said.

Vallyn shrugged. "We've really annoyed them. I
killed a Gray Gardener, Kellius here burned down their
guillotine, and we had the bad taste to escape in the
process. That's sure to kick them into a gallop."

"You shouldn't have done that," Drelm told the
wizard.

"Peace, Drelm," Elyana urged. His dark look fixed on
her, but he looked away and took a long swig from his
own wine sack.

"I'm glad Kellius burned down the guillotine." A
hint of passion had crept into Elyana's voice. "I wish
he could have truly destroyed it."

"What do you mean?" Renar asked. "He did destroy
it."

"There's souls trapped in the guillotine blade, boy,"
Vallyn said tiredly. "Every person ever killed by the

blade. Burning down the wood will set the Galtans gnashing their teeth and get some carpenters paid for a few days, but they'll just build a new one. The blade can't be destroyed short of some kind of magic ritual."

"Oh." Kellius sounded disappointed.

"I thought it fine work, Kellius," Elyana told him. "You have a sense of style."

"Oh," he repeated, brightly this time. "Thank you, Lady."

"How did you get away?" Elyana included Renar and Vallyn in the question with a sweeping gesture.

Renar answered her, knowing a surge of pride. "Vallyn raced into the room where we were . . ." His voice trailed off and picked up lamely, ". . . talking with some priestesses." Renar exchanged a quick look with Kellius. The wizard reddened, but said nothing. It wasn't as if anything had happened, as much as Renar had hoped it would, and he tried to stop his own face from flushing. "Vallyn told us the Galtans were coming. Then he cast this fabulous spell that opened a hole in the air. Kind of, I guess."

"What sort of spell was that, anyway?" Kellius asked. "That was very skillfully done."

Vallyn bowed his head. "It was nothing. A little something I picked up. I wish I'd known it back in the old days, Elyana."

"What does it do?" she asked.

"It's a kind of teleportation spell," Kellius said, sounding impressed.

Vallyn laughed, clearly pleased. "It allows me to open a passageway between my current location and another place within a few hundred feet. It can't take me nearly as far as your lost ring did, but it's safer. It got all of us out."

"How did you know the Galtans were coming?" Drelm asked gruffly.

Vallyn shrugged. "I have a friend in the temple." He tapped a point between his pectorals and they heard a dull clunk, perhaps a charm hidden beneath his shirt.

Renar shook his head and let out a low whistle. "One thing's for sure: I see why you hate the Galtans so much. They're a little crazy, aren't they?"

"Boy," Vallyn told him, "you don't know the half of it."

It was good to see the camaraderie growing between them. Elyana allowed herself a faint smile as she watched the others fall into easy banter. The bard shifted smoothly into a story about their old days in Galt. Drelm, though, seemed nearly immune to any feelings of good fellowship. He stood, walked to her side, and crouched down.

"How long until they catch up to us?" he asked. Always he sounded as though he were making a demand rather than seeking to have a question answered. If nothing else, she would have hoped their little venture had cemented his trust.

"They're half a day behind," Elyana replied. "They're likely to have remounts, but once we're negotiating passes, it won't make much difference." That's why she'd pushed them so hard today. Luck was with them—only two of the horses had gone lame. They'd be left behind, but there were still enough animals to carry them forward.

Renar had given his attention over to them. "I thought we were on the border with Kyonin," he said. "Won't they be afraid to cross it?"

"Galtans will cross any border in defense of liberty, boy," Vallyn said, then added, "Bastards."

"Don't the elves kill anyone who crosses into Kyonin?" Drelm asked.

Elyana felt all eyes upon her as she answered. "We will be on its border, but not in Kyonin proper."

"I hope the elves appreciate the distinction," Vallyn quipped.

Elyana was exhausted beyond her normal resources, and allowed the others to take the first watches. She sat back against a rock, cleansed mind and spirit, and rested, letting her mind wander in a disconnected way that led soon to a dreamless sleep. When Kellius woke her before dawn she wasn't precisely refreshed, but she felt better. The stars shone white and cold from on high, and a frigid wind swept down off the mountaintops.

Even the wizard could see the campfires in the plain below, four leagues closer than Elyana would have guessed. The Galtans were less than a quarter-day behind, now.

"They must be riding their beasts to ruin," she said.

"Could it be sorcery?" Kellius asked her.

"How do you mean?"

"A potion. A special feed. Something to keep their horses going so long. So far."

"That sounds expensive," Elyana replied. "And awfully well prepared. I have a hard time imagining it."

Kellius nodded his homely head. "Perhaps you're right."

As she marshaled her grumbling companions and got them moving in the cold hours of the early morning, though, the wizard's words got her to speculating. Could he be right? After all, their group had destroyed a guillotine, or at least its scaffold, and it might be that the Galtans were determined to punish them for that slight alone.

Daylight found them deep in the foothills, riding up toward a narrow pass between two rocky heights. The old map had depicted a clear way through and Elyana had no other choice but to believe it.

Over the next hours they worked their way into the cold heights, and the wind swirled and danced, thick with little flecks of snow, as they walked their horses along a path worn away to little more than a goat trail. The earth was still too warm at this altitude for the snow to accumulate, and it melted as it hit the ground.

By evening they had passed the gateway peaks, riding a high trail with a steep right drop. Elyana wished she'd stopped an hour back, before the trail narrowed, but she kept forward. She trusted Persaily's footing well enough to stay mounted, but the others all led their horses, concerned that the beasts might misstep and send them plunging into the canyon a mile below. From time to time Elyana looked back to check their progress. All but Drelm hunched shoulders against the cold. They needed a rest, especially the wizard, who stumbled every few steps.

It was another hour before they reached a miserable little stopping point, a gently sloped shelf of snow-swept rock some forty paces wide. It didn't matter that the wind whipped through like the shriek of a thousand angry spirits—there was room enough to set up their tents.

Most of them snatched only a little rest in between shivering. An hour before dawn Elyana finally gave up and got everyone moving. Drelm was the only one of them not sluggish.

On they wound, tired folk leading worn-out animals along that high, cold trail. As the sun rose, they saw hawks flying free and clear above. The birds could wing away from trouble, or seek a better angle in the wind.

Elyana and the rest had only the one angle, blowing ever east through their clothes, their skin, and seemingly their bones.

Elyana led the way, forcing them on more by example, feigning some measure of Stelan's iron constitution. The breaks they took that morning and afternoon had to be while kneeling against the side of the cliff, only inches from the deadly drop to the river glittering below. The horses dug at the occasional clumps of green stuff thrusting out from between frozen stone and snow.

Finally, come the late afternoon, Elyana rounded a sharp corner and saw that the trail was sloping down, and that the path widened before them into a broad flattened space ringed by the wall of the mountain. She let out a little cry of triumph, encouraged Persaily to move past, then turned to tell the others. Only then did she see they were under attack.

Three translucent humanoid figures hovered ten feet out from the drop. Each was formed entirely of whirling currents of air. Their heads and upper limbs were indistinct, their lower bodies changing at the waist into twisting dust devils. One swept a lengthening, swirling arm at Renar.

Elyana had battled fire elementals and even faced a kind of beast shaped of black earth, but she'd never fought an air elemental. She did not think arrows or blade could harm them.

Drelm gamely swung an axe at one who struck at Renar, but the blow passed through it. The elemental sent a gust of wind roaring into the half-orc. He teetered precariously on the edge of the drop.

Elyana called out to the captain's horse. The frightened beast understood and bit down on the flailing half-orc's arm, then trotted forward, pulling the surprised guard captain to the cliff wall, where he grabbed hard to an exposed tree root.

The other horses took this as a sign to be followed, and pushed into the men in front of them. Elyana shouted at them to hold position, but the animals hurried on, too frightened by the commotion to heed her. One bowled right into Renar, who threw himself against the cliff wall. The horse stepped into the side of his boot. The wind carried Renar's curse away.

Farther back, Vallyn produced his lute and vanished in a sparkle of golden motes.

Elyana sidestepped the oncoming horses and completely missed the fourth air elemental coming up from behind. A gust of wind from its arms set her stumbling along the edge. Below her loomed a drop of more than three thousand feet, and while she had earlier been dreaming of green lands and fair rivers, she hoped not to reach them this way.

An iron grip closed around her wrist, and a great heave slammed her back into the cliff. It was Drelm, fresh blood still staining his arm from where the horse had bitten. Renar's horse plunged from the ledge, screaming. Renar hung determinedly to a root in the side of the cliff even as an air elemental blasted at him with both arms.

Kellius was working a spell, but Elyana could not hear his words. He did not complete whatever he planned, for one of the elementals tripped him with a blast of air. The wizard struck the cliff wall and then bounced off. He reached frantically for the stone of the mountainside, and missed. Arms whirling, he tumbled backward off the ledge.

Chapter Eleven
The Mountain and the Vale

Elyana had a brief glimpse of Kellius dropping to the glistening river far below, and then the elementals swirled toward her. There was only brief time for anguish, and then she had to focus solely on her own survival. Drelm had a firm and painful grasp on her shoulder as he himself clung stubbornly to a thick knob of rock. One of the elementals leveled both arms and sent winds surging into their faces. Elyana turned her head, blinking against the snow and grit blowing into her eyes. Drelm's grip tightened on her and she realized he must be afraid he was losing his hold.

Suddenly Vallyn glittered into existence at her side, cradling his lute. She snatched at him with her free hand. The force from the elemental's constant wind tore at his instruments and pushed his hair back over his receding hairline. Teeth gritted, the bard swung a hand down to his strings . . .

And then she and Drelm and Vallyn stood upon the stone beside the horses.

"Get Renar!" Elyana told him. There would be time for thanks later.

Vallyn swept his hands across the lute. The wind carried all but a tinkling hint of the melody away from her. The bard vanished to reappear beside the young knight, still clinging with both hands to the mountainside. Vallyn strummed again, reaching out to touch the boy at the last minute, and then both reappeared behind Elyana.

The elementals quit their cliffside attack and drifted on toward Elyana's new position. She yelled for her people to back toward the snow-covered boulders, hoping there might be a cave against the mountainside.

As she scanned their line of retreat, a tall, lean figure stepped from behind a large rock so suddenly he might well have appeared by magic. He was garbed all in white furs, and his ungloved hands glowed with a nimbus of sparkling white energies. Where a moment before had been only a rocky highland dusted with snow Elyana now saw more than a dozen men, similarly clothed. Three moved to gather Persaily and the other horses. The rest of the strangers raised arrows against beautifully carven bows.

"Elves," Renar said, and glanced to Elyana for confirmation.

Their hoods hid their ears, but Elyana knew the boy was right from the shape of their faces and their large eyes, not to mention their height. The matter was obvious, just as it was obvious from their solemn, fixed faces that the natives were none too happy to see visitors.

The elven wizard shouted to the air elementals in a fair, musical language and the beings retreated from him, then sped away into the upper air. In a matter of moments they were lost to sight behind the mountains.

Immediately thereafter the wind lessened its roar, and Elyana could hear the question of the wizard as he turned to face her.

His words came swiftly, and she had to pause to think about their meaning. "Cousin," he said sternly, frosty vapor rising from his lips, "who are you, and why have you brought strangers to our land?"

Elyana bowed her head once. While she knew the elven tongue, it had been long since she heard it.

Before she could answer, the elves tensed. Their heads swiveled to the right along with their bows.

Kellius floated up over the edge and lit upon the ground as lightly as a bird, though he panted heavily. He looked just as surprised to see the elves as they were to see him.

"He is with us," Elyana said quickly, before the tightening bowstrings could loose arrows.

"Flying spell," Kellius said weakly. None of the elves looked especially amused. Their leader turned to Elyana with narrowed eyes.

"What are they saying?" Drelm growled.

"Instruct your beast that he is to remain silent," the leader told Elyana.

"He asks you to be silent," Elyana translated. "Cousin," she told the wizard, "we do not bear you any ill will. We do not mean to trespass—"

"What greeting is this?" The leader stepped closer, peering at her. He was the first person in a long while with the height to stare Elyana down. His face was long and sharp, with a thin, refined nose and arched white eyebrows almost the same color as the furs that clothed him. His eyes were a clear, light brown. "You are of the blood, are you not?" he demanded. "You have come to my land, so you announce yourself to me by name and family."

Elyana bowed her head to him. "I am Elyana. You must forgive my manners, cousin. I was raised by humans after the death of my parents, and I did not learn the ways of my own people until I was much older."

"I more fully understand," he said. "What is your family name?"

"Sadrastis."

He nodded once. "Elyana is not a traditional name."

"I keep it in memory of the human woman who raised me."

Again came that stare, and a slight inclination of the head that might have been acknowledgment. "I am Alavar, a Sentinel of Elistia. My magical guardians are deadly. You were fortunate that we had detected your coming so that I could reach you before they did. It was a near thing."

"I thank you."

He accepted this with the barest of nods, then took in her comrades with a single glance before facing her once more. "Why do you come into my lands with humans and an orc?"

"He is but a half-orc," Elyana answered quickly. She'd thought that would be obvious. Alavar's frown deepened at her correction. "We seek aid for an ailing friend, father to that child, baron to these twain." She indicated Kellius and Drelm.

Alavar's lips narrowed pensively. "Humans are unwelcome in our lands; orcs are to be shot on sight. What am I to think of you, who travel with them?"

"I do not care what opinion you hold of me," Elyana said, which raised both of Alavar's eyebrows. "These humans have risked life and blood to ride with me, and so has the half-blood."

"The orc."

"A half-orc, through no fault of his own."

"An orc is an orc through no fault of his own," Alavar said, as though explaining an obvious matter to a child.

The elf's tone struck a sour note with her. "His name is Drelm," she told him, "and he is captain of the baron's guard. He has risen far in the esteem of my friend the baron because he has worked hard to follow the path of Abadar."

"The god of the counting house."

"The god of a good and noble knight. And," she said, saying more than she intended, "a good and noble half-orc."

"Good and noble?" Alavar repeated in astonishment. "Until now I have never heard such words associated with an orc of any blood. Tell me, young one who calls herself Elyana, of the bloodline of Sadrastis, if I take this creature into my lands, will you accept responsibility for him? If he troubles my folk, I shall judge him harshly, and his penalty shall be yours. Think quickly!"

Elyana studied the half-orc, glowering at the elves who ringed him: two with bows and a one with a leveled spear.

"Do you trust him with your life?" Alavar pressed.

"Yes," Elyana said, and realized that she did.

Alavar considered her for a long moment, then raised a hand. "Lower weapons," he commanded.

Instantly the bowmen did as he bade, returning arrows to quivers. The fellow with the spear on Drelm withdrew his weapon with visible reluctance.

"We can be trusted utterly," Alavar told them in the common speech of Taldor. His accent was very slight, and Elyana had no trouble understanding him. His manner, though, remained stiff. "If you act as guests, you will be treated as such."

"We thank you," Vallyn said with a bow. Renar and Kellius followed suit, Drelm a moment later, his bow slow and deep.

"I, too, thank you," Elyana said.

A thin smile crossed Alavar's lips, and once more he spoke only to her, in Elven. "You are very interesting, Elyana. Do you know, a nephew of mine once met one of your bloodline."

She herself had only met a few of them. "I regret that I am unacquainted with many of my kinsmen."

"You will find none here, alas, but you will doubtless take pleasure in my people, who will welcome you, and share food and lodging, and sing for you."

"I welcome your hospitality," Elyana said, hoping she remembered the proper response to Alavar's formal invitation.

Only Elyana was allowed to keep all her weapons, though the elves permitted everyone to retain their knives. Drelm's scowl made it clear he was especially skeptical about relinquishing his arms.

Vallyn sidled up to Elyana as they started along the trail. "That was tense," he whispered. "You're a better diplomat than I remember."

"I didn't know you spoke Elven."

The bard shrugged. "How could I not? Your folk have too many good songs."

The nearest elven warrior, a dark-haired woman, eyed them curiously for a long moment, but did not return Vallyn's smile. To his eyes, Elyana remembered, all elves would look beautiful.

Their trail took them to a wall of massive stone, dotted in frost, unremarkable save that a set of footprints had emerged as if by magic from its face. No entry point was visible. Alavar stopped at the stone and whispered a word; a ten-foot section of the wall swung inward soundlessly, and Alavar strode after it.

He was followed first by a trio of his own soldiers, and then Elyana. She walked into a hallway of smooth stone, just tall enough that she could not reach the ceiling without stretching her arm full length, and just wide enough for three, if they were very close. To human eyes the way would have seemed dimly lit, but the phosphorescent green fungus strategically growing on low niches every thirty paces was more than enough light for her.

The horses nickered, nervously, only to be calmed by the elves who led them behind the group. Elyana glanced back to look over her charges, both equine and human. And half-orc, she thought. Vallyn looked curious, but subdued. The wizard and Renar peered at everything in great fascination. Drelm met her eyes, his expression wary. She nodded her head slightly to him, meaning to be of some reassurance, but he did not respond.

He had saved her life there on the cliff, just as she had called to his horse to pull him to safety. She did not really care for his look, or his manner—or, for that matter, his smell. And he was rude. What did it say about her that she was more comfortable with him than with her own people? She frowned at the thought.

The corridor curved gradually as it wound into the mountain. At times they passed entrances to other passages, some of which stretched away on a level track; others veered up, and some sloped sharply down. Each was demarcated by an alcove with a life-sized statue of an elven warrior and a word or four at eye level beside the opening. The elven words were carved deeply with precise skill, directing readers to such places as Rainbow Tier and the Outer Walk. At no time did they pass other elves. The hallways, however, seemed well tended. There was no dust, and the only intruders, aside from themselves, were occasional pale insects that she spotted upon walls and floors.

They walked through the cavern for more than half an hour, stopping finally at another wall. This one, though, opened before them without Alavar raising a hand. Elven warriors mailed in green lacquered breastplates and helms waited tensely on its far side, their hoods cast back across their shoulders. Alavar exchanged greetings and left his guests waiting while he held a quick conversation with the tallest of his warriors. This fellow asked one or two questions, then slipped away.

Alavar turned back to them with a proud smile. "Welcome to the Hold of Elistia, Fortress of the Bluffs."

She repeated the greeting to her comrades, who bowed, even Drelm, following Vallyn's example.

Elyana nodded a greeting to the dour guards and stepped into the sunlight after Alavar and his lieutenants. Hundreds of feet overhead hung a stone ceiling that gave way to a horizontal cave entrance a mile wide, the entire chamber forming one monumental niche in the mountainside. The sun streamed in sideways from the opening to warm tall, spindly buildings shaped from rock and brick. Walkways stretched between their upper stories. The chatter of folk reached her ears, including the laughter of children and the clack of their play swords. Somewhere, too, was the strum of a harp, and a trio of female voices soared in heart-rending harmony. The smell of baking bread and spiced tombor root washed over her. So sweet was the scent that she had to gulp back saliva.

Alavar ordered all but three of his men away and told them to see to the care of the animals. He then tasked the remaining trio with the care of their guests.

"Enjoy our hospitality," Alavar told the newcomers in lightly accented Taldane. "Take your rest and eat of our goods, though you should not fill yourselves. There will be a dinner tonight in your honor." He did not need to add that he was not sure that his guests deserved it, for it was clear from his tone.

"Captain Drelm, is it?" Alavar said, then continued without waiting for an answer. He was not, Elyana noticed, actually looking at the half-orc. "Be advised that your kind has never before been welcomed here. Move carefully, and make no sudden movements, lest your intentions be misunderstood."

Drelm's head bowed curtly. "I understand."

"Elyana. I would be honored if you accompanied me."

Elyana raised a hand to her companions and then left with the wizard lord.

Though outwardly calm, Elyana was troubled, for she was not certain that her limited time among the elves of Kyonin would see her in good stead in this place. She was certain she would forget proper forms of phrase or praise, or that she would simply behave in a human way and be judged rude and uncouth. There was nothing to be done about it, and she had enough wisdom to shrug off her discomfort, but she was still ill at ease.

Alavar led her toward the sunlight of the cave entrance, which caught whiter highlights in the sentinel's hair. He was trim and athletic, and Elyana found herself wondering just how old he was. Were he human, she would guess late forties, but she was around elves so rarely she had little experience gauging their ages.

After a few dozen feet they climbed a worn wooden staircase, the handrail of which was smooth with the passage of uncounted hundreds of years. The steps hugged the side of a building for three stories and stopped at a terrace, from which Elyana could look down over a vast open garden.

The elves of Elistia had found a long cavity in the mountainside and shaped it into their home. Looking right and left, Elyana perceived that the cliff dwelling stretched at least a half-mile wide, and sat a good quarter-mile into the rock. Gardens and trees grew in the space, for they were well below the level of the heights over which they had but recently climbed. There was yet a hint of chill in the air, but it was just a kiss, not a bite, and while the elves strolling in the gardens or tending its many colored fruit below wore long sleeves, the plants they tended seemed to flourish.

"We have a kind of paradise here, Elyana," Alavar told her.

"I see that. The view is striking."

Beyond the garden she saw the cavern rim, and a hint of greenery below. Beyond the rim lay the brown and gray mountain wall on the other side of the river gorge, ornamented with an occasional stubborn tree or shrub.

"How high up are we?"

"Elistia was built within this narrow cavern that lies only a few hundred feet above the floor of the canyon," Alavar answered. "A few small homes stand on the river shore, guarded by a tower. But most of our people dwell here. All elves," he said with a pointed look, "are welcome."

"Thank you."

He glanced at her from time to time as they strolled together, making sure he had her attention. "Sometimes folk are called away, to seek their brightness, or for wanderlust. I have never completely understood their yearning, but it is well enough. Folk like yourselves, though, who are torn from us, always sadden me."

"You do not need to feel sorrow upon my account."

"But I do," he said quickly. "You know what you are called."

Well she did, and it was an apt enough descriptor. "Forlorn."

"Yes. And forlorn you seem. But how could you not be, raised apart from your folk, exposed constantly to the death and cruelties of the lesser races?"

Elyana stiffened, but did not look at him. Neither her family nor her friends were of lesser races. It was not now time to correct him, but she was not sure that she could resist if the slights were to continue.

"Sometimes," he continued gently, "when the Forlorn return, they are seen as strange outsiders, and are made to feel unwelcome. I wish you to know—I pledge to you, Elyana—that you *are* welcome."

Elyana inclined her head. "That is very kind of you."

"I am certain that you hunger for both food and drink. These things you must have, and then you must meet the lord of Elistia. To him you will have to explain your reasons for bringing visitors to our land."

Elyana bowed her head.

Alavar clapped his hands once, and a young elven woman hopped down a smaller set of stairs from a veranda above. She smiled brightly at Elyana.

"Elyana, this is my niece, Aliel. She will see to your needs. Aliel, Elyana will have to be made ready for the High Lord in two hours' time."

"I will see to it, Uncle." Aliel's voice was bright and clear. She smiled so infectiously that Elyana could not hold off smiling in return.

"Come, cousin!" The young lady offered her hand and Elyana took it.

Aliel led her deep into the halls of the building attached to the veranda, one Elyana realized was at least partly given over to Alavar's family. She gained a vague impression of halls set with wide windows, balconies blooming with flowering plants, and finely crafted floorboards covered with intricately woven rugs, but so quickly did Aliel lead and so quickly came her questions that Elyana kept pace only with difficulty.

"I almost never see strangers," the woman said pleasantly. "Is it true that you come from beyond the mountains? And with humans? How many are with you?"

As quickly as Elyana answered one question, more followed. Chiefly they concerned the habits and customs of humans, particularly their appearance, the speed of their growth, and the sorts of food they enjoyed. The young lady was insatiably curious, and it was with some relief that Elyana encouraged her departure from the room with the bath. Most elves she'd met had no trouble chatting while naked, but Elyana had been brought up by humans and preferred privacy.

Aliel swooped back in after Elyana's bath was complete, speaking so rapidly that Elyana had to ask her to slow down so that she could understand the Elven words.

"I've picked out any number of dresses for you to select from this evening," Aliel repeated cheerily. "So many of the ladies were ready to give theirs up to you that I couldn't refuse any of them. Don't you know? They're all so thrilled that you've come from so very far away and are dying to hear all about it!"

"How nice," Elyana said, still drying her ears with a towel. She'd wrapped herself in a thick brown fur robe and now stood, a little wet and bemused, contemplating a bed heaped with a bewildering array of dresses in a rainbow assortment, though all were long-sleeved and seemed to approximate her build.

"There certainly are a lot of dresses there," she offered lamely.

"Don't you think they're lovely?"

Elyana allowed that they were. "I had planned merely to wear the change of clothes I had in my travel pack."

"Those things?" Aliel failed to conceal her amazement. "No, no, no. Those might be fine out on the road, but you really don't want to wear them here, do you?"

"Um. A sword will look awfully strange on my hip while I'm wearing a dress."

Aliel stared at her a moment, then laughed. "Oh, you're so droll! I like that. That's funny."

Elyana settled on a calf-length dress of brown and violet, then left with Aliel for another chamber set with lavender-scented candles and many mirrors. Here the young woman helped Elyana arrange her hair, braiding it into two intricate knots behind her head, arranging the rest of her hair to hang long and straight. It was a far more elaborate look than Elyana had used for many years, but the result did not displease her. As she turned her head right and left to consider her profile, she imagined that she might have looked thus if her birth parents had survived to return with her to Kyonin all those years before. Then she might feel less like she were playing dress-up.

"I think you look wonderful," Aliel told her.

They then sat together before a window seat and listened to the trilling of song birds outside while they consumed the light pastries her folk were so adept at making, and drank of a sweet wine superior even to the

Galtan vintage. Once Elyana settled back, content and fairly relaxed, Aliel asked if she were ready to meet the lord. Elyana said that she was.

Aliel reached for a shelf on her right, lifted a little chime, and rang it.

Elyana was amazed. "You summon your lord with a bell?"

"Why should I not?"

Elyana wasn't sure she could explain. She couldn't imagine someone summoning Stelan that way, no matter that he was the most humble of knights. It simply wasn't respectful.

When Elyana turned at the sound of a soft footstep in the doorway she saw Alavar standing under the arch. He had changed from travel clothes to more regal raiment, complete with a glittering golden diadem seated in his smooth white hair. His leggings were of jet black, so dark she could imagine stars shining in their depths, and the matching doublet over his white shirt sparkled with gold thread.

Elyana rose and bowed her head respectfully. Too late she remembered that she wore a dress, and lifted up a handful of the garment to curtsy as Aliel was already doing.

Alavar responded with a regal inclination of his head. "Greetings, niece, and Cousin Elyana." He faced Elyana. "I hope that you have found our accommodations hospitable?"

"Very much so, thank you, Lord." She added the last after the slightest hesitation.

"I am pleased to hear it. Thank you, Aliel. That will be all for now."

"It was my pleasure, Lord and Uncle." Aliel curtsied again, and another smile bubbled up on her lips as she straightened. "I shall see you soon, Elyana!" With that, she glided away.

Alavar then considered Elyana once more.

Although Elyana was fully dressed, from flowered hair to pearl-sewn slippers, she felt strangely exposed. This was the first time in a long while that she had walked anywhere without at least a knife at her belt.

The lord misinterpreted her expression. "Those clothes suit you well, Elyana, but you appear troubled. Are they uncomfortable?"

"I did not know that you were lord, Lord."

"While I am abroad I am merely the captain of the Sentinels," he said dismissively. "Unless I am in my official capacity, I insist upon being addressed as Alavar, or Uncle, in my niece's case. I do not care overmuch for ceremony, or the court life, or I would not have requested service at this outpost. Please, sit." Alavar walked forward and indicated the table with its two chairs by the open window. Elyana returned to her seat.

Alavar slid in across from her. "Your campaign to stamp out the shadow wizards of Galt and Taldor is not unknown to some of us upon the border. Your blood cousins spoke of you with a peculiar pride, saying that your grandfather's spirit ran strong within you. It is his sword you bear, is it not?"

"It is," she said in surprise. "If you recognized my name, why did you not say so?"

"I wished to confirm your identity. I understand that you were challenged for the right to bear the sword when you once returned to visit elven lands, and that you overcame the challenge with a pronounced success."

"That is true."

Alavar smiled thinly. "Even when speaking your true tongue, your answers sound like those of a human."

"I don't agree," Elyana replied. "Some humans are just as long-winded as elves."

Alavar favored her with a bland look, then smoothed out his doublet. "You are an interesting enigma to me, Elyana, and I would like to be of help to you. I hope you do not object terribly to this more formal audience, which is still less formal than custom might demand."

"I do not object," she said, wondering as to his tone. He seemed to have taken it upon himself to instruct her in etiquette.

He nodded gracefully to her. "Allow me to compliment you on your wardrobe. In such garments, your natural beauty shines all the brighter."

Was that flattery, more polite conversation, or an icy attempt at elven seduction? She could not entirely tell, but bowed her head. "Thank you. I like your crown."

Alavar laughed. "Ah! By sweet Calistria, your unpredictability amuses me." He eased against the rear of the chair, his back still regally straight. "Be so good as to tell me why you have come to these lands."

"If you do not mind, Lord, there are one or two things I would ask. Aliel was a delightful hostess, but I could scarce get a question asked of her."

Alavar arched an eyebrow, then indicated his permission with a minute inclination of his head. "What would you know?"

She would start with simpler questions first. "Are we in the elven kingdom? I though the border lay farther east."

"You are quite right," he said with a regal nod. "This is merely an outpost."

"It is quite an impressive one." In her experience, outposts were usually a small fort with a hamlet.

"I am delighted that the beauty of my home impresses you. From here we can monitor the border for nearly a hundred miles to north and south. We have eyes in the heavens." Alavar smiled at Elyana's curious look. "I refer to our falcons. Some of the finest falcons in all of Kyonin are trained here. They scout far and wide for us."

"Is that how you detected us?"

"It was the primary means for watching you, yes, although there are other methods for monitoring this area of the Five Kings range."

Means he obviously planned to keep to himself.

"Is there more you would know?" Alavar asked. "Why are you so curious about the border?"

"Because I hoped not to trespass."

Alavar waved her concern off.

"I mean to enter the Vale of Shadows, Lord Alavar. What can you tell me about it?"

At mention of the valley, Alavar's expression clouded. "I was afraid that you were going to say that. My people forbid access to the vale."

"And I was afraid *you* were going to say *that*."

"No good can come from that place, Elyana. Few who enter return alive."

She watched him warily, wondering how best to continue.

"Why would you even want to go inside the place?"

"I intimated the problem earlier, Lord. My friend has been cursed. He is baron of Adrast, and Renar is his son. Drelm and Kellius are his retainers."

"I am sorry to hear about your friend. What has any of that to do with the Vale of Shadows?"

"I believe Stelan's cure is hidden inside."

The lord studied her silently. "Your speech is so very simple," he observed finally. "It is as though you have no time to contemplate longer ideas. I expect it comes of being raised by folk with such short lifespans."

"I expect it does."

Alavar frowned briefly and leaned forward. "Elyana, am I correct in assuming that this baron is a human?"

"You are." Elyana tried to keep her tone neutral.

"How old is he already? You must ask yourself—"

"Do not finish that sentence."

Alavar's eyebrows rose precipitously. All but the smallest children knew that it was the height of rudeness to interrupt someone while speaking, especially for elven children, as Elyana had been told during her time in northern Kyonin. She could easily imagine Alavar saying something very similar, and did not give him the chance.

"However many years Stelan has left before him," Elyana said, "they are just as precious as mine. Or yours. Perhaps even more so, because he has so few to begin with."

Alavar eyed her in consternation.

"I mean to enter that vale, Lord. If it is not within Kyonin, you have no right to stop me."

The lord of Elistia settled into his chair, back straight, expression bland. "Your manners are more than a little brusque, Elyana. I blame not you, but those who raised you."

"I do not mean to offend," she answered. "Just as I'm sure you did not mean to insult the memory of my parents."

Alavar blinked in surprise.

Elyana had grown tired of Alavar's prejudices. "I lost my parents in a boating mishap when I was very small. I barely recall their faces. My foster parents almost died trying to help them. They were strangers. They had no call to aid my blood parents, or to take me in and raise me as their own. Yet they did so." She stared directly into his eyes, hoping to hammer home her point. "I am sorry if my speech troubles you. But please do not malign those who raised me because their customs are different from your own."

By his expression, Alavar recovered swiftly from his surprise, but he did not speak for a long moment. Finally he said: "I shall keep that under advisement. You must have been very close to your foster parents."

"I was."

He nodded slowly. "I do not like to think how difficult it must be for you to live amongst the humans. I would find it very challenging."

"I have little with which to compare it."

He conceded this with a wave of his hand. "You are set upon this errand to the Vale of Shadows."

"Yes."

"You spoke aright, earlier. It is not my right to forbid those not of my nation from entering the place. But I wish you to know exactly what you are venturing toward. What do you know of the place?"

She hesitated momentarily, for her ignorance embarrassed her. "Little more than its name."

"I think if you knew more, you would be far less eager to travel there."

"I am hardly eager, Lord. It is duty, not pleasure, that takes me there."

"Of course." He gathered his thoughts for a moment. "Our sages say that it has been scarred for millennia, almost since the dawn of time. The Rough Beast, Rovagug, was mightier almost than all the other gods combined, but they overthrew him at last. He could not be killed, so the gods split Golarion itself and entombed him and his followers inside. They healed the seams in the world, but some points were weaker than others, and these were reinforced. One of these points is the Vale of Shadows."

Elyana did not tell him that she already knew this; she did not wish to appear rude again.

Alavar continued. "Over the millennia, the seal on the vale has deteriorated. *Things* seep up from below, and from other places, as well, for the energies used during its construction weakened the borders between the planes of existence. It is one of my duties to patrol near the vale, so that we may protect this area from whatever might creep forth from the nightmare realms contiguous to the vale."

"What does the vale look like?

"It is a blight upon our reality," he said with vehemence, "filled with shifting energy from the Plane of Shadow. From outside it looks as though it is permanently shielded by the darkest storm clouds. I have ventured inside a handful of times. It is not a pleasant place. Creatures drift in and out from other realms, sometimes bringing twisted landscapes with them. There are no colors to be seen inside. There is a tower there, but neither I nor my predecessors have allowed anyone to enter. I assume this tower to be your goal?"

"It is."

"And you are still intent upon reaching the place, knowing what I have told you?"

"Yes."

"I also assume that you have no other option before you."

"I have pledged . . . the item we seek to the clerics who are keeping my friend alive."

"Why do you not wish to name it?" he asked her.

She smiled sadly. "If I do not name it, you cannot forbid me from removing it."

He chuckled. "Should you be so fortunate to survive a journey within, you will have earned whatever you find there. But you may keep your secret."

"I thank you."

"Don't you worry someone else has found that which you seek? The tower has stood there for a very, very long time. Someone might have penetrated its defenses."

"If they have, my friend is doomed."

Alavar chose his next words carefully. "Please do not take this the wrong way, Elyana. But I must wonder. Would a true friend have sent someone on such an impossible quest?"

"He did not send me. He lies unconscious."

"So you took this upon yourself. The strength of your friendship is to be praised. But surely a true friend would not be pleased were you to kill yourself in aiding him."

"He would do the same for me."

The lord's chin lifted ever so slightly. "Then he is worth your sacrifice. A loyal friend is the brightest treasure of all." He fell silent. "Very well. If you are determined to follow this mad enterprise, I will guide you there. Once inside, you will be on your own, but I can leave soldiers to guard your mounts until your return, should you be so fortunate. I do not think you would wish to ride your horses within."

Elyana was fairly sure she could ride Persaily anywhere, but she bowed her head in acknowledgment. "Thank you. You are most kind." She hoped that sounded more formal and polite, though she was certain her sentences still lacked the polish expected here.

"It is my pleasure," Alavar said. "I now have another question for you. There is a large force of humans trailing you. I believe them to be Galtans. Why are they following?"

Elyana did not bother asking how Alavar knew; if his birds and sorcery had detected *them*, surely it could find the Galtans.

"Years ago, my friends and I crossed through Galt to fight the shadow wizards. I made enemies there, and rediscovered them when we passed through this week."

"They appear very determined. I'm not inclined to interact with so large a force unless they come upon Elistia. They will have trouble enough in the mountains."

The humans sometimes said that elves were cowards because they let the ground and the environment do the fighting for them. Elyana understood the elven viewpoint on this matter. For a race so long-lived, with offspring so rare, it was better to let time and the elements do the fighting rather than risk elven blood.

"Do they seek the same thing as you?" the lord asked.

"I don't know how they could. I did not speak of it to them."

He nodded. "These new Galtans are even stranger than most humans. Orcs are far simpler to understand. Not so long ago, I would sometimes ride down amongst the humans and sample their wines. I have not gone amongst Galtan lands for almost sixty years. They are a strange race, humans."

"They are capable of great courage, and loyalty."

"So you lead me to understand," he said. "Many human generations ago there were some that I was fond of. But I never named one friend."

Interlude
Ring of Shadows

Darkness wrapped them only moments after they were through the doorway. Cold pierced their flesh like thorns. One of the men screamed, and there was the sound of metal clanking on stone, protesting as it was crushed and rent.

Stelan's voice echoed through the dark chamber. "Arcil, light!"

A brilliant flood of white energy lit the space an instant later, and Elyana finally saw what they faced. A reptile the size of an ox lashed its spiny tail near bookcases which ornamented the curving two-story wall behind it. The dragon seemed fashioned from plates of shadow wrapped around a skeleton. Its head twisted from side to side, its fierce red eyes blinking against Arcil's flaring ball of light that burned high in the vast, cathedral-like space.

Black vapor drifted from its fanged maw. Under one claw the knight Daramont lay twisted, blood trickling out from multiple rents in his armor to gather in a widening pool.

Eriah cried out at sight of his twin. Elyana advanced. If there was hope for the fallen knight, there was no way to give aid until they stopped the dragon.

"Run!" Young Nadara backed frantically toward the archway, her voice rising in panic. "He's summoned an umbral dragon!"

They had thought only to find Lathroft, the shadow wizard who'd fled before them. They had not expected this horror. Elyana knew it was small, as dragons went, but that made the creature no less deadly.

She charged forward on the left, Stelan on the right. There was no hesitation. After so many years, they reacted with rapid precision to every challenge. It was no surprise to hear Vallyn's voice raised in a martial melody, or Arcil shouting something in cryptic words.

The dragon swung toward Stelan, hissing, its backswept horns pointing to Elyana. A draconic wing brushed down at her at the same moment its tail lashed. She ducked under the one, her hair streaming out behind her, and leapt the whipping appendage in a crouch. She landed nimbly, then noticed a strange blur in the air a few paces to her left.

Stelan cried out to Abadar and shouted as he swung at the creature's darting head. Elyana's eyes were rooted on that widening whirl of energy. A human hand in a dark sleeve thrust out from its center.

She had found the shadow wizard.

Elyana's leap carried her into the blur and through into a strange, dark place occupied only by the wizard; her sword came down across Lathroft's hand and severed it at the wrist. Blood weltered as the hand flew free. The hooded wizard howled and dropped to his knees, stump pressed to his chest. Elyana noticed that her blade's swirling, intricate runes glowed here as they did when the weapon was wielded against creatures of shadow. Their light bloomed even more fiercely as her second strike swept down through cowl and skull; brain and blood sprayed out and the wizard fell, gurgling and twitching.

So died Lathroft, the second most powerful of the shadow wizards. It was hard to believe him truly finished, and Elyana stared down in wonder.

They'd tracked him for most of the last year, finally honing in on this last location when his own niece had decided to turn on him. Elyana had not thought to fell him so easily. She supposed the running battle through the fortress had exhausted a lot of his spells, and it was probably no easy task summoning a dragon.

In any case, Lathroft looked like he'd moved well past dying to dead, so she rotated slowly to scan the rest of the space.

She stood in a black-and-white version of the room she had just quitted. While Elyana had never before entered the Plane of Shadow, Arcil had told her that there was a place from where the shadow wizards drew their magic and conjured their monsters. Instinctively she knew she was in that place, and she wheeled quickly to verify that the portal was still open behind her. The rip in reality hung in the air, its edges blurred and shimmering. She shouldn't have worried. She could sense its presence even with her back turned.

A quick survey of her environment showed twisted walls that did not quite meet at right angles, and a bizarrely slanted ceiling. All else was just the semblance of reality. Where there were books in the real world, here were only dark recesses, and there were no counterparts to the living beings she'd left behind.

Her first impulse was to jump back to her own reality, but she then understood she could use her position to her advantage. Lathroft might be dead, but his severed hand still radiated a magical nimbus. She bent cautiously beside it. Even an idiot would have been able to guess that the ring upon the long index finger, emanating an aura of darkness, had created the opening. Arcil would want that, she knew.

She glanced back through the portal. She heard Arcil call for her even as the dragon roared. The thing had turned its back to the opening. There was no better time.

Inured to gore by long years of exposure, Elyana snatched up Lathroft's hand by the wrist and jumped back through the portal. She was reluctant to handle the ring itself without Arcil's advice.

She dropped the bloody hand as she came clear into the normal world. The dragon's roar seemed insanely loud, part growl, part high-pitched whine, as though steel were being ripped in two at the same moment a pack of wolf hounds growled. The Plane of Shadow deadened noise, she realized—everything in the real world seemed louder now.

She aimed for the dragon's wing joint, and struck with a two-handed blow. The monster shrieked. Its injured wing beat at her, but she ducked and rolled, the floor cool against her palms. She came up on one knee only to find herself facing the dragon's open maw. That looked bad.

But Stelan was suddenly beside her, brandishing his great two-handed blade. The dragon's maw swung and cocked hard left, birdlike, before letting loose a cloud of darkness. It enveloped Stelan completely.

Elyana sprang with a keen slash even as the beast's ghastly, emaciated head whipped back. She suddenly found herself facing a cavernous maw of silver-black teeth. Her blade split scales along its jaw and it hissed, snapping those teeth together only inches from her face.

"Elyana!" Arcil shouted. "Down!"

She dropped. A great clap of thunder and a blinding flash of light followed. The dragon keened and threw its head back in agony. The tail lashed out and struck a wall of books, sending dozens of volumes flying off the shelves. Blue electrical energy danced in long lines all across the dragon's head and neck. It scuttled backward.

Eriah charged up from Elyana's right and hacked into the head, shouting something about vengeance as black ichor flew forth. And Vallyn was weaving a spell with another song.

The cloud of darkness still overhung Stelan, but the knight staggered free. His greatsword hung loose in his grip. The dragon saw him and scrambled further back, its claws scraping against the tile.

"I can kill you all," it said in a harsh, rasping voice.

"Back to the hell that spawned you," Stelan shouted, and struck again. The dragon raised its head, but the mighty blow cut deep into its chest. Stelan stumbled in the track of his swing, off-balance.

Elyana dashed out, grabbed Stelan's arm, and guided him to safety, yelling for Eriah to retreat. Daramont's brother was too slow. A great blow from a flapping wing sent him careening into a wall.

And then Arcil let loose with another blast of magical energy. An even brighter arc of blue electricity lit the dragon's underside and it reared up, mouth wide.

It hit the ground, hard. Lightning still played across its scales. Its tail lashed, its wings beat the air. It backed away, battering into the walls. Books plummeted from the shelves left and right. Old and faded papers were shredded or wafted down from on high, torn free from their bindings. Arcil came out from behind his column to curse at the dragon as it bled copiously over the scattered tomes and pages.

The beast sank down, blinked once, twice, and then stared sightlessly at them.

Elyana watched it for a moment, then checked over Stelan. He was shaking.

"I'm all right," Stelan told her. "Just cold. See if there's anything that can be done for Daramont. And keep your eyes sharp for Lathroft—"

"Lathroft's dead," Elyana said. She stepped over to the downed knight.

Unfortunately, there wasn't anything to do for Daramont. A quick check showed her that he'd probably bled to death after that first blow.

His twin brother Eriah joined her, all but inconsolable, and talked of erecting a monument to him from the stones of the building—after they demolished it. Elyana patted his shoulder, still concerned about Stelan.

Stelan sat heavily against one of the pillars. She joined him quickly. His skin was cold beneath her palm. "What's wrong with you?"

Nadara had crept from her hiding place and stared around the room with bright eyes. "Where's Lathroft?"

"I killed him," Elyana said.

"Truly?" Nadara said, still sounding stunned. "Where's his body?"

Elyana indicated the rift, still hanging open. The dead hand lay just before it. Nadara walked dazedly over. "Is he really dead?" she repeated.

Elyana watched her until Stelan spoke wearily. "The dragon's breath leached strength and warmth from me. I just need rest."

She laid her hands on him and discovered his assessment was basically accurate. He was physically drained, but he had no injuries other than those accrued during the battle that had won them entrance to this final chamber.

Vallyn stood helplessly beside Eriah and Daramont. Nadara peered cautiously into the rift. She'd been nervous for weeks, and Vallyn had told them she was afraid Lathroft would discover her betrayal, or that their band would fail and he would take vengeance upon her. The bard was the only one who could get more than a few words out of the girl.

Elyana walked around them all to check on Arcil, who'd taken a dart in the shoulder in that final fight up the corridor.

Arcil stared at the pile of ruined volumes, oblivious to the line of dark dragon ichor spreading slowly across the flagstones. His mouth was open in anguish.

As Stelan and Elyana walked closer he dropped to his knees and sought furiously among the books, lifting one, then another, to read the spines.

"Sorry about the mess," Stelan offered.

"You should have stayed down," Arcil said savagely. He spared him only a brief look. "My blast would have finished him without this."

"Do you want me to apologize for killing the dragon?" Stelan offered. Elyana started to laugh, but Arcil spun with such an intense look of hatred that her smile vanished, stillborn.

"You strutting . . . You can make of joke of that? This was their library! Anything we wanted to learn about them—their habits, their practices—was here!"

"There's plenty left to read," Vallyn offered.

"Shut up, Vallyn."

"Your priorities are misplaced, Arcil," Stelan said, a steely note creeping into his voice despite his fatigue. "One of our comrades is dead."

Arcil scowled, as though that too were an inconvenience. He looked about to say more, then caught sight of Elyana and stared hard at her. His expression slowly lost its rancor, and he looked away. He stood. "Did I hear you say Lathroft's dead?"

"He lies on the other side of that portal," Elyana told him. "It leads to the Plane of Shadow. I think it's controlled through the ring on his hand. It's over there."

"By the gods!" Vallyn bent low. "Did you slice this off, Elyana? What a sword arm you have."

"He had a weak wrist," Elyana offered, and the bard laughed.

Arcil stepped lightly over to Nadara and steered her away from the portal. She retreated as if in a daze, and looked up at Vallyn. She was a slim waif, and Elyana supposed that she was pretty in a way, though her eyes were a little small. Certainly Vallyn was drawn to her, but then the bard was closer to her in age, and always ready to charm a new woman.

"If Elyana says he's dead, he's dead," Vallyn offered, and flashed a smile. Nadara accepted the information with a short nod.

Arcil turned and stared into the depths of the portal, like a man inspecting his reflection before a mirror. "By the heavens," he breathed. "That's actually the Plane of Shadow?"

"It looks just as you always described," Elyana answered. "I don't know how long it will stay open, though. Isn't it dangerous to keep it that way?"

Arcil didn't answer. He dropped carefully to one knee and almost touched the glowing ring. He let out a low, appreciative noise.

Vallyn sidled up to Elyana. "You've made him very happy," the young man told her softly, adding, "How proud you must be."

"Vallyn," Elyana said, her tone a warning.

The bard was not dissuaded. His voice dropped even lower. "How long do you think it'll be before we have to track him to a shadow lair of his very own?"

Chapter Twelve
Social Engagements

Bright melodies and joyous laughter rang in the air. Elyana barely noticed them. Instead, she stared at the finger around which she'd worn the dark ring for so many years. It had not taken Arcil long to divine the ring's usage, but then, he'd studied the texts of the wizards who used shadow magic. Would the Gray Gardeners fathom its use as easily? And if so, could they employ it against her?

Then again, it might be that one of the soldiers had slipped it off her finger when she was captured, and it was even now on the black market.

"This is so amazing," Renar said beside her. He'd been saying the same thing every few minutes for the last half-hour, just as soon as the plates were cleared from the tables and the singing and dancing had begun. It seemed like the whole of the settlement had gathered that night in an open space upon the green. Glowing lights drifted back and forth overhead, shining now red, now yellow, now blue. Their constant drift meant no place remained long in shadows.

Dozens of the elven folk were up singing or playing their instruments, their voices raised in sweet harmony, and even more of them spun and skipped in a complicated group dance Elyana thought might be called a gabriole. She and Drelm and Renar were the only folk still seated, and she was feeling less and less comfortable by the moment. Sooner or later some merry elf would drag her to the dance floor, and then she would be even more out of place.

Kellius had downed glass after glass of the sweet elven wine until he'd lost all restraint and trotted out there to join the dance lines, red and yellow flowers in his cap and an idiotic smile plastered across his face. She'd warned all of them that elven wine was more potent than it seemed, but Renar was the only one who'd taken her seriously. Vallyn had gladly sipped his fill, then joined the musicians. He stood on the table among them, strumming his lute and looking a little lost and a little lovestruck at the same time.

"Amazing," Renar repeated. He had a hard time tearing his eyes from the flow of elven dancers, entranced by the long-limbed elven girls with their flowing skirts and curtains of hair. Elyana followed his gaze, smirking, and caught sight of Kellius, shifting his beanpole frame back and forth among the dancers, out of step and falling in and out of time.

There was a flurry of motion by Renar's side, and Elyana turned in time to see Aliel beside him, hands reaching out. "Come, dance with me!" she ordered.

It looked as though Renar had been thunderstruck. Aliel was tall and slim and young, not quite grown into a graceful neck and long legs. Hers was a filly's beauty, but her eyes were radiant and her face flushed with excitement, her hair a wild tangle. Elyana wondered if her oath to protect Renar included heartbreak, and decided he would have to wend that path alone. Renar rose, grinning foolishly, and took Aliel's slim hand.

The girl laughed and led him out among the dancers.

Elyana wondered why she wasn't more pleased that no one had yet come to ask her hand. She was fairly certain that she didn't want to dance.

Drelm sat on her right, drinking slowly from a battered dwarven stein. The elves had provided the rest of them with fluted, elegant drinking cups shaped from wood. Drelm seemed not to have noticed the insult. It might be he preferred this vessel to the smaller ones given the others.

"I never thought to see so many of your folk," Drelm said finally. "They are so swift, and fragile."

"Yes."

"Their moods shift like water," Drelm said.

Elyana nodded.

"You are not like them."

"No. No, I don't suppose that I am."

He took a long draught. "I used to hear your laughter in the castle, and I thought you flirted with the baron." He glanced at her sidelong. "You do not laugh like that at other times."

"You don't laugh at all," Elyana countered.

Drelm grunted. His tiny eyes set on Renar. The boy's spirited stomping and hand waving made him seem as clumsy as Kellius, but he tried bravely to match the flowing pattern of the dancers around him. He beamed all the while at the delighted beauty beside him.

"Your folk are naturally happy. But you are sad." Drelm drank. "I too know sadness," he said as he sat the mug down, "and through the strength of Abadar have not let the sadness become rage."

This was swiftly becoming the longest conversation Elyana had ever shared with the captain. She eyed him in curiosity, for she sensed that he had more to say.

"I have come to understand why the baron values you," Drelm went on. "Loyalty is your byword. The bard tells me you pledged your life for mine."

"I did."

He took a long draught. "I will not forget."

That seemed to satisfy the guard captain, who finished off the mug and set it down with a thunk. He reached for the half-full wine carafe and poured another draught. "Too sweet," he said.

Strange, she thought, that here surrounded by her own people, relaxed and garbed in their clothing, she still felt a greater bond with the half-orc they would have attacked on sight. His words had fired her own curiosity. "What is your sorrow, Drelm?"

A frown pulled down one corner of his mouth, exposing the root of one tusk. "I do not discuss it." He looked at her sidelong and seemed to come to a decision. "I have made my weakness a strength," he admitted with a hint of pride.

"What is your strength?"

He thumped his chest twice with a closed fist. "My strength is honor. My strength is loyalty. I know what others say of me. They think me a brute and a coward. Yet my word is strong. All who see me know it."

Elyana's expression softened. No, she thought, they do not. And more was the shame.

Drelm spoke on. "I have prayed over it many times. The baron showed me how. He is a great man." This last point was unnecessary, for Elyana heard the reverence in the captain's voice whenever he mentioned Stelan.

"He is. One I hope has many years left before him."

A long moment passed. Drelm drank, glanced at her, drank again, then fixed her with an intent gaze. "What is it like," he blurted out, "to have so many years to live?"

She considered him.

His voice grew soft. "How old are you, Elyana?"

She thought for a moment. "I shall be a hundred and eighty-nine this year. Sometimes it is hard to keep track of them."

Drelm shook his head. "No wonder your family is dead. But you live."

"Yes."

"I did not know my family," he said, his expression darkening. "I shall die by my fiftieth year, if not before. But you and I are warriors. Death will find us before we reach our natural span." Drelm lifted his stein in salute, and she raised her own cup.

"Honor," he said. She repeated the word, and they drank.

She heard Alavar's voice at her side. "At these mellifluous festivities you sit idle, merely drinking?"

He did not need to say that she sat drinking with an orc—Alavar's bewilderment was plain enough. At her look he bowed and broke into a smile. He extended his hand.

Gone was the lord's diadem, though he retained the rest of his raiment. Tiny points within the ebon garb shifted with the lights. "Come, my extraordinary guest. Allow me to lift your feet."

"Dance," Drelm urged her when she looked back at him. "Grab happiness while it lies before you."

And so Elyana kicked off her slippers and joined the lord upon the grass, taking steps she but half-remembered. Alavar proved a fine leader. He guided her easily through the paces, and after the first minutes she was smiling and laughing like all the others, almost forgetting that a vast gulf of understanding divided her blood kin from herself. Were they truly as removed from worries as they seemed, when they became one with the music and the dance, or were they merely better accustomed to concealing their pain?

What did they think as they passed by the table where the half-orc sat like a lonely gargoyle, sometimes illuminated brightly in colors that painted him orange or blood red, and sometimes hid him in shadow? Were they reminded, as was she, that all life was fleeting, and not all folk were as fortunate as the elves? One could not know it by their laughter.

In the end she begged off after dancing with or near lord Alavar for more than an hour, saying that she had to rest. Neither Vallyn nor Kellius nor Renar paid any heed to her warning look. Drelm alone stood ready, and nodded once to her. She understood that he would take care of ushering the others away, and bowed her head in thanks.

Alavar himself escorted her to her room. He linked her arm through his own, and the sound of the music receded as they strolled from the place.

"While the guest accommodations are quite fine," Alavar said, "my own quarters are more aesthetically pleasing. If it is your wish, I would share them with you this night."

He was a fine-featured man, and it had been long since she had shared a night with another. She met his eyes, and the passion she saw directed at herself pleased her. But she did not answer.

"You do not have to remain alone and apart, Elyana. You can learn our ways. You have already found happiness here; it comes easily to elves among their own folk."

She shook her head, for she knew that it was not true, even if he believed it.

"What do you fear, my lovely one?"

She leaned forward and kissed him lightly on the cheek. He blinked, startled. Did elves not court one another that way? She raised a finger to his own lips, noting the pale band of flesh where her ring had sat. "This is not the night, Alavar. I do not know how long my friend can last. I must rise early, and make haste so that we may return to him in time."

He took her hand and gently squeezed it, bowing his head. He led her on down another corridor, and she found herself before an opening hung with gossamer fabric.

"Your room, lovely lady." He bowed and pressed his lips to the back of her hand. "I very much enjoyed your company this night."

"And I yours."

He bowed to her, and she curtsied formally to him.

"I look forward to seeing you in the morning."

"Likewise," she said, which prompted a merry laugh from him.

"I so enjoy your manner of speech, Elyana," he said, then bowed again. "May you rest well."

"And you," she replied, a little confused, then turned to part the fabric door before she could give him further cause for amusement.

She thought that she'd handled herself well, and felt a twinge of discomfort that she had still presented herself, somehow, as uncouth or unpolished. The mattress was slender, soft, and immeasurably comfortable. Yet it was a long while before she felt at ease, even after she closed her eyes.

Elyana woke in dim light before dawn. A morning dove called softly, and somewhere far away a lone piper played a melancholy melody. Elyana discovered her freshly mended garments folded neatly just inside the door, and equipped herself. She'd heard Drelm's deep voice thanking an elven escort last night, after she had lain down, and this morning she heard him knocking into something and groaning in his own quarters across from her. They stepped into the hallway at about the same time.

"Good morrow, Captain."

"And to you, Lady."

"Let's rouse the others."

That proved more easily said than accomplished, for neither Vallyn, Kellius, nor Renar lay in the rooms set aside for them. Drelm scowled at this discovery.

"They promised they would follow shortly," he said with a growl.

"You believed them?"

Drelm actually looked away with chagrin. "I thought the bard old enough to know better. And I could hardly command the young baron."

Elyana sighed. "What about Kellius?"

Drelm hesitated a moment, then straightened and threw back his shoulders, as though he were a rank-and-file soldier addressing an officer. "I lost sight of him."

She groaned.

"I am sorry, Lady," Drelm said.

"Be at ease," she told him. How could a half-orc compete with the allure of elven wine? And elven women, for that matter.

"They should all know better." Drelm furrowed his brows. "And I am ashamed at the young lord. Does he forget his duty to his father? Do they all forget their duty to the baron?"

"We will send word for them while we eat," Elyana said smoothly, "and then saddle the horses."

An elven youngster awaited them on the patio outside their rooms, and he presented them with freshly cooked eggs and a selection of pastries and nuts. It was too early in the season yet for fresh fruits.

Elyana sent him off to find their companions. "Tell them we leave shortly," she instructed, "and that they must be ready for departure."

"They'll be eating cold eggs if they don't get here soon," Drelm said, chewing. "I hate cold eggs."

No one else had turned up by the end of breakfast, so Elyana asked another young elf to lead them to the stables.

Persaily was happy to see Elyana, although the mare hadn't suffered in her absence. Her coat had been so carefully brushed that it shone with a high gloss. Burrs and cockles had been combed from her mane. Even her saddle had been polished.

"Huh," Drelm said. "Your folk know horse care. I'll give them that."

Kellius arrived as Elyana was fitting in Persaily's bit. The wizard looked bleary-eyed but happy, and munched on a hard roll. A wreath of little white flowers decorated his hat brim.

"You're late," Drelm told him.

"Yes . . . I'm sorry about that. I'm afraid I lost track of time."

Elyana looked over at him. "It might have been wiser to ensure a good night's sleep. The vale is but one day off, and you'll need all your strength."

"Indeed." Kellius rubbed his forehead. "I've not had proper time to study my spells."

"That was folly," Drelm told him, and Elyana did not naysay the judgment. It interested and pleased her that since yesterday the half-orc had adopted the role of her lieutenant.

Renar came jogging up next, pasty and out of breath. His hair was wet. "Sorry—I was in the bath."

"Your father would not delay so," Drelm told him, and Renar lowered his eyes.

Elyana did not correct that judgment, although she was not so sure it was true. Stelan had sometimes lingered for extra time with a particular elven maiden, as she well knew.

Renar tried to look busy and useful by double-checking all of their equipment. Elyana had already done that, but she left Renar to his charade.

Vallyn did not stroll up until Lord Alavar himself had appeared. Unlike the other two, he looked neither embarrassed nor bleary. His eyes were tired, true, but he had a spring in his step.

Drelm glared at the bard but did not rebuke him. Either he thought the bard outside the rank structure, or knew well enough that the bard would simply shrug off the criticism, or turn it into a joke.

Alavar bade them all good morning, and told them that there would be one overnight before their arrival. "There are few hazards upon the way, although we will pass through some dense wilderland. My hunters keep the most menacing predators clear of our perimeters." As he spoke, Aliel walked up, and he waved her forward. "My niece Aliel will be accompanying us as well. I believe she has already met some of you."

Aliel wore riding pants and boots this day, and her hair was tightly braided. Elyana bowed her head in greeting, but the elven girl barely had eyes for her. The full force of her beauty was directed like a ray of summer sun onto Renar, who caught it and smiled stupidly back.

Elyana held off groaning. Did the boy think he had found love, here? Elven love with humans was a fickle thing . . . though hers had not been, she reminded herself. Was she too jaded, or had she grown old and cynical?

And it might be, she realized, that she was jealous of their happiness.

Their packs replenished with elven breads, nuts, and dried meats and fruits, they climbed into their saddles. Alavar led them down the switchback trail to the river canyon.

They emerged on a narrow strip of land beside the river. Warriors looked down from what she first took to be a rocky outcropping. As the elven sentinels raised hands in greeting she realized that they stood atop a high tower cunningly worked into the cliff side.

Alavar guided them on past a collection of small outbuildings and rows of furrowed ground. Elyana heard Aliel explaining that they'd terraced the soil to grow crops that needed more moisture.

Drelm eyed the fortifications with interest, and Elyana imagined him noting the deceptively decorative walls and defensive points along the ramp. As beautiful and idyllic as the elven hold might seem, with its walls and towers decorated by flowering vines, it would be no easy task to win. The river and the canyon were barriers, just like the overland route and its tunnels with multiple choke points.

A quarter-hour's ride alongside the river brought them to Elistia's westernmost outpost, a fortified tower built beside the cliff face, looking like nothing so much as a weathered pillar of rocks until close study revealed a sturdy door and arrow slits. An arched stone bridge stretched across the river beside it. While all the buildings and structures Elyana had seen in the last day looked delicate and organic, the bridge itself had been fashioned with blunt, simple lines. Its stone was so smooth that she perceived no mortar. Water had rounded the lower reaches of the great bridge pylons, but near the two arches their lines were straight and crisp.

Once they'd passed through the gate and up the ramp to the bridge, Elyana saw the thing was practically level. Perhaps perfectly so. There was no stone railing, as a human or elf might have constructed.

"Lord Alavar," Kellius called from behind. "Who built this bridge?"

The lord addressed him over his shoulder. "I wish I could say, young wizard. Elven scholars have spent long years studying it, but the bridge is barren of marker or engraving or obvious stylistic identifiers. It may be dwarven work, for it is certainly sturdy enough to be fashioned by the folk of the deep rock, but there are no other signs. And scholars tell me they can detect no impact of hammer or chisel, only marks left by natural degradation. It is as though the whole thing were crafted at once from a single block of stone, yet there is no residue of magic."

"Perhaps it's so old that it has faded." Kellius, usually timid while on horseback, was glancing furtively from side to side at the river roaring forty feet below. Elyana noted that he was not concerned with the water foaming between the arches. Most of his attention was reserved for the stone beneath their horses' hooves.

Before long they had left the mystery of the bridge and were climbing up a cleft that Alavar told them had been smoothed over by elven wizards to make an accessible path. "In olden times there was naught here but an ancient, featureless stone stair, much like the span we so recently vacated. It was poorly suited for horse travel."

There must have been a large number of steps, because summiting the ramp alone took more than an hour. They were not quite up into the frost, but the wind in the highlands proved cutting and cold.

They pressed on, stopping at midday for a sumptuous meal of fresh fish, subtle cheese, delicate bread, and more elven wine, then remounted. In the late afternoon the trail descended once more into a wide valley flowering with ragwort and aster, and it was here that Alavar declared they would set up their camp.

"The vale lies but a quarter-day on," he told them. "Aliel will take care of you thenceforth."

"You're returning, Lord?" Elyana asked. He must have already planned to do so, she noticed, for two of their four escorts were turning rein with Elistia's ruler.

"I want to be on hand should your pursuers draw closer to Elistia." Alavar raised a hand in parting, speaking Elven. "Fare you well, Elyana. I hope that we shall set eyes upon each other once more, and that your comrades survive along with you. Aliel and my Sentinels will deliver you to the valley and await your return for four cycles of the sun. After which—we can offer only prayer."

"I understand," Elyana told him with bowed head. "We are grateful to you for your aid."

"It is my pleasure." He answered her first in the common tongue, then finished in Elven. "I hope that your baron appreciates the enormous risks you take upon his behalf."

With that he turned his horse with an effortless nudge of his knees, and in moments he and his escort had vanished over the crest of a hill.

Chapter Thirteen
Into the Vale

Aliel was all sweetness and light across the campfire that evening, begging them to talk of themselves and their experiences, but Renar was the only one of them she successfully drew out. Soon the two of them were speaking of childhood memories, lost in each other's eyes.

The two elven guards kept apart. They seemed altogether nonplussed with their assignment and spent no extra effort attempting conversation with their charges. One had already crawled off to rest by meal's end, and the other stood watch at a distance.

"Looks as though Renar's elven vacation is going to last a little longer than mine," Vallyn said wistfully as he watched the couple, then stretched his arms. "I think I'd best turn in early. It was a late night."

"Vallyn's right," Kellius said. "I've studying to do, and I'm already tired. I'd best get at it."

Vallyn retreated to his tent, although he did not sleep immediately, for Elyana heard the light strumming of his lute for almost an hour. Kellius sat close to the fire as the wind picked up, studying his spellbook and jamming his wilted-flower-bedecked hat more tightly on his head during violent gusts. Renar and Aliel wandered back to a tent, hand-in-hand, still chattering happily.

"Get some sleep, young lord," Drelm growled at his back.

The light was dim, but Elyana was certain she saw the young man's cheeks redden when he looked back over his shoulder at the half-orc. If Renar felt embarrassment, it could not have been for long, for once he disappeared into Aliel's tent he and the maiden could soon be heard laughing together.

The half-orc sucked at his wine sack for only a moment, then set it aside, and he and Elyana stared into the fire. She wondered if Arcil were watching them even now, and, not for the first time, wondered how she would stop him. How long would the cleric of Abadar be able to keep Stelan alive if she found the crown but could not get it to work? Had the clerics even managed to keep Stelan alive this long?

Drelm interrupted her thoughts. "The baron moves well, for an old man," he said softly. "I would like to have seen him in his prime."

"He's not an old man, yet," Elyana countered. Or was he?

"He is certainly not young. You are fortunate to have seen him in battle."

"Yes," Elyana agreed. Drelm looked as though he felt talkative again, but she didn't, not with so many worries crowding up behind her. She bade the half-orc a good night and crawled off to her tent and her bedroll and lay down again alone.

She rose before dawn, refreshed and alert, and after her morning stretches she stood to gaze at the distant

peaks. She thought of the stirring speeches Stelan used
to give before combat. They were short and direct and
usually involved a prayer. She would be leading none
of those. Instead, after breakfast she left Aliel and her
guards aside and gathered her meager force.

"You have all seen the Plane of Shadow," she told
them. "We will face something very much like it. In
such a place, the borders are fluid and shifting. There
is constant movement. Don't worry about things on the
horizon or more than a few hundred feet away. Worry
instead about the closer details. Where to set your feet.
Why something seems to move when there is no breeze."
She checked over their faces and found all attentive.

"Once we are in the valley, we seek a tower, and any
such structure is likely to be well guarded, though not
necessarily in any obvious way. There will be magical
hazards we may not see, so Kellius will need to examine
the approach and the entrance carefully."

"Shadow magic's no joke, lad," Vallyn told Renar.
"Your father and Elyana and I faced it too many times.
Half the folk that rode with us didn't come out, and one
of them turned." The bard's eyes roved over them all,
but fixed intently upon the young man. "If *you* want to
come out alive, we'll have to keep an eye out for each
other. It's not just about watching out for yourself. Keep
alert for dangers to your friends."

Renar put his hand to his hilt, looking ages older. At
least he seemed to be taking the venture seriously.

"Kiss that pretty elven lass again too, boy," Vallyn
continued, "so you remember how sweet life is."

The young man blushed at that and looked down at
his feet. This time, though, Elyana caught a hint of a
smile and knew that he was proud to have found love,
and to have others notice he had done so.

They packed up the camp and climbed back into the saddle. The sun was bright, and as the path sloped down the air grew warm. It would have been easy to imagine they rode off for a picnic, or a summer idyll.

Then they reached a ridge looking over the valley and stopped to gaze down into an expanse of roiling darkness lying between the slopes of two steep mountainsides. Black vapor drifted up from its edges and into the sky, dissipating as the wind of the heights swept it up.

"There's only one way in," Aliel said in her clear, high voice. "There are magical wards, but I will open them for you."

Elyana listened to her only distractedly. The clouds of the vale were black as thunderheads. She could faintly perceive the outline of what might have been treetops far below the darkness, but everything was hazy and indistinct.

"Does the valley always look like this?" Elyana asked.

"I have seen it but three times before," Aliel answered. "Twice it has looked thus. Once the shadow was far dimmer. Uncle says sometimes it is all but imperceptible, like an ache gnawing at the back of your skull."

"And why is it worse sometimes than others?" Kellius asked her.

A slight frown marred her clear features. "Our sages do not know, and have not been terribly inclined to investigate at length. The changing conditions seem unconnected with season or weather and obey only some unseen ebb and flow on the Plane of Shadow itself."

Elyana lifted her hand and gestured to their guide. "Show us the way in."

In another quarter-hour they stood at the top of a gentle slope and the edge of darkness that looked much like the shore of a tarry sea.

Elyana turned in her saddle and faced her comrades. "Drelm and I can see better in the murk, so rely on us. Captain, you take left flank, I'll take right." Elyana swung down off of Persaily and pressed her reins into the hands of one of the stoic elven Sentinel's hands. She faced Aliel.

"She is a fine, fine horse," Elyana told her. "If I do not return, take good care of her."

Aliel blinked at her, eyes wide in astonishment. "Oh, I am certain you will return," she said, sounding affronted that Elyana would discuss mortality.

"Regardless, see to her."

"That I shall, and with great pleasure." Aliel smiled as she rubbed the mare's nose. Persaily snorted in response.

The others dismounted and ran a final check of their gear. Renar finished first and spent a long moment holding Aliel's hands and staring into her eyes, then, needing no inspiration from Vallyn, kissed her once more. His obvious reluctance to depart gave Elyana the opening she'd sought for a long while.

"Renar, we must speak."

The young lord looked surprised, but stepped away with her.

She waited until they'd drawn more than a dozen paces off, then lowered her voice. "I think you should remain."

Renar's eyebrows arched and his mouth opened, but she shushed him.

"You do not have the experience of the rest of us."

"Kellius has precious little himself," Renar countered.

"He commands powers that you do not. You have come this far, and it is enough that you were determined to enter. You need do no more."

He frowned. "I'm the lord; I'm in charge."

"You have not been in charge since our departure, and you well know it."

Renar hesitated a moment, then lifted his chin. "I outrank you."

She had to struggle to keep her amusement from her voice. His pose resembled that of a stubborn child, but she'd do well not to point that out to him. "Indeed you do, but as your father would say, I have almost no respect for rank."

"So you're not going to let me?" Renar lifted his hands in exasperation. "How are you going to stop me?"

"You mistake this expedition for something simple. Your father and I dared nothing like this until we were seasoned."

"You don't think I'd survive."

How to impress upon him the very real danger they faced? "I'm not sure that *we'll* survive. What will your barony do if both you *and* your father perish? What will your mother say if I return with only your body?"

The boy set his lips in a tense line.

"You can stay here, with Aliel, and await our return."

"You want me to stay with a *woman* while you and the others risk your lives?"

Her voice was sharp. "You think women are soft, Renar, and that you are soft to stay with one?"

"I—yes—no—" He sputtered on, his eyes meeting hers and then drifting away. "What will Aliel think if I stay here?" He asked softly. "I am not a coward."

"She will know that I commanded you to remain."

"But you cannot command me. I am the baron. The acting baron."

"That is a fiction, and everyone knows it."

His jaw set. "I'm going with you, and you cannot make me stay." Though the declaration was childish, the words that followed were better chosen. "I would be ashamed for the rest of my life if I were to wait here holding a maiden's hand while the folk I will one day command risk their lives for my father."

She considered him for a longer moment, then inclined her head. She had advised him, but she would not force him into her choice.

"I thank you again for your counsel," he said, then strode off to bow formally to Aliel.

He would probably die, Elyana thought, but she had done her best. Not that Lenelle would understand. He was his own master now; she had no right to do more.

Renar returned, and she assigned him to stay beside Drelm. Kellius took the middle, and Vallyn stood on her left.

"Let's go," she said, and they started forward with her.

It was strange to walk slowly into the darkness. She watched as it climbed over her boots, her hips, her shoulders . . . and then it was above her head.

Once inside she experienced the same deadened sense of sound she knew from the Plane of Shadow. And she felt no wind. There was grass, but it grew short, thick, and black. She caught Renar glancing over his shoulder and hissed to him to keep his eyes forward.

By the time they reached the bottom of the slope they'd descended almost a quarter-mile from the height above. Before them was a long row of black crystals, tall as obelisks, thrust up from the ground at sharp angles. A few lay supine, but some poked up at diagonals, and others were ramrod straight. As they neared them Elyana saw that the crystals stretched as far as she could see to right and left.

"Don't touch them," she told the others.

"No worries there," Vallyn answered.

Elyana unslung her bow and set an arrow to it as she stepped forward.

The strange forest of crystals ended after only ten paces, and then they emerged upon a sward of longer, finer grass stretching out for the next few miles. It was as though by passing the crystals they had more surely entered the true realm of shadow.

"I wonder if these crystals are a power source, or a boundary marker?" Kellius asked, reading her thoughts. "I wish we had time to examine them."

"Don't get to studying shadow magic, wizard," Vallyn said.

In the distance she saw the tower clearly. It was much shorter than she had expected, rising no more then twenty feet. It had been built in a precise, twelve-pointed star, although time had canted it a few degrees to one side, and five of the slim, decorative spires that crowned its roof were broken off.

Drelm held up a hand, and as the others obeyed his signal to halt, he crouched, axe gripped in his other hand, and bent his head into the grass. Elyana thought she heard snuffling noises, and then Drelm rose, bearing a skull. He held it in his palm and showed it to them. The mandible was missing. Elyana had never seen such an elongated crown, or such wide orbits.

Drelm dropped it gently to the turf.

They soon discovered that the grasses hid great swaths of bones. After the first few Elyana stopped looking to see if she could determine race. Far more important was the cause of death, and the length of time that they'd lain there. It was all too easy to assume that they were all remnants of some long-ago battle.

She and her companions were a half-mile in before they saw the first shift. A few hundred feet ahead the air blurred, and suddenly a half-dozen scaly things in blackened armor were shoving spears against winged humanoids bearing burning swords. They were there only long enough for Renar to mutter "Abadar" and for Elyana to raise her bow. They vanished without so much as a puff of smoke or a sparkle.

"Was that an illusion?" Vallyn asked. From the sound of his voice, he clearly did not think so. "By Holy Calistria, I *hate* the damned shadow magic. I can't believe you got me involved in—"

They heard a roar behind them and whirled. A lake of dark, bubbling oil had appeared, and a creature bobbed on its surface, its huge reptilian head full of razor-sharp teeth that now stretched toward them at the end of a long, long neck.

Elyana's arrow sank deep into the scaly head, but the beast was too stupid or hungry to notice, and the maw plunged down toward them. Even as Kellius's fireball blasted from his fingers, the creature blurred and vanished along with its lake.

"Holy Abadar," Renar said.

"Abadar's got nothing to do with this," Vallyn retorted.

"What's going on?" Drelm demanded.

"These aren't illusions, and that's not shadow magic," Vallyn answered.

Elyana turned to the wizard. "Kellius, any speculations?"

He shook his head and adjusted his hat. "I'd guess this entire place is unstable. It's not just that an ancient spell lingers over the valley. This place is weak, dimensionally. It's not just pulling things in from one plane."

"Plain language, wizard," Drelm urged.

"Things are getting sucked into this valley from all over the other planes. Near and far. I don't know if that's someone's deliberate design, or an accident."

"Is there any way to predict when the next shift will happen?" Elyana didn't think there would be, so wasn't exactly surprised when Kellius shook his head.

Arcil, she thought, would at least have made an educated guess. But she had Arcil to blame for them being here in the first place. Kellius was a better man, and did not deserve the comparison.

"Let's keep moving," Elyana told them.

"Quickly," Vallyn added.

"No," she corrected, "deliberately. Eyes sharp. And we should spread out a little. If something opens up beneath one of us, then the others can help out."

"What if it opens beneath us then takes us along when it shifts?" Renar asked.

She'd been hoping he wouldn't think of that. "Let's hope we don't find out."

Chapter Fourteen
The Tower

In the next quarter-hour they experienced three more intrusions, the most spectacular of which occurred in the clear space in front of the tower. Two groups of mailed figures on serpentine steeds fought to the death for almost two minutes before vanishing, the battle's outcome still undecided.

Black and gray trees stood off in long clumps five hundred feet to either side of the tower. Elyana guided them toward the edges of the woodland, reasoning that they wouldn't be as obvious to whatever appeared if they weren't striding through the open.

As they drew nearer to the tower, Elyana saw that the structure was larger than she'd first thought. But she did not long dwell on that, for she heard the crash of some large animal plowing through dry vegetation. A half-mile ahead something erupted from the trees and soared out onto the field, just in time to reach a pair of strange opponents. A six-armed lizard on some furred, cyclopean mount saw the dropping shadow and swung his oddly shaped trident up too late—the dragon shape snatched him up with a claw and bore him away. The lizard-man's feathered combatant shook his dark sword and brought it crashing down into the skull of the lizard-man's mount, and then those two vanished. The dragon, however, glided on, bearing its prey in its claws, until it reached the other screen of trees and landed.

Elyana urged the others deeper into the woods. She ordered Drelm to watch for approaches within the forest, and peered out from behind a tree bole.

Vallyn stood just behind her, cursing lightly. "By all that's holy, I never thought I'd see another shadow dragon. And that one's a hell of a lot bigger."

Elyana did not bother responding. She watched the dragon bite the head off the writhing humanoid and then pick his armor apart with obsidian claws, like a man shelling a lobster. The long, fanged maw tore into the body with such vigor that the four of them could hear the crunching across the clearing, despite the strange sound-deadening effect of the Plane of Shadow.

Vallyn looked pale. "I'm fond of old Stelan—comrades forever and all that—but no way in hell am I going to fight *that*."

This beast was a good three times the size of Lathroft's dragon, stretching thirty feet from corded, spiny neck to whiplike tail. It looked smaller when it wasn't flying, curled like a cat toying with a mouse. It was even beautiful, in a gaunt and horrible way—a finely fashioned engine of destruction, blacker than midnight.

"I say we just teleport out of here," Vallyn said, speaking with nervous rapidity. "I have a couple of the spells readied—I can take almost all of us to safety, or to the edge of the crystals, at least. But we'd best do it now, before it knows we're here."

"It knows we're here," Elyana said softly. She had not taken her eyes from the thing.

Vallyn crouched down beside her. "How do you know?"

"It's putting on a show," Elyana said softly. "It's toying with us and seeing what we'll do."

"That's . . . that's just wonderful. You're sure?"

"Pretty sure."

"So what do we do?"

"I'm thinking."

She crept quietly back into the forest. She was almost certain the dragon knew she was there, but there was no point in making it aware that she knew it played a game.

Little light reached them under the canopy of dark leaves. Nothing grew beneath it, either—there was only bare earth, scatterings of rock, and the occasional rounded hump of a skull.

Once Elyana had briefed the others, Drelm was swift to suggest a course of action. "We stay to the trees. If it attacks us here, it will be hampered. We'll use the ground to our advantage."

"You're insane," Vallyn told him. "If that thing attacks us, we're done for. We need to retreat."

"If we retreat, it will attack," Elyana said. "Your spells can't get us far enough to get out, and they can't transport all of us. I'm not leaving anyone behind."

"We can't go back," Renar said determinedly. "We're going forward. If the dragon attacks, we'll beat him down, just like my father did."

"Oh, blessed Calistria," Vallyn said, disgusted, "spare me." He shook his head. "We faced a little dragon, boy, and it nearly killed us—did kill one of us. And we had Arcil on our side. No offense, Kellius, but Arcil was pretty good."

"I think you underestimate Kellius," Elyana said, though she feared Vallyn spoke the truth. "And you surely underestimate yourself. Your teleportation spell can't be the only trick you've learned in the last twenty years. But I do not mean us to attack it unless we must. Drelm is right: if we stay to the trees, we stand a better chance. It's watching to see what we'll do because it doesn't yet know our real strength." Elyana glanced at each of them in turn. "We move forward."

Vallyn grumbled, but when Elyana set out through the trees, he fell in behind her. If anything, his step was even more certain now than it had been in his youth. "I can't believe what my promises get me involved in," he muttered. She did not acknowledge him.

They advanced along the edge of the forest. Elyana was fairly certain she knew from what area the dragon had come, and she wondered if they would find a nest or the entrance to a cavernous lair when they reached that section of the forest, or if their proximity would prompt its return.

"Elyana," Vallyn said quietly at her shoulder. "I do have one idea."

"What is it?"

"If we can get close enough to the tower, within a few hundred feet, I can open a portal to the top."

Elyana gauged distances as she walked. Beyond the greater gloom of the trees, the darkness of the plain flowed suddenly with movement, but it was not the dragon—rather, it was a wave of gray water, man-high and rolling outward.

"Grab a tree," Elyana commanded, but even as her lips closed over the last syllable the water struck the line of woods. Liquid sprayed out and the scent of it hit her a fraction of a moment before the water itself—a cloying, rotten smell, as if something long dead had made its home in the wave before its sudden arrival.

The trees broke up much of the wave's impact, but when the water hit it was with a stinking slap that curled her lips. All managed to maintain balance, but Drelm recovered first, calling their attention to further activity on the plain.

A vast, white worm-thing had reared up in a spiral, and now the dragon was on wing, flapping to investigate.

There might be no better chance. The wave had brought the monster, and who knew when the strange magics of the valley might take it back.

"Now," Elyana urged, nose wrinkling at the scent of her own clothes. They ran on through the trees.

Elyana had to slow herself, for she quickly outpaced the others. In a test of endurance the humans and Drelm would certainly defeat her, but in the woods, at speed, she could have lost them.

Behind them the dragon was rearing back and blasting at the white worm with an immense cone of darkness.

The front third of the worm was obscured by shadow, and Elyana was glad that she was nowhere close.

Renar and Vallyn reached her first, then Drelm and the winded wizard. They looked out from the safety of the trees at the oddly shaped tower, fashioned all of slim gray stones, almost as if someone had built the thing by stacking and mortaring a vast collection of headstones.

"Vallyn," she said, "is this close enough?"

"Aye—I can get two others up with me, but there are only so many spells of this magnitude I can weave in a day."

"Only two?"

Vallyn shrugged. "That's all I can manage."

She'd have to leave two behind, then, and she was loath to abandon anyone on the plain with the dragon . . . although the dragon looked like it might be busy for a while. She thought quickly. She'd love to have Drelm with her in the tower, for she was certain it would have guardians. But that would leave Renar and the wizard to fend for themselves, and they were the greenest members in the party.

"Drelm, you and Renar keep to the forest. Find a sturdy tree, and stay on guard."

"We should not split up," Drelm said.

"I don't like it either, but we've not much time."

"We have to play the cards we're dealt," Vallyn added. Drelm seemed unconvinced.

"May Abadar protect you both," Elyana said. She meant it, this time. "Vallyn, get us up there."

"As you wish." Vallyn slung the instrument from behind his back and strummed quickly, left hand pressed lightly to the strings so that the sound rose muffled. It would have been hard to hear much over a disturbing noise from the vale that sounded rather like an enormous creature vomiting.

Renar was in mid-protest when a sensation of light-headedness swept over Elyana. As she blinked away the dizziness, she discovered that the ground had tilted beneath her and her surroundings altered utterly. She had arrived upon a worn stone floor canted to her right by about five degrees. They were not, as she had first thought, a mere twenty feet above the ground, for the tower stood in a deep cleft at the valley's edge. The plain dropped steeply into the cleft a good bowshot from the tower's edge, and Elyana saw that the tower itself, seated in that low spot, was at least a hundred feet tall.

The entirety of the roof's surface was covered with blocky glyphs and symbols. There might once have been a spire at the end of every star point, but several were broken at various points, and all were weathered.

They had materialized only a few feet from one pointed edge, a proximity both Kellius and the bard hurried to correct by stepping quickly to the central body.

Elyana moved to the farthest point to better view the lay of the valley, so confident in her balance she scarcely minded her step as she advanced to place a hand upon a spire. She could not see her companions hidden in the woods, but there was no missing the titanic battle underway between the ghastly ribbed worm and the dragon. The worm leaked dark ichor, but, even as Elyana watched, some other lighter substance sprayed out from a set of holes upon its back and struck the dragon's neck. The shadow creature shrieked and beat its wings, rising through the air.

"One more place I never want to visit again," Vallyn muttered.

"All the other creatures vanished as swiftly as they came," Elyana said. "This one remains."

"Then Calistria smiles upon us," Vallyn said. "Why question fortune?"

Why indeed. Elyana moved away from the edge and joined Kellius, who was crouched on the stone, studying the engraved figures. "Can you read it?" she asked.

"I think it's a ward," the wizard replied. "But I don't have a clue as to what it does."

"If it were designed to keep us off the tower, we'd already be blasted out into empty space," Vallyn said.

"That's not necessarily true," Kellius objected. "Some wards are more sadistic. There might be something already slowly at work upon us—"

"We'll worry later," Elyana cut in. "We need to move while the dragon's distracted. The roof overhangs a floor that's open below us."

"How do you know?" Kellius asked.

"I could look under the overhang from the edge of the star point. If I hang out I might just be able to swing in."

Kellius pursed his lips. "That's a long drop if you miss. I can cast a flight spell on the three of us."

Elyana mulled that over. "Save your energy. The two of you ought to be able to carry me."

Kellius nodded thoughtfully. "I believe so."

The wizard worked fast, whispering a few cryptic phrases and passing his right hand across first himself, then the bard.

"There's not much to controlling the spell," Kellius said to Vallyn. "You simply will yourself where you wish to go."

The bard was already floating a few inches above the roof. "How long will this last?"

"Only a few minutes." With an apologetic smile, Kellius grasped Elyana's left bicep, his fingers tightening after the initial contact. He used his other hand to hold down his hat. Vallyn sank to the roof, stepped over, and grasped her other arm.

Then, suddenly, both men were airborne, with Elyana carried between them. They drifted slowly to the edge of the roof. Elyana tried to ignore the drop, and the thought that all that lay between her and a messy death were the grips of two men suspended in the air by nothing whatsoever.

Kellius dropped more swiftly than Vallyn so that she sagged to the right, then hastily corrected himself as she sucked in a sharp breath.

Elyana kept her eyes on the tower.

The stone of the roof was a foot thick, and overhung the floor below by three feet. Swinging in might not have been as simple a matter as she had thought.

Vallyn and Kellius floated under the overhang and into the shadowy level below. This tower's designers possessed the same disregard for safety demonstrated by the bridge builders near Elistia. Like the roof, the space was completely open, without railing or even a curb. There were only some stone columns of support, and a sealed door to a thick, squared-off structure in the center. There were no spiders or bats or any obvious hazards, which was both a relief and a concern, for it almost surely meant that there would be something more . . . unless the detained dragon were the guardian. But even at its length it could not be an ancient dragon, or even an especially old one. These towers were supposed to have stood for millennia.

Kellius and Vallyn dropped gently to the floor with her, and both men released her arms. It felt good to have something solid under her feet. While Vallyn and the wizard approached the tower's center, Elyana glanced once more over the valley. Worm and dragon still battled, though the worm leaked even more ichor than before. The dragon was not unscathed. Both wings displayed great, jagged rents, one of which was trailing black smoke.

Vallyn faced his lute forward again across his belly while Kellius advanced toward a stone panel set at head level into the structure at the tower's center. No hinges, handles, or pulls were obvious. The stone was smooth and featureless, but as Elyana centered her own magical energies upon it she discovered that the panel was magically inscribed with a disturbing symbol—a skull with chains hanging from the orbits of its eyes.

"Zon-Kuthon," Vallyn said in disgust. "It just keeps getting worse."

"It's hardly surprising, though," Elyana said, wishing she'd better prepared herself for dealing with the dark god's faith. "Arcil said he's the one who put up the towers."

"How are we going to get through?" Vallyn asked. "There's no handle. There aren't even hinges."

"I may be able to open it." Kellius stepped closer, hands outstretched, fingers quivering.

Elyana exchanged a quick glance with Vallyn, who was clearly concerned.

"Are you going to touch it?" the bard asked.

Kellius didn't answer.

It was not a time to stand and ponder mysteries. The dragon would have to triumph before too much longer, and then their challenges might become insurmountable. Their exit was in question. Elyana looked over her shoulder to the titanic battle and saw the dragon retreat before another spray of green ichor from the worm.

Kellius lowered his hands. "There's a gap, here, in the stone." He knuckled one hand as if to rap on a thin gray brick that framed the panel, but did not touch it. "This brick's an illusion, and there's a tiny chamber beyond. I think you're supposed to put your hand inside."

"A blood sacrifice," Elyana said.

"You're kidding." Vallyn sighed in disgust.

"Probably you're supposed to lose a little blood in reverence to . . . the god." Kellius hesitated, as if reluctant to say the name. "I just don't know if it's going to take a little blood, or your whole hand."

"With this god," Vallyn said, "everything *but* the hand might be seared off."

Elyana sighed inwardly. "Very well. Move aside."

"Are you serious?" Kellius asked her. She didn't answer, but raised her left hand. "Which stone is it?"

Kellius frowned, took a deep breath, then pivoted and thrust his own hand at what looked like an ordinary block.

"Kellius!" Elyana cried. The mage's fingers passed straight through and his lips immediately pulled back in a grimace. His back arched and he rocked with pain. She started forward to assist him, but Vallyn held her back.

"It's *his* ritual," the bard said. "Interference could get both of you killed. Don't speak, lad," Vallyn urged. "Not a sound. Hold it in . . ."

At the same moment, a door-sized section of stone adjacent to the panel and stretching through the stones below it simply vanished, revealing a flight of stairs descending to darkness.

Elyana caught Kellius by one shoulder as the mage breathed in again and pulled his hand free. Panting heavily, the magic-worker looked first at his palm, then flexed his fingers experimentally.

"That was very foolish," Elyana told him.

"You've taken more than enough risks for all of us," Kellius said.

"What did it do to you?" Vallyn asked.

"It was . . . painful." Kellius' sober look added extra weight to the final word. "As though my hand were being scorched with flame while being skewered with a hundred tiny knives."

"A pain test," Vallyn mused. "Good thing you didn't shout. Something worse might have happened."

Kellius rubbed his hand, still looking over it carefully. "That's a pleasant thought."

"Are you sure you're all right?" Elyana asked.

The wizard nodded distractedly. Vallyn was already peering into the stairwell, although he permitted Elyana to lead the way in.

Beyond was nothing but silence, and the smell of stone and dust. She started down the stairs, and soon found herself in a round room bounded by the tower's walls. The star points had apparently not been incorporated into the interior design. Light from the stairwell opening illuminated a sprinkling of diamonds and gems set into the chamber's mortar, but she paid little heed even as the bard whispered a prayer of thanks. Elyana's attention had been captured by a jumble of large brown bones lying along one wall.

She drew her sword and advanced carefully. She noted with disinterest that the gems that had set Vallyn smiling were arranged in pictographic images of Zon-Kuthon inflicting pain in a variety of ways upon great swaths of humanity. Most of her attention was on the bones.

"What was it?" Kellius asked at her elbow.

"It looks like it's been dead for a long, long time," Vallyn said. "Let's hope it stays that way."

The bones seemed uninclined to move, which was refreshing in such environs, and she risked another glance to take in the room.

The stairway stretched down from the ceiling and turned in the floor's center to continue farther down. Its left wall was open, without rail or banister, although three support pillars rose at even intervals along its edge.

Kellius spoke a short, sharp word and a feeble white light blossomed in the chamber.

"Wouldn't it be wonderful if the tower's guardian had just up and died?" Vallyn said. "It wouldn't make for much of a story, but it—"

Kellius interrupted. "Elyana, Vallyn, come here." The wizard was peering down the stairwell, his expression troubled.

Elyana joined him. "What is it?"

"Something moved down there. Something white."

"So much for your hope, Vallyn," Elyana said.

By way of answer, the bard strummed a quick succession of chords. "I'd like you both to have a little inspiration." The song was different from any she'd heard him weave before, and more powerful, for Elyana felt stronger, taller even, as though more life flowed within her than she usually knew.

She nodded her thanks and, after a last glance at the motionless bones, started down. In the old days, Stelan would have been at her side. Now she was in the forefront, the wizard following, Vallyn to the rear.

The chamber proved entirely different from that above. Light shone upon every wall, for each was carved with illuminated figures of surpassing loveliness, endowed somehow with grace and a sense of movement. Elyana did not dwell upon the walls, despite her interest, for two floating apparitions draped in white waited at the landing.

Elyana was no stranger to ghosts, and her neck hair prickled with a sense of dread as she looked upon them. These two, though, were different from the three disfigured crones she had encountered in the Galtan cemetery. These had been lovely women, and their faces were not diseased or twisted in rage. They looked only sad. Though they themselves looked human, their garments appeared elven in their simplicity of design, flowing but not voluminous, so that the dresses were both feminine and flattering without being constrictive or revealing. Both ghosts wore necklaces depicting a long-tailed bird, and Elyana recognized the symbol with a start as that of the goddess Shelyn, sister to Zon-Kuthon. The white thread of the necklace stood out along their paler necks, and the birds themselves glowed with a pale light.

The ghosts hovered just beyond the foot of the stairs but did not attack, and Elyana found the dark places where their eyes had been too disturbing to meet.

One of the ghosts drifted a half-step before the other and raised her head. Her lips moved. Elyana was not altogether sure that she heard the voice so much as felt it.

"Who are you that comes to pay respect in the chapel of Shelyn?"

Elyana heard Vallyn's sharp intake of breath. "In a temple to her brother?" he asked. Elyana started to speak, but Vallyn suddenly brushed past her and halted on the last foot of the stair to bow respectfully.

"We are wayfarers," the bard said, "come to visit this tower to pay reverence to the mistress of light and song."

"We bid you welcome." The lead ghost inclined her head.

"What's a temple of hers doing in a star tower?" Kellius asked quietly of Elyana.

Elyana wasn't sure. The two were brother and sister, but Zon-Kuthon was master of pain and suffering, while Shelyn was the mistress of art and music. Zon-Kuthon was said to be obsessed with his beautiful sister, but Elyana was still shocked to find a temple to her within a structure to a god diametrically opposed to her beliefs.

The second spirit drifted closer to her companion. "Sister," she asked softly, "how did they gain entrance? There is no priest or priestess with them."

"Perhaps they knew the holy word."

"Sisters," Vallyn said with a ready smile, "we have come from very far away. Do you not have welcome for us?"

"They have come for the treasures," the second ghost told her companion, then raised a hand to Vallyn. "This is no place for rest. You must turn back."

"But we need your aid."

"Much as we would like to render succor," the second ghost told them, "this is a chapel only for those with a sacred duty to take up arms against the beasts of Rovagug. If you have not come in service of that duty, you must depart."

Elyana could think of nothing clever; that was Vallyn's duty, and she looked to him.

The bard licked his lips, then presented his best smile once more. "Ladies, please. You can see into our hearts. You know that we—"

"Deceivers!" the second cried. "Sister! They are thieves! Thieves! Shelyn, aid us!" And her mouth opened wide.

The shriek that emerged from the ghost rattled through the whole of Elyana's body and set her trembling. She backed away with little of her own volition, her sword raised in a shaking hand. She knew the fear was irrational, and that it came not from her, yet she could do naught but heed it. The phantom shape drifted up the stairs, one hand cast toward her, its ghostly sleeve billowing in an unseen wind as it came.

Vallyn scrambled back up the steps, his face pale in panic. Elyana fought her fear and plunged her sword into the advancing spirit. The ghost's face flickered in agony as the elven blade swept through its incorporeal form, and then it was Elyana's turn to feel pain as the slim fingers passed onto and through her upper arm and shoulder.

She knew a sensation that was somewhere between searing cold and burning heat. Her sword arm ached from deep within; sinew, muscle, and bone felt brittle and withered. Then too there was the irrational fear that left her scattered and nervous.

Kellius shouted from behind her. "Get back, Elyana!"

There was nothing she wanted to do more; Elyana retreated two steps, teeth gritted so that she would not scream. The ghost glowered at her and she heard the strum of Vallyn's lute. Kellius pushed past and shoved a gray wand almost directly into the face of the spirit. He uttered a single, sharp word and a blast of freezing energy expanded outward from the tip.

Elyana felt the cold radiating from the wand even from behind; the dead priestess, exposed to the wand's direct blast, moaned in agony, throwing up hands and arms to shield against an attack that passed directly through her. The energy had clearly harmed her, and she drifted down and away even as Vallyn's own magic went to work. This time he played a swift, intricate pattern. The wounded ghost cried out in pain once more.

The first of the ghosts had watched, confused. Now she opened her mouth to scream. Kellius's wand blasted a second time as the wizard advanced down the steps, striking both spirits. Ice and snow slicked the lower stair and the stones that lay at their bottom.

The first spirit shrieked. Elyana did not feel the effect as strongly as the original attack—perhaps she was already scared enough.

"Not working," Vallyn muttered, striking up a more martial song. Even as his spell faded, one of the ghosts lunged up at Kellius. The sudden change caught the wizard off guard and he brought up the wand too late; he tripped back as he met the phantom's stare, his mouth wide in a scream he was too weak to voice.

Elyana fought against her terror. They were pinned in—better if they could spread out. She slid around the pillar to her left and dropped to the floor. She landed lightly and came up on Kellius's attacker from the side. The ghost was turning her head as Elyana slashed once through her torso. Elyana pivoted and swung once more, through the spirit's arms and neck. The ghost raised both hands to her face and then broke into dissolving fragments of vapor.

The other spirit rushed up the stairs toward Kellius only to meet a third blast of frost. She threw back her head in a soundless scream, and then fell into dissipating fragments of mist.

All that remained of the battle were their own aches and wounds and a light coating of snow and ice that left the stone pavement glittering like a fairyland decoration.

Elyana quickly took stock of the rest of the room. There was the stairwell, which stretched down another level. There were the walls decorated with images of a slender, lovely woman in simple, flowing garments. In one she played a harp, in another she watched benevolently over a trio of pipers, and in a third, rays of different shades of white and gray beamed from her hands over folk who bowed in gratitude. All the depictions lacked color, of course, but Elyana felt their vibrancy as surely as she saw the gentle curve and slope of the masterfully rendered figures.

Below the third illustration was a stone byre, and on that byre, arranged in the shape of a man, was an elaborate set of light armor, a lance—and a crown.

"Blessed Calistria," Vallyn breathed. "There it is." He started to move toward the treasures, but Elyana's hand stopped him.

"Careful," Elyana said. "There may be unseen protections." She motioned to Kellius.

The wizard moved forward, taking care not to approach the items too closely. While his fingers and lips moved in a spell, Elyana stepped over to the stairwell and peered down. This was a high tower— what else might it contain?

"This has to be what we're looking for," she heard Kellius say, and she stepped back over, one eye still cast toward the open stairwell. "Each of these pieces has been fashioned with immense magical energy." The wizard's voice was low with awe. "I've never seen anything like them."

"Is there any kind of ward?" Vallyn asked him.

"No," Kellius answered. "These items are simply. . . sitting here. Well-preserved. Tended by ghosts. For what purpose?"

"Hmm." Vallyn reached down and tentatively touched the crown. It was fashioned from two thick strips of metal that snaked about each other, one light, one dark. "It seems to me that these poor women were placed here to guard this armor, long, long ago. And they've continued to guard it."

"But why?" Kellius asked. "What's the armor for?"

"*Who* is it for, you mean." Vallyn looked thoughtful. "If the star towers were places where the gods reinforced Golarion when it was stitched closed, maybe they're weak points. And should one of the Rough Beast's minions escape from their prison, maybe these are tools to fight them. Look at the symbol on the armor."

Elyana and Kellius both stepped closer. A swirling sigil was emblazoned into the cuirass, but it was one unfamiliar to her: a swooping shape that evoked a harp—one that was broken.

"It symbolizes both music *and* loss," Vallyn said. "I think it's consecrated to both gods together."

"Why?" the wizard asked.

"So a cleric of either could wear it, I suppose. Or maybe because a human champion set to fight Rovagug's minions would need the help of both. That's a frightening thought."

And currently unimportant. Elyana walked to the crown. "Kellius, what does your magic tell you of the power of this device?" She wanted to make sure they'd found the right thing.

"As I've said, armor, crown, and lance all have mighty enchantments. Their power surpasses anything that I've ever seen."

Elyana nodded once. "Our friends wait, and the dragon will not be long distracted. If we can depart now, we should."

Vallyn glanced at her quickly. "You don't think we have time to . . . scout out the rest?"

She smiled to herself. Of course—she had promised him a cut. "Take a look below while I pack these things to take with us. But there's gems enough on the floor above."

Vallyn nodded, humming to himself. He reached out to lightly finger the edge of the crown, his eyes bright with interest, then turned away and headed to the stairs.

"I'll pack," Elyana told Kellius. "See if he needs help. Urge him along."

"Of course."

Elyana knelt beside the treasures. She had heard of magical bags that never ran out of room, but she had never seen one. All she possessed was a small pack. She wrapped the crown in her spare shirt and placed it inside. Then she examined the rest of the gear. There was a breastplate embossed with the broken harp symbol and a complete set of matching scale armor, complete with gauntlets and boots. These she might take with her, but how to transport them? They wouldn't fit in the bag. And how to carry the lance, inscribed with delicate, swirling symbols that resembled musical notes? She reached out to touch it and felt a throb of energy from the dwarven bracelet wrapped around her upper arm. She studied the notes on the haft, deciding that they depicted a simple rising melody. Perhaps she should leave them here, in case a champion should one day come seeking them.

The bard and the wizard returned only a few minutes later. Vallyn, grinning, patted a bulging packet at his waist. "Diamonds. They were on a wall in the outline of a giant, blood-drenched spike."

"Lovely. Are you ready to use your transportation spell again?"

"Certainly. I can't carry much extra weight, though. Are you planning to take that giant pig poker?"

"No. We leave all this."

"All of it?" the bard was astonished.

"Someone's likely to need it, someday. It's bad enough we're taking the crown."

Vallyn shook his head in disbelief. "Elyana, those things are worth a fortune."

"Time is wasting, Vallyn. Get us out of here."

The bard sighed, lifted a hand, twitched fingers, and then brought it down across the strings.

Elyana felt the flow of magic gather around them, but nothing happened. Vallyn frowned. He set his hand to the strings more forcefully, producing a louder sound.

Still nothing.

Vallyn cursed. "There must be a magical barrier to keep people from teleporting in or out."

"I've heard of that," Kellius said. "It makes sense that the place is protected."

"We'll have to fly back out, then," Elyana said. "Hurry, you two."

They hurried up the stairs, Vallyn sighing regretfully as they passed more gems. The stairwell had remained open, but closed the moment the last of them stepped free.

A moment later, Kellius cast another flight spell upon himself and the bard, and once more he and Vallyn lifted Elyana, compensating better for her weight this time. They floated with her up through the hole, around the overhang, and set down on the roof.

The wizard was no more comfortable with the edge than he had been before, and hurried away from the edge as soon as he released Elyana's arm.

She turned promptly to take in the view. On the plain below there was no sign of the dragon, only the motionless carcass of the gigantic white worm. She searched the horizon. Could the great lizard have gone after their friends?

Vallyn too had advanced toward the center, though he was a pace or two behind Kellius as he slung his lute into place.

One moment there was nothing on top of the roof but themselves and the dark, skeletal fingers cast across the stone by the tower's spires. The next moment the dragon melted into existence from the shadows and snatched up the wizard with one great claw.

There came a sickening crunch, and then bodily fluids were leaking all down the black scales and great curved claws. Kellius was already limp.

The dragon bared its teeth.

Before Elyana had fully registered the awful moment, Vallyn strummed a single chord and vanished.

The dragon turned to focus on Elyana, dropping Kellius. The wizard's ruined body struck the roof with a sick thump.

"What strange treats the morning brings," the dragon said. "Don't any of you intend to fight?"

Chapter Fifteen
Abandonment

There was no time to mourn. Elyana reacted without thinking, dashing for the ledge. The dragon's head whipped after. She heard the teeth, each half her body length, clamp down just behind her. For all the creature's violence, she knew that it was just playing with her. If it wanted her dead, it could already have killed her with ease.

Elyana had only a vague inkling of a plan; the first part involved getting off the roof alive. She stepped to the edge even as the roof shook under the beast's great weight, then dropped. Her hands caught the ledge and she hung there, contemplating the dizzying drop and the impossible gap between overhang and the floor beneath. At any moment she expected to be blasted off the side of the tower by the creature's breath. There was no hope for it. She'd just have to leap from the overhang and hope she hit the floor with her feet. She swung once, twice, heard the dragon cackle, and arced out across space.

Her boots struck the floor. Above her she caught a brief flash of dragon snout, and then overhang and roof blocked her view. Her waist had barely crossed the ledge, but the rest of her hung out over empty space. A vast dragon leg swept down as she contorted herself sideways to grasp the stone with her hands. The dragon's claw thumped into her armored back, inadvertently propelling her to safety.

She scrambled to her feet, dashing for the stairwell, only then remembering it was closed.

Once again she was bereft of options. She thrust her hand into the space and experienced for herself what poor Kellius had described—though it felt not so much like she was being burned as that her skin was being flayed while spikes were driven through her flesh. The pain was so intense that her vision blurred and her knees buckled; she was not sure she could have screamed if she had wanted to, for her throat muscles were clenched shut in agony.

The dragon's head swung down to consider the space, blotting out the light on the tower's south side.

The door opened. Gasping, Elyana dashed through it and down the stairs.

A blast of darkness missed her by handspans, saturating the air around it with cold. She leapt off the left side of the stairs.

Seasoned warrior though she was, Elyana had done too much, too quickly, and her landing was hard. She came down awkwardly on her left leg and stumbled.

"Don't you want to *play*?" The dragon's voice echoed from above.

But Elyana was already running down to the next level, favoring her left leg. In the respite she cursed the bard. Vallyn would only have had to take a few steps to carry her along with him. She held out a faint hope that he'd gone for aid, then found herself wishing he wouldn't. Coming back with Drelm and Renar would only get someone killed.

The ice and snow at the foot of the second flight of stairs had mostly melted, though the stone still glistened wetly. She cast down her pack and bedroll, thrust her head through the patterned breastplate, and was buckling on one side before she heard slow, deliberate footfalls on the floor above. Human footfalls. The dragon's voice came again, but altered. The harsh lower tones were gone, leaving only a lilting feminine soprano. "You don't really think you can get away from me, do you?"

Elyana felt a cold stab of fear. She snatched up gauntlets, pack, and lance and backed toward the lower stairs. The breastplate was a little wide and a little short, and banged into her as she moved. It might have been a shade more comfortable if she'd had the time to buckle the other side.

She pulled her shirt out of the pack and lifted it clear. She didn't know the full extent of the crown's powers, but she was sure she'd find them useful.

There was no crown. In its place was only a small flat rock.

For the briefest moment, Elyana thought the crown had slipped out from the shirt and must be lying loose . . . and then she understood with great clarity. Vallyn had touched the crown before her, while humming. He'd cast a spell and somehow transported or switched the crown right in front of her eyes. There'd been no magical pulse from her armband when she touched the crown, while she'd felt one the moment she clasped each of the other artifacts. She should have noticed. But why should she have suspected Vallyn?

How long had he planned the betrayal? Was that, like his vanishing act, a split-second choice?

She didn't know, and there was no time to ponder. She tossed down the pack and slipped on one gauntlet. She heard the slow, methodical impact of feet on the stairs, one after the other.

By all that was holy . . . She tilted the lance toward her, studying the notes. It had been many human generations since she had sat at her father's side, holding the old choral book, and she could not be sure these musical symbols were even in a proper register. The staff lacked a line along the top.

"There's really no point in hiding." The dragon's voice floated down toward her with false cheer. "Although I do enjoy a good game just as much as the next lady."

Elyana backed up beneath the stairs, rotating the haft to better study the music.

The footsteps reached the bottom of the stairs. She heard the scuff of slippered soles on the stone.

"Hmm, where might you be hiding?" The dragon sounded as though it were an adult playing a hide-and-seek game with a small child.

Elyana gulped.

The creature that stepped around the edge of the stair was garbed in a flowing black dress. She had a beautiful white face framed in the most luxurious and silky black hair Elyana had ever seen. Her lips were cruel and sensual, and her eyes glowed darkly with mischief. Fine black eyebrows were upswept above lovely brows.

The lips parted in a short laugh. "An elf, cowering under the stairs with her armor half on, wearing one glove. Really, what did I do to deserve this? Must my entertainments always be so poor?"

"You didn't enjoy the worm, then?" Elyana asked levelly.

The mouth bent in a frown. "That was your doing? I did not sense that level of power in the wizard I crushed above. Was he a friend? Say yes. I hope he was a friend. Did you like to see him dripping?"

"You're pathetic, dragon." Elyana held the lance casually pointed away from the thing with the woman's shape. "No more refined than the worm itself. Your nature would only have been more apparent if you'd snapped off his head."

The delicate brows furrowed in anger. "You *mock* me?"

"Why did you leave these treasures here, I wonder, rather than take them with you to your lair? Wouldn't it have been easy to cart them past the ghosts?"

"The treasures belong to my lord, Zon-Kuthon."

"So you were afraid to take them."

The lips flared to expose perfectly white teeth. "Do you think you're funny, thief?"

"Not especially. But I am a fine singer."

The first few notes were out of her mouth before the dragon's eyes narrowed. The creature raised a hand, and Elyana saw her fingers twitch with the beginnings of a spell.

But Elyana finished her song and the lance tip glowed. Elyana lowered it to charge, and at thought of the imminent impact, a searing bolt of white light projected from the pointed end and blasted the dragon's assumed body into the wall.

The dragon-woman screamed as she struck the picture of Shelyn watching the pipers. She slumped to the ground. Elyana breathed no sigh of relief, however, for her adversary climbed rapidly to her feet, dark eyes blazing.

Elyana sang again, but before she could complete the melody all sound fell away from her—she could hear nothing. The dragon lowered glowing hands and smiled wickedly.

The grinning mouth moved, then frowned as the dragon realized Elyana could hear none of its taunts. This, too, annoyed the creature. It seemed to Elyana that the dragon lived in a constant state of egotism and irritation.

Elyana could not be sure just how badly she had harmed the dragon, or how much damage the monster had sustained in her battle with the worm. She didn't think the thing could be at full strength. But how weak might she be?

Not weak enough. The dragon-woman's lips were moving once more, and it raised its hands again. Elyana charged, the lance gripped in both hands.

Clearly the creature was unused to humanoids running *toward* her, for the dragon-woman's eyebrows rose not so much in worry as in astonishment as Elyana closed the distance.

As the tip closed in, the dragon-woman reached out with one hand and tried to bat the weapon away. The moment her flesh made contact, she cried out in pain and snatched her fingers back. Elyana drove the point into the creature's chest.

The lance pierced flesh, but even in human form the dragon was dense. Though all Elyana's weight and considerable momentum were behind the blow, the weapon barely pierced the creature's flesh.

Elyana was pulling the lance free to jab again when the dragon's lovely mouth opened wide and darkness poured forth.

The ebon cloud blotted out all light in the chamber save one; the symbol upon Elyana's breastplate, which glowed brilliantly.

Weakness washed over Elyana, and her right hand's grip was suddenly too feeble to stay fixed around the lance haft. The left hand was shielded by the gauntlet, but it alone wasn't strong enough to maintain her grasp when the weapon was struck a heavy blow.

Elyana tottered backward, breathing wearily, and drew her sword. The broken harp in her armor blazed more brilliantly, and suddenly the darkness itself was dispelled, as if burned away. Elyana felt her strength return to something approaching normal levels. Her hearing too was restored, though it was soon obvious that effect had little to do with the armor.

"I want you to hear me, elf!" The dragon had stepped away from the wall. Elyana did not see where the lance had been cast, but she heard it clanging down the stone stairwell toward the next level.

"You sound irritated, dragon," Elyana said. She could not quite keep the breathlessness from her voice.

"And you sound tired."

"I think you're the tired one. First the worm, then an elf. Are you starting to think it was a mistake to come in after me, yet?"

The dragon spat. "Kedretitas does not make mistakes. Those are for lesser beings." The woman stood glowering, and Elyana felt a wave of fear crash against her, then break somehow against the breastplate, like the ocean parting against a reef.

The dragon screeched in fury. Her head swayed and bobbed in a reptilian way as the woman-shape sprinted forward in a fluid rush. One of her hands latched hold of Elyana's sword hand as the elf swung. Somehow it had gotten under her guard. The creature's speed was astonishing, and Elyana's brows rose in amazement as the dragon-woman lifted her by the wrist, grinning into Elyana's eyes. She twitched her fingers playfully as she reached for Elyana's throat with her free hand.

The pain lancing through Elyana's forearm was excruciating; she felt the bones grinding together and knew that she was moments away from hearing the bone snap. She inadvertently let go of her sword, which clanged into the stone behind the creature.

Out of desperation, Elyana slammed her gauntleted hand onto the dragon's shoulder. The result was better than she could have hoped: The beast whined in pain and released her. Elyana landed on her injured leg, grimacing.

Her arm throbbed and her ankle was afire with pain, but she smiled as she limped toward the retreating dragon.

"That hurt, did it?" Elyana asked.

"You're *nothing* without your little magical toys," the creature snarled. "They're not even yours. They belong to Zon-Kuthon and his loyal servants."

"Then why do they hurt you?"

"Their intent is shaped by their wearer, idiot!"

"If you want them, come and take them."

The creature screamed at her; Elyana didn't wait for whatever attack would come next. She dove for the beast's legs. The moment her armored hand struck the dragon, the creature's scream transformed into a cry of agony. Elyana's weight would not normally have staggered the creature, but the touch of the gauntlet did.

Elyana slammed into the ground, and the armor smashed into her chest, but even as she struggled for breath she pushed forward so that both gauntlet and breastplate touched the dragon's calves. The creature cried out in agony and wrestled away, kicking out a foot as she fought clear. The blow caught Elyana near the elbow, and she heard a snap at the same time pain washed through her arm.

Elyana clambered to her feet, panting. Even the slightest movement jarred her broken arm and sent waves of agony coursing through her body. The dragon lay unmoving, and Elyana's sword rested a few paces to the right. She hesitated only a moment to catch her breath and focus through the pain, but it was a moment too long. The dragon pushed herself up, her eyes bright red, one hand already shaping a symbol in the air.

Elyana lurched forward and grabbed the spellcasting hand with her gauntleted fingers. The dragon-woman's hand spasmed, and she screeched. Elyana clamped hard and dragged the thing with her.

"Wretch!" The dragon cursed her with unfamiliar words and fought to stay Elyana's progress by digging fingers into the stone. But they were human fingers, despite the dragon's great strength, and while her nails drew furrows in the stone, the creature still lacked good purchase. She was leveraging her feet beneath her when Elyana's hand closed on her sword.

Elyana's arm was bruised and broken. When her hand wrapped around the hilt and lifted, she screamed in agony as the weight of the blade pulled on the wounded limb, then screamed again, almost at a pitch with the dragon as she drove the weapon down through the gaping rent the lance had left in its dark dress.

The shock of the blow was so painful that the room momentarily blanked out around her. Elyana's hand slipped from the sword.

She came to a moment later, slumped down, her left hand still clasped about the human wrist of the creature dying beneath her. The dragon strove in vain to reach for the sword as black blood drained out from the wound. Elyana was spent, yet something troubled her; she wished she could remember what it was. Something about the dragon.

The dragon-woman stared up at her, her expression troubled. As her life passed, the face settled into a mask of disbelief.

Elyana gazed down at the still form for a long time before she released her hold with the gauntlet, then sank to her knees. Her sweat-soaked hair hung down across her eyes.

She was never sure how long she sat there, the dead dragon and the throbbing pain her only companions. Gradually she roused herself into motion, wondering how she might possibly leave the tower in her condition. She hadn't seen a ground-level door when she'd looked from above, but it might be hidden as the entrance above had been. If there were no way out below, she'd somehow have to lower herself from the tower—a monumental task, given her condition. First, she'd have to wrap and brace her arm one-handed, which was already more challenge than she desired.

And then Elyana realized what had troubled her. This was the dragon's assumed shape. It was a spell, and spells faded. How long would this one last?

Elyana lurched to her feet, taking her sword up in the gauntleted hand, for the other hung useless at her side. Every staggered step sent pins of agony through her arm. She gritted her teeth and soldiered forward. It would be good, she thought, to grab her bow—but how would she carry it? And how much time did she have?

The dragon's spell wore off. One moment there was a humanoid corpse in the room. The next, a massive black dragon occupied a space that could not possibly contain it. The creature's great skull slammed into the stone wall and her body bowed, straining against stones until they yielded, shattering the wall and flinging hunks of masonry into the open air.

Elyana was too slow, too tired, and too injured to reach the stairwell, and the tail lashed back from the wall and caught her in the chest. She was flung over the altar where the rest of the armor still lay and instinctively threw out her bad arm to catch herself. She landed on the arm, and knew only a moment of pain before blessed darkness finally claimed her so thoroughly that even the symbol glowing in her armor could not pierce it.

Chapter Sixteen
A Familiar Face

"Drink, Elyana."

She did as she was bade, for the voice was familiar, and kindly. Someone was holding a cup to her mouth, and she felt the pressure of the rim and the liquid against her lips. As she swallowed the bitter drink her senses swam back into focus and she grew aware of a hand supporting the back of her head. Beyond Arcil's troubled face she perceived the bulk of the dead dragon, a rough hole in the wall, the open sky beyond.

She blinked.

Her arm ached, but a tingling sensation spread down through her torso and out to her limbs as liquid passed into her throat. Almost immediately the pain in her extremities faded.

Arcil smiled down at her as she blinked again and raised her hand. Nice to be able to do so without pain, without shaking. Although she was still so very weary.

Arcil?

She struggled to sit up, assisted by Arcil's hand. "What are you doing here?" She was still too groggy

PLAGUE OF SHADOWS

to convey the depth of wrath she'd intended, and her delivery sounded more grumpy than threatening.

"I thought I was rescuing you," Arcil said drolly. "But apparently you did that all by yourself."

She stared at him, and all of the recent events clattered back into a kind of order.

He chattered on as though they were long-lost friends who'd chanced upon each other in the market. "Imagine my surprise to find the beast already slain. I happened to have some healing elixir, which you were sorely in need of."

Of course he'd been monitoring. The smile of satisfaction left no doubt in her mind.

And this, clearly, was the real Arcil, not another impostor with an illusion spell . . . although he hadn't aged, and was more handsome than she had recalled. His chin was a fraction larger, his nose a shade smaller, his hairline . . . it *was* an illusion spell, just one that was worn by the real Arcil.

She could see him watching her as she inspected him, and his smile thinned.

"Murderer," she growled.

His eyebrows rose minutely. "I believe I've just saved your life."

Elyana climbed to her feet, waving off his hand. "Kellius is dead because of you, and I was nearly—"

"I came," Arcil said forcefully, "as quickly as I was able." He actually sounded as though he were the injured party. "It took longer than I hoped to get here because I thought I needed a greater spell . . ." He fell short at her look. "You do understand that I'm the one who distracted the dragon so you could get to the tower, don't you? I'm the one who summoned the worm."

"An appropriate choice."

Arcil bared his teeth, then visibly mastered himself.

His manner astonished her. "You're insulted?" she demanded. "After all this, you're *offended*? You killed Calda, cursed Stelan, butchered poor Kellius . . ." She broke off as the image of the wizard's twisted corpse swam before her eyes and her throat tightened. She took a breath, then fixed his now stony face in her vision instead. "It's your fault I was lying here half-dead next to a dragon carcass!"

He did not answer. Only the fact that he'd most likely just saved her life kept her from immediately cleaving him in half, and she glared at him while she gathered her thoughts.

He wore dark leggings and boots, a well-tailored vest, and a shirt with an embroidered collar. Expensive, and likely of various colors, though in the shadow realm it was all gray to her. A shoulder bag lay at his feet.

"I see that you've donned some of the tower's garb, but not the crown," Arcil observed. "Where is it?"

"Hell if I know, and you're not getting the damned thing in any case."

"Vallyn stole the crown, didn't he?"

Elyana simply glared. "I won't let you have it."

Arcil gave a long-suffering sigh. "Yes, well, neither of us have it at the moment. And don't you need it for Stelan in any case?"

"Because you cursed him."

"He was being unreasonable!" Arcil's voice rose. He closed his eyes, and once again took a deep breath and visibly calmed himself. "I know how fond of him you still are."

"People are fond of dogs, Arcil. I love Stelan."

"I'll dismiss his curse—will that make you happy?"

"*Happy?* That might be a good start—"

"But I need the crown," Arcil said, talking over her.

Elyana's eyes narrowed in fury.

"I need the crown. I have no other option, Elyana. And now I've helped you. You know that you could not have left the tower without my healing."

"I owe you nothing."

"I believe you know better."

"I'm not in debt to you! You owe me for Stelan's curse and the death of Kellius—and for putting all of us through this."

"I am sorry about the wizard," Arcil said neutrally.

"You're always sorry, but you keep doing what you want!"

"I'll remove the curse from Stelan if you help me find the crown. How's that?"

"No." Elyana stepped away to her pack. She could walk from the tower, now, assuming she could scale the cleft.

Arcil groaned behind her as she secured the other strap of her breastplate. She had decided to take the armor and to let the future champions worry as they may about dealing with evil earth-rending gods.

"You don't even know how to wield the crown," Arcil continued. "And I know you don't have access to anyone that can help you understand its workings. There is no need for this. Help me recover the crown from Vallyn, and I'll cure Stelan."

He had a persuasive point, but she wasn't about to admit that to him. "'Cure' is an interesting word, from the man who afflicted him."

"My word is good, Elyana. I lied only once to you, and have vowed never to do so again."

She closed her eyes. "How long do you need it? A week? A day?"

"You're mocking me."

"Words cannot encompass what you're doing, Arcil. How long do you need it to assemble an army of shadows or whatever it is that you want?"

"In truth, I only require it for a few moments. What do you intend to do with it?"

"That's my business," Elyana said slowly, grimly enjoying the look of frustration on the wizard's face.

He scowled but remained silent.

Elyana sighed inwardly. As much as she hated to acknowledge it, her best course lay clear. "I'll help you, Arcil. But you have to lift Stelan's curse. Now. And I must have the crown when you're through."

His penetrating gaze might have given the dragon pause. He took a long, deep breath. "Very well."

"Lift the curse."

"Gather your things, and I shall do so."

"As easy as that? You don't have to teleport to him, or—"

"I must cast a spell," Arcil said. "We are agreed, then?"

"I suppose we are," she said, trying not to dwell on her anger. If Arcil had been this straightforward to start with, none of this—the deaths, the journey, the pain— would have been necessary.

She gathered her gear, and the armor, and the lance, which she found lying cockeyed on the stairs, and then they started up. Arcil said nothing until he began his spell.

After only a short while he declared that he was done. She thought about challenging his veracity, but knew he'd only repeat that he'd only ever lied to her once.

"We can teleport down to Stelan's boy from the top of the tower," Arcil told her.

She gestured for him to precede her on the stairs.

The portal closed behind them the moment they stepped clear.

"Stand ready," Arcil said.

"Don't we need to be on the roof to teleport?"

"No. It's the walls that are warded to prevent departure."

He noticed her crestfallen look. "What is it?"

"Nothing." Nothing but a tragic error. If they hadn't returned to the roof, unthinking, maybe Kellius would still be alive.

Or, she thought, if they had teleported from the tower and all five had faced the dragon without benefit of the armor, maybe all five of them would be dead.

Elyana's eyes drove up toward the ceiling, above which Kellius's shattered corpse probably lay. "Goodbye, Kellius," she said softly.

Arcil's hands stirred the air and he spoke harsh syllables in a stentorian voice. Black swirls formed around him and spiraled out in an expanding circle to envelop both them and the equipment. In a moment the rest of the tower dissolved. This spell did not evoke the sense of confusion and dislocation of the bard's magic. It was more secure and certain, somehow. Perhaps it was due to the ease with which Arcil cast it.

In a moment the trees took shape as though Arcil had conjured them into being. Elyana turned to take stock of their surroundings as Drelm appeared on her left.

His gaze shifted between her and the wizard, and his expression slowly darkened.

"What's going on?" he demanded.

"Where's Vallyn?" Elyana asked. She saw Renar scrambling down from a large tree.

Renar moved toward Elyana. "Praise Abadar! It's good to see you." She saw him searching behind her, consternation narrowing his eyes. "We saw you enter the tower," he continued, perplexed, "and we watched, and we saw the dragon fly up there . . . I tried shouting a warning to you, but—where's Kellius, and why's Vallyn wearing Arcil's disguise?"

"This is no disguise," Arcil said calmly. "I arrived in time to save Elyana. There was no help for Kellius. Has the bard returned to you?"

Drelm was lifting his greataxe.

"I don't understand," Renar said.

Arcil's well-groomed eyebrows lowered as the half-orc stepped close. "Be careful."

Drelm did not leave off.

"Hold!" Elyana commanded. "I asked a question. Where's Vallyn?"

Though puzzled and angry, Drelm managed to divert his attention to answer. "He was with you."

Elyana cursed quietly.

"What's wrong?" Renar asked. "Is Kellius really dead?"

"The dragon slew your wizard," Arcil said matter-of-factly.

Elyana wanted to add "thanks to you," but held back.

"Where's the dragon now?" Renar demanded.

"I killed it," Elyana said bluntly.

"By yourself?" Renar asked. Elyana's withering look was all the verification required.

"That is a mighty deed," Drelm said affably. "And now you've captured the wizard! But where is Vallyn?"

"Vallyn stole the crown." Elyana was aware that Arcil waited politely to correct the half-orc, so she continued quickly, "and Arcil is assisting us by his own choice. He has lifted the curse from your father, Renar."

"He has? Wait a moment—this is really Arcil?"

"Do you believe him?" Drelm asked.

Elyana looked at the wizard for only a moment. "I do." She turned to the others. "Vallyn stole the crown. Have you seen him?

"The last we saw, he was with you," Renar answered, still staring at the wizard.

"He must have teleported to another point in the valley. There's no telling how far he's gotten. Arcil—any idea how long I was unconscious?"

"A few minutes at most."

"So the bard has less than a quarter-hour lead," Elyana said. "But magic can fix that. Arcil, can you teleport to him?"

"I have to know a place, or scry it, before I can teleport to it."

"So scry it!"

"I can't."

"Why not?"

The wizard looked distinctly uncomfortable. "There are two problems with that. The first is that I have a limited number of powerful spells I can throw before I exhaust myself."

"What's the real reason?" Elyana demanded.

"Well," Arcil answered after a moment, "I don't actually know how to scry, myself. I had another wizard create an artifact for me some years ago so that I could use it."

"So you don't have to use a spell—that's even better."

Arcil cleared his throat. "Please don't take this the . . . there's nothing prurient in it—I would never . . ." At sight of her narrowing eyes, he spoke quickly. "It's centered only upon you."

Gods. Elyana's hands clenched and the wizard inched away. "You've been spying on me?" Her voice was low, dangerous.

"No—no . . . I just wanted to look in on you from time to time. On my friend Elyana. To make sure you were all right. I swear to you that was all it was."

"Do you want a medal for that? Gods!" She gritted her teeth and breathed in deep. "Do you have *no* decency?" Elyana turned on her heel. "Gather our things." She indicated the armor and lance with a wave, then tore off the breastplate. "This is for you," she told Renar.

"But . . ."

"Do as she says," Drelm instructed him.

Renar persisted, lowering his voice. "Vallyn's our friend, Elyana. Are you sure he stole the crown and it's not some trick of this wizard?"

"I can kill you, boy," Arcil said softly.

Elyana glared at her old comrade. "Arcil may be twisted, amoral, and soulless, but he's only ever lied to me once. Vallyn must have been planning to steal the crown from the start."

"But he's our friend," Renar repeated lamely.

"Time's wasting," Elyana told him. "Pack up the gear and move."

His head still swimming with the sudden shift in alliance and attitudes, Renar was only tangentially aware of the strange and marvelous armor with which Elyana had returned. He replaced his own breastplate and gauntlets with the finely made stuff. It was lighter than his own, and unmarred by even the smallest dent or flake of rust. He then helped Drelm wrap the rest of the armor and his original breastplate in their bedrolls, making cumbersome backpacks.

."What kind of symbol is this?" Renar asked Drelm, patting the broken harp thing on his chest. Arcil glanced at him then looked away. The elder wizard stood apart, and Elyana waited with her back to him beside a tree bole.

"No idea," Drelm replied.

"A symbol of two gods," Elyana said without turning.

Renar wasn't sure he felt comfortable wearing something sacred to any god other than Abadar, but withheld further comment as they started back, staying to the trees. "I can't believe Kellius is dead," he told Drelm quietly.

"He was brave," Drelm said. "I imagine he died well. The lady will tell us the tale when she is ready."

"He was a good man." Renar had difficulty believing the kindly spellcaster was really gone, and wondered, perhaps, if he had simply fallen off the tower edge. Might he come flying after them, as he had when they'd first thought him dead?

Surely Elyana would have told them if there were hope. She was being remarkably quiet, though. "It's hard to believe Vallyn was a traitor."

Renar was aware of Arcil keeping pace a few steps to their right, but the wizard's sudden pronouncement startled him all the same. "I never did trust him," Arcil said.

No one replied.

Elyana led them, watching the terrain. Somewhere in this valley was likely a small fortune hidden in a dragon's cave or hoard, and it would make some adventurer very happy one day.

It was odd that the forest never shifted, only the plain. The peculiar shifting landscape erupted twice after they exited the woods. The first time, a battalion of hyena-headed men marched suddenly into view with leveled pikes, only to disappear as quickly as they'd come. The second time a small hill laden with blooming flowers materialized on the valley's far side, bringing with it a sweet honey scent that lingered pleasantly even after it vanished.

Elyana glanced back at her charges and flexed her mended arm. She had not been able to keep from doing that, no matter that it seemed fully restored.

Once she had the crown, she was going to demand the degenerate wizard turn over whatever it was he'd used to scry on her, and then she'd smash it into a thousand pieces. She couldn't remember when she'd been so angry, but she strove not to give in to the fury. The landscape was too dangerous to lower her guard. Later, she could be livid. Later she could mourn the death of noble friends and old friendships.

The crystals covered the black earth ahead of them. She loosened the sword in her scabbard. There'd been nothing in the crystal forest the first time, but there were no guarantees.

Worries crowded in around her. What was Vallyn really planning? Later, she told herself. And then she heard the faint hollow clatter of wood against wood. As of an arrow against a bow.

"Down!" she roared, even as she threw herself flat.

Renar and Drelm cast themselves to the ground after Elyana. Arcil was a second slower.

Renar noticed that an arrow was sticking out of the wizard's shoulder when he dropped. His respect for the hated Arcil rose several notches when he observed that the man tugged the thing out with nothing more than a dark oath. Were all of his father's old comrades this tough?

"Lose the pack, young baron," Drelm hissed to him, then crawled for cover as figures popped out from behind the crystals. The identity of their attackers was no longer a mystery, for after the first arrow someone with a Galtan accent was cursing and another was ordering a second volley.

Renar contorted himself to stay flat as he wrestled off his cumbersome backpack. He followed on his belly after the captain, who was heading for a boulder.

And then darkness dropped all around them, so thick he could see nothing, not even the hand in front of his face.

"It's mine, Elyana," Arcil cried, and Renar realized after a moment of confusion that he meant the blackness.

"Too much!" came Elyana's response. "I can't—oh, to hell with it!" Her words were replaced by the sound of steel being drawn.

"Nice," Drelm growled. "Stay back, young baron," he said, and then came the sound of his footfalls, warring now with shouts of consternation from their Galtan attackers. Renar swore. Did they always have to keep him from the action?

The darkness was not absolute to Drelm. To his half-orc eyes, the Galtans stood revealed in their armor, leaning against the crystals with one hand as they hugged their bows in another. Restraining the urge to howl, he sprinted toward them.

As quickly as it had begun, the darkness ended, but by then Drelm was at close range, splitting the chest of a surprised Galtan with a savage blow that splashed blood to left and right. He yanked the gory weapon free as the man fell screaming, then threw up an armored forearm to catch a blade thrust tentatively his direction. The half-orc scarcely felt the blow, but his Galtan opponent reeled past, clutching at the hole where half his face had been.

Finally able to see, Renar hurried to his feet, his heart pounding. His sword was already drawn. He charged into the crystal forest and heard a variety of screams, all male. Of Drelm there was no sign, nor of the wizard Arcil, but off to his left he thought he heard the sounds of shouted mystic words, then a thunderclap and more screams.

He stepped over a Galtan who lay face-up beside a crystal, an arrow through his throat. He stared overlong at the blank eyes and almost missed the two soldiers backing toward him.

They saw him at the same instant. One muttered something incoherent and pointed. The other charged him with a sword.

It was then that Renar's training paid off. Days and months and years had made some fighting tactics a routine that removed thought from the equation, so that when the first soldier swung from his left, Renar was able to judge how far to step without even thinking. The blow missed him, and Renar exploited the opening with a quick slash that tore through the rusting hauberk and sent the soldier lurching with a cry of pain and a welter of blood. Renar parried an overhead blow from the second soldier with the flat of his blade, then drove his gauntleted fist up under the man's grubby chin. There was a surprising crack and the fellow dropped, limp. Renar had a moment to consider that his first real battle kill was with his hand rather than his blade, and then the first Galtan was on him again, screaming about liberty.

The man's swing was mad and desperate. Renar caught the blow, but on the edge, and could almost hear his father's cry of disapproval. He knew his father would not have minded so much the quick step and slash into his opponent's open side. The second strike in the same area was too much for the fellow, who reeled away with a cry of anguish, his sword ringing against a crystal as it dropped from his hand.

Renar scanned for more foes, flush with adrenaline and a little pleased with himself.

Then he saw Elyana.

He'd been pleased to finish off two Galtans. Elyana was advancing against a knot of six that called rude encouragement and brandished their weapons. He knew she was deadly, but that looked like suicide. He bit back a warning.

As the first two advanced, Elyana leaned almost gently into the one in the lead. He dropped, clutching his throat even as the blade twisted in her hand like a living thing and cut off his companion's sword hand. Blade and digits spun away as he crumpled. Elyana vaulted over him to swipe through the neck of the fellow immediately behind. As the head dropped free, her effortless backhand carved through an arm with raised sword and into the snarling face behind it.

Renar gaped. In less than a five-count, four opponents were down, and Elyana was still on the move.

HOWARD ANDREW JONES

She sidestepped a blow from another soldier, then whirled as he followed. Renar called to look out, for he'd seen a man with an axe rushing her from behind.

He needn't have worried. Elyana stepped clear at the last moment, and the axeman brained his ally. A cool thrust took the axe-wielder under the arm and through his heart. He fell gurgling.

It was the most astonishing thing Renar had ever seen. He roused himself from being a mere spectator, raised his sword, and ran after.

Of the Galtans Renar and Elyana faced together, the elf slew all but three. She flashed Renar a dangerous smile and left him panting to dash toward the sound of further conflict.

It was all over in a few more minutes. Renar was standing on the border of the crystal forest, watching tiredly as four Galtans hot-footed it toward the slope out of the vale, when Arcil stepped up beside him.

"You might want to cover your eyes," he said, and before Renar could ask why, the wizard raised one hand toward the fleeing Galtans. Arcil spoke a set of words in a twisted language Renar did not recognize, then lightning flashed from the wizard's fingertips. Renar turned his head too late and discovered that an imprint of the lightning's pattern seemed seared over everything he looked at. He blinked, and saw that where the running men had been were now twisted and smoking bodies.

"It will fade after a time," Arcil told him dispassionately, then stepped back into the crystal forest.

The four of them rendezvoused there. Elyana and Drelm were splashed with gore from head to foot. The half-orc grinned with savage joy. The bloodletting had clearly gone only a little way toward alleviating Elyana's anger, and she simmered still as she scanned for more foes.

Arcil looked pleased with himself. He showed no outward sign of damage, other than dark stains against his knees, presumably from grass. Renar was about to ask him about the shoulder wound—shouldn't there have been blood there?—when Elyana addressed the wizard.

"I thought I saw you with a live one."

Arcil pointed down at a gray-robed figure. "We can question this one."

"He's dead!"

Arcil smiled. "Oh, he's dead, but this Gray Gardener will tell us what we want to know."

Elyana frowned at this, and then her expression softened. She looked thoughtful.

"How'd Vallyn get past them?" Renar asked.

"A better question is how they got to us," Elyana asked. She then added, "We'd best check our friends."

For a moment Renar wasn't sure what she meant, and then his stomach lurched. How many Galtans had they faced? Twenty? Against three elves left with their horses? *Aliel*. He turned and meant to run.

"Renar!" Elyana stepped quickly over and seized his arm. She stared hard at him. "They're either alive and hiding, or they're dead. Don't rush. There may be Galtans out there still."

"If they've hurt Aliel," he declared, "I'll kill them all."

Chapter Seventeen
Among the Dead

Elyana and Drelm did most of the killing for him. A dozen Galtan soldiers had been left behind to guard the horses and the camp. There were a number of unfamiliar mounts, and all but one of theirs, along with the pack animals. But Persaily was gone.

Elyana found Aliel's body under one of the collapsed tents, apparently dead by her own hand. She had to show the young woman to the disconsolate Renar, who sank to his knees and wept.

The elven soldiers were slain, their bodies looted and naked save for undergarments. They'd been tossed away from the horses, and flies now gathered on their bruised and bloodied skin.

And Persaily was gone.

All the Galtans were dead, but that was no salve to Elyana's rage and sorrow. Numbed by it all, she joined Arcil.

The wizard had dragged the corpse of the Gray Gardener up from the crystals and into the clean air. Elyana would have thought she'd be happy to see colors again, to walk on green grass under a blue sky, but there seemed no joy left within her.

She watched as Arcil methodically, almost tenderly, straightened the dead man's limbs and removed his mask. The Gray Gardener's pock-marked face was fixed in a look of surprise. Elyana hadn't seen Arcil take down the spellcaster, but had heard the battle, and cause of death was clearly the blackened patch of clothing and flesh over the man's heart.

Arcil produced a squat black candle from a pouch at his waist and bent to the body.

Elyana looked up as Drelm approached, a shovel over one large shoulder.

"I thought I would get started digging," he said. "What's he doing?"

"Talking to the dead."

"Huh. Elves do get buried, right?"

"I don't actually know," she admitted slowly. "I never saw a funeral ceremony conducted by elves."

Drelm grunted and started to step away, but he stopped short as Arcil finished lighting the candle in the dead man's hand. Smoke rose from the little flame, thickening quickly.

"What do you mean 'talking to the dead'?" Drelm asked, and Elyana saw his hand tightening on the shovel.

"Grave candle," Arcil announced without looking up. "Extremely useful. But we only have five questions, so we need to make them count."

"Only five?" Elyana bristled.

"It will be fine," Arcil soothed. "I have experience with this sort of thing."

"I bet you do."

Arcil frowned a little, as though she were being uncharitable.

The candle smoke did not drift, but hung thickly, growing more and more substantial. Soon a smoky mirror image of the dead man had taken shape, complete to the face frozen in blank astonishment.

"Where is Vallyn going with the Crown of Twilight?" Arcil asked.

Elyana thought it dangerous to assume that the bard's theft had anything to do with the Galtans, especially since they had only five questions, but said nothing.

The ghost's mouth moved and his voice rose in answer, passionless and bland. "He has entered the shadow realm on his way to Woodsedge, where he shall take the crown to our mistress."

"He was a spy?" Drelm asked Elyana quietly.

Elyana's voice was tight. "He must have planned on betraying us from the start."

Arcil raised a quizzical eyebrow to Elyana. "Since when has Vallyn had shadow magic?"

Elyana winced. "He must have taken my ring."

Arcil, still cool and collected, held up a hand and spoke once more to the spirit. "And how did *you* come here, past the elves?"

"I am a master of travel magics. Our agent left us a sign."

"They must have meant us to run the risk, then take the crown," Elyana said to Arcil. "A strategy that probably sounds familiar."

A pained expression crossed Arcil's face, but he did not reply.

"That's why our escape from Woodsedge was easy," she said to Drelm. "Vallyn didn't kill *any* Gray Gardeners.

Easy enough to get the clothing and our weapons. And my ring. But why did they capture us in the city?"

Arcil must have decided that a worthwhile question, for he turned to address the hanging spirit. Tendrils of smoke continued to climb from the candle to weave into his form. "Why did you apprehend Elyana in the city if you meant to follow her?"

"There are many factions of liberty," it answered with disinterest. "Sometimes the right hand is unaware of the left. Elyana is wanted, thus one group apprehended her when she was recognized in the temple. Then the other managed her release."

Arcil turned to Elyana. "We have but two questions left, and one of them must be to ask for the Gray Gardener sign and countersign. Is there anything in particular you have to know?"

"I wish you'd kept one alive," Elyana said. "There's an awful lot I'd like to know. How long Vallyn's been their spy. What they're planning to do with the crown. Who their mistress is . . ." Elyana stopped short. "I bet it's Nadara."

"Lathroft's niece?" Arcil asked her, incredulous.

"I thought you'd been scrying us. Yes. She was there to help us escape."

"I can't watch you constantly," Arcil said. "Are you sure it was Nadara?"

"I'm certain."

Arcil turned to consider the ghost, then looked back to Elyana. "Gray Gardeners may not know the true identity of their leaders. That's part of the reason they wear their masks. It would probably be a wasted question. I'd like to know what they want with the crown."

"Ask, then," Elyana told him.

He did. "Why are you looking for the Crown of Twilight?"

"The mistress tasked us with its recovery."

Arcil grimaced. "I should have phrased the question more carefully."

"You should have left him alive," Elyana pointed out again.

"Easier said than done. There is one thing more I wish to know, Gardener. What is your sign and countersign?"

"When challenged, this week I am to say 'beautiful and blue.'"

With that final word, the image within the smoke faded away, and the vapors themselves were carried off by the wind at the same moment the tiny flame burning along the wick extinguished itself.

Arcil bent down to retrieve the spent and melted candle, then the dead man's mask and hat.

"Gods!" Elyana dearly wanted to kick in the dead man's head, but she satisfied herself with another long curse. "He stole my ring, and my horse. He stole my horse! And we've no way to catch him."

"I was always suspicious of Nadara," Arcil said thickly. "I've often wondered whether that girl had meant to lead us into her uncle's trap, and didn't know what to do when we survived."

"It looks like she took up the craft for the Galtans. I knew Vallyn was interested in her, but—" Elyana sighed. Vallyn had been interested in about any girl with a pretty face. What had led to continued contact with the niece of a shadow wizard? What had led him to do any of this? She'd thought him a friend, and Elyana did not use that word lightly.

"I can get us to the Plane of Shadow," Arcil said. "And I'm sure you can track him there, can't you?"

"Possibly," Elyana said. "But he's got a head start."

"Then we waste time."

"We have to bury the dead," Drelm said.

Elyana had almost forgotten he stood there.

Arcil chuckled then glanced at Elyana. "What a solicitous orc you ride with. Is this your doing?"

Drelm snarled. "I am half-*man*, wizard, and better acquainted with honor than you!"

Arcil arched an eyebrow threateningly.

"We bury the elves," Elyana said to Drelm. "I don't give a damn about the Galtans."

"They can feed ravens," Drelm agreed.

"Must we really dig?" Arcil said. "I thought you wanted—"

"What I want and what is the right thing to do are sometimes different things. We bury these dead. They'd have done the same for us."

"You think so?" Arcil said, skeptically. "I thought you didn't know any elven rites."

"We shall give them the respect they're due," she said tightly. "I'd treat any ally the same. Even you." She faced Drelm. "Let's get to it."

They had brought only one shovel of their own, but found three others among the Galtan supplies. That was enough for each of them, although Arcil abstained.

There was no time for deep graves, and after only a little while she and Drelm were casting dirt over the pale faces of their two elven chaperones.

A red-eyed Renar bore the corpse of his love from the tent they had shared only the night before, then lay her beside the grave he himself had dug.

"Is there nothing that can be done?" he asked Elyana quietly.

Her heart sank. "I'm sorry, Renar. That kind of magic is far beyond me."

Renar licked his lips and slowly, ever so slowly, looked over at Arcil. "What of you? What about this Crown of Twilight? If we bear her with us, will it . . . can it bring her back? Might it bring all of them back?"

Arcil's reply sounded almost kindly. "No. The subject must still be alive, or . . . preserved in some way."

The boy seized on this faint hope "We can preserve her. Can you help me do it?

"That's not what I meant." Arcil was still patient. "Her soul is fled."

Renar stared at him for a long moment, then bowed his own head. He put one hand to the bridge of his nose and Elyana saw him crying, quietly. She motioned to Drelm, then helped the half-orc lower the girl gently into the rectangular hole. They stepped back, and Drelm unceremoniously tossed in the first shovelful of dirt.

After a moment, Renar joined in, tears tracking down his face all the while, and bit by bit the beautiful elven girl disappeared beneath the soil. When the mound was high enough, the three of them set down their shovels and leaned against them.

"We should say a few words," Renar managed in a choked voice.

Arcil's sigh was not terribly loud. Elyana shot him a warning look anyway.

Renar lay the shovel down, spread his open hands and looked into the heavens. "Holy Abadar, I know that you were not the lord of these folk, but they died on a mission to aid one of your most faithful adherents. I ask only . . ." here he faltered before quickly regaining his composure, "only that you help to guide them on their way and shield them until they find the light of their own god or goddess."

"We also ask that you guide the soul of our friend Kellius," Drelm said.

Renar nodded. "Yes. Glorious Abadar, the wizard bravely gave his life trying to save the life of my father, who has dedicated his life to you. We pray that you welcome Kellius into your heavenly vault."

"Amen," Arcil said, just a hair too quickly. Elyana pretended not to have noticed.

"Now a moment of silence," Drelm commanded gruffly.

And so Elyana bowed her head, thinking that Stelan had taught Renar well, if he could speak so easily over the burials. She thought again of the stern and competent elven warriors. Their lives had been lost because they'd come to safeguard Elyana's band. And then she thought of poor Aliel, so young by elven standards, scarcely grown. The slow-birthing elven race would mourn her long after there was nothing left of Renar but dry bones.

She felt Arcil's eyes upon her. His expression was solemn. What did he believe she was thinking? He tipped his head a fraction of a degree toward the others, whose heads were still bowed.

Ah. He thought that they two were comrades and knew better than these hangers-on. Perhaps they did.

She realized that all three men were looking at her.

"We are ready," Drelm told her.

Renar wiped tears away and nodded. His cheeks were red and raw.

Elyana had allowed her thoughts to scatter. She marshaled her discipline. "Arcil, you can teleport these two straightaway to Stelan, can't you? You know the place."

"I could. Are you ready?" he asked the others.

"You will not use magic upon us," Drelm said with a low growl.

Arcil paused briefly, and his eyes glinted. "Well, I suppose you can walk back to Adrast, then. Good luck on your journey." He turned to Elyana. "Shall we?"

"We can't let Vallyn get away," Renar interjected.

"Arcil and I will find him. I gave my word to help, but I did not pledge your aid as well."

A deep rumble rose from the half-orc's throat. "Lady, the crown is promised to the holy church."

Arcil gasped in horror. She'd forgotten that he hadn't known what she planned with it.

"Abadar honors those who honor their promises," Drelm said. "I will ride with you. For the crown. And because it pleases me. And because the bard needs killing."

"That he does," Renar said fiercely, surprising Elyana a little. "Besides, we can't let the Galtans get the thing. Didn't you say it allows the power over life and death? What will they do with that?"

"They've an endless supply of bodies," Arcil said. "Mostly headless, all ready to be animated as wights—or worse. Knowing the Galtans, they're planning an invasion to bring 'liberty' to Taldor or the River Kingdoms."

Renar's eyes widened. "An invasion?"

"I don't know," Arcil said. "It's the blunt and obvious thing, which is typical of Galtans. That or an army of shadow beings are their most likely aim."

"Abadar preserve us," Renar said, then eyed Arcil suspiciously. "Why do *you* want it?"

"That's private."

"Private," Elyana repeated. And suddenly her composure snapped. "It's anything but 'private,' Arcil!

People have died because of you. Now you're telling us that Vallyn might be giving the Galtans a powerful weapon? They wouldn't have access if you hadn't sent us after the crown."

"I didn't send you after it," Arcil pointed out. "And it's not my fault that Vallyn's a backstabbing traitor. Although I could have told you that."

"You have no honor," Drelm spat, and the wizard bristled.

"You have no idea who you're speaking to, you ignorant savage!" All civility had vanished. "I can slay you with a wave of my hand. You know nothing about my honor!"

Elyana held up a hand to Drelm, but as she looked over Arcil she could not keep from a final statement, her words dripping with disgust. "You think that honor is merely keeping your word, and being loyal to the few you deem worthy."

"I find it charming you think it something more," Arcil snapped. His voice took on a sanctimonious note. "You have an endearing notion that kindness begets kindness. But most people are only out for themselves. How much kindness did you give to Vallyn? And he betrayed you. In a lifetime you might encounter but one or two people who are really worth your trust."

It was long past time that she might have been able to get through to him about matters of honor. There was one point, though, that he had to be made to understand. "Drelm is an ally. You will cease threats against both him and Renar, Arcil."

"So long as they do not threaten or insult me."

"You heard him," she said without much enthusiasm. Drelm grunted. Renar remained silent.

"All right, you two. I welcome your company, and thank you for it. So does Arcil," she added. "Gather our horses and some spares. We're going after another one of my old friends. You know the funny thing, Arcil? He always predicted we'd have to hunt *you* down."

Interlude
The Last Gathering

"Well," Stelan said, uncharacteristically hesitant, "what do you think?"

He stood in a ray of sunlight that beamed through the wide window of his great hall, his arms raised high at his sides, palms up, as though he were a priest urging his congregation to their feet. But he spoke only to Elyana and Vallyn.

Fine white robes with blue piping draped him. Elyana had just finished knotting a matching blue sash about his waist.

She stepped back to admire the effect, glancing over at the bard. Vallyn sat on the nearby mead hall table, one leg dangling off its edge, the other propped on the nearby bench. Servants would shortly be gathering in the hall to set the places for Stelan's wedding feast, but for now they were alone.

"You look wonderful," Elyana told him. And he did—the sunlight shone down on the neatly combed hair, granting him a false halo and highlighting a few curling strands that had refused to remain ordered. In the bright light his hair looked almost blond, and his eyes shone. With his broken nose and scarred face, he could probably not be called handsome, but he was fair, and she loved him. And he was hers no longer.

"You look so good I'm thinking about marrying you myself," Vallyn quipped, and Stelan chuckled.

The baron's eyes tracked to the narrow archway through which they had all come a quarter-hour before. Just visible were the first of the worn steps that wound up to the living quarters.

"Where are Eriah and Arcil?" Stelan asked.

"They were still drinking when I went to bed," Vallyn replied.

"Arcil, drinking?" Elyana had rarely seen the man indulge himself with anything, most especially drink. He hated being out of control.

"Oh, yes," Vallyn answered. "Surely you saw. He was in an even worse mood than usual."

"I don't know what he has to be mad at you about," Stelan said.

Vallyn shook his head. "It was foolish to invite him. He went bad a long time back."

Stelan made a half-hearted scoffing noise.

"He's been treading the dark path a long, long time," Vallyn continued.

Elyana thought that assessment a little too simplistic, but she did not correct the bard; it was she who'd insisted that Stelan invite their old companion. They hadn't seen him in more than six months, not since they'd parted ways outside the keep.

Vallyn would not leave off. "He's been studying those tomes, and they've rotted his brain. We should've burned them."

"He was a loyal friend to us," Stelan said. "It would be ungracious to leave him out. It is you who never liked him."

Vallyn shrugged. "He never liked me."

"Well," Stelan said, "I like you both. Let's hear no more of this." He clapped his hands, and after a short moment a pageboy came running. The lad's hair was newly shorn, and a little unevenly. His red tabard, emblazoned with Stelan's coat of arms, was improbably clean. Elyana could not believe that he was wearing it with two hours left to go before the wedding ceremony, but someone had allowed him access to the garment, and he was so proud to be dressed in it he practically strutted. The boy bowed grandly and gazed up with eyes shining in adoration. "Yes, Baron?"

"Go look in on master Eriah and master Arcil, if you please. If they are not awake, rouse them. But gently."

"Yes, Baron." The boy bowed deeply and then dashed off in such a hurry he almost missed the stairwell. He scampered up the steps and his footfalls could be heard against the stone in quick succession.

Vallyn cupped hands to his mouth and called after: "If they don't get up, send for me, and I'll wake them with a bucket of water!"

"Now that you say it," Stelan said, "you'd best follow. That boy might be in for a rude surprise if they're both hung over."

Vallyn grinned, hopped down from the table, and started up the stairs, though at a far more relaxed pace.

Then Elyana found herself alone with Stelan in his wedding raiment. Judging by his expression, Stelan had just realized the situation himself. For weeks, he'd been quite careful that they not be alone together. Lenelle remained keenly aware of their past relationship.

"So," Elyana said brightly, stepping closer. "This is your wedding day."

Stelan spoke as if unaware that anything were awkward. "It is good to be surrounded by friends. We have done so much together. None of this would have been possible without you. My lands restored. The people on them safe. The shadow wizards dead or driven into hiding. I owe so much to you." Stelan cleared his throat, and an awkward silence settled between them.

"Stelan," Elyana began softly, "have you told her everything?"

"She knows that we were intimate," the baron answered uncomfortably.

"That I gathered when her attitude grew even colder."

"Be more generous, Elyana. It is only natural to be jealous of you."

"Is it because she knows you still love me?"

"I don't want to do this again."

Neither did Elyana, really, so she fell silent.

Apparently Stelan hadn't quite had enough, though, because he kept talking, almost shyly. "I shall never forget you. But . . . we're too different."

"We are far more alike than we are different," Elyana reminded him.

Stelan looked away from her. "Revisiting this isn't like you, Elyana. We've made our choices."

"You don't have to make this choice. I don't think you really want to marry her. You like her; you think you can grow to love her, out of duty. You do not have to grow to love me. You already do."

"I do," Stelan conceded. "But what of it? How does that help my people? Will there be children?"

"There might be."

"If you wish it. And you do not. I must have children—you saw what happened to the realm—"

"Then appoint a successor."

"It's not just about you, Elyana," Stelan said, sounding disappointed. "And it's not just about me," he added, so low that she barely heard him.

"There are other ways, Stelan. This is our last chance. When you pledge your vows—"

"Would you take up the call of Holy Abadar, Elyana?" He stepped forward and roughly clasped her hands. "Would you do that? You ask me to give up hope of a son and heir, for you. Would you do that, for me?"

She looked into those dark eyes. "Why must you cling to that god—"

"The god of my family, for generations."

"So I should take up your religion because it is habit? He is lord of the moneychangers!"

Elyana grew conscious of a patter of feet on the stairs. The pageboy, from the sound of things, coming at a run. She might have paid more heed if she'd not been watching Stelan's brows darken.

"He is a lord of balance," Stelan said, his voice rising. "Do not blaspheme!" He thrust her hands away. "You will never bend. You wish me to give all, and—"

"Lord! Baron!" The page burst out of the archway and stared at them, panting. "Something horrible—Lord Eriah's dead—Lord Vallyn says you must come—"

Stelan looked at the boy as if seeing him for the first time. He fixed Elyana with a brief, dark stare, then hurried toward the child. Elyana started to go after him.

"Elyana!" Arcil's voice. She turned to find him hurrying toward her from the servants' entrance to the kitchen, lean and regal in his dark tunic and leggings, beard carefully trimmed.

Stelan did not slow his race after the boy, and soon disappeared up the stairs. Elyana paused at the bottom step, waiting for Arcil to reach her. "Did you hear that?" She meant about Eriah's death, but Arcil, as he frequently did, failed to understand her true meaning.

"I heard everything," he said, stepping closer.

"What?"

A wiser man, or one less desperate, would have been warned off by the lowering of her brows.

"You insist on wanting him, Elyana. You think he's a partner, an equal. But he has never been."

"Oh, gods. Arcil, that page said Eriah's dead—"

Arcil took a determined step forward, holding her eyes with his own. "He's a fine warrior, Elyana—an accomplished swordsman. But think back. It was always you who did the best thinking. Who dropped through the portal to fight the dragon? Who outflanked the Galtan sorcerers? Who planned the escape from Woodsedge?"

"Arcil, your timing is—"

She fell silent as he came closer than he had ever before dared and rested one hand against her shoulder. His gaze was steady, his breath fresh and smelling faintly of mint. "You only imagine that Stelan is your equal because you are lonely. You see something more than is there. Stelan knows it. He's known it for a very long time."

Slowly, reluctantly, he released her. "No one has ever mattered to me more than you, Elyana. No one. I—"

"Arcil." She spoke his name with deliberate slowness. "Eriah is dead. Do you hear? Do you care?" And with that, she turned her back on him and started up, wondering that she could care about someone so callous and self-absorbed. She heard Arcil following behind her, though he said nothing.

Up the stairs she went, then into the upper hall and the chamber with the open door, outside of which a pair of maids waited nervously. They stepped aside when they saw her and Arcil.

Within was only a small room and a small, narrow window, its shutters thrown wide. Light poured through it in a focused stream to illuminate the blankets on the bottom of the bed. Eriah had not made it beneath them; he lay across the crimson covers, one boot on, one off, his face locked in an expression of utter terror.

Alive, he and his twin had always been remarkably good-looking, with fine, even features, sandy hair, and charming smiles. But Daramont had died under the dragon's claw and Eriah had died . . . how?

Stelan stood staring grimly down at his dead friend. Vallyn waited beside him, and his expression twisted in fury the moment he saw Arcil.

"Where have you been?" the bard demanded.

Arcil scowled. "What business is it of yours?"

"Eriah's dead by wizardry!" Vallyn shouted. "And what other wizards do you see around here?"

"You think I would kill him?" Arcil asked haughtily. "Why would I do that?"

Stelan's voice was low, controlled. Elyana recognized that his temper was but barely held in check. "The maids heard you arguing with him late last night. Do you deny it?"

"I do not."

Stelan pressed on, a threatening undercurrent in his voice. "Did you kill him?"

"I did not," Arcil replied evenly.

"He's lying," Vallyn spat.

"I never lie!" Arcil countered.

"What would you have me believe, Arcil? How do you explain the death of the man, in my home?" Stelan's voice rose. "On the night before my wedding day?"

"I don't know, Stelan," Arcil answered stiffly. "But I know that I did not kill him."

"What were you arguing about?" Elyana asked.

"That is a private matter."

"You and your private matters," Vallyn sneered. "It's not private now, wizard. I know how you keep your word. If your magic killed him, does it mean you did not? Is that how you think you're a truth-teller?"

Arcil's lips twisted up and he stepped toward the smaller man.

"Enough!" Stelan roared. He moved between them with arms outstretched. He gave Vallyn a brief, warning glance, then turned the whole of his attention to Arcil. "Are you responsible for his death?"

Arcil drew himself up slowly. "I am not."

Stelan eyed the man for a long, long time, then finally let out a breath. "That is good enough for me."

Vallyn made a scoffing noise. "What does Elyana say? She'll know whether he's telling the truth or not. And I could compel him—"

"The day I let you throw a spell on me—" the wizard began.

"He speaks the truth," Elyana interrupted. She stepped over to the body. "It might be that an old injury finally did him in. Or the drink. It happens sometimes."

Vallyn looked back and forth suspiciously between her and Arcil.

"Say nothing of this to my bride," Stelan said. "She will not think it a good omen. That we should bury a guest, a friend, on the day we are to wed—"

"Say no more," Vallyn said quickly. "We'll carry on as though nothing's happened. And I can handle the burial arrangements."

"I'll speak to the servants," Elyana said. "You should ready yourself. Today you celebrate—tomorrow we shall speak over our friend."

"There are prayers that must—"

"Eriah was no follower of Abadar," Elyana said. "I will summon a cleric. Let us care for him, Stelan. You must think of your bride, and the wedding."

"Elyana's right," Arcil said.

Stelan nodded slowly, and Vallyn reached up to put a guiding hand on his shoulder. "Let's get you back downstairs. You should probably eat something, too. Wouldn't want you getting a nervous stomach before the ceremony."

Stelan nodded and glanced speculatively at Elyana as the bard led him away.

Any opportunity for their final words had now passed. It had been her last chance to reach him. She dared not allow her simmering anger to master her, for Stelan needed her aid. She called for the maids after his departure, and spoke to both them and the page, impressing upon them that the baron would be sorely displeased if word of the death were to reach the ears of the mistress this day. They assured Elyana that they would keep things secret.

Arcil waited the while, looking out the window. He did not turn back to her until she dismissed the servants and shut the door.

"That was good of you to protect me," he told her.

"You think I lied for *you*?" Elyana's voice was thin and cutting. "Why did you kill him? He was our friend, Arcil! What were you doing?"

"He planned to court you—I lost my . . . it was a mistake, and—"

"You killed him because he planned to court me?" Elyana's voice rose shrilly. She stepped closer, feeling a murderous rage of her own take shape. "You thought I would want him? You thought he could just take me?"

"I was drinking."

"You lied to me."

He looked away.

"How did you excuse your earlier words, Arcil? Vallyn was right, wasn't he? You killed him with a spell so that you didn't personally lay hands on him."

"It was . . ." his voice trailed off. "I lost control because . . . because I love you, Elyana. I have always—"

"You know nothing of love, Arcil! You confuse it with ownership!"

"I'm no fool!" he countered. "You owned Stelan's heart, and he yours. But I never understood why. His strength? His looks? Eriah was far better-looking and had that same kind of strength. And he was younger—"

She slapped him hard enough that his head twisted hard to the left. The sound of the blow echoed through the room. His hand rose, but he did not retaliate.

"It's always about you! Edak died that night because you couldn't bear to wake Stelan first. You killed Eriah because you thought he could take me—as if I would want a handsome simpleton!"

"He announced he would win you or—"

"It's my choice, Arcil!"

"Your choices make no sense!" he shouted back. "Why Stelan? He has neither your skill nor your intellect!"

"And you have both?"

"I do. And you know it."

"You are a murderer. You think first of yourself, always."

"No—I think first of you!"

"Of possessing me! That's not love. Do you think I lied to Stelan to protect you? I lied to protect *him*. It is bad enough you killed someone on his wedding day. But if he were to know that you did it? Gods, you're a selfish bastard!"

"Elyana, please. All I've ever wanted is you."

"Get away from me."

"No, you don't understand. I can—"

Elyana stepped back. He started to follow, but she flung up a hand, her mouth a thin line. "I can and will kill you with my bare hands, Arcil." She spoke slowly and carefully. "Stay away from me. Forever."

Then she backed toward the door, leaving him shaking and breathing in great gasps.

Arcil did not turn up that afternoon at the ceremony, and no servants reported his departure. Elyana would not see him again for more than twenty years.

Chapter Eighteen
From Shadow to Nightmare

Elyana watched the portal to the Plane of Shadow swirl into existence. The immaterial edges of the gateway Arcil summoned with his wand were hazy and blurred, but the dark land beyond was distinct, crisp. Black and white and gray. Depressing.

"I've come to hate shadows," Renar said.

Elyana wondered if he recalled that Vallyn had voiced very similar opinions. And then she scowled at thought of the bard.

Her gelding shifted nervously beneath her. The horse laid back his ears as Elyana guided him through.

The others followed swiftly, and then Arcil closed the portal. The Galtan mounts and the pack animals whinnied back and forth in agitation until Elyana urged them to settle.

Finally she could scan the horizon. The long black grass of the shadow steppes grew in every direction. The mountains rose on the horizon like the teeth in an ebon saw blade, and clouds hung like tattered banners in the gray sky.

Elyana slid from her mount and bent to search for tracks.

Arcil's horse was especially shy, both of the place and of him. The animal danced nervously as the wizard waited. "I wish we could just teleport and wait for him outside the city," he said.

"Can you do that?" Renar asked. The harp symbol on his breastplate glowed like a beacon in the Plane of Shadow.

"I can," Arcil said, "but there's no guarantee Vallyn will make it out of here alive."

"Not if we catch him," Drelm said.

Elyana swung up into her saddle. "Let's ride."

It was difficult to judge time and distance in a place with no sun, where the land shifted subtly and the stars drifted overhead like the clouds. Still, Elyana knew there could be little doubt as to Vallyn's direction; he'd taken the only obvious pass through the brooding crags. Sure enough, after what she guessed was half an hour, they picked up Vallyn's trail proper. He had been pushing Persaily hard, rarely letting her walk. The bard was a practiced enough horseman that he knew better, and Elyana seethed.

Soon they were riding steadily through a wide, twisting canyon, mountain slopes on either side so dark they might have been fashioned from black marble.

"There are those who say that the land really has no geography," Arcil was saying to the others. He sounded completely at ease and unwinded.

Arcil continued his impromptu lecture. "The wizard Corwin once wrote that you shape shadow to your own needs as you ride through it, though I have often thought he likely referred to a different kind of shadow."

"How many different kinds are there?" Renar asked.

The question seemed to please Arcil. "You're more curious than your father, boy. Why, I might spend a dozen lifetimes studying them all."

"There's something following us," Drelm called from the rear.

Elyana wheeled and cantered back to the half-orc, who held both reins in one hand while he pointed back with his right.

She stared into the narrow mountain pass behind them and perceived a cloud of dust raised by riders dimly outlined within. They were all of darkness, but the beasts they rode had manes of white flame and hooves that struck ivory sparks whenever they touched ground. Three rode in front, and there were at least four behind.

"Nightmares," Arcil said. "Ridden by some kind of shadow or fiend."

"Are they after us?" Renar asked.

"They are now," Arcil answered. "They might have sensed Vallyn's passage, or ours."

Drelm grunted. "Did the Galtans send them?"

"I think not," Arcil replied. "There are living beings here, creatures which hate our life force and crave it."

"I'd say we've about a half-hour," Elyana said, "if we ride hard."

"Can we outride them? Drelm asked. "Our horses are fairly fresh."

Arcil shook his head. "Those are nightmares. We must either exit the plane or even the numbers if we are to have any chance at all."

"Then we'd best ride until we find a place to make a stand." Elyana kicked the gelding into gallop, and the others followed.

Neither the mountains nor the pass were directly analogous to the landscape in the real world. Before very long at all they had passed through them both and returned to the steppe.

Drelm rode at the rear, and soon called up that perhaps eight of the animals were following. "They're gaining on us," he added.

"They've been galloping this whole time," Renar noticed after a backward glance. "How do they keep galloping?"

"They're nightmares," Arcil answered. "They don't really tire."

"We could just leave," Drelm said. "And come back."

"There are several problems with that," Arcil said. "We have Vallyn's trail, now. If we leave, we may not be able to get back to the same place, even if we remain at the same point in the real world."

Drelm grunted.

"And if these fellows catch Vallyn," Arcil added, "then they'll have the crown."

"So do something," Renar said. "You have other spells, don't you? Didn't you send a shadow hound and other monsters against Elyana and Drelm and poor Kellius?"

"Let's keep riding," Elyana said. She was still holding out for better fighting ground.

Drelm seemed to have guessed her thoughts. "There's nothing but grassland here," he objected.

"That's all we can see now," Elyana replied. "The Plane of Shadow shifts."

She would have preferred to have her point demonstrated to the half-orc in some dramatic fashion—a sudden upthrust of rock, say, or a wooded hilltop. But the steppe stretched on, and the horsemen followed relentlessly like a tide. They could be no more than ten minutes away. Elyana dared not push the horses faster, for fear of losing Vallyn's trail.

And then they arrived at the river.

She slid off her horse and advanced to look into the inky, featureless darkness. It looked barely wider than a stream, but there was no seeing through to its bed. Within she could discern no sense of motion or flow, either—the liquid might as well have been glass.

Elyana searched the ground for Persaily's tracks and discovered that they'd stopped abruptly about ten feet from the edge. Probably the bard had used another of his teleport spells. He'd claimed to have only one left. It hadn't been his first lie.

"Is this the river we crossed in the real world?" Renar asked. "Near Woodsedge?"

"Maybe. Or it might not have a true analogue. Arcil, how safe is this to cross?"

"It's not." Rather than explaining, Arcil produced his wand with a dramatic flourish and pointed it toward the river. Its tip glowed as a thin line of darkness stretched over the river, then widened to five paces as though it were an ebon plank.

"Clever," Elyana said, though she doubted the horses would find it especially comforting. She urged her own mount out, but the gelding was doubtful. He reached the river's edge, whinnying in complaint. She was too distracted calming him to pay heed to the pack animal she led. It was so frightened that it jerked away with great violence, parting the worn leather lead line Elyana had tied to the saddle ring. The animal tore away at a hard gallop along the stream's edge, trailing the severed rope.

There was no time to follow. Elyana urged her horse the rest of the way across, then called for the others.

Drelm managed it with both his spare animal and his own, but Renar's pack horse was frightened out of its wits. It bucked so wildly that Renar had to draw his sword and slash free the lead line before he or his own mount was injured. Freed, the crazed horse galloped after Elyana's.

Arcil rode last. His animal's ears were flattened and its eyes showed whites, but it seemed calm until an arching, segmented body surfaced beside the bridge. At sight of the monster the horse reared, and Arcil was cast off the saddle. His arms flailed uselessly for purchase, but there was nothing for him to grab, and he plunged sideways into the ebony liquid.

Elyana was off her mount and running forward as Arcil's horse and the spare tied by lead line to his saddle galloped madly over the shadow bridge to their side. She dodged their hooves and stood at the river bank.

"Arcil!" She screamed out his name, sword in hand. At some level she was surprised to learn how worried she sounded—an instinctive reaction for an old friend? It was not, she realized, merely her worry that they needed him to get out.

Drelm swore colorfully, and Elyana heard all the horses shuffling, snorting, and whinnying to each other.

"Keep them calm!" Elyana called. She was astonished by the Galtan horses. She would never have pronounced such poorly trained animals ready for service.

Arcil pulled himself up to the riverbank. She reached out a hand to aid, then saw what the river had wrought and stifled a cry of terror. The clothes hung on an emaciated frame, and browned, dried skin clung to Arcil's skeletal fingers.

His head swung up, and Elyana saw that where his eyes should be there were only two flaming points of light. He had no nose, only a gaping black hole. What hair had not fallen away to expose his mummified head was stiff and unkempt.

The lipless mouth moved, and Arcil's voice rose from the creature. "Aren't you going to help?" he asked indignantly.

It was then she understood that this had not been done by the river. "Arcil—what did you do to yourself?"

From somewhere close by, Renar cried out to Abadar and urged her to kill it. But she could not tear her eyes from the wreck of her old friend.

Arcil looked down at his withered hand as he pushed himself up to the bank. He climbed to his feet and resolutely met her eyes, as if daring her to say more.

"Kill him, quickly!" Drelm urged.

Elyana heard the captain thump up beside her. "Hold!" she snapped without turning to look at him.

A ropy black tentacle lashed out of the liquid, fastened about the wizard's ankle, and tugged. Arcil fell hard on that bony face and was hauled back toward the inky river with lightning speed.

Elyana grabbed his arm, pulling, half afraid the dried skin and bones would rip off in her hand. It was no good, though, for she was being pulled off balance.

The tentacle and the foot it clasped hung just over the liquid. She threw herself flat against the riverbank next to Arcil, grasped his bony upper thigh through his pants as the creature drew him further, then stabbed down. The blade lit the river incandescently, though she could not see the thing it stabbed. The moment she made contact, though, the tentacle relinquished its hold and snaked away.

Elyana scrambled back, cast down her sword, grasped Arcil's hands, and pulled him to safety. They both backed away from the river, watching the surface. It was smooth and tranquil again.

The riders, though, were close enough now that Elyana could pick out details on their armor.

And Arcil was a lich.

Drelm and Renar still waited to the side. The young man's face was twisted in revulsion. Drelm was deadly serious, and had his greataxe poised for use.

"Gods, Arcil," she said. "Look at you."

"Now do you see why the matter is private?" Arcil hissed. He grasped the links of a chain hidden by his collar, then pulled the links up until he'd lifted a pendant.

Elyana waved and the half-orc backed off, though he watched cautiously.

The thing that was Arcil cradled the pendant in the palm of his skeletal hand. Through his fingers she could glimpse a small golden oval set with an amethyst that almost perfectly matched the shade of her eyes. There appeared to be writing upon it, and a clasp, but it was small enough that the details were hidden in Arcil's palm. "The river must dampen or cancel some sorts of magic," he muttered, and opened the lid of the pendant. He twisted something inside the necklace between thumb and forefinger—and his appearance was restored.

He closed the jewelry with a snap and slipped it back under his shirt, then stood to consider them all.

"He needs killing," the half-orc said.

"You would die trying, orc," Arcil told him. "Only my affection for Elyana leaves you whole, after what you have seen. Do not test me. Do you understand now, Elyana? Why I couldn't come to you, or Stelan?"

"Holy Abadar," Renar whispered softly.

"Arcil . . ." Elyana managed softly. "What happened to you?"

He met her eyes as if to communicate something significant, then looked down and away. "Immortality did not turn out as well as I expected," he said bitterly.

"I thought the crown couldn't help if you were already dead," Renar said.

"I'm not dead . . . not entirely. My soul still lives. If I reabsorb my soul while wearing the crown, I shall be restored."

"You should just have asked," Elyana said softly.

"You told me you never wished to see me again."

"This is . . . this would have changed things." Her eyes swept out to their oncoming foes. As fascinating as all of this was, there were more important things to worry about. "I don't like these odds, Arcil. Do you think the nightmares can get through the water?"

"They can fly if it pleases them," Arcil answered.

"Great. Maybe we should just teleport to Woodsedge and wait for Vallyn there."

"You know as well as I that he might already be dead somewhere on the Plane of Shadow."

So might we, soon, she thought.

"I will summon aid," Arcil told her. "Stay clear." The wizard stepped apart from them.

She turned to the others. "Renar, string your bow. We'll aim to take down the mounts. Unless those warriors can fly." She glanced at Arcil for confirmation, but he was in the midst of complicated hand gestures, his lips moving as he studied the distance. "We'll assume they can't." She stepped to Renar's horse and unlashed the star tower's lance from where they'd secured it to the side of the saddle.

"But he's . . . he's dead," Renar said.

"Mostly. It doesn't change the fact we promised him aid, does it?"

"No," Renar answered, adding after a moment's hesitation, "you're right."

Renar cast off his gauntlets and grabbed his bow. Across the river, Elyana could now pick out individual flames upon the nightmare steeds. Their heads were little more than ebon horse skulls wrapped in fire. Smoke rose from their nostrils, carried backward by their speed.

"Put on your helm," she told the young knight.

"I can't see as well with it," he objected. "How will I fire?"

"You'll have more trouble seeing without your head," Drelm instructed. "Put it on."

"Plant a row of arrows," Elyana told him. "Like we used to practice. And stand ready. We only have a few minutes at most."

Elyana heard Arcil in conversation and turned to find him talking with an armored woman bearing a long, heavy sword. The stranger looked up after a moment and walked toward Elyana. Arcil swept his hands into the air once more.

"The master said you are to lead me," the woman told Elyana doubtfully.

The stranger's dark leather cuirass was overlaid with ring mail that stretched down to her thighs, and her gloved hands were wrapped in lighter chain. Metal greaves were strapped over her calves. For all that, and her size, she carried herself with feminine grace.

"Who are you?" Elyana asked.

"I am the master's most trusted servant, Sareel." Her voice was light and smooth, in direct contrast to her threatening appearance.

Elyana had never seen anyone quite like her. Small, segmented horns curled from Sareel's dark bangs. The woman was broad-shouldered, and taller even than Elyana by a few inches. Elyana wondered what color her eyes were in the real world, for here they were a brilliant white.

"How well do these two fight?" Sareel indicated the others with a single nod.

"Renar is capable though mostly unseasoned. Captain Drelm is reliably deadly."

"That is good to hear."

Elyana motioned Sareel to come with her, and she stepped over beside Renar. The warrior woman followed. "Position yourself here. Have you a distance weapon, Sareel?"

"I do not."

"Renar, we're aiming for the nightmares."

The boy nodded in his helmet, then removed the thing and set it beside him.

"Your father would have kept his armor on."

"I'm not my father."

"So I see. Drelm, you and Sareel stand ready. Some of them are likely to make it over." She raised her voice a modicum. "Arcil, you've got the right."

The wizard was still in the midst of an incantation, but she knew of old that he'd know what to do.

Elyana fitted an enchanted arrow to her bow. The river was ten feet off, the nightmares and their dark armored riders no more than seventy feet beyond. She breathed deep, pushing all other distractions aside, and nocked arrow to string. She focused intently upon the glowing white eye of the central horse, and let fly.

The arrow soared, its point winking against the darkness. Elyana readied another arrow.

Her first mark tore through the horse's right orbit. The animal's head flung up and its front legs folded. It rolled and crushed its rider beneath it. The flaming mane sputtered—and then the fallen body was hidden behind the remaining animals.

Elyana fired again. This time the creatures watched with human intelligence, scattering to left and right. Her second shaft missed. But as the animals veered, a shadow hound leapt baying at a cluster of them on the right. Arcil had made his move.

One animal dodged the hound easily; the other stood up on its back legs and pawed at the air as its rider fell backward over its rump. Elyana planted two regular arrows in its exposed chest, and then the hound bowled into it.

There were six then, twenty feet from the river. The lead animals struck ground and rose into the air, their legs racing as though they galloped up invisible slopes. Two of the mounted warriors spurred toward the shadow hound, and the beast darted around their long, flashing swords.

The nightmares were sinisterly beautiful in their flight. Fiery manes streamed out behind them, and their hooves glowed with sparks that gleamed like stardust. The teeth in their black skulls parted, as though they grinned with the sheer pleasure of their flight.

Elyana shouted for Renar to fire. His arrows found their marks, and with her help they counted for another, which crashed down on the far shore and lay with its broken rider, whinnying pitifully and struggling to rise on broken legs. Arcil wrapped one rider in long black tentacles of shadow, then crushed the struggling figure and dropped it into the stream.

The dead man's mount dropped down to their side of the river, the remaining nightmares landing with it and cantering forward.

"Drelm, Sareel!" Elyana shouted. "Renar, put on your damned helmet!"

Stelan's son dropped the bow and fumbled with the armor. Elyana could spare him no more attention. She turned and raised the lance toward a grinning nightmare that galloped toward her. She sang the five-note melody. A bright beam of searing light streamed up from the lance to spear through the nightmare's neck. It shrieked in an unhorselike way, then fell silent forever and dropped flat. Elyana aimed at the rider and sang the melody a second time.

The battle soon fragmented, Arcil directing his shadow hound and warping shadow with his wand, the horned Sareel dodging and weaving and delivering blows against two unhorsed riders. Elyana and Renar fought within sight of each other, though just barely. It was challenging to see through the smoke rolling constantly from the gleeful nightmares. The beasts were so eager for the fight that they practically pranced into battle, tails and manes licking like white flame. Elyana caught glimpses of Drelm wading into the creatures and dealing blows with his mighty axe, but the fumes from the breath of nightmares obscured her vision.

A mounted warrior rode hard toward her. Elyana leaned away from a powerful swipe and felt it brush a whisper above her head. The noxious fumes set Renar coughing behind her. She feared the young man would shortly be overwhelmed, magic armor or no, and struck with desperate fury into the flank of the animal that had passed her.

The blow sank home, and the nightmare whinnied in pain as its back legs collapsed. She had no time to worry whether or not it was down for the count, for its rider twisted on the dying mount and leapt for her.

She missed the rider's stabbing blade by throwing herself sideways, but his gauntleted left hand clipped her in the shoulder, and she landed hard on her back. She rolled to her feet, only to find the knight already up on one knee. Worse, she'd inhaled some of the smoke, and began to cough. She unsheathed her gleaming blade and darted forward, only to be deflected with undisguised ease. The nightmare's rider climbed the rest of the way to his feet. Renar shouted in pain to her left. She could not spare time to look.

Her opponent was large, strong, capable, better armored, and almost as swift as she. Elyana did not care for her odds, let alone Renar's.

The armored figure struck out at her with a level slice. She nimbly sidestepped. The moment the point slid past, she ran in, driving with full speed. So much for finesse. Her blade struck the armor full on and plunged through the breastplate. She could not pull her weapon free. The shadow warrior, transfixed, shook in pain and struck out, smashing her in the chest so hard it knocked her flat. Suddenly she was confronting a pair of gleaming hooves suspended above her as a nightmare reared. The thing whinnied in expectation. Before the blow could be delivered, though, the creature's flesh was enveloped in a nimbus of flame that ate up first its skin, then its bones, until it vanished completely in ash.

Elyana blinked in surprise. Arcil leaned over her and grinned, extending a hand.

She pushed herself up rather than take his proffered help. She coughed. Smoke still obscured much of her vision, but she saw Sareel striding the battlefield, sword ready.

"Renar needs aid," Elyana told Arcil. She wrenched her sword free from the shadow warrior, and by her blade's glow found her way to Stelan's son.

Renar lay still beside a slowly dying nightmare. It kicked at her as she neared; Elyana sidestepped and hacked deep into its neck. It stopped moving after that.

She knelt beside Renar and loosened his helm. He was pale, and blood trickled from his mouth. His eyes rolled. He'd taken a nasty slash through the thigh from a blow that had found a gap in his armor. He was bleeding out.

She pressed hands to his forehead, coughing in the acrid smoke. She centered her magical energy. And then another series of coughs racked her, disrupting the spell.

She put fingers to his neck. The boy's pulse was slowing. Elyana was overtaken by a coughing fit. She couldn't concentrate.

"Elyana?" Arcil knelt at her side. She saw a stoppered leather vial in one hand. "Are you all right? Are you hurt?"

"Renar—" she said weakly, and coughed again. "I'm fine. Renar's dying."

"I only have the one left—"

Elyana snatched the vial, ripped the cork free and tossed it aside. Her fingers shook as she coughed again, and she had to steady them with her other hand. She bent the vial to Renar's open mouth, then tipped it in. The liquid gurgled through the pale lips. She steadied the vial against him, and, still coughing, cradled the back of his head with her other hand, lifting him up so that he wouldn't choke.

"We need to get both of you out of the smoke," she heard Arcil say. "Sareel!"

A good suggestion. Elyana staggered to her feet and did not fight off Arcil's steadying hands. She grasped Renar by the arms and started dragging.

"This way," Arcil said. And then Sareel was lifting Renar's legs and moving him became far simpler.

They set him down in the dark grass and Elyana knelt by the young man while Arcil watched. After a moment she had her breath back, and she looked up in search of the half-orc.

The smoke was drifting slowly from the battlefield, revealing the carnage. Drelm leaned heavily against his axe as he surveyed the field of twisted limbs and bodies. One of the nightmares was still flaming, twitching its legs, but all others were motionless.

Renar coughed and struggled to rise. He grinned weakly up at Elyana.

"Are you all right?" she asked him.

"I'm fine. I think. Thank you for healing me."

"Thank Arcil. It was his elixir."

Arcil smiled thinly at him.

Renar bowed his head in acknowledgment. "Thank you."

"You're welcome," Arcil replied with gravity.

Elyana helped Renar to his feet. She had to use the last of her magic on a deep wound in Drelm's arm. Sareel was unhurt, though still coughing. No one else had any healing spells, so there was nothing to do for a wound in Drelm's thigh save to clean and sew it closed, which Elyana did while Arcil fretted and Sareel stood watch.

It took a few minutes for Renar to round up the remaining horses, who'd had the good sense to gallop to safety.

Elyana longed for nothing so much as a good long rest, but she climbed wearily back into the saddle. "Let's go. The trail grows colder by the moment."

The others followed her example, Sareel taking one of their extra animals.

Elyana pushed on as hard and as swiftly as she dared. She would have been thankful that the tracks were so easy to follow if it had not been because Vallyn had forced Persaily to a near continual run. The poor mare had been bred for endurance, but even she would have to be giving out by this point.

Elyana's calm grew increasingly strained the longer they rode. Signs of Persaily faltering grew more and more frequent. There were constant twitches in the trail as the mare stumbled.

It couldn't have been that Vallyn was so frightened of pursuit. Likely he hadn't even expected Elyana to survive and track him. It was fear of the shadow realm that had kept him galloping, on and ever on, hoping for some landmark he might recognize. He had no companion to calm him or jest with him, only the laboring horse and the endless miles of darkness and quiet. Then too, he might have glimpsed strange things in the skies, or pursuit of his own.

Perhaps it was his own conscience he feared.

After another long while the character of the steppe altered. There were slopes before them, and when they topped one Elyana saw a cluster of dark square shapes on the horizon.

Renar came up to the hillock and looked with her. "Is that a city?"

"It looks to be." Elyana pointed down the sandy slope, where there were clear marks. "Vallyn was pretty eager to find it."

"How far ahead is he?"

"No telling. He might be in the city." Elyana nudged the gelding down the slope.

The trail grew more obvious in the shorter grass and dry soil.

When the walled black outline of the city still lay what looked like four to five miles off she saw a low shape in the grasses and knew immediately it was no boulder or dirt mound. The gelding was weary and slow to respond, and she had to kick him into a gallop.

There, crumpled in a heap, fur slick with foam and swollen tongue hanging out, lay Persaily. Dead.

Elyana swung off and stared at her horse.

The others soon reached her, watching helplessly as the elf sank to her knees and wept like a mother who has lost her child.

They dismounted, but by mutual consent did not advance to comfort her.

"It was a special horse," Renar told Arcil quietly.

"She was always sentimental," Arcil replied gently. "It is something I like about her."

"She is soft," Sareel said.

"Silence!" Arcil hissed, fury clouding his features.

The warrior woman bowed her head. "I beg forgiveness, master." She dropped to her knees.

Arcil readied to backhand Sareel, then felt Renar's eyes upon him. He lowered his hand, frowned at Sareel, and hurried over to the elf. The soil crunching beneath his boots seemed loud as thunderclaps.

Wonder of wonders, she leaned against the side of his leg, her shoulders shaking as she sobbed. He stroked her hair gently, making soothing noises. He hoped that they didn't sound as awkward to her as they felt. The moment was marred for him only because he had lost most of the feeling in his fingers years before.

All too swiftly, Elyana regained her composure and leaned away. She climbed to her feet, taking in the bleak tableau. Sareel and the others looked on. Her eyes fell once more to her horse.

"I'm going to find him, and I'm going to kill him," she promised. "But going into Woodsedge, now . . ." she shook her head.

"Are these your saddlebags, or his?" Arcil pointed down at the leather bags slung over Persaily's motionless flanks.

"His," Elyana answered.

Arcil crouched, unfastened the saddle bag, and reached inside. He stood a moment later, holding up a ball of fabric.

"It's a shirt," Drelm said.

"It is," Arcil said, and his teeth showed in a predatory grin. "But it will have his scent. And if it has his scent, I can summon a beast to track him."

"Do so," Elyana told him.

He stepped aside, and in moments his words had conjured a small black winged thing with which he held a whispered conversation.

Renar watched the wizard in conversation with the strange little creature, aghast. It looked like some kind of little demon or devil. Renar wasn't really sure of the difference. Elyana rejoined him, her eyes red. "Put on your cloak," she said sharply.

It took a moment for him to follow her reasoning. If they were to enter Woodsedge again, he finally realized, it was best not to do it in such attention-grabbing armor. And so he fumbled with his gear, one eye still upon the elf woman.

Her gaze was directed at neither her dead horse nor the shadow city, nor the wizard crouched by his familiar. She looked instead upon some point visible only to the mind's eye. Her face was lined with worry, and for the first time Renar could ever remember, she seemed worn and old. He shrugged himself into his cloak, then stepped over to her.

He gently plucked at her sleeve. "Elyana?"

She turned slowly.

"I'm sorry about Persaily."

She did not respond, and Renar turned away to see Arcil's familiar vanish in a puff of black smoke. Arcil stood, his head bent over something that glinted in his hand. A small mirror, Renar thought.

"Renar, Drelm, eat something," Elyana said distractedly. "Drink. We'll be heading in soon."

She left them and went to sit cross-legged beside Persaily's body, head bowed. Renar thought that she might be praying. He had never seen her do that before.

Drelm grunted and sat to dig into his dried rations.

After a moment, Renar joined him. He looked forward to seeing the sun, and the sky, and the green grass. All of his former wants and longings, though, had become bittersweet, at thought of the love that had flared so brightly and then died away. The ache was so deep he was not sure he would ever feel the same.

Still numb, Elyana finished her silent meditation and climbed to her feet. She discovered that Sareel was staring at her, and Elyana could not help feeling that she was being sized up as a potential opponent. She wondered whether she could take the warrior woman in battle. She'd glimpsed how swift Sareel was, and how accomplished, and could guess she'd have a longer reach.

"Elyana."

The wizard was walking toward her, the silver mirror shining in one hand. He looked worried.

"What's wrong?" she asked.

"We're too late. Vallyn doesn't have the crown anymore."

"Who does?"

He shook his head. "I don't know."

Elyana clenched her hands into fists. "Then we'll track down Vallyn and ask him."

"That's going to be more challenging than you might think. The Galtans have thrown him in a prison cell."

Chapter Nineteen
Renewed Acquaintances

The aid of a wizard of Arcil's power made everything simpler. Only a few whispered words of incantation altered Drelm and Renar. In a moment, Drelm looked like a muscular farm hand, and the lance from the star tower that Renar carried seemed only a simple spear. Sareel did not fare as well—with more human features she looked like a hulking farm girl rather than a dangerous and exotically pretty warrior woman. As for Elyana, Arcil offered his mirror to her, showing blackened hair, and ears reshaped until they were almost human.

"You are still a striking woman," Arcil told her, "but you do not look like Elyana."

"It's true," Drelm agreed.

Arcil was all for teleporting immediately to an alley near the jail, but Elyana was insistent that the horses not be abandoned in the Plane of Shadow. He grumbled a bit about wasting energy, but sent all the living animals away in a wink of white light.

"There, Elyana," Arcil said. "Now they're standing in our plane in the fields outside Woodsedge."

"Let's get on with the rest, then," Elyana told him.

They materialized in the same shadowy alley his familiar had observed. Elyana breathed in the city's stink as its sounds assaulted her. They faced a weathered brick wall. It might have been dirty, but it was red, and the sky just visible in a line between the roof eaves was blue-gray and thick with heavy clouds. They'd been on the Plane of Shadow so long that the colors themselves seemed otherworldly.

Elyana wished that they could have teleported directly into the cell, but Arcil had detected wards placed to prevent magical entrances and exits from the jail.

Arcil led the way from the alley and Elyana discovered a familiar square. The industrious Galtans had finished a new guillotine, one with an enormous arch, all the better for watching the blade drop. As the device already sat on a platform raised above the square, the frame from which the blade would fall reached almost to a nearby third-story window.

Early afternoon, Elyana thought. So much had changed in only a handful of hours. A butcher vendor eyed them suspiciously as they filed into view, then lost interest as a squat woman challenged him about the freshness of his stock.

Merchants hawked goods from stalls set up all around the square: dried gourds, cloth, breads, even wine and desserts. Smoked meat was offered by half a dozen different butchers, and some folk had brought their own small livestock for slaughter. If not for the guillotine and the self-important pairs of soldiers, it would have looked like the market section of any city.

Arcil, his features hidden by his deep hood, led them through the maze of people and goods. Though disguised, they really didn't blend in with the Galtan crowd, and Elyana wasn't terribly surprised that someone behind them called for them to halt. Arcil kept on, pretending not to hear.

"You there, in the hood! Halt, I say!"

Arcil froze.

The crowd behind them cleared away as surely as if they'd heard someone declare their little group had the plague. As the liberty-capped guardsman strode forward, Arcil turned suddenly and pulled down his hood.

The shoppers and merchants had turned from their own tasks to become a crowd, and they gasped almost with one voice. Arcil wore a gray leather mask and tricorne. The garb of the Gray Gardeners.

The two guardsman stopped a few paces off, and Elyana saw the blood drain from their faces.

"I am on business, citizen," Arcil said menacingly. "Is there some way that I can help you?"

"No," stammered the pug-nosed man on the right. "No, citizen."

"Good." Arcil pulled the hood back up and stalked away, the cloak belling behind him. A trifle dramatic, really, but the Galtans loved drama, and it had silenced them.

The wizard then boldly walked up to the postern gate of the gaol, showed mask and hood, and when challenged for the password spat: "Beautiful and blue."

The guardsman stood quickly aside, and Arcil strode on as if he owned the place. Elyana did not stare at the grounds, and tried not to dwell on the outer wall of the jail they had but lately escaped. Been allowed to escape, she corrected. Was this, then, some other strange ploy? Surely not. The Galtans could not be anticipating her return. So why had they imprisoned Vallyn?

Arcil, head thrust forward as if he strode into a stiff wind, walked straight for the dark stones of the prison and set his hand to the door latch.

Before long they were moving again through narrow corridors and up twisting stone stairs. The first-floor cells were full once more, for guards were pushing a squeaking cart heavy with food trays into a hall, and Elyana glimpsed fingers wrapped around the cell windows, as though inmates were pressed against them in anticipation. On the third floor they saw but two guardsmen, who played dice on a battered table. At sight of Arcil as Gray Gardener they hopped to their feet, ashen-faced. They quickly turned over cell keys and lantern to Arcil. The wizard unlocked the gate and they passed through, leaving the guards gulping behind them.

The sky rumbled outside.

"This was our hall," Drelm noted.

Arcil was counting softly under his breath. He stopped at "twelve" and faced left. He peered through the door's barred window, then slid a key into the protesting lock and turned it. He hauled it open, and Elyana stepped to his side.

The bard peered up at them from his seat on a straw pallet. While the hairline was the same, his face was so distorted that Elyana at first did not recognize him as her old companion. His upper lip was purple, his cheek bruised, and one eye was swollen shut. His nose was broken. He raised his hands and Elyana heard the rattle of chains. Manacles wrapped his wrists, which were tethered to the wall with a short, rusty chain.

He did not recognize either of them until Arcil removed his mask.

"Arcil." Vallyn's one good eye rolled over to Elyana, then widened slightly, recognizing her garments and the way she carried herself. "Elyana. Of course. Of course you saved her."

"On the contrary, my old friend," Arcil answered pleasantly. "She slew the dragon with no help from me. Or you."

"I didn't think either of us had a chance, Elyana," Vallyn explained.

Arcil answered for her. "It is good to see you . . . having gotten something like what you deserve."

"You must wonder how I got myself here." Vallyn's voice was cracked and strained.

"Not especially," Arcil said. "I just want the crown."

"And Elyana's helping you with that?"

"We have an arrangement."

"I can help you find it," Vallyn promised, "if you let me out."

Arcil smiled and his voice went on, precise and measured. "Or I can kill you, and compel your soul to purge itself of secrets. That would be faster, I think."

Vallyn's one open eye rolled toward Elyana, who stood still as death.

"What should we do with him?" Arcil asked conversationally.

"You killed my horse, you miserable bastard."

"I . . . I had to ride fast, Elyana. I knew the kind of things that live in the shadow lands—"

"You are a coward."

"Yes . . . yes, but I had no choice. I had to take them the crown. I had to—"

"Where is it?" Arcil demanded.

"Why?" Elyana asked, setting one hand on the door frame.

"Do you honestly care?" Arcil asked her.

"He was my friend, once," Elyana said. "Or a fine, fine liar."

"The latter, I think."

The bard spoke quickly. "No, I am your friend, Elyana. I panicked when I saw the dragon—I'm sorry about that. But I had to get the crown away. I had to—"

"Your friends killed the elves," she told him. "All three of them. Including the girl." She glanced to her left where Renar watched tensely.

"The Galtans had already done that," Vallyn said. "I had nothing to do with it. You've got to believe me."

"So it was an accident?" Elyana's voice rose in outrage. "Is that what you're saying? That there was no way to warn them?" Elyana's voice grew hard. "Gods! What's wrong with you?" She looked at Arcil as well. What was wrong with both of them?

It was as though Arcil heard her thoughts. "I wished no one to see my weakness," Arcil said. "As for him . . . he's probably not telling the truth."

"I am!" Vallyn whispered, then strained against the chain so that he could lean a few feet closer. "You must believe me. I had no choice. They would have killed me years ago if I hadn't supplied them with information. Names. Locations. Everything. It took me *years* to get where I was. I wasn't lucky enough to be born to privilege. I had to fight my way up from nothing, and they were going to take it away!"

"Greed," Arcil said. "His sin is greed and mine is pride." The wizard sounded as though he were enjoying himself. "What's yours, Elyana? If we were going to live a parable, we really should have seven sins, don't you think?"

"Let me out," Vallyn begged. "Let me out, and I'll take you to the crown. I can do it. I know what they're doing."

"Tell me where the crown is," Arcil said, "and she'll think about it."

Vallyn licked his puffed and bloody lips and searched Elyana's face for sympathy. He found none.

"They were awfully eager to see me," Elyana said. "So they want me dead, and you told them where I was, why haven't they come after me?"

"I don't know," Vallyn said. "I figured you'd been taking care of them. Nadara's sent out at least three assassins in the last five years, for you *and* Stelan. They never came back."

"Assassins?" Elyana repeated. There'd been a few bandits, and a wolf pack, and an occasional murder. No personal threat to her or Stelan . . . She looked over at Arcil.

"I told you," he said woodenly, "I've been monitoring you. Stelan too. I knew you'd be upset if he died." At her strange stare, he continued. "After the first assassin, I kept a few servants on the perimeter of Stelan's holdings. No one else got as close."

Vallyn's dry chuckle sounded more like a death rattle. "Arcil the guardian angel," he said.

"You ridicule me?" Arcil's hand rose as though he cupped an invisible ball, and a cold light flickered in his palm.

Elyana stilled him with a hand on the wrist and faced the bard. "You'd be pitiable, Vallyn, if you were worth the trouble. You're not. They dropped you here because they finally thought they'd gotten all they could out of you, didn't they?"

"Nadara swore!" Vallyn said, indignant. "She swore this would be the last thing! She even promised she'd leave you and Stelan alone if I just got her the crown! I swear that I didn't mean anything bad to happen to you!"

"The crown," Arcil said. No hint of humor remained in his voice. "Where's the crown?"

"Nadara's got it." Vallyn drooped. "They're planning something big, tonight. There's going to be a huge speech with all the city dignitaries."

"She doesn't waste time," Elyana said.

Vallyn shook his head. "She's been biding her time for more than twenty years, inching her way into power among the Gray Gardeners. And she has her uncle's notes, and the knowledge. You should have seen how excited she was when I told her you were headed for the crown—"

"Enough story," Arcil said. "Where is she?"

"Let me out and I'll take her to you."

A line of blue lightning shot out from the wizard's hand and struck the bard.

Vallyn convulsed as the energy danced over his body. His head crashed with a thunk into the wall behind him and his mouth opened in a silent scream.

"Stop it!" Elyana snarled.

Arcil dismissed the spell with a careless wave.

Vallyn slumped in his chains and wheezed. Elyana bent down to grasp his chin. She turned his bruised face up and glared into his good eye.

"You have lied to us. You have betrayed us, and our allies. You stood idly by when you knew assassins came for me."

"I didn't know—" Vallyn objected.

She dug her fingernails into his chin. He whimpered and fell quiet.

"And you rode my horse to death. All for what, Vallyn, the promise of wealth? Was Nadara *that* good in bed? Don't answer. Where is she?"

"Promise you'll let me go."

"I promise not to kill you if you tell me where she is. Now."

"You trust *him*. Over me."

"You should worry about me, Vallyn."

Tears trailed down from the corners of both his eyes, the swollen one and the good. "There's to be a demonstration at the parliament steps. They will either be there, or in the Chamber of Liberty."

Elyana released his chin and considered, frowning.

"That's the tall building beside the guillotine. The Gray Gardeners meet in the third floor. Above the square. Now please—"

"How many will we face, Vallyn?" Arcil's voice was soft and sinister.

"At least seven are wizards or sorcerers. A few are swordsmen and political folks. They'll be backed up by the army. Elyana, don't go. You won't have a chance. I don't know what kind of deal you made with Arcil, but I can—"

"No deals, Vallyn. No arrangements. No words. Arcil, pass me the keys."

Arcil's eyebrow arched, but he pressed the jangling ring of keys into her hand.

"Thank you, Elyana," Vallyn sobbed. "Thank you."

"And you have no idea what the Gardeners plan?" Arcil asked.

"Nadara's going to unite the factions. With the crown. I don't know how, but she seemed awfully amused. Please, Elyana."

Elyana had not yet set the keys to the manacled wrists offered up to her. Galtan factionalism was almost as mysterious to her as finances and organized worship. She did know that national and regional Galtan office terms were finished by Madame Guillotine with surprising regularity, and that various factions inevitably rose and thrived in the resulting chaos. These scrabbled constantly for access to Galt's failing resources.

"Why do the Gardeners wish to end the chaos? It keeps them in power."

"Nadara's going to rule Woodsedge. Through the Gardeners. With the crown. I don't know how. Please, that's all I know."

Elyana set the keys down beside the bard. "It's time to go."

"Wait," Vallyn protested. "You're taking me with you, aren't you?"

"I'm leaving you the keys. How you escape from here is your own affair."

Arcil looked at her dubiously as she shouldered past, then smirked at Vallyn and followed. Renar and Drelm stepped to the cell doorway.

"Renar, please. Reason with her! I can't possibly survive if you just abandon me—"

"It's a better chance than you gave Aliel," Renar said bitterly.

"That was an accident," Vallyn said quickly. He was fumbling with the keys as he spoke, twisting his hand to fit the key into the manacles. "You know that I couldn't possibly have meant for anything to happen to her! You have to know that."

Renar stepped away. Drelm glowered down at Vallyn for a moment, watching as he freed himself from the first manacle. Then he closed the door with a thunk and followed the others. There was the click of a lock.

"No!" Vallyn shouted. "That's not fair!" He scrambled to his feet and pressed his face to the bars. He screamed after them in fear and anger. "Don't leave me here!"

Drelm did not look back.

Chapter Twenty
Citizen Assembly

The five o'clock bells were tolling as they exited the jail, but there was no sign of the soldiers who should have been gathering for mealtime. A lone soldier walked the upper wall above the gate, and two dejected-looking guards manned it. They didn't seem surprised by the sight of a Gray Gardener and a small group of followers, and allowed them through without challenge. Arcil drew up his hood as they left, and passed the hat and mask to Sareel to stow in a backpack.

The streets outside were packed with long streams of men, women, and children walking for the central square.

Elyana wished they'd grabbed a few liberty caps off of their opponents in the Vale of Shadows. One out of every five people was wearing one.

They stayed with the crowd, walking among them toward the square. Soldiers were clearing the vendors away, and folk gathered to face the wide stone steps that fronted the parliament building. A podium had been erected under its impressive portico, which was supported by a half-dozen stone pillars. Soldiers stood along the bottom row of steps, keeping the crowd back from stage, podium, and row of chairs behind.

Some enterprising children had clambered to sit on the ledge of the platform that supported the guillotine, gaily swinging their legs and chattering among themselves.

A mob bore crude placards. Some of them Elyana understood simply enough—"Death to the Tyrants," "Liberty," "Down with Taxes"—but others mystified her. Several men carried wooden signs with symbols of horses and vegetables, and they seemed almost as agitated as a knot of burly men holding signs labeled with such slogans as "Support your Builders' Guild" and "No Stones, No Liberty." She wondered if the letterers understood the irony in the last statement, for escape from Woodsedge to liberty had been far simpler before the construction of its wall.

A handful of vendors remained, calling attention to their goods: cheese, bread, and fried meat on sticks. They did a brisk business. Drelm sniffed—a peculiarly loud sound to rise from a human nose, and it earned him a quick glance from a beady-eyed merchant before he turned to badger other passersby.

"I'm hungry," Drelm muttered.

Elyana could hear folk talking about all sorts of things: whether or not it would rain, how hungry they were, irritation that they had to gather for yet another speech. Others had heard rumors that all the city leaders would be in attendance and looked forward to the political sparring that would surely transpire.

Arcil slid up to Elyana's side. "There's a great deal of magical energy emanating in a wave toward the stage," he told her softly.

"From where?"

Before the wizard could answer there was a flurry of motion on the steps of the parliament, and a trio of men in gold-trimmed blue waistcoats ascended the stairs. They lifted brass trumpets to their lips and blared out a fanfare that was more loud than skilled. The fanfare stuttered to a halt, then the musicians launched into a ragged rendition of "The March of Liberty," one of the informal anthems of the Galtan revolutionaries.

The massive entry doors of the parliament hall were thrown wide, and a dozen well-dressed men and women strolled onto the steps, waving at the crowd. The throngs erupted with cheers, waves, and a few catcalls. A chant about wall-building rose from the sign-shaking citizens, but died before reaching much momentum as another trumpet blast rang out. A fat but handsome man with wavy black hair stepped up to the podium, hands raised high. Almost unnoticed, a trio of robed and masked Gray Gardeners had also come through the doorway. They watched quietly from the shadows as the speaker thanked the assembled citizens for coming.

"The magic's centered all around the people on the stage," Arcil whispered to Elyana. "They practically glow with it. I believe that the magic on the stage is linked to whatever's going on . . . over there."

Elyana's eyes followed the line of Arcil's gaze toward a tall, grand building behind the guillotine, directly across from the parliament. The Chamber of Liberty, Vallyn had named it. The shutters on three wide third-story windows were thrown open, but unlike all other windows around the square, no one leaned against the sills.

"There's a great deal of sorcerous energy wielded by both the gardeners and something on the top floor of that building. And it's connected."

"Where's the crown?"

"I can't tell. Honestly, it might be on either side."

Elyana realized that the whole mess wasn't going to get any simpler. Wouldn't the clerics of Abadar be perfectly happy with the blessed armor, which was clearly of great worth? And hadn't she already risked enough for Arcil— who, after all, was a murderer and a blackmailer?

Yet even though the thought of his unseen eyes upon her was cringe-inducing, Arcil had apparently been safeguarding her and Stelan for years. Did she owe him for that, and for his assistance in the tower? She would have been unlikely to survive without him. Did those actions balance out the long list of his transgressions?

They could not. But she had given her word. "Do we wait, or move now?" she asked.

Arcil had apparently been wondering the same thing. "Now, I think. I don't know what they intend. Suppose they drain the crown's power?"

Elyana nodded.

"You and those two can go look into the Chamber," Arcil said. "I will remain here."

"Is that wise?"

"I can watch you through this." Arcil pushed his hand through the edge of his robe, showing her a small violet globe. "I can send you aid, or reach you myself, almost instantly."

"Don't you have to concentrate to use that?"

"No."

She frowned. So it was essentially a window to her at any time. "When this is all over, I want you to smash that."

"It's practically unbreakable," he said, then, upon seeing her brows darken further, added, "but I'll see that it's destroyed."

She told Renar and Drelm to follow and struggled through the crowd until they reached a side street. Behind her, the first speaker had called for unity, and then a woman's voice rose shrilly over the din of the crowd. Her voice grew fainter as the three of them moved away. "It's long since time to put petty factionalism behind us," she was saying. "It is I, your sister in liberty, who says this. Do you not trust me?"

Thunder rumbled in the distance.

Elyana took a right turn, thankful that near the central square the streets of Woodsedge were mostly straight. The route should lead them to the rear of the correct building.

After another right they saw no one in the lane but themselves and a figure lying against some crumbled stairs, hugging an empty bottle. The distant crowd broke into another shout, then died as a speaker, his words too distant for coherence, began to harangue them.

A few dozen paces on, two helmeted guards suddenly stepped forward from an archway at the back of a white stone building. The shorter of the two raised his hands.

"Turn around, citizens," he said. "Your presence is required in the square."

Elyana gave him her best smile as she advanced. "Drelm," she whispered from the side of her mouth. "Axe."

The men were bored, but they were professionals, and they put hands to sword hilts as Elyana's group closed the distance. When they were but twelve paces away, the short one again ordered them to halt, then drew his sword.

Drelm's hand snapped back, and an axe flew forward. It caught the short soldier in the forehead and he sank in a welter of blood.

His companion had just cleared his scabbard when Elyana struck. He blocked the first strike, but her flashing sword darted in and found his throat before he had time to shout a warning.

A moment later, Elyana was walking beneath the stone archway while Drelm and Renar dragged the bodies after her.

The door opened into a grimy cellar.

Drelm dropped his guardsman on top of Renar's and then closed the door. The light dimmed to a tiny line under the boards.

Elyana searched the gloom, stepped around a line of crates stacked neatly against a wall, and started up creaking wooden steps. The door at the top was old and warped. And locked.

"Drelm," she said, "smash us a way clear."

She jumped down, and the half-orc took her place. It took him but two good kicks to open the portal. The door swung wide on its broken hinges and slammed into a cabinet, and Elyana winced at the racket. She followed Drelm through, sword to hand.

There was no one there.

They moved down the dark back hallway to a large kitchen and pantry. All were deserted. Elyana raised a hand for them to be still. Listen though she might, she could hear only the sounds of the crowd outside.

It might be that the mass of people had completely drowned out their arrival. She could hope.

She led the way out of the silent kitchen and into the brown-paneled hallways. They took the narrow servant's stair up two floors and stopped in front of a dark oak door. Elyana waited there, listening. Still she could perceive only the sound of the clamoring throng carried through the building.

The character of the place changed on the other side of the door, becoming a structure of white stone walls and polished wood floors overlaid with decorative runners. The hall was hung with paintings of landscapes and heroic peasants. Elyana paid them little heed, her attention straining instead for sign of Gray Gardeners.

The hallway stopped at a set of double doors carved with an elaborately detailed Galtan liberty cap circled with breathtakingly accurate laurel leaves.

What had probably once been elegant brass doorknobs had been worn down over the years to a dull metallic color. She knew better than to grasp one if there were wizards on the other side. The doors would be warded; she was certain of it. She motioned the others back.

"Do you wish me to kick it?" Drelm asked quietly.

She shook her head. An old couch sat in an alcove to their left. "Pick that up. Renar, stand ready."

The young man cast off his robe while the half-orc took up the couch. "Won't this make a lot of noise?"

"That's why you're going to be ready to move fast," Elyana answered. "But not so quickly that you're going to walk into whatever spell it sets off. Drelm, heave away."

The half-orc nodded once, then hefted the furniture to chest level and flung it side-first into the doors.

The wood splintered with a crash as the doors flew open. The couch and doorframe were drenched suddenly in a storm of ice shards that materialized from thin air. Elyana threw up an arm to block the pelting ice. Drelm grunted and lifted his throwing axe. The storm petered out after only a few moments. The couch lay broken between the doors, and the half-orc vaulted over it, heavy feet crunching on the ice.

There was no time for careful consideration of the audience hall beyond. Elyana had the sense of a large space with a high ceiling. Three gray-robed targets presented themselves in the room's center, and all were turning toward Drelm. The half-orc paused only to hurl his throwing axe, and then he faltered, groaning in pain as he fumbled for his larger weapon.

From behind him, Elyana saw the half-orc's axe strike one Gray Gardener in the chest. Blood flew, and the man opened his mouth in a scream even as the crowd outside burst into applause, drowning out the noise.

At the same moment a wave of pain swept over her, and she bit back a shout. There must have been a second ward. She managed only a single shot, taking one of the three Gray Gardeners through the knee. He dropped, howling.

Elyana struggled for breath as she nocked a second arrow. The pain was intense, as though every one of her muscles was suddenly on fire.

The room was wide and long. Dozens of desks, tables, and chairs had been pushed to the walls. In the clear space beside the Gray Gardeners were six coffins tilted against chairs facing the back of the room. Each contained a body, and Elyana was astonished to find herself staring at a face she recognized. Even over the sting of the spell she felt a chill, for she could hear the black-haired man speaking to the crowd at the same time she gazed upon his still corpse, dressed in the same clothing he wore below, even to the sash that stretched diagonally across his chest.

One Gardener remained upright. He faced them, but did not act.

Drelm advanced, lifting his greataxe. The wizard with the arrow through his knee raised a hand from the floor planks where he reclined, and a shimmering ray of energy struck the half-orc, now only a few paces away. A befuddled expression spread over the captain's features and he sagged to the ground, as if even his own body were too great a burden to bear.

Renar charged past Elyana and the row of bodies, aiming the lance straight for the lean Gardener who had not yet acted. Stelan's son felt only a glimmer of the ward's power before the armor turned it aside.

The Gardener axed by Drelm raised bloody hands. Renar saw the fingers glowing with eldritch light and winced in anticipation of the attack. No spell struck him, though, for an arrow stoppered the wizard's mouth and he fell sideways, gurgling blood.

Renar sang the melody Elyana had taught him and the weapon in his hands fairly vibrated with energy. A beam of pure white light shot from its tip and struck the Gardener in the center of his chest. The man curled up as though he'd been dealt a haymaker to the gut, his hat tumbling free to expose a black gleam crowning his brow. The force of the blast flung the fellow backward through the open window, his feet clipping the sill as he spun out and down.

Renar saw him strike the top of the guillotine and then land with a sick crunch on the guillotine's platform, right beside a fat man holding hands with a small boy.

Few had taken notice, though, for at the moment Renar's blast hit the wizard a cry rose from the crowd outside. The parliament speakers were dissolving, drifting apart like smoky shadows. Already screaming people were pushing and shoving to escape the square.

Drelm collapsed on top of the crippled wizard who'd cast the spell on him, his knife still embedded in the man's chest. Elyana hurried past him to the window, teeth gritted against the lingering ache of the spell. She reached the sill in time to see folk leaping off the edge of the guillotine platform and away from the body of the Gray Gardener that had plummeted into their midst.

"Elyana," Renar said, pointing down to the broken man below, "I think he's wearing the crown!"

As interesting as that was, Elyana's attention was caught by further pandemonium spreading through the mob. As though the Galtans were not already frightened enough, Arcil and Sareel appeared beside the podium in a flash of light. The wizard drove tentacles of darkness against the Gray Gardeners while Sareel guarded his back. A few of the soldiers rushed to aid; the rest were carried away by the crowd, or were already running with them.

"See if you can hit the wizards with your lance," Elyana told Renar. She glanced back at Drelm and saw the half-orc lying prone. He waved her on. Good enough. They were all alive still, somehow, and the crown was below. All she needed was that, and then Arcil could get them home.

Home.

She gathered her aching limbs, slung the bow over one shoulder, and climbed into the window. She leapt out for the top of the guillotine.

If she could have dropped straight onto it, she would have done so, but there was a gap of more than four feet between sill and the top of the device. The stabbing pain in her calves and triceps distracted her only a little, but even that was too much. She knew she'd misjudged the moment she launched.

The top of the guillotine was a thick beam suspended over two wide columns, designed to support the blade as it rose for its long, deadly drop. She had intended to land with a graceful acrobatic twist. Instead, her toes slipped on the wood, and while she managed to turn herself, she landed on her belly across the beam. Her armor absorbed part of the impact, but the wind was knocked out of her. Worse, she had no purchase. She scrambled frantically to establish a grip on the beam's edge. She failed, but managed to right her trajectory as she dropped so that she landed solidly on the platform beside the blade housing, on the side where Galtans usually kept the head basket.

The frightened mob was still fighting to exit the square. They fled, leaving dozens of dead or wounded trampled in the street. No one seemed to pay her any heed, for which she was thankful. She breathed a sigh of relief as she bent down beside the dead masked man on the platform. She could see the dark gleam of the metal band on his balding brow. She had only to snatch it up and signal to Arcil, and they could be done.

And then she saw that it wasn't the right crown.

Chapter Twenty-One
The Crown of Twilight

The crown she'd seen on the stone bier in the tower had been fashioned of two interwoven bands—one dark, one light, rising and falling around one another in a wave. Suddenly understanding dawned, and she cursed herself for her stupidity. She hadn't found the wrong crown, she'd just found half of it. The thing must come apart, like the metal puzzle toys blacksmiths fashioned for children.

She pulled the crown from the dead man's brow. The moment she grasped it, she felt her armband thrum in response to the vast reservoir of power stored within the artifact.

The metal was so black that it did not give back a reflection. Elyana stood, the artifact gripped tightly in her left hand, then absently rolled the dead wizard off the platform with one booted foot. The body struck the cobbled stones below with a thud muted by the screaming crowd. She debated how to go about contacting Arcil.

The wizard had thrown up a glimmering shield of energy, and so too had one of the Gardeners opposite him, the magic distorting features so severely that Elyana could not pick out details. At Arcil's side, Sareel hewed through the arm of a warrior. Around them were a jumble of bodies, some hacked and bloody, others merely twisted and still. The corpses of two Gray Gardeners lay among them.

Whomever Arcil fought was immensely gifted, for he or she lashed the wizard's shield with a blistering rain of blue lightning. Was it Nadara? Mystic energy flared against the shield, and Arcil reeled under the onslaught.

Elyana had already turned to shout up at Renar when there was a flicker across the square. Arcil's opponent had vanished. She spun to see Nadara slide smoothly from the shadow of the guillotine's beam.

Her pretty face was made ugly by her sneer. Her long, dark hair, flecked with gray, whipped in a tight tail pulled back from her head. She was garbed like a man, in gray trousers and waistcoat. The scorched remnant of a Gray Gardener mask was roped about her throat like a necklace.

Most importantly, a white-gold twin to the crown in Elyana's hand glittered on her forehead.

Elyana went for her sword, but Nadara was faster. At her gesture, the shadow from the guillotine snaked up to snare Elyana's arms above the elbow. The cold, dark force turned her with irresistible strength, pressing her arms to her chest. Elyana brushed the hilt of her sword, but was yanked off-balance toward the dead man's bed of the guillotine. She was slammed down onto the wood with such strength that she was momentarily stunned.

The shadow arms pulled her along the bed, and as she blinked to clear her head she was not altogether

surprised to see another pair of shadowy tendrils lifting
the gleaming, deadly blade from its housing, carrying
it up the guillotine channel. The startling thing was the
music coming from above—not from a lute, but from a
harp, and the soft voice of a bard.

Vallyn! From where had he come, and on whose side
would he fight? And why hadn't Renar or Drelm done
anything to aid her?

Nadara's eyes were alight with vindictive glee. Elyana
heard her name being called and turned her head to
find Arcil running from the far side of the square,
dodging around bloody bodies. Sareel sprinted after.
The warrior woman's sword blade dripped gore. Above,
the shadow arms had lifted the blade two-thirds of the
way toward its apex, and those that restrained Elyana
had pressed her into line with the shining weapon's
path. Nadara had not bothered to slam down the neck
brace that would lock her in place—the shadow arms
did that well enough.

Elyana might be the metaphorical damsel in distress,
but she couldn't wait for rescue. Who was her hero—
the boy with the lance? The treacherous bard? The half-
orc lying huddled in pain? The lich?

Elyana knew her own magic was dwarfed by that of
the wizard beside her, but she still had one resource: her
half of the crown. All she needed was a way to wield it.

In the building above, Renar's spirit rebelled against
what it was being told to do by the bard, who'd appeared
a few moments before, plucking away on a half-strung
harp only partially in tune. Struggle though he might,
that magic had kept Renar from employing the lance
to aid Arcil. Now Vallyn commanded him to use the
thing, and against his will Renar's voice rose in song.

A blaze of magical energy streamed forth and struck Arcil squarely in the side. The wizard caved inward as though struck by a great fist and went tumbling past his bodyguard, robe smoking.

Vallyn erupted in gleeful laughter. Renar struggled, but could do nothing without Vallyn's voice instructing him.

"Mistress!" Vallyn slid closer to the window. Renar watched helplessly as the guillotine blade neared the top of its channel, readying its plunge toward his elven friend. Vallyn raised his voice, shouting, "I saved you, mistress! It's me, Vallyn!"

Drelm had little strength left, and the pain was a living thing that writhed within him, a serpent that twisted all about his muscles, nerves, and organs. But pain was an old companion to him. He pushed himself slowly to his knees even as the bard worked his magic upon Renar. The half-orc was dazed, and stars sparkled on the edges of his vision, but he could still focus. And so at the same moment Renar fired the bolt from the lance into Arcil, Drelm lumbered to his feet and ambled slowly toward the bard. He was not altogether clear what he would do, only that he would stop him. He could not even attempt stealth. He built up speed, shuffling, then jogging. He was eight paces from the bard, five, four . . .

At the last moment Vallyn whirled, and Drelm saw the man's eyes go round in shock. Though his clothes were still torn and bloody, Vallyn must have cast a healing spell over himself, for his handsome face was clear of blemishes. Vallyn lifted up the harp as if to use it as a barrier, and then Drelm crashed into him.

Drelm had meant to grab for Vallyn's neck, but the instrument spoiled his blow. No matter—the half-orc's weight slammed into the bard and his arms encircled him, harp and all.

Vallyn screamed, trying to cast a spell, but his fingers could not close on the strings. Drelm felt the shock as the bard's back slammed into the edge of the window, and then they were falling, falling . . .

The bard's head and shoulder struck the pavement, and Drelm knew a moment of satisfaction as blood and brains erupted into his face. Then he too struck the ground. There was a sharp pain, and then all sensation left him.

Elyana's range of motion was limited by the shadowy arms encircling her, but not entirely restricted. Crown clasped tightly, the elf bent her arm to pass the artifact through the band of shadow holding her to the dead man's bed. The restraints parted the moment the metal touched it.

At the same moment, Nadara released the guillotine blade, and it plummeted, rumbling in its wooden tracks.

Her left leg hooked under the dead man's bed, Elyana pulled hard against the shadow gripping her right side, tearing free at the last instant. The blade sliced off her trailing hair and the shadow holding her right arm, as well as the armor on her right shoulder and a hunk of muscle beneath. She gasped, grabbed the crown from her crippled arm, and set it on her head as she rose.

Power hummed through her, dulling the pain. Everything around her glowed with a corona of energy, especially the guillotine blade and the brow of the shadow wizard that furrowed at her even as the woman lifted another hand.

Elyana kicked out, booted foot catching Nadara in the kneecap with a crack. The woman dropped with a cry along the edge of the guillotine platform. Her hand went up, crackling with dark energy.

Elyana's hand closed on her sword hilt. Nadara cast a weave of darkness at her like a net. It battered Elyana back, clogging her breath, freezing her with its icy touch . . . and slid away as the crown on Elyana's brow bathed her in light. The shadows couldn't be used upon someone wearing either side of the crown, she realized.

Nadara must have understood this at the same moment, and was mouthing another spell even as Elyana's blade crashed down and pierced through cloth and sinew. Nadara's casting arm dropped bloody and separate on the planks. Nadara had only begun to scream when Elyana followed up with a thrust through the woman's throat. The elf pulled the other half of the crown free while the Gray Gardener was still writhing.

The square was almost completely empty now, save for twisted bodies. A few folk still looked from windows in horror, and from down the street came the sound of hoofbeats. A cavalry detachment was on its way, banners waving, feathered helms bobbing. Lightning flashed within the clouds above.

Renar burst through the front doors and raced to where Drelm lay crumpled on the pavement. Sareel, cradling Arcil's upper body, called for Elyana to hurry.

She could feel all of their energy: Renar, pulsing with the vibrancy of youth, ringed by protective magic. Arcil, cold and small beside Sareel's mighty life force, his lesser energy swiftly draining into the ether. Drelm, broken and near to death.

She also felt the power of the guillotine, the shrieking of the souls trapped within its blade. She could sense them straining against the bonds of the weapon and understood that if she just focused the power she might learn how to release them. If she had but a little time . . .

But there was no time. The cavalry thundered on, and Renar was calling to her. Sareel was shouting her name. And if they didn't teleport home before Arcil died, they would all be trapped in Woodsedge, at the mercy of the local justice.

Renar was manhandling the half-orc, dragging the limp captain by the shoulders. Elyana sheathed her bloody sword and leapt down from the platform, feeling the pain that coursed through her body only at a distant level. The crown enabled her to tune it out. She reached Arcil's side at the same moment as Renar.

The magical attack had burned through Arcil's illusion as well as his robe. His mummified face stared up at her from above his charred and smoking garments. The glow in his eyes was dim. His hand fumbled for her, but Elyana didn't grasp it until she had stretched for Renar, the other half of the crown dangling like a giant's bracelet around her wrist. Renar's gauntleted hand touched her left one; her right clasped the dry fingers of the lich, and she had a moment to stare up at the guillotine and the oncoming cavalry before everything faded and they sat suddenly before her tiny wooden house with its green eaves.

Here in Taldor, the sky was clear and blue and white clouds drifted easily by. To the east was a distant storm front. Birds sang. A few of her horses looked up from their contented grass munching, then bent back to the task that occupied most of their lives.

"The crown," Arcil was saying, "give me the crown."

"The blast shattered his soul," Sareel said. And she rose toward Renar. "You little bastard!"

"The bard compelled me!" The boy raised his hands in protest.

"Leave him be!" Elyana spat. The warrior woman halted, looking back and forth between Arcil and Renar, even as Elyana turned the two pieces of the crown over to the shaking hands of the lich.

"It's in two halves," Elyana told him. "Let me—"

He was too feeble to resist her as she took the two portions away, desperately striving to slide them together. Without the crown on her head, though, the effects of the pain spell returned. Her shoulder was agony, and her fingers fumbled even as Arcil slumped.

"Arcil, hang on!" she urged. The crown halves slid into place, and she passed them to the wizard, only to find he was too weak to grasp them. She cradled the horrible head with its sunken flesh and placed the crown there. She sensed a surge of energy run through him.

Arcil felt like a drowning man given a brief gulp of air. He could think clearly, and felt for the power of the crown, reached for the energy he needed to wield. He had to restore his soul to his body—if even a little bit returned to him, the rest would find its way, and the crown would heal him. He had stored his essence in the supposedly unbreakable scrying sphere. Yet the magic from the lance had cracked it. His soul had leaked away.

Exhaustion overcame him, and he sank back against Elyana's arms. "There's nothing left," he said.

Elyana nodded. Tears streamed down her face. "I wasn't sure . . ."

Power over life and death. He'd been so blind. Shadow magic was illusion. The Crown of Twilight could destroy, and it could shield from shadows. It could trick the body into healing itself. It could even shape shadows into a semblance of life, just as Nadara had done with the images she'd formed of the Galtan leaders she'd killed. But it could not return a departed soul.

He let out a long sigh and considered Elyana. She still wore the illusion spell he had placed upon her.

No matter the energy of the crown—it wasn't enough to sustain him much longer. Without it, he would already have expired.

He raised a shaking hand and dismissed the illusions, suddenly desperate to see Elyana as she truly was. One last time he stared into those violet eyes, now misty with tears. He watched her push back that glorious auburn hair, and felt her hand on his own scalp as she touched him. He always hated to see her sad. He regretted that.

"I'm sorry, Elyana . . ."

Elyana alone heard the whispered words. She was staring into those dead sockets as the red light within them flickered out. And she wept.

"Heal him!" Sareel screamed behind her. "Use your magic! Use the crown!"

"He's dead," she said. And Arcil looked as though he had been so for a long time. But Drelm was not, or at least he hadn't been a few moments ago. Still weeping, Elyana turned to where the heavy body lay.

A meaty hand closed on her good shoulder and flung her around. "Save him!"

The horned warrior woman was electric with rage. Elyana saw her clearly for the first time since their return. Sareel's chin was swollen. Gaping rents stood out in her armor.

"The crown can't do that!" Elyana said.

"You lie!"

"It can't heal him!" Elyana shouted, grief fueling her anger.

"Then *you* heal him!" Sareel's voice was hysterical. "I've seen you heal in that stupid crystal ball! Why won't you heal him?"

"He's dead—but I can still save Drelm."

The woman's face contorted in fury. Her sword came up and she spun for the half-orc. Elyana knew a brief flash of horror. Sareel meant to finish Drelm.

Elyana's entire body protested as she flung herself into Sareel. It was more a stumble than a tackle, and she shouted in pain as her damaged shoulder smashed into Sareel's side.

Both women went down in the grass behind the half-orc, and in the fall Sareel's pommel struck Elyana's skull. Half stunned, the elf could offer no resistance as Sareel pushed her savagely away. She was faintly aware of Renar screaming for Sareel to halt, and of Sareel shouting back that she'd kill Drelm if Elyana didn't save her master. A booted foot crashed into Elyana's side, and a new wave of pain rolled through her.

"I'll kill you, too!" Sareel declared.

And then Renar sang a happy little melody. Elyana heard a thud, accompanied by the scent of scorched metal and roasting meat. She pushed herself up with her good arm, stomach churning.

Renar was suddenly there, offering a gauntleted hand. "Elyana! Abadar preserve you, you look awful!"

A half-dozen witty quips rolled through her head, but she had not the strength. "Help me to Drelm." Her voice was a hoarse whisper.

Renar pulled her up, supporting her as he walked her to Drelm.

Elyana sank to her knees beside the captain. She caught a glimpse of her shoulder and wished she hadn't. It was a black and red mass of skin and bruises, leaking blood. She was sure she had seen exposed bone through the mess of muscle and armor.

She was so dizzy. She needed something, and couldn't recall what it was. It was close, she knew.

Elyana's gaze traveled the area, fell upon Sareel. The warrior woman's face was still twisted in fury, but her eyes stared sightlessly toward the heavens. A smoking, fist-sized hole had been blasted through the center of her chest.

"I wish I hadn't had to do that," Renar said beside her.

Elyana had used up her magic healing Drelm on the Plane of Shadow, but there was one last chance. "Crown," she said, so softly that Renar had to ask her to repeat herself. She sagged over Drelm's body. It took nearly all her remaining energy to explain. "Crown."

Renar hurried to Arcil's grisly remains and gently lifted the crown from his brow. He knelt down by Elyana and placed it on her head.

The moment he did so the pain ebbed. She felt it still, like an unwanted visitor lingering on the doorstep, and knew that her own energies were dangerously low. "Ride for help," she told Renar.

He nodded, then shot to his feet and whistled for a horse. Elyana heard the clop of hooves, then the rustle as he vaulted onto the animal and kicked it into gallop. She supposed he was holding on to its mane, riding bareback. Dimly she perceived the sound of the hoofbeats receding.

Elyana did not imagine it was wise to tap into energies beyond her own, especially when she herself was so close to unconsciousness. But she sensed that the half-orc's life was dimmed almost to nothing. There was no time to wait for a cleric. She put her hands to the sides of his bruised head and stared down at his eyelids. And she called on the power of the crown.

It came instantly, sliding through her body in a torrent she was almost too weak to control. She gritted her teeth, forcing herself to concentrate, and sent her life force questing out toward Drelm's own. She found it, a dying ember cradled in a broken hearth, and poured incredible energies toward it, trying to shape them into the waves she knew.

The energy was too great. One moment she was at the forefront of the wave; the next she was consumed, floundering within it. Everywhere was the energy, and it drew her down, down, swirling powerlessly away.

Chapter Twenty-Two
Final Words

As Elyana stirred, she thought for a moment that she lay in her own bed, and it was time to rise and saddle Persaily.

But the scent wasn't right. She smelled stone, and the blankets were softer than those on her own bed. She was accustomed to only one flat pillow, and she lay propped up on a very thick one. As she opened her eyes, she perceived that the light slanted in from the wrong angle to be the window in her bedroom. A figure stood silhouetted in profile by the sunbeam, looking outside. Stelan.

As she noticed that this was a room in the keep, all the recent events came flooding back to her. She looked down at her body and saw herself under thick blankets, the collar of a blue sleeping gown open at her throat. A tapestry she had always liked hung on the wall to her left, one featuring huntsmen on finely fashioned horses racing gaily, not after game, but for the sheer thrill of the speed that the weaver had captured in the horses' raised tails and flared nostrils.

As she'd turned her head, something about the way her hair lay on her neck felt odd, and she reached back. Her probing fingers discovered that her hair had been trimmed short, now stopping midway down her neck rather than at her shoulders. At first she was affronted, then remembered the guillotine had probably made a proper mess of her hair. It was only after she reached up that she recalled how the shoulder she now used had recently been aching. Throbbing. Now there was no pain anywhere in her body at all. She felt blissfully cleansed, though still very tired.

Close at hand was a small table with a pitcher of water, and a glass. She realized just how dry her throat felt.

She sat up slowly, the bed creaking beneath her, and reached for the glass. Stelan turned at the sound and came over immediately, watching as she drank.

She smiled at him as she set the glass down, and it was almost like old times as he dropped eagerly down on the edge of the bed. He took hold of her hands and squeezed them tightly but did not speak. His dark eyes were filled with such concern he might not have trusted himself to say anything.

"You are cured," she said.

"And you are well?" he managed. He looked thin, careworn. But he was alive.

"I am," she said. "And Arcil kept his word and lifted your curse."

"He must have," Stelan said.

"Drelm," she said suddenly. "Gods. Did he make it? I lost control of the spell. Is he alive?"

"He is."

Elyana breathed a sigh of relief.

"You nearly died in saving him, Elyana." Stelan's voice was strained but quiet. He was striving, none too successfully, to conceal the depth of his relief. "The cleric healed you days ago, but you would not wake. He feared your mind had been shattered by the magic."

"It's still here, I think."

Stelan gave her a half-hearted smile and squeezed her hands so tightly it pained her, though she did not ask him to let go. He released his grip after a moment and looked away from her. "I was worried for you."

She almost teased him over the obvious understatement. She restrained herself.

"You risked everything for me and my family," Stelan went on. "I will never be able to thank you properly."

"The strength of your friendship is thanks enough," she replied, wishing that he would take up her hands again, though she knew he should not. "How is Renar?"

"He is well. He is stronger now than I remember him. And a little sadder. Those few days he was gone . . . aged him. He has spoken of an elven woman of great beauty."

They had lost so many, and poor Aliel's death had been one of the most senseless losses of all. The pain of the young girl's pointless death burned afresh at thought of her. "I must pay respect to her family," Elyana said slowly.

"So must we. Renar says the elves were of great help to you. I would like to thank them personally."

Elyana shook her head. "No—I do not think that would be the wisest course. Perhaps you could offer a gift, or a poem. But I will deliver it. I think it would be more proper."

Stelan nodded absently. She sensed that he wished to touch her again just as much as she desired it, which was probably why he still would not meet her eyes. She forced brightness into her voice. "What of the crown?"

"Given over to the holy temple of Abadar," he said, finally managing a brief look in her direction. "As you promised it would be, in payment for keeping me alive." He paused. "Lenelle did not think you would return," he added softly, then seemed to regret it.

"I wasn't sure myself that we would. Renar has told you everything?"

"Everything that he knows. I don't think he's learned to tailor his stories much, yet, though there are some details he did not share with his mother. I still don't understand Vallyn. What was his real aim?"

She hadn't had much time to draw her own conclusions. "He wanted the praise of the Galtans. Or the love of Nadara. They had something over him . . . maybe it was his little inn on the border. But I can't claim to completely understand. They beat him badly and locked him in a cell, and still he turned on us in the end."

"Renar said that Vallyn had been aiding you all along the way. Was it just so he could use you to please his masters?"

"I wish I could say, Stelan. He went out of his way to give Renar advice to protect him. Whatever Vallyn felt, in the end we didn't matter as much to him as his own skin. He knew the Galtans wanted us dead, and never warned us."

"He always did look out for himself. I knew he was a little bit of a coward, but . . . I thought he was our friend."

"People change," Elyana said.

"Some of them," he replied. "Nevertheless, I will pray for his soul."

"I hope that you will pray too for Kellius."

"I have." Stelan's head rose in conviction. "And I will. He died nobly in my service, and his name will not be forgotten. I am commissioning a statue of him so that we will have a place to burn offerings."

That sounded appropriate. She wondered if the thoughtful young wizard would have approved. A statue seemed so formal, and Kellius had been so approachable. "Perhaps you should plant a flowering garden in his honor," she said.

"That can be done as well."

Elyana smiled sadly, trying not to think of the brave young wizard's last moments, and his final agony. It put her in mind of what she herself had recently undergone. "The Galtans had some kind of pain spell on me. Was it a curse?"

"No. The healer dismissed it. It would have faded in time. He was amazed that you'd still been on your feet with it activated. He doesn't know you very well." Stelan chuckled. "You never stop until something knocks you down."

"Drelm had that spell on him, and some kind of strength draining magic, and he still fought on. You do what you have to do."

"So did we always."

Elyana pulled up the corners on the right side of the bed and slid out, her bare feet cool on the stone. She stepped for the wardrobe. "Are my clothes in here?"

"Yes. I can have someone help you with that—"

"I'm fine." The wardrobe door creaked open at her pull.

"Perhaps I should go." Stelan rose and stepped quickly away.

Elyana turned. She'd been so comfortable talking with him that she'd momentarily forgotten that a married man should not see his old lover naked. She smiled sadly. "I don't need to dress immediately, I suppose. It's just that this gown . . ." She gestured down at the fabric stretching to her ankles. "It's not really me."

"Yes. I understand."

It was, she supposed, what she would wear to sleep if she were a wife to a baron.

"Elyana," Stelan began, then hesitated before edging forward.

"Yes?" she prompted.

"Renar said that Arcil was . . ."

What word was he struggling for? Helpful? Powerful? Evil? Good?

"A dead creature," he finished.

"He was."

"I saw him. The cleric said that he was an abomination, but Renar demanded that he be buried properly, with full rites. He was adamant about that."

"Was he?" Elyana was secretly pleased.

"What do you think? I would not have an unholy thing in the hallowed ground of the village cemetery. The priest thinks we should burn him."

"No," Elyana said without thinking, wondering at her answer even as she spoke on. "Renar is right. He should be buried. He said he was sorry."

"He did?"

"Those were his last words. I think he meant to say more, but he died."

"Do you think there is hope for his soul, then?"

"I'm no expert on souls, Stelan. A whole lot of people died because of him."

Stelan brushed at his beard, frowning thoughtfully. "Renar told me that he didn't think Arcil was all bad. What do you think?"

"I think Arcil would have ripped out your liver if it had been useful to him," Elyana answered. "He'd have been polite about it, of course. But he was a black-hearted bastard, only out for himself."

"Then why are you crying?" Stelan asked gently.

"The hell if I know." Elyana wiped a tear from the corner of her eye.

"I shall pray for him as well," Stelan said with quiet dignity.

"You are a good man, Stelan."

"Not as good as I would like to be." His lips worked quietly, portraying some deep inner struggle, and then he sank to one knee before her. He reached up and tenderly clasped her hands. He kissed her fingers, then pressed the back of her hand to his face. He remained thus for a long while.

She closed her eyes and felt new tears sliding down her cheeks. Her heart thrummed.

"If I had but three words left for you," Stelan managed finally, "I would also say that I am sorry, Elyana. Sometimes I wish . . . Sometimes I think—"

"Shhh." She took one of her hands from his and set it atop his head. "Don't say it."

His eyes held only her, and bored deep into her soul, as they had not done for long, long years. "I will not be here much longer for you to save, Elyana. Old age comes on apace. Would you really have wanted to see that? To be with me?"

"You know the answer. Stelan, you are wiser than this. You love your wife, and she you, and Renar would not exist without the two of you. He is a good man. He will be a good ruler."

Stelan wiped something from his eye, and stood. He let go of her hand and drew himself up. It was almost as if he slid a mask back into place. "I hope that you will join us for dinner," he said formally.

She responded by lifting the hem of her nightgown and making a deep curtsy. "I will be delighted to accept."

He bowed his head and departed to let her dress.

Over the next few days, Elyana spent more time at the keep than she had in years, and even Lenelle seemed to welcome her to dinner, hugging her once with such sincerity that Elyana understood the depth of the woman's appreciation.

Yet even as the baron's home was opened to her in ways she had never known, she understood that Adrast and the keep, and even her stables, could never again be hers. That they might never have been. As her strength returned and the mark the ring had left upon her finger faded, she realized that it was time to go.

She told Stelan and Renar that she must return to the elven lands and pay respects to the family of the deceased. She saw by Stelan's look that he knew her true aim, but he did not attempt to dissuade her.

Renar, though, clearly missed Elyana's real purpose until she called him to her cabin to leave detailed instructions for the care of her animals. He might still be somewhat naive, but he was no fool.

"You're leaving for good, aren't you?" he asked.

Elyana checked the height of her stirrups and stroked the neck of Persaily's sister, a calm roan. "I may be gone for a while, Renar. It's probably time I better knew my own people."

"So how long will you be away?"

"I cannot say."

"Elyana."

She heard him speak her name in a different way than he had ever said it before. It was not wheedling, or needy, or petulant, or respectful. He had addressed her as an equal.

She met his eyes.

"You mean to miss my father's death, don't you?"

She swung up into her saddle. "Stelan will have many years left, Renar. Perhaps I shall return to meet your children, and teach them to ride. And hunt. Show better sense than your father and I, and stay here. This is a lovely little village, and far from trouble. Don't go looking for any."

He took her horse's reins near the bit and absently stroked the mare's cheek. "Is there anything you wish me to say to father?"

"He knows all that I would say. Thank him for me."

"Thank him?"

"For his friendship, Renar."

"Thank you, Elyana. For . . . everything."

He looked as though he was struggling to find a way to convey more, but his meaning was clear to her. "You're welcome, Renar." She hesitated only a moment, then turned to impart a final piece of advice, something she wished she had said to Arcil, or Vallyn, in younger days. "It is the way of humans to crave always what they do not have, and begrudge the things that are near at hand. You would do well to remember that."

"I will," he said seriously. She hoped he would.

She urged her horse forward with the barest nudge, leading another behind her, burdened lightly with saddlebags.

She looked back at him, there beside the fencepost, hand raised in farewell, and wondered what he would look like in another twenty years. She would have to come back and see.

The road through the village would take her too near the keep, and too close to familiar faces, so she cut southeast around it, rejoining the dirt track a quarter-mile past the last farmstead. She was startled to discover a thick, sturdy figure waiting there under an oak, his warhorse cropping grass nearby.

She drew up her reins. "Drelm. What are you dong here?"

The half-orc stood, stretched his great shoulders, and walked for his mount. "Riding with you."

He must be confused, she thought. Did he not know that she was leaving the village? "I am going back to Elistia."

"So am I." He climbed into his saddle with a grunt.

She stared at him, faintly amused. "I don't expect that you'll find it a comfortable home. You didn't like the wine, remember?"

"You won't stay," he assured her. "You will ride on. And I will go with you."

"Why?"

He rode up beside her, his horse snorting in greeting. "The young lord will be the baron's captain now. And in his time, he will hire a captain of his own. As for me, there is more of the world that I would see. If you do not mind the company."

"I would not," Elyana decided without need for reflection, and their horses fell in step.

"Do you think we'll see more shadow wizards?" Drelm asked.

"Gods, I hope not."

"Me too." Drelm was quiet for only a moment. "What about Gray Gardeners?"

"I hope to avoid them as well."

Drelm nodded slowly. "You do think, though, that there will be things to fight?"

"Most assuredly."

"Good." The relief was clear in his voice, but he seemed to think further explanation necessary. "That will please me."

Elyana laughed, and the two of them rode out together under the warmth of the rising sun.

About the Author

When not helping run his small family farm or spending time with his wife and children, Howard can be found hunched over his laptop or notebook, mumbling about flashing swords and doom-haunted towers. He has worked variously as a TV cameraman, a book editor, a recycling consultant, and a college writing instructor. He was instrumental in the rebirth of interest in Harold Lamb's historical fiction, and has assembled and edited eight collections of Lamb's work for the University of Nebraska Press. His stories of Dabir and Asim have appeared in a variety of publications over the last ten years, and led to his invitation to join the editorial staff of *Black Gate* magazine in 2004, where he has served as Managing Editor ever since. His first novel, an Arabian historical fantasy titled *The Desert of Souls*, was published in February 2011 by St. Martin's Press imprint Thomas Dunne Books. He blogs regularly at **blackgate.com** and maintains a web outpost of his own at **howardandrewjones.com**.

Acknowledgments

Special thanks go to Bob for scouting the terrain; to Pete and Chris, who guided me through the pass when they had battles of their own to fight; and to Shannon, who led the cavalry through a mighty host of foes.

Glossary

All Pathfinder Tales novels are set in the rich and vibrant world of the Pathfinder campaign setting. Below are explanations of a number of key terms used in this book. For more information on the world of Golarion and the strange monsters, people, and deities that make it their home, see the *Pathfinder Roleplaying Game Core Rulebook* or any of the books in the Pathfinder Campaign Setting series, or visit **paizo.com**.

Abadar: Master of the First Vault and the god of cities, wealth, merchants, and law.

Adrast: A small barony in northwestern Taldor.

Athalos: A deceased wizard specializing in shadow magic.

Avistan: The northern continent of the Inner Sea region.

Calistria: Also known as the Savored Sting; the goddess of trickery, lust, and revenge.

Cheliax: A devil-worshiping nation in southwestern Avistan.

Chelish: Of or relating to the nation of Cheliax.

Elves: Long-lived, beautiful humanoids who abandoned Golarion millennia ago and have only recently returned. Identifiable by their pointed ears, lithe bodies, and pupils so large their eyes appear to be one color.

Five Kings Mountains: A large and ancient mountain range in southeastern Avistan. Primarily inhabited by the dwarven nation of the same name, though surrounding nations such as the elves of Kyonin also have settlements there.

Forlorn: Elves raised in human society—so called because the difference between human and elven lifespans causes them to outlive generations of human friends and family.

Galt: A nation crippled by constant, violent democratic revolution. Fond of beheadings.

Galtan: A person or thing from Galt.

Golarion: The planet containing the Inner Sea region and the primary focus of the Pathfinder campaign setting.

Grave Candle: A magic item that allows you to speak with a corpse, but only for a few questions.

Gray Gardeners: The masked secret police of Galt, who dispense harsh revolutionary justice to those who cross them or the state.

Half-Orcs: Bred from a human and an orc, members of this race are known for their green-to-gray skin tone, brutish appearance, and short tempers. Highly marginalized by most civilized societies.

Hell: A plane of absolute law and evil, where evil souls go after they die to be tormented and transformed by the native devils.

Hellspawn: A human whose family line includes a fiendish taint, often displayed by horns, hooves, or other devilish features. Rarely popular in civilized society.

Hold of Elistia, Fortress of the Bluffs: An outpost of the elven nation of Kyonin situated in the Five Kings Mountains.

Inner Sea Region: The heart of the Pathfinder campaign setting. Includes the continents of Avistan and Garund, as well as the seas and other nearby lands.

Kyonin: An elven forest-kingdom located in eastern Avistan.

Lich: A spellcaster who manages to extend his existence by magically transforming himself into a powerful undead creature.

Mount Rein: One of the easternmost mountains of the Fog Peaks range between Taldor and Galt.

Nightmare: A monstrous, horse-like creature with mane and hooves of fire. Highly intelligent and completely evil.

Orcs: A bestial, warlike race of humanoids originally hailing from deep underground, who now roam the surface in barbaric bands. Universally hated by more civilized races.

Plane of Shadow: A dimension of muted colors and strange creatures that acts as a twisted, shadowy reflection of the "real" world.

River Kingdoms: A region of tiny, feuding fiefdoms and bandit strongholds, where borders change frequently.

Rovagug: The Rough Beast; the evil god of wrath, disaster, and destruction. Imprisoned deep beneath the earth by the other deities.

Sentinels of Elistia: Elven soldiers and lookouts from Kyonin, based in the fortress of Elistia and used as border guards.

Shadow Hounds: Predators from the Plane of Shadow—vaguely wolf-like in shape. Capable of causing intense, debilitating fear with their howls.

Shadow Magic: Magic focusing on the manipulation of shadow and/or calling forth the creatures and power of the Plane of Shadow.

Shadow Wizards: Wizards specializing in shadow magic.

Shelyn: The goddess of beauty, art, love, and music. Long-suffering and good-hearted sister of the evil god Zon-Kuthon.

Star Tower: One of many towers created by Zon-Kuthon to help stitch the world shut again after Rovagug was imprisoned in its center.

Taldan: Of or from Taldor.

Taldane (Common Tongue): The most widely spoken language in the Inner Sea region.

Taldor: A formerly glorious nation, now fallen into self-indulgence, ruled by immature aristocrats and overly complicated bureaucracy.

The Rough Beast: Rovagug.

Tregan: A tiny Taldan town on the border with Galt with a large population of refugees from the revolution-torn nation.

Umbral Dragon: A dragon affiliated with shadows and the Plane of Shadow.

Vale of Shadows: A strange valley in the Five Kings Mountains filled with shadow magic, surrounding a star tower.

Wight: An undead humanoid creature brought back to a semblance of life through necromancy, a violent death, or an extremely malevolent personality.

Wizard: A spellcaster who masters the art through years of studying arcane lore.

Woodsedge: A city in western Galt.

Wyvern: A brutish draconic creature not as intelligent or cunning as a true dragon.

Yanmass: A city in northern Taldor.

Zon-Kuthon: The twisted god of envy, pain, darkness, and loss. Was once a good god, along with his sister Shelyn, before unknown forces turned him to evil.

For half-elven Pathfinder Varian Jeggare and his devil-blooded bodyguard Radovan, things are rarely as they seem. Yet not even the notorious crime-solving duo are prepared for what they find when a search for a missing Pathfinder takes them into the gothic and mist-shrouded mountains of Ustalav.

Beset on all sides by noble intrigue, curse-afflicted villagers, suspicious monks, and the deadly creatures of the night, Varian and Radovan must use sword and spell to track the strange rumors to their source and uncover a secret of unimaginable proportions, aided in their quest by a pack of sinister werewolves and a mysterious, mute priestess. But it'll take more than merely solving the mystery to finish this job. For shadowy figures have taken note of the pair's investigations, and the forces of darkness are set on making sure neither man gets out of Ustalav alive . . .

From fan-favorite author Dave Gross, author of *Black Wolf* and *Lord of Stormweather*, comes a new fantastical mystery set in the award-winning world of the Pathfinder Roleplaying Game.

$9.99
ISBN: 978-1-60125-287-6

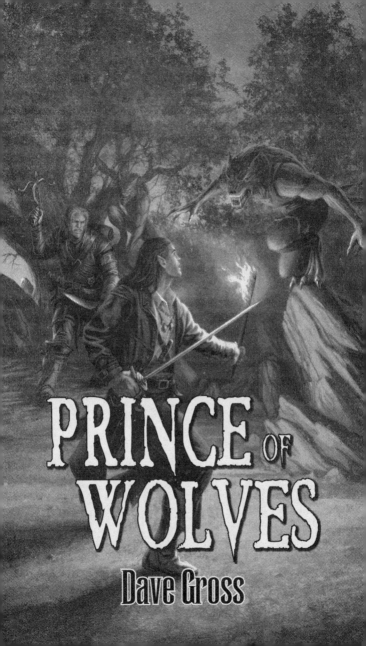

PRINCE OF WOLVES

Dave Gross

Winter Witch

Elaine Cunningham

PATHFINDER

TALES

I n a village of the frozen north, a child is born possessed by a strange and alien spirit, only to be cast out by her tribe and taken in by the mysterious winter witches of Irrisen, a land locked in permanent magical winter. Farther south, a young mapmaker with a penchant for forgery discovers that his sham treasure maps have begun striking gold.

This is the story of Ellasif, a barbarian shield maiden who will stop at nothing to recover her missing sister, and Declan, the ne'er-do-well young spellcaster-turned-forger who wants only to prove himself to the woman he loves. Together they'll face monsters, magic, and the fury of Ellasif's own cold-hearted warriors in their quest to rescue the lost child. Yet when they finally reach the ice-walled city of Whitethrone, where trolls hold court and wolves roam the streets as men, will it be too late to save the girl from the forces of darkness?

From *New York Times* best seller Elaine Cunningham comes a fantastic new adventure of swords and sorcery, set in the award-winning world of the Pathfinder Roleplaying Game.

$9.99
ISBN: 978-1-60125-286-9

In the foreboding north, the demonic hordes of the magic-twisted hellscape known as the Worldwound encroach upon the southern kingdoms of Golarion. Their latest escalation embroils a preternaturally handsome and coolly charismatic swindler named Gad, who decides to assemble a team of thieves, cutthroats, and con-men to take the fight into the demon lands and strike directly at the fiendish leader responsible for the latest raids—the demon Yath, the Shimmering Putrescence. Can Gad hold his team together long enough to pull off the ultimate con, or will trouble from within his own organization lead to an untimely end for them all?

From gaming legend and popular author Robin D. Laws comes a fantastic new adventure of swords and sorcery, set in the award-winning world of the Pathfinder Roleplaying Game.

$9.99
ISBN: 978-1-60125-327-9

THE
WORLDWOUND
GAMBIT

Robin D. Laws

"AS YOU TURN AROUND, YOU SPOT SIX DARK SHAPES MOVING UP BEHIND YOU. AS THEY ENTER THE LIGHT, YOU CAN TELL THAT THEY'RE SKELETONS, WEARING RUSTING ARMOR AND WAVING ANCIENT SWORDS."

Lem: Guys, I think we have a problem.

GM: You do indeed. Can I get everyone to roll initiative?

To determine the order of combat, each player rolls a d20 and adds his or her initiative bonus. The GM rolls once for the skeletons.

GM: Seelah, you have the highest initiative. It's your turn.

Seelah: I'm going to attempt to destroy them using the power of my goddess, Iomedae. I channel positive energy.

Seelah rolls 2d6 and gets a 7.

GM: Two of the skeletons burst into flames and crumble as the power of your deity washes over them. The other four continue their advance. Harsk, it's your turn.

Harsk: Great. I'm going to fire my crossbow!

Harsk rolls a d20 and gets a 13. He adds that to his bonus on attack rolls with his crossbow and announces a total of 22. The GM checks the skeleton's Armor Class, which is only a 14.

GM: That's a hit. Roll for damage.

Harsk rolls a d10 and gets an 8. The skeleton's damage reduction reduces the damage from 8 to 3, but it's still enough.

GM: The hit was hard enough to cause that skeleton's ancient bones to break apart. Ezren, it's your turn.

Ezren: I'm going to cast *magic missile* at a skeleton.

Magic missile creates glowing darts that always hit their target. Ezren rolls 1d4+1 for each missile and gets a total of 6. It automatically bypasses the skeleton's DR, dropping another one.

GM: There are only two skeletons left, and it's their turn. One of them charges up to Seelah and takes a swing at her, while the other moves up to Harsk and attacks.

The GM rolls a d20 for each attack. The attack against Seelah is only an 8, which is less than her AC of 18. The attack against Harsk is a 17, which beats his AC of 16. The GM rolls damage.

GM: The skeleton hits you, Harsk, leaving a nasty cut on your upper arm. Take 7 points of damage.

Harsk: Ouch. I have 22 hit points left.

GM: That's not all. Charging out of the fog onto the bridge is a skeleton dressed like a knight, riding the bones of a long-dead horse. Severed heads are mounted atop its deadly lance. Lem, it's your turn—what do you do?

Lem: Run!

NOW IT'S YOUR TURN . . .

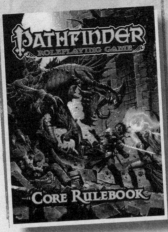

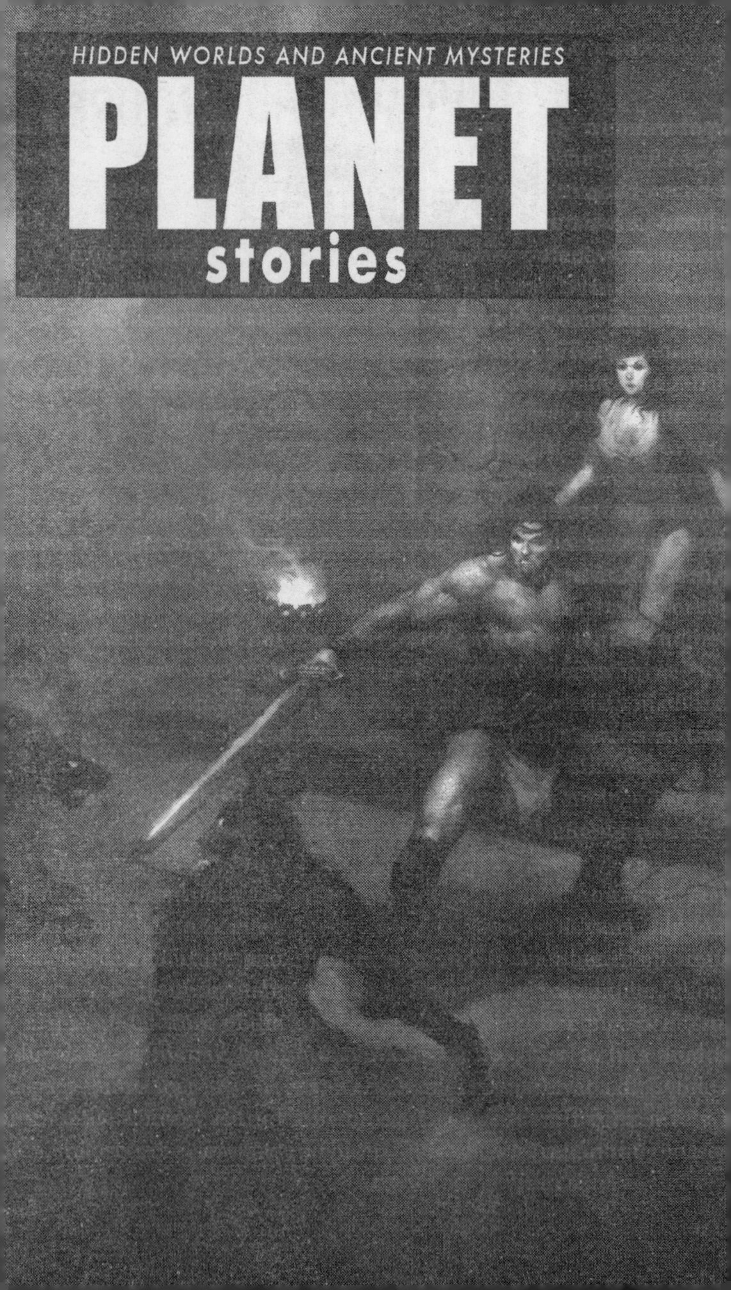
HIDDEN WORLDS AND ANCIENT MYSTERIES
PLANET
stories

EXPLORE NEW WORLDS WITH

PLANET STORIES

CHINA MIÉVILLE PRESENTS
HUGH COOK

THE WALRUS
& THE WARWOLF
A Chronicle of an Age of Darkness

INTRODUCTION BY JAY LAKE
MATTHEW HUGHES

TEMPLATE
A NOVEL OF THE ARCHONATE

First Works From Science Fiction Greats
**BEFORE
THEY WERE
GIANTS**

Edited by James L. Sutter

Strap on your jet pack and set out for unforgettable adventure with PLANET STORIES, Paizo Publishing's science fiction and fantasy imprint! Personally selected by Paizo's editorial staff, PLANET STORIES presents timeless classics from authors like Gary Gygax (Dungeons & Dragons), Robert E. Howard (Conan the Barbarian), Michael Moorcock (Elric), and Leigh Brackett (*The Empire Strikes Back*) alongside groundbreaking anthologies and fresh adventures from the best imaginations in the genre, all introduced by superstar authors such as China Miéville, George Lucas, and Ben Bova.

With new releases six times a year, PLANET STORIES promises the best two-fisted adventure this side of the galactic core! Find them at your local bookstore, or subscribe online at **paizo.com**!

SEE WHAT FAMOUS WRITERS ARE SAYING ABOUT AUTHORS IN THE PLANET STORIES LINE

"So highly charged with energy that it nearly gives off sparks."

Stephen King

"The most remarkable presentation of the utterly alien and non-human that I have ever seen."

H. P. Lovecraft

"Vastly entertaining."

William Gibson

"The essence of genre adventure, with excitement and horror . . . what more can a reader ask?"

Piers Anthony